For my cousin Sahar: appreciate your freedom and never take it for granted. Stand up for human rights and speak up for those whose voices are stifled by unconscionable leaders. Here is to you and here is to liberty and equality for all humanity.

Acknowledgements

A thousand thanks to my mother who helped me get reacquainted with the Muslim way of life and my father who provided me with books from Iran written in Arabic and interpreted into Farsi and English, who helped with my research and translation and who shared his wisdom about the Muslim community. I am also grateful to my brother for his knowledge of the stock market, real estate and sports, my editor and friend, Heidi Dvorak, for her analytical ability and her drive for excellence, Rick Wroblewski who worked in Abu Dhabi and helped provide answers to my numerous questions regarding the Arab society and all the brave Saudi activists who work diligently to unveil the many secrets the Saudi government tries hard to hide. Thanks to my family and friends for their input and their continuous support of my work, Jonathan Gullery for the wonderful cover design and the staff of RJ Communications for helping authors succeed in a competitive industry.

PREFACE

Why did I write about Saudi Arabia instead of Iran was the question many people asked. I chose Saudi Arabia because in order to understand what constitutes today's Iranian government, you must first understand Islam and in order to truly comprehend Islam, you must go to the source of where it all it started – the *Wahhabis* known today as the Saudis who believe that they are the unifiers of Islamic practice.

In 550 B.C, Cyrus the Great established the first Persian Empire known today as Iran. He ordered the release of Babylonian slaves, accepted all cultures and tolerated all religions. He put his Babylonian address in writing carved on a clay cylinder which was later found in 1887. Recognized as history's first charter of human rights, this clay cylinder can be found today in the united nation's building in New York City.

Zoroastrianism, recorded in history around 6th century B.C. and based on the teachings of Prophet Zoroaster, became the main religion of the Iranian people. Their code of conduct was good thoughts, good words and good deeds. When the Arabs conquered Iran around 640, they introduced *Jizya*, a special tax declared on the non-Muslims – nonbelievers. It was first used on the Zoroastrianism in Iran. Many Zoroastrians fled the country. Others who stayed could not afford to pay and eventually were forced to convert to Islam. Anyone who later changed their mind and wanted to convert back to their prior religion or to another religion was judged as apostate and condemned to death.

The conquest of Iran by the Islamists forever shaped the struggle between the modernists and the fundamentalists. I left Iran long before the Islamic revolution of 1979 and grew up in the U.S. However, my memories of Iran are vivid such as going to the beach with my family and running around in our bathing suits, my mom dressing up in sexy dresses when she went out to dinner with my father and his friends. There were concerts and dances with lively music and picnics in lush green forests with men and women mingling.

I also recall the religious fundamentalists of Iran such as my uncle's wife who always wore a black chador with only one eye showing. She wasn't able to have children and had insisted on adopting me. "You already have two other children, why don't you give this one to me," she had told my mother. The reason my uncle's wife had wanted me was that I was family and thus I would not have to cover up in front of my uncle and since I was a girl, my uncle's wife would be allowed to remove her chador in front of me. Fortunately, my mother refused her offer.

I remember my two cousins who were pushed into marriages they abhorred. One of my aunts, a fundamentalist, and her son, a bully, forced my cousin to marry a man she did not love. My mother said I was 40 days old when she attended her wedding. She told me tears poured down my cousin's face as the musicians played and people danced. After her marriage, my cousin got pregnant. Depression caused her to get sick and she ended up in a hospital for six months. Years later, my other cousin who was a year younger than me, wanted to marry a man she loved but her brother made her marry another because he was rich. Both these marriages ended up in divorce.

As I recalled these marriages, I wondered what would have happened to my cousins had they refused to marry men they did not love? And so I created female characters and placed them in the most impossible situation – Saudi Arabia. Because even in today's Islamic Republic of Iran where many rights have been taken away from women, women are allowed to vote and have positions in the parliament. They are more educated, have better jobs and more freedom than the Saudi women.

The Dawn of Saudi
In Search for Freedom

ONE

They buried her in an unmarked grave. Only in death did Saudi women and men receive equal treatment. Her father's face was grim, his body cold as ice. Her grandfather thought she was a disgrace to the family name. Her mother didn't shed a tear – not because public displays of grief were frowned upon since Saudis consider all stages of life and death as submission to God's supreme will – but because she knew her 22-year-old daughter, Sahar, was finally free. She was going to miss her daughter's generous nature of giving away her belongings to those who needed them: her beautiful chocolate eyes that sparkled when she laughed; her spunky aura that brightened any room she entered. *Oridol horeyata* – Sahar often said – I want my freedom. Perhaps it was all for the best, Asima thought, almost fainting from the sweltering August heat underneath her black cloak. She squeezed the hand of her youngest daughter, who had insisted on accompanying her, as she turned around and began walking back toward the family's Rolls-Royce.

"Will I ever see my sister again?" Asima's 8-year-old daughter asked as she got in the back seat of their car with her mother and her uncle Nadim. Her father, Saad, sat in front with the chauffeur.

"Someday in heaven," her mother said, looking one last time in the direction of Sahar's grave and hoping that she would be liberated at last.

A limousine behind them followed, carrying Asima's unhappily married eldest daughter and her brute of a husband. *How lucky for Sahar that she was dead,* the eldest sister thought. *If she had the courage, she would follow suit and escape this life of bondage.*

There had been much speculation about exactly how Sahar's life in Riyadh ended. Those who attended the wedding believed she was so stressed from being forced into marriage that she suffered a heart attack and died on her wedding night. Her immediate family thought the beautiful young bride was depressed and committed suicide. But the headlines printed in bold letters and announced over television and radio prior to the six o'clock news to entice people reported: *The bride of Saudi business tycoon, Husam bin Zaffar, died on their wedding night.*

One TV reporter said:

Sahar bint Saad bin Kadar Al-Hijazi (Sahar, daughter of Saad and granddaughter of Kadar Al-Hijazi.), the third wife of Husam bin Zaffar bin Amjad Abdul Samad (Husam, son of Zaffar, grandson of Amjad Abdol Samad) collapsed on their wedding night, went into a coma and died within an hour. Her physician reported that she died of an aneurysm.

International newspapers added:

Friends and family declined to comment, but an anonymous source reportedly stated, "The stress of being forced into a marriage she abhorred was more than likely what caused the vessel to burst. Sahar was a happy loving girl who none of us will ever forget."

Cynthia Crawford's eyes bulged when she read the news. She had sumptuous thick lips, an hourglass figure and lush black and silver hair that reached her shoulders. "Drew, have you seen this morning's paper?" she asked as she burst into the sunlit breakfast room dressed in her charmeuse robe and pajamas, looking for her husband. Theirs was a marriage on paper. They lived separate lives, but when it came to business and money matters, they collaborated.

Andrew Jason Crawford II of the Crawford Enterprises, a debonair man, the same age as his wife, 63, looked up in surprise. He rarely ran into her as early as seven in the morning in their Pasadena mansion, about a 15-minute ride north of downtown Los Angeles. "I was about to read it when you interrupted," he answered creasing his high forehead hidden underneath his full head of softly layered gray hair. He opened the Sunday paper and spotted the article about Sahar's death. "Good lord! That poor girl.

I must call and extend my condolences to her husband." Husam was soon to be one of Crawford's major investors due to his association with Sahar's family.

"Such a shame," remarked Cynthia. "They don't show her picture here but I read somewhere that she was lovely."

"Was she? Aneurysm. Who would have thought? I suppose this will postpone his visit to the U.S."

"What's going to happen to the merger, now?" Cynthia was nobody's fool. She may not have bothered with the day-to-day office business, but because she owned 50 percent of her husband's assets, she made sure to keep up with current events that could affect their finances.

The Crawford Enterprises, a Real Estate Acquisition, Inc., was a publicly traded multibillion-dollar business with American and international investors. Andrew Crawford and his 37-year-old eldest son, Jason, sat on the board of directors.

Kadar, Sahar's grandfather, was a famous Saudi multibillionaire. A well-known businessman, he owned 65 percent of his company and the rest was owned equally by seven foreign investors who were not involved in the day-to-day activities of the partnership. Kadar's businesses hadn't been doing well lately. He was a major shareholder in Crawford enterprise.

Sahar's widower, Husam, was also a well-recognized multibillionaire businessman. He owned diverse businesses such as manufacturing, retail, real estate and technology all over the world and his prospering company was privately owned. Husam's company was supposed to merge with Kadar's. If their companies didn't merge, then Kadar would have to file bankruptcy and sell his businesses and shares in Crawford Enterprise to cover his debts. This would, in turn, not only devastate Kadar's business partners but would also make the Crawford shares tumble. However if Kadar joined forces with Husam and their conglomerate became one, their enterprise would become one of the largest in the world, thus boosting investor confidence, increasing the value of Crawford Enterprise and making Kadar's partners content.

"Damn! The merger!" Drew blurted. He threw his linen napkin on the table and called for his chauffeur to bring the car around.

Upstairs, Jason Crawford III, lean with a muscular torso and strong legs, dark blonde hair and thick eyebrows, was changing into his golf clothes. He had a master in entertainment technology and an MBA from Carnegie Mellon. His new girlfriend, Tiffany, was listening to the business news when she heard about Sahar. He was about to put on his lucky green socks when Jason heard Husam's name. "That's our client. I can't believe his wife died on their wedding night. Talk about a bad omen."

"That's what I call extremely bad luck," said Tiffany, lying underneath the cashmere blankets. Even with her lustrous brown mane, big breasts and curvy body, there was nothing particularly special about her. And just like Jason's prior girlfriends, she wasn't going to be around for long. He preferred variety, even if he did date similar-looking girls.

"I wonder if the merger is going to go through now," he said, more to himself than to Tiffany. "I'd better cancel my golf game, go to the office and make some calls," he added changing out of his golf clothes into pants with cuffed hems and a sports shirt, his usual weekend business attire.

"I guess we won't be going sailing this afternoon," she said. Jason didn't even hear her.

"If that merger doesn't go through, our stock could fall." He looked at Tiffany blankly. "Did you say something?"

"Never mind," she said and picked up the phone to call a male friend. Tiffany was not one to sit home and wait for her man. Men were simply entertainment. Her relationships were here today, gone tomorrow, and her family was her bank account. She was a lawyer at her father's firm but only put in half the time the other employees did.

In Riyadh, women like Tiffany caught in bed with men that weren't their husbands would be punished by the *mutawan*, the religious police of vice and virtue. The first part of punishment was anywhere from 60 to 490 lashes with a flexible leather whip. If they had sex with a stranger, they would be stoned to death, perhaps drowned by a male family member or decapitated. The fate of all women, royalty or otherwise, was the same. The only difference between the rich and poor was that the former lived in a golden cage and the latter in a metal one. Affluent women were able to travel and have all the clothes, jewelry and chauffeurs they desired, but they still were at the mercy of their husbands, fathers and brothers. A woman was always considered the property of her husband or male guardian, and that male was allowed to treat her any way he wanted, even kill her without being prosecuted.

Only recently had the Saudi government issued ID cards to women, much to the dismay of hardliners who protested against women's faces being unveiled for their photos. The cards were issued to prevent fraud and embezzlement. Women used it to open bank accounts or to start a stock portfolio. The only problem was that the ID wasn't honored by many institutions. Oftentimes they sent the woman back and asked her to bring two male family members who could vouch for her. When a woman wanted to leave her house, she had to be escorted by a male relative. Traveling without a man's permission was forbidden.

Like all Saudi women, such was Sahar's fate as her situation worsened when she turned 22. According to Saudi tradition, she was too old to get married. Men preferred their women as young as one year old. There were no laws in Saudi Arabia defining the legal age for marriage. The prophet Mohammad was the model they followed. Aisha became his wife when she was six years of age, and the marriage was when she was nine. The younger a woman married, the better. She would be more subservient. Perhaps that was why it was too late for Sahar. She was too mature and independent to be subservient. Against her culture's popular belief that a woman's purpose in life was to bear sons, she expected more.

So often she had refused to leave her house, not wanting to be covered with an *abaya* – a black cloak covering the body from head to toe – with a head scarf and dark veil over her face. She thought it was unjust that she wasn't allowed to breathe the same fresh air that men did, that she was forced to look at the beautiful blue sky through the blackness of her veil, and that while men fornicated before marriage, she had to be a virgin and was not allowed to have as many husbands as men were allowed to have wives. She often wondered *which god supported such cruelty toward women. Which god created such inequality among men and women? After all, weren't all humans supposed to be equal? How much of this inequality was religion and how much was it the interpretation of men of her culture?* She hadn't an answer but could no longer accept the life she was born into. She needed her *al horeyat* – her freedom.

TWO

May 1, a week after her 22nd birthday, Sahar's father, Saad, started sending over one suitor after another to abide by his father, Kadar's, wishes. Sahar's 10-bedroom pale-golden villa – as homes in Saudi Arabia were referred to – surrounded by date palms and high, white concrete walls to prevent passersby from seeing inside, was tended to by six maids, three gardeners and a pool man, thanks to her paternal grandfather's wealth. Kadar had multiple sclerosis, which had progressed into paraplegia. He used a wheelchair to get around and lived on the premises in his own quarters with two entrances, one leading to the street and the other to a hallway that connected to his son's house. That way, if he became ill, he could call in through his intercom to his son or daughter-in-law.

Both Asima and Sahar disliked Kadar. They especially disliked his interference in their lives when he tried to choose a husband for Sahar. Today was again one of those days that Sahar was going to be angry with her grandfather when Rubilyn, her Filipino maid, entered her bedroom.

"What on earth are you doing in my room at this ungodly hour?" Sahar asked, her head resting on her silk pillow.

Middle-aged and sweet, Rubilyn had tan skin, big cheeks, slanted eyes and a flat nose. "Ungodly hour? It's 11 in the morning, child," Rubilyn complained looking at Sahar's puffy lids and large eyes that resembled Bambi's. "Most people are getting ready to have lunch," she replied, clacking her tongue against the roof of her mouth, which was what she always did when she disapproved of something.

"Well, I'm not most people." Sahar had been so depressed lately that all she did was sleep. Gone were her days of traveling and studying abroad. Growing up, she had a gift for languages. With the help of an American tutor at the age of five, she spoke English flawlessly. She wanted to continue her education in international law and become a lawyer, but her father wanted her to get married first. Now, Sahar was trapped in Riyadh until she married a chosen husband.

"I can see that," Rubilyn answered, planting her hands on her wide waist. Widowed at a young age with no one to support her, she had been working in the household for 25 years. Fortunately for her, she had been able to secure a job with the Al-Hijazis without anyone confiscating her passport or hurting her.

Often young Filipinos with work permits in Saudi Arabia were treated like slaves and had their passports taken away by their employers so that they could never leave the country. They were beaten by the owner of the house or raped by male family members while the Saudi courts ignored it.

The bright sun filtered through the large windows like film through a projector, and Sahar was annoyed that Rubilyn had pulled back the burgundy taffeta curtains. "Stop that. I need my rest," she said, pulling the covers over her head.

Rubilyn's pudgy body leaned over Sahar and she shook her with agitated hands. "You must get up. Your suitor is waiting downstairs and growing very impatient." She began picking up her clothes from the floor, folding her custom-made shirts and hanging up her expensive dresses.

"My what?" she asked, sitting up in her cream-lace pajamas. A color poster of Daniel Craig in *Casino Royale* on the wall behind her bed glowered over her. Her uncle Nadim had bought it for her on the black market, knowing how much she liked him.

"Your suitor – the man your grandfather wants you to marry."

Alabalkabir Kadar – Grandfather Kadar – looked like a Swiss-booted goat with his long face, small eyes and a beard that only grew underneath his chin. He was a hypocrite just like many other Saudi men. Before his illness, he used to violate the laws of his country and religion by drinking alcohol, taking illegal drugs and engaging in extramarital sex whenever he traveled outside of his country.

"Oh damn," she blurted, pushing the thick scarlet velvet covers away. "Get me my *abaya*."

Shocked, Rubilyn stared at her. "But you haven't even brushed your teeth."

"Don't panic Rubilyn, I will not be sitting close enough for him to smell my breath."

"But you're not dressed."

She got off her bed and went to fetch her *abaya* herself.

Rubilyn watched Sahar's tall, slender figure rise as she reached for her cloak. "You're still in your nightclothes. Won't you change?"

"What for? I'll be wearing this horrible black sack over my head. No one will know."

It was unheard of. Wealthy Saudi women groomed themselves with care and attired themselves in high fashion under their *abayas*.

"At least brush your hair," she told her, looking at Sahar's unruly waist-length golden brown hair. "Don't you want to feel pretty?"

"For a man my father's age? No."

"Then put on some makeup."

She rolled her eyes. "You win. Give me that red lipstick." She pointed at a silver tube sitting on her vanity.

Rubilyn gloated. At least this one time the girl she had helped raise since she was a baby was listening to her. She handed over the lipstick.

Sahar twisted the cap off and began painting her face like a clown.

Rubilyn was horrified. "You can't go down there looking like that."

"Watch me." She pulled her veil over her face and trotted downstairs.

Ahmad, her suitor, was waiting for her on the sofa by the window clad in his *thobe,* a loose, white cotton garment with long sleeves that covered his entire body. Saudi men wore these as dictated by their religion – a man should be judged by his deeds and not by his appearance. The *thobe* expressed equality.

Ahmad was accompanied by his 69-year-old mother, Badra, who had a wide bottom and a limp. She wanted an opportunity to see his bride before he married her. His first wife hadn't been able to give him sons, so he was taking on a second.

Sahar sat next to her mother in the *majlis* – a room used to entertain family and guests – decorated with two ivory-brass mirrors, crimson velour carpet and a teak table set with small cream stones. She stared at Ahmad with displeasure from underneath her veil. He was her cousin's brother-in-law. In Saudi Arabia, people usually married within their own clan for two reasons: One, because their families didn't approve of marriage to outsiders and, two, it was difficult for strangers to meet in private and get to know each other due to segregation of the sexes. Sahar's mother, Asima, married at the age of 14 to her second cousin Saad when he was 25. She was now 39, her eldest daughter was 24.

"Your father told me you're 22 and well educated."

"Yes." At five-feet-three-inches tall, he was seven inches shorter than Sahar, was 34 years her senior – his mother gave birth to him at the age of 13 – had a big mole on the side of his nose and was hairy. *Who in their right mind would base a lifetime decision on one visit?* Sahar thought.

"And you speak English and Spanish?"

"Yes."

"You must be quite bright."

"No."

"You're modest. I like that," he chuckled. "When we're married, I expect you to be just as modest and, as long as you obey me, you may have anything you desire."

Sahar kept quiet, hoping that he would leave soon so she could go back to sleep.

"I'm meticulous about punctuality. I forgive you for being late today, but in the future, I expect you to be on time."

She did not respond, so her mother nudged her. Asima was slim. Underneath her *abaya*, she dressed in a caftan embellished with floral embroidery around the neckline and sleeves.

Sahar started coughing incessantly.

Ahmad clapped his hand and a maid ran into the room. "Get her water. She seems to be choking on something."

A servant brought a glass of water, but Sahar said, "No, thank you. I'm better now."

"May I have a look at you?" Ahmad asked. In the Saudi culture, people married without ever laying eyes on each other, but in the more modern families, the groom asked to see the bride or at least look at her hands or face.

"I'm sorry," Sahar responded, "but I don't feel comfortable exposing my face to you."

"She's rather shy," Asima lied.

"Then perhaps my mother could have a look at her."

"Of course," Asima interrupted before Sahar could protest. She grabbed her daughter's hand and dragged her reluctant body to the women's quarters, which overlooked a rose garden. Ahmad's mother followed.

The room, like many rooms in Saudi households, had low sofas and coffee tables, which made guests feel as though they were seated on the floor. Here Asima entertained the wives of her husband's business associates. Men and women had separate quarters. When a husband and wife were invited to someone's house, the woman entered from the women's entrance in the back and the man entered from the men's entrance in front. Men dined on the floor in a room where dishes and meals were already set up for them. The wives ate in the dining room, out of sight of men. Muslim women were only allowed to remove their veils and *abayas* in front of other women, their fathers, brothers, husbands, children, grandchildren, fathers-in-law and uncles. In front of anyone else, such as their brothers-in-law, they ate with their veils on as they discreetly lifted a small portion of their veils in order to put food in their mouths.

Badra addressed Sahar when they were in the back room in the women's quarters. "I have already seen a picture of you sent to us by your parents. You're very pretty and have no reason to be shy," she said, taking a seat on the sofa next to Asima.

"I do not wish to remove my *abaya*," Sahar said, adamantly, standing in the middle of the room.

"Please remove your veil and let me have a look at you," Badra ordered, clearly frustrated. The real reason she wanted to see Sahar was to make sure that her potential daughter-in-law had no deformities before her son married her.

Sahar shook her head no once again.

"Do as you're told," Asima demanded firmly from underneath her sable gabardine veil. Although she was more open-minded than most of her culture, she knew that it was time for her daughter to marry or she would be called a spinster.

"I'll do as I'm told, but you're not going to like it," Sahar said, shedding her veil and black robe.

Badra gasped in horror. Sahar's unruly hair was sticking out from all angles and red lipstick started at one cheek and extended to the other. She looked like she should be locked up in an institution, and her breath smelled like garlic. "This meeting is over. My son will not marry your... your...crazy daughter." She stormed out of the room, whispered something in her son's ear and the two left.

Sahar looked at her mother with a smirk, dropped into a chair and said, "Well *Alomm* – Mom – I think that went well, don't you?"

Asima, still seated on the sofa, her body numb, removed her *abaya* and veil, revealing her long radiant brown mane that reached below her shoulder blades, and shook her head in disappointment. She had always desired that Sahar have all the things she never had. Asima regretted marrying at a young age and pushed her eldest daughter to do the same at 16. She had wanted Sahar to enjoy herself and experience different cultures before taking on a life full of responsibilities.

"This is not your fault, it's mine. I should have never introduced you to the western culture," she said, looking at her daughter with discontented hazel-brown eyes. "You have lost all respect for your family."

"I'm sorry for disappointing you, but we're talking about my future, not yours. I'm not going to ruin it by marrying a man who expects me to obey him. What he needs is a dog, not a wife," she replied, retying a loosened string on her pajamas.

"Sahar, you have got to get married. You're getting too old, and people are talking."

"I'm still young. Women in America don't get married until they're well into their 30s."

"You are not in America."

"Oh, but I once was. We used to go to New York all the time, or have you forgotten?"

"No, I haven't forgotten. But you need to put all that behind you."

"I can't, and I will not be treated like an object. Didn't you even hear what he said? Obey him. As if I would. I would die before I obey anyone."

"Me and my damn liberal ways. Had I raised you more conservatively, we wouldn't be standing here arguing over what is natural."

"Natural? You think being forced into marriage is natural?"

"In our culture, yes. I didn't know your father well before I married him."

"You're from a different generation. There are many families here in Riyadh who let their children choose their spouse."

"And if I had a talk with your father, would you at least consider choosing your husband?"

"No *Alomm*, I don't want to get married right now."

"You know what you're asking is impossible. Your *Alabalkabir* Kadar would never allow it."

Her grandfather was a mean, old, controlling man whose acquaintances were ruthless, greedy businessmen. He invested his money in foreign properties and traveled often until he became a paraplegic. His illness only made him more resentful as he made everybody's life miserable.

"I don't understand why *Alab* – Dad – lets that old man control our lives."

Eleven years her senior, Saad had a friendly smile, warm eyes, a trimmed mustache and a bearded chin. He loved his wife very much. And even though she hadn't been able to give him any sons, he never took on a second wife, however hard Kadar tried to change his mind. But in other matters, Saad did what his father asked out of respect.

"I don't like it either, but we have no choice. We live in a culture where women don't have rights. The sooner you accept this, the sooner you will get on with your life," Asima said. Suddenly, she heard her husband slamming doors and stomping around. "He must have heard about what happened. You'd better stay out of his way. I'm going to go fix the mess you made."

Why couldn't more men be like her *Alkal* Nadim, Sahar thought as she snuck out the back door and went to sit by the pool. Not yet married, Uncle Nadim was her mother's youngest brother. Fascinated with the Hollywood entertainment industry, he had attended school in the U.S. seven years ago to study to be a makeup artist on film sets, specializing in bald cap – making a person look bald – but soon found out that it was difficult to break into the business without connections. Disappointed, he had returned home and gone into the import-export business with his father.

Alakal Nadim disapproved of how the men of his country treated women. He believed in equal rights and preferred women who were educated. Sahar loved to be around him. They talked of books, politics and the arts. He was like the perfect older brother Sahar never had. But not even he could help change her grandfather's mind.

Suitor after suitor came by with marriage proposals over a period of one month, but Sahar managed to push them all away. Each time she thought of a new scheme to get rid of them, but she was running out of ideas. Today she sat on her bed eating lunch when Rubilyn entered wearing her long-sleeve tunic and loosely fitted pants that overwhelmed her short stature. She was there to pick up Sahar's laundry but when she saw her with a plate of lamb, sautéed garlic and a huge pile of garbanzo beans, she said, "You're not going to eat all those, are you? You know you can't control your gas when you eat so many beans."

Upset at her father, Sahar had decided to eat alone. Saad was planning to sit in on today's marriage proposal and do everything in his power to get his daughter married.

Rubilyn pushed her short black hair behind her ears and repeated herself. "Please stop eating all those beans. You know you can't control yourself when you eat all those beans."

"Rubilyn," she said irritably, "That is precisely why I'm eating them."

"Ooooh, ooooh, I don't like this," she answered, clacking her tongue and shaking her head. "Your father is going to be very displeased."

"Damn my father. Doesn't anybody care about how I feel? For the past month, men have been coming here and staring at me as though they were purchasing meat. You would think that they would've heard all the rumors about me not being submissive."

"Sweetheart, you come from an old respectable family. No man's going to be able to resist you even if your behavior is less than proper."

Coming from a praiseworthy family and the same tribe was oftentimes more important to a man than marrying for love or money. If one belonged to a tribe, it meant that one was a pure Saudi. Not belonging to a tribe meant the person migrated from other countries long ago and settled after Hajj in Mecca or Medina. Often, someone from a tribe was forbidden to marry a person without a tribe.

"Less than proper?" she sniggered. "I believe the word you're searching for is *insane*." She put another spoonful of beans in her mouth, pitying her next suitor. Earlier for breakfast, she drank prune juice and milk and finished off her meal with broccoli and cauliflower. She looked almost pregnant now and the gas formulating inside her was starting to bother her stomach. She ran to the bathroom.

"Are you alright in there?" Rubilyn asked when she heard her moaning.

"I'm fine. Now please *ebtaed anny*," she told her – go away.

"But...."

"*Atrokni vahdi*" – she yelled – leave me alone.

"Perhaps I should make you tea to soothe your stomach," she suggested with persistence.

"*Atrokni, atrokni vahdi.*"

Three hours later, Rubilyn came into her room to help Sahar with her clothes but she was already dressed. "Are they here yet?" She asked about her suitor and his mother and sister who were supposed to accompany him.

"They should be here soon, but I have to admit, I'm surprised you're ready and early too. You must finally be accepting your fate."

"You may think that if it makes you feel better, but I will never surrender."

"Now, now, I don't want to hear any of that talk. Be a good girl and behave."

The doorbell rang. Sahar smiled underneath her veil and mumbled, "Let the show begin." She went downstairs. Her parents were already there waiting to see what disaster might occur this time. Sahar glanced around the room before greeting everyone.

The mother and sister were clothed in *abayas* and veils; the suitor was wearing a three-piece head cover as it was a custom in the Kingdom – *taqiyah* – a cap filled with holes that helped keep the *ghutra* – a square-shaped-white-cotton folded into a triangle – from slipping off the head. During summer, a white fabric was worn; in winter a s*humagh* – a red-and-white checkered cover – dressed the head. On top of this was an *igal* – a black rope-like double cord – holding everything in place.

Sahar greeted the two women by kissing them once on the left cheek and three times on the right – as it was customary to give four kisses in this manner. She said *As-Salamu 'Alaykum* – Hello – to her suitor and went to sit on one of the red, cream and gold chairs as she loudly passed gas.

The stench was so horrible that everyone quickly cleared the room and went outside into the garden. "Where's everyone going?" she asked, sarcastically.

Her father, a sturdy man of high stature, came back covering his nose with one hand and grabbing her hand with the other, dragging her outside. Sahar let out another smelly fart that not even the outside air could diffuse. The suitor looked at his mother and then at Asima and said they had to leave because there was somewhere they had to be. When they were gone, her father started yelling.

"Sahar, this was your last chance, and you blew it," he shouted, his voice like thunder. "By the end of next month, you will be married and that's that." He stormed out and drove off in his Rolls.

Sahar started crying.

"Please, don't cry. It's not so bad, being married," her mother said, trying to comfort her. "You're really lucky to have so many people who would want to marry you. It's a rarity these days."

Lately in Saudi Arabia finding a husband was difficult and the divorce rate high – due to men divorcing women, not vice versa. And since women weren't allowed to be intimate with men outside of marriage, many had *almesyar* – weekend marriages – where they relinquished their rights to financial support and men didn't have to report them to family or other wives.

"But I don't want to get married." She heaved a sigh and sat on a bench in the garden.

Rubilyn entered in her *abaya* and a *khimar* – a cape-like scarf covering her head, wrinkled neck and saggy bosoms, to see what was going on. It broke her heart to see Sahar so sad.

"What is it, Rubilyn?" Asima asked.

"I heard fighting and was worried."

Asima's face was tense, her aura dark. Sahar was too independent and stubborn. She almost wished she hadn't let her attend a high school in Vancouver and an American/Spanish university program in Barcelona. Sahar was too well educated. "We're okay, Rubilyn. What Sahar needs to understand is that her tricks have gone too far this time. We're an honorable family, and now everyone is going to talk about our crazy daughter."

"Miss Sahar is not crazy," Rubilyn protested.

"I know that and you know that but outsiders don't."

Sahar started to head out of the garden.

"Just a minute young lady," her mother said.

But Sahar never looked back. There was no way that she was going into a marriage without a fight. She fled to her room and closed the door behind her.

Her thoughts drifted back to her best friend Dawn Parnell, who she met while attending college in Spain. From Utah, Dawn was tall and slender like herself but with short red hair and lovely dark-blue eyes. She made the mistake of falling in love with a Saudi old enough to be her father. At 19, she and Sahar used to take classes together and would horseback ride and play tennis in their free time. Dawn taught Sahar how to ride a bike. In Saudi Arabia, bicycles were forbidden for women because the orthodox Muslims thought that the movement of the legs and hips was provocative.

When Dawn met the Arab at a nightclub in Barcelona, she fell in love, decided to drop out of school and convert from Mormon to Muslim. Soon after that, her parents disassociated themselves from her.

"How do you say 'freedom' in Arabic?" Dawn had asked Sahar while sitting in a café drinking sangria.

Like some Mormons and Muslims, Dawn and Sahar drank socially when they were away from their homes even though it was forbidden in their religions.

"*Al horeyat.*"

"Here's to *al horeyat*," Dawn yelled out, clinking her glass with Sahar's. "I'm free from my parents and their rigid beliefs."

"Are you sure this is what you want to do? Marry a man from my country?"

"Yes, I've never been more certain in my life."

"In America, you are free to do as you wish even when your religion dictates otherwise but in Riyadh all your freedoms will be taken away. You will not be able to drink sangrias. You will not be allowed to leave the house without a *mahram* – a guardian – who would either be your husband or a close male relative like a brother

or an uncle. You will not even be allowed to drive or ride a
bicycle."

Saudi Arabia was the only country in the world where women
were not allowed to drive cars.

"Can't you be happy for me? I'm marrying someone I love."

"I'm happy for you, but you talk about how important your *al
horeyat* is to you. You will not have *al horeyat* in Riyadh. In fact,
you will have the exact opposite."

"My boyfriend loves me. He said we would live in a western
compound and travel all the time."

Sahar knew all about compounds. They were apartment
buildings where westerners lived and men and women were
allowed to mix and dress the way they wanted. Some were much
nicer than others. They had a grocery store, swimming pool, a
large yard where the tenants could play sports and an entertainment
room where people drank, played music and danced. Women and
men were even allowed to sit around in their bathing suits, make
homemade alcohol from smuggled yeast, and watch films in a
movie theater, which was all *haram* – forbidden on the outside.

In Saudi Arabia public swimming pools were segregated by sex.
Rich women whose *Mahram* owned boats went into the water in
the middle of the ocean fully clothed in their *abayas* and veils.
Alcohol and nightclubs were illegal. And although people watched
films through satellite TV and on DVDs at home, public movie
theaters were nonexistent.

"Yes, but you would still be confined to the compound. As soon
as you leave, you'll have to cover up, especially since you're a
Muslim now."

Foreign non-Muslims had to wear *abayas* but were allowed to
show their hair. Even then, they had to always carry *hijabs* with
them in case they were caught by a power hungry *mutawan* who
would force them to wear their head scarves. A Muslim from any
country was always forced to cover up from head to toe while in
Saudi Arabia.

"I think it's kind of neat to wear an *abaya* and a veil. It's so mysterious," she giggled. "Men are always wondering who is behind the veil."

"Maybe it'll be neat at first, but when you're walking around in 120-degree weather under a black heat-trapping shapeless garment with sweat pouring down your body and your feet sweltering, you'll want to rip it all off and swap clothes with a man wearing a cool white cotton *thobe* and slippers."

"None of that matters when you're in love."

At that point Sahar stopped talking because she knew that no matter what she said, her friend had already made up her mind.

Dawn got engaged at age 20 and was married weeks later. After her marriage, she moved to Riyadh but not in a western compound, which her boyfriend had promised, but in a house located in an Arab neighborhood. The man she had married lied to her about his liberal ways in order to manipulate her into marriage. She learned to speak Arabic, yet that didn't improve communication between them.

Perhaps he had loved her at first, but soon all of that changed. He had an insatiable hunger for intercourse, at least several times every day. He hurt her by biting, punching and whipping her until she couldn't take it anymore. She had tried several times to go to the Saudi court to complain to officials, only to be sent back to her husband, telling her that she didn't have any proof. The officials requested that she obey him. The proceedings always went like this:

"I would like to divorce my husband."

"Why?" the official would ask.

"He beats me all the time and has broken my arm twice."

"Yes, what else?"

Dawn soon found out that it was nearly impossible for a wife to get a divorce from a husband, but incredibly easy for a husband to divorce a wife. All he had to say was "I divorce you" three times.

A week after Sahar's last suitor, another named Husam came to see her. Her father had warned her about her behavior, but she wasn't as afraid of him as much as she was of her grandfather. She sat quietly in her living room. Her 68-year-old prospective husband stared at her and wondered what she looked like underneath her veil. Husam was her grandfather's younger cousin, tall with a Buddha belly, acne scars, a salt-and-pepper mustache and a gray beard that started from his sideburns and grew all the way around his face.

Husam's sister, who accompanied him, asked Sahar to join her in another room. She then asked her to strip her veil. Sahar obligingly did as she was told and when the veil lifted, Sahar was expecting a loud shrill, but instead Husam's sister merely smiled. "I was told about you and your dumb tricks," she commented, looking at her bald head and nonexistent eyebrows while admiring Sahar's tall figure and soft hands, "but believe me, my brother will marry you anyway." Sahar fit the profile her brother had given her. He was looking for a slender wife with large eyes and light skin.

"Don't you care that I'm bald and have no eyebrows?"

"No, I don't. I know that your uncle studied to be a makeup artist in America and has fixed you up well. And I'm sure there is a beautiful head of hair underneath that awful bald cap on your head."

Everyone who knew the Al-Hijazis well also knew about Sahar's *Alakal* Nadim, and each time something went wrong, they blamed him even when he had nothing to do with the incident. Loving a good prank, Nadim had played many as a young boy, like the time he attached an invisible wire from one side of the dining room to the other to trip the servants as they rushed back and forth to serve the guests their meals; or the times he made obscene phone calls to stuffy family members while changing his voice and accent, or when he dropped dead worms into the drinks of unsuspecting guests at a wedding party.

"I will not marry your brother," Sahar replied with conviction.

"Oh, yes you will. Your grandfather has already drawn up a business contract with him. And after your marriage to my brother, the papers will be signed. So, you see, it's a done deal. Husam's company will merge with your grandfather's, so you have no choice but to marry him."

"I will make his life hell. Why would you want your brother to marry someone as obstinate as me?"

"You have it all wrong. It is he who will make your life miserable. For the first three insolent behaviors you will get warnings and on the fourth, you will get a sound lashing, then broken ribs and, after that, I will see to it that he will scar your pretty face with a knife." She stared at Sahar and the look of horror on her face made her grin. "This is your first warning. You have two more," she said and walked out.

Sahar stood there thinking she would drink poison before she would ever let that woman's brother touch her.

THREE

Husam agreed to marry Sahar and bought her an intricate gold watch embedded with pricey canary diamonds as a symbol of his affection for his soon-to-be bride. In June, 10 days after the marriage proposal, he joined his partner Kadar's son, Saad, on a business trip to the U.S. He usually traveled with Emad, his interpreter, but because Saad spoke English fluently, there was no need. And since Saad was Sahar's father, traveling together would help solidify work and family ties. Their private jet landed in Los Angeles and a white chauffeur-driven Lexus picked them up. Forty-five minutes later, they were dropped off at the foot of the San Gabriel mountains in Pasadena in front of an elegant hotel built in the 1900s, situated on 20 acres of manicured grounds. After waiting for them to check in, freshen up and change from their traditional Saudi attire into suits and ties, the driver took them to a high-rise owned by the Crawford Enterprises, in the business district of downtown Los Angeles. Once inside, a cylindrical transparent elevator with a view of the city took them up to the 47th floor. When the doors opened, the men were greeted by a courteous male receptionist, who asked them to have a seat.

Yumiko, Jason Crawford's young assistant, a leggy Asian girl in a skirt suit, greeted them and waited for either Saad or Husam to extend their hands before she shook them. A business woman had to wait for a Saudi man to offer his hand because some men did not shake hands with a woman. A Saudi man was never allowed to shake hands with a strange Saudi woman. Saad shook hands with Yumiko but Husam did not. She then led them through a long corridor, past a series of offices, eventually inviting them into an oblong, air-conditioned, smoky-gray glass walled conference room.

"Can I get you something to eat or drink?" she asked, looking at Husam and thinking how cold and distant he seemed and then at Saad's kind and friendly visage. He was wearing a pair of pale-brown-lens Valentino glasses and a beige linen suit and tie. His hair parted to one side.

Saad requested a cup of tea and plate of dates; Husam asked for a Scotch and soda.

"I'll be right back," she replied. Jason's efficient assistant always ordered dates and imported Indian tea when she knew Saad was coming to town.

A few minutes later, Jason who was walking toward the conference room in his three-piece navy suit ran into his two brothers who were supposed to join him at today's meeting.

"Sorry but I can't make it to the meeting. I promised my son to attend his basketball game," his youngest brother lied. He was actually going over to his mistress's house. Her husband was going out of town.

"And I have to go pick up my daughter from ballet," his middle brother said, trying to get out of work early. His daughter wasn't going to be finished with her lesson till three hours later.

"Yes, by all means go. I'm so glad that I can always count on the two of you," Jason replied sarcastically as he turned away, opened the door to the conference room and walked in.

"It's great to see you as always," he told Saad warmly.

"Likewise," Saad replied. "This is Husam, my father's new business partner."

"Nice to meet you," Jason replied, shaking his hand and thinking that he looked a lot like Kadar with his brown saggy skin, protruding jaw and stern countenance. "I trust that your trip was comfortable."

Saad translated for Husam and answered, "He says thank you, it was."

After the men sat down, Jason passed them two black folders.

"I had someone translate all the papers into Arabic for Husam, so if you turn to page two, we can get started."

Yumiko served their refreshments and left.

The three men discussed a shopping mall they had recently purchased on the west side of Los Angeles, the tenant leases, renovations, expansion plans, marketing strategy and projections as to when they would break even and then start turning a profit. Jason showed them some potential projects, hoping they might invest.

"And where are these buildings located?" Saad asked, glancing over a glossy photo of a hospital and large office building.

"They're both located in downtown Los Angeles. We can have a look at them tomorrow morning if you'd like."

Saad relayed the message to Husam, who agreed.

Husam was an astute businessman who was never satisfied. The more he owned, the more he wanted. He knew that money meant power, and one could never have too much power.

After a four-hour discussion, they moved to the executive dining room; two servers in cute French maid dresses served them a late lunch. The meal was carefully planned by Yumiko and included Jason's favorites: onion soup, coq au vin, a cheese platter and crème caramel. At one point Saad left the table to use the bathroom, and in no time, Husam's tongue wagged at one of the servers as she gave him his third scotch and soda. Jason observed him and wondered what it would be like to have three wives. Wouldn't they get jealous of each other and be hard to manage? And what about the number of children he would have from each spouse? He shook his head at the thought of having 10, 15 or 20 kids and was glad that he was single. He tried to imagine what Husam's new bride looked like. She probably had long thick black hair that smelled like jasmine, mesmerizing dark eyes and luscious lips. As Saad returned, Jason cleared his throat and coughed a few times to get Husam's attention so that Husam's soon-to-be father-in-law wouldn't see him salivating over the French maid.

"I've been meaning to congratulate you on your daughter's forthcoming nuptials," Jason said, and then turned to Husam, adding, "I'd also like to congratulate the soon-to-be groom."

Saad relayed the message to Husam who replied, "Thank you. We are happy that soon our families will not only be business partners but also close relations."

Husam's eyes glinted over his meal like those of a lion's that was about to capture his next prey. Jason watched him carefully, analyzing his every move. George, Jason's friend from childhood once told him: "One can tell a lot about a man not by listening to what he says but by watching his actions." George and Jason were supposed to open up their own virtual reality and computer game firm after college, but Jason's father Drew had convinced him that he was much needed at the Crawford Enterprises, so Jason had caved in to his demand. Andrew thought that his younger sons lacked strong leadership qualities. Years later, Jason regretted his decision, but by then George had started working for a computer game company. And Jason was stuck at a job he didn't enjoy.

"Delicious," Husam said to Saad in Arabic as he devoured his food. He had a disproportionate body, with extra weight around his belly.

"Yes, the soup is very good," Saad answered, eating a small portion of the cheese that topped it, glad that his daughter was finally getting married. He had often been worried about Sahar adopting the ways of western culture and wanting to be with a man outside of her faith. Marrying Husam would eliminate all that.

In Saudi Arabia, a woman who married a non-Saudi without the king's permission was condemned to death by her family and the courts even if she lived outside the country. Often the family would hunt the woman down in another country and execute her. And although Saad loved his daughter, he knew he would have to follow the same rule if she ever disobeyed him. That was the main reason why he was so content. He was relieved that she was finally settling down with the right man.

Jason took a forkful of salad and said to Saad, "Husam seems to be enjoying himself."

"Yes, well, Husam is a big eater. He never seems to get enough food in that stomach of his," he chuckled.

He's a lot like your father, Kadar, Jason wanted to say. Instead he said, "Then I must invite him to dinner at my house."

"Unfortunately, we will not have enough time for that. We'll be going back to Riyadh the day after tomorrow."

"So, soon?"

"Yes, we have to prepare for my daughter's wedding. But before we leave, we'd like to fly out to Las Vegas tomorrow after we have had a look at two buildings. Husam wants to see the hotel and casino we bought last year."

"Yes, of course. I'll make arrangements to join you. Should I have my driver pick you up at eight?"

"Nine would be better."

"Then nine it is."

"I would like some wine to wash down my meal," Husam said to Saad. "And why aren't you eating? You have hardly touched your food."

I think you're eating enough for the both of us, Saad wanted to say. He told one of the girls to bring over a glass of merlot.

"Certainly," she nodded and left.

Jason didn't care much for Husam. He already knew Saad and his father Kadar from their previous trips. He never cared much for Kadar either and didn't trust him, but his father thought that doing business with Kadar would increase their fortune. And when Kadar's condition worsened, making it difficult to travel, he sent his son abroad instead, Jason was pleased to work with him. Unlike his father, Saad was more reserved, less demanding and better mannered. But Husam reminded Jason of Kadar and hoped that he wouldn't have many dealings with him in person.

They ate quietly, especially Husam, who liked to concentrate on his food. When dessert arrived, Jason broke the silence. "Are you planning to come back and visit us after the wedding?"

"Not me, but Husam and his interpreter will. By then, the merger will have gone through and Husam will be representing our firm."

"Oh." He paused, trying to think of a nice reply but instead became interested in his crème caramel.

"Is something wrong?" Saad said, selecting a piece of Gouda from the platter.

"No, I was just thinking about how much I enjoyed our working relationship," Jason replied and then looked at Husam, wondering whether or not it would be easy to work with him.

"Me too," Saad answered, "but my father isn't able to get around as well as he used to and wants me to take over some of his operations. I am one of the few he trusts, so I will have my hands full and not be able to travel as much."

"I'm sorry about your father's health. Perhaps, if the opportunity presents itself, I will come and visit you in Saudi Arabia."

"I would like that," Saad said. Husam nudged him, asking him to translate their conversation.

Saad noticed the disappointment in Jason's tone and said, "We were talking about my father's health."

"Are you sure that's all you said? You seemed to be talking for long time. The English language must require a lot more words than ours," he said, thinking that they were talking about him because Jason kept glancing over.

"Yes, well, we made some idle conversation but nothing of importance."

"Emad always translates everything for me."

"Then perhaps you should've brought him with you," Saad answered curtly, "because I don't have the patience to translate idle conversation."

"I'll keep that in mind next time," he huffed.

Jason could tell from Saad's tense face and his raised voice that the two men were bickering. "Husam, would you like another glass of wine?"

Saad translated and Husam said, "No thank you, I would like to go back to my hotel and rest so that I can get an early start tomorrow."

Jason called the chauffeur to bring the car to the front entrance of the building, and a few minutes later, his guests got in and headed toward their hotel.

FOUR

While Husam and Saad were occupied with business dealings, Sahar's mother, Asima, and her Uncle Nadim were shopping for wedding clothes and planning the big event. Sahar's repugnance toward the groom made both the Al-Hijazi and Abdol Samad families anxious to tie the knot quickly. Motivated by greed, Kadar pushed the hardest. His businesses weren't doing as well and working with Husam was essential to his company's survival.

Sahar, Asima and Nadim were at a shopping mall somewhat like the ones in the west. Malls in Saudi Arabia, however, were high-rises catering mostly to the wealthy with floor after floor of high-end merchandise. The mannequins were headless since it was forbidden to show hair and facial features.

"How do you like this one?" her mother asked pointing at a window display of a conservative white bridal gown with a floral beaded pattern. Asima was petite with impeccable taste in clothes. Under her *abaya* and triple-layer georgette veil she wore an ankle-length silk chiffon dress, Dior flat sandals, and carried a Pucci handbag.

The mall was coed except for the third floor, which was for women only. Women-only malls also existed as well as malls with special hours for men and families.

"I wish these mannequins had heads," Nadim said, playfully as he straightened his white *gutra* and glided along in his *thobe*.

The custom in Saudi Arabia was always to conceal rather than reveal and although men had more freedom than women, they preferred conformity by dressing in loose-fitting robes. White cotton *thobes* were worn during hot weather, dark wool for cool, and on special occasions such as a wedding, a *bisht* or *mishlah* – a cloak trimmed in gold – was worn over the *thobe*. At a meeting in a room full of men, one had to study faces very carefully since everyone dressed similarly.

"They would look so much better with heads," Nadim added. He often wished that the laws of his country were based on civil laws instead of Sharia – a code of law derived from the Koran and teachings of Mohammed.

"Nadim, you're hardly helpful. We should've left you at home," Asima complained, looking at her brother's boyish face, his black sparkling mischievous eyes and devilish smile.

Unlike most men who would rather have their teeth pulled than accompany women to a shopping mall, Nadim wanted to help. Without Nadim, Asima and Sahar would not have been allowed to leave their house. And men and women had to always carry their identity cards with them in case the *mutawan* stopped them for questioning.

"I thought I was the designated driver," he replied.

Women were allowed to own cars but not drive them. The only time they were permitted to sit in front was when their *mahram* was driving. Women without means whose husbands were at work were trapped at home; the middle class took taxis and the rich employed chauffeurs. However, because of the *Mutawan*'s ruthless treatment of women, it was always safer to leave the house with a *mahram*.

"You know very well that our chauffeur could have driven us to a women's mall." Drivers would drop women at ladies-only malls and pick them up later.

"Oh, but I would've missed all the fun," he teased. Nadim wore a goatee and was lanky.

"Fun?" Sahar said. "I'd rather have my head cut off at the chop-chop square than go shopping for this wedding."

The Sa'ah square, also known as the chop-chop square, was an open courtyard near the gold *souks* – shops – where locals drank tea and talked while their children ran around. On Fridays the square was deserted and became the chop-chop square before the noon prayer, when prisoners were flogged and limbs and heads were cut off while a crowd gathered and watched. The government did this as a lesson to others in case they had any notions of breaking the law. Men caught in the company of unrelated females were flogged. Thieves and burglars lost their hands and feet. Adulterers, drug traffickers, murderers and rapists were beheaded with a large curved sword. Afterwards, low-paid Indian employees hosed down any leftover blood and body parts. Proud of their laws, Saudis always boasted about their low crime rate.

"Lower your voice, for heaven's sake, and stop talking like that. Let's focus, we don't have all day," Asima told her.

Sahar, disobedient as ever, started walking ahead of them and ducked into a CD shop. Underneath her *abaya,* which covered her feet and made her stumble at times, she dressed like an American – vintage faded jeans, Abercrombie & Fitch baby T-shirt and a pair of fuchsia and white tennis shoes. She picked up *The Best of Cher.* On the cover, a black shawl was painted over Cher's sexy dress.

"That'll be 94 riyals – 25 dollars," the male Pakistani sales clerk said.

All the employees working on the mixed floors of the mall – floors where both males and females were allowed to walk – were male foreigners, even on floors where bras and underwear were sold. The Saudi religious leaders preferred that men and women not work together. They were only allowed to work concurrently in hospitals.

Sahar paid and walked out. Her mother started yelling at her. "What's the matter with you? We don't have much time."

"We have plenty of time," Nadim interrupted. "Let's not panic here."

They began walking back toward the department store where they had seen a wedding gown in the window. Sahar went through the racks and picked up the ugliest, cheapest dress she could find and gave it to Asima.

Saudi bridal gowns were much like gowns from anywhere else in the world – white, beaded and jeweled. A Saudi wedding was usually an extravagant one, but with the downfall of the economy in the region, many brides and grooms rented their elegant clothes. In Sahar's case, with the dowry that Husam provided her, plus her family's wealth, she could well afford to buy anything she wanted.

"Aren't you going to try it on?" her mother asked, picking out a nicer dress for her daughter.

"No, it's the right size."

Nadim said, "You should try it. The length might need alterations. Why don't you go up with your mother to the women's-only floor and try it on?"

Because of the fear that men and women may hide in the fitting rooms and fornicate, the mixed floors didn't have dressing rooms. Instead, women had to put down a deposit and take garments to the women's restrooms to try them on. But in this mall, an entire floor was devoted to women reachable by a ladies-only elevator. The security guards and salespeople were females, dressed in western-style clothing such as pants, short-sleeve shirts and knee-high dresses instead of *abayas* and traditional Saudi clothing called *jallabia* or *thawh* – a long, loose dress with long sleeves that came in different colors and covered every part of the body. Customers could check their *abayas* in the complimentary *abaya* cloak room and wander around in jeans and fitted tops. Even so, many women felt uncomfortable taking off their *abayas,* but Sahar and Asima removed theirs as soon as they reached the floor. Nadim stayed downstairs and went to have a soda since he wasn't allowed on the women's-only floor.

The white gown Sahar selected sagged around her bosom and was too short for her. "Perfect," she said, "let's take this one."

"No honey, this gown looks terrible on you; try on this one," Asima said, pointing at the nicer one she had chosen for Sahar earlier.

"Who cares? I'm never going to wear it again, nor am I planning to keep it."

"Sahar, I know that you don't like Husam. But you have to at least keep up appearances for our family's sake."

Part of Sahar's dowry consisted of fine pieces of jewelry, perfumes, silk materials from which she was to create her elaborate trousseau or *addahbia*. It was a custom to wear brand new clothes once married, a symbol of starting a new life.

"Let me have the dress," she said, reaching for it.

Her mother looked at her skeptically and handed it to her.

Sahar put it on but didn't look in the mirror. Instead, she faced her mother and asked, "Do you approve?" But she already knew the answer from the tears in her mother's eyes.

"You look beautiful." Asima looked at her daughter in the white, strapless beaded lace gown. See-through short sleeves with a floral motif had been added and a charmeuse sash started from underneath her bosom, wrapped around to her back and draped down to the floor. "With the veil from my wedding and the diamond and pearl tiara, your outfit would be almost complete," her mother said enthusiastically. "All we need now is to get you a pair of long gloves, shoes and a purse to complete the ensemble."

Sahar felt saddened that she was such a disappointment to her family, especially to her mother. "Thanks Mom. It's too bad that you will never see me happily married," she said, taking off the dress and changing back into her jeans and T-shirt. Asima looked at her watch. In 10 minutes it would be prayer time.

When *salat* or prayer time came in the Kingdom as it did five times a day – before sunrise, at noon, in the mid-afternoon, immediately after sunset and before midnight – all Muslims had to pray because Saudi Arabia followed the orthodox Islamic school of thought. They believed that prayer was the most important pillar of Islam and the greatest of religious duties. Those who abandoned it were called evildoers and were regarded as criminals who would go to hell. If one neglected prayer, then she or he would be separated from God and be deprived of his mercy, the abundance of his favors, and the plentitude of his generosity.

Muslims who did not pray were considered infidels. The *mutawan* often walked around and looked for the Muslims who avoided the prayer time and flogged them. Shiite Muslims who combined their *raka* – repetition of prayer cycle – and only prayed three times a day were also considered nonbelievers. Thus when prayer time arrived, no matter where one was in Kingdom, the lights were dimmed, the doors were locked and the checkout counters were closed. Anyone in line had to wait 15 minutes before business resumed. Non-Muslims waited. Muslims headed for a nearby mosque.

Mosques were plentiful and since people scheduled their daily lives around prayer time, they always knew where to go. Many businesses and restaurants had a praying area in a back room for customers. Others prayed at home in solitude. Some malls and buildings had a mosque inside.

Ritual purification preceded all prayers. Larger mosques had ablution fountains or other facilities for washing in entryways or courtyards. Worshipers at smaller facilities had to head for the restrooms to perform their ablutions.

Because women must be covered from head to toe when entering a mosque in Riyadh, Sahar and Asima dropped off the wedding gown at the cash register and told the sales clerk to hold it for them. Then they picked up their *abayas* from the cloakroom and headed for the restroom. During the ablution ritual, which took about 10 minutes, they cleansed three times in the following order – washing hands and wrists, rinsing mouths and nostrils, wetting face from hairline to chin and ear to ear, bathing the right arm to the elbow followed by the left. They dampened their heads where their hair parted and the inside and outside of their ears once. After that, they bathed their feet and ankles three times. When the ablution ended, they recited in Arabic, "I bear witness that there is no God but God. I bear witness that Mohammad is his slave and messenger," followed by "O Lord, make me of those who turn to you in repentance and of those who are not defiled." Once finished, Sahar and Asima threw on their *abayas* and headed toward the mosque in the mall.

Women prayed in a separate room from men. Men got to see the *Imam*, who led the prayer. Women simply listened to him over a speaker. Sahar and Asima entered a beige room with red and navy carpet, removing their shoes before entering. They stood facing Kaaba – a Muslim shrine in Mecca toward which Muslims recited Qur'anic passages as they assumed specific postures – bowing, prostrating and standing up again with *raka*, a repetition of prayer cycles. After prayer time, Asima and Sahar returned to the store to finish their shopping.

"What time is it?" Sahar asked. Her stomach was growling.

"Where is your watch?"

"The battery died, and I forgot to bring it to have it replaced."

"Why didn't you wear the watch Husam bought you?"

She shrugged and mumbled, "Umm...I don't know."

"Please don't tell me that you gave it away," Asima said as they approached the store.

Sahar had a habit of giving all her expensive belongings away to people who needed them. She hated how the rich in her country squandered money while the poor starved to death. "Hakim's son was sick and he had no money to take him to the doctor." Hakim was one of their servants from Pakistan.

Although all Saudi citizens had health insurance coverage and received some benefits from the government, a non-Saudi resident or foreigner received nothing. Even children of non-Saudi parents who were born in the Kingdom were not considered citizens.

"Do you realize how expensive that watch was?"

"Yes, but what good would it do on my wrist when I can use it to help save a life?"

"What about the diamond necklace your father bought you? I haven't seen it on you in a long time."

"I...I..." she coughed to clear her throat, "I gave it to Rubilyn."

"What for?" her mother frowned. "She has no place to wear a necklace like that."

"Remember when she went to visit her family in the Philippines last year?" Sahar said as she and her mother dropped off their *abayas* and veils once again at the cloakroom.

"Yes."

"She sold it and used the money to buy them gifts and her airline ticket," Sahar had no regrets about what she had done. Too many clothes, shoes and jewelry were symptoms of boredom, she thought.

There were no bars, clubs, movie theaters or concert halls. Only five percent of the female population worked. The new rich generation without work experience didn't like taking on menial jobs and preferred employment in high positions. So, many didn't work and lived off of their parents and trust funds. This left a few options in life – eating, visiting family and friends, shopping and more shopping.

Asima's jaw dropped open. "You're out of your mind," she said, raising her voice. "Your father is going to be very angry with you when he finds out."

"*Alab* doesn't pay attention to such things; not unless you bring it up," she said as they walked up to the cash register.

Asima paid 56,000 riyals – $15,000 – with her debit card for the dress and asked the salesperson to send it to their house. Then she and Sahar picked out a pair of long gloves, crepe and satin round-toe pumps and a small purse with a semi-circular silver handle decorated with crystals. She also bought her daughter a ruby necklace embedded in a vintage-looking platinum setting.

"I don't want a wedding present. I will refuse to wear anything associated with this event."

"It's not a wedding present. It's something I want you to have to always remember me by."

"I don't need a necklace to remember you. I will always love you, no matter what."

"Will you try it on and let me see how it looks on you?"

Sahar did as she suggested and looked at herself in the mirror, but all she saw was a miserable girl whose life was about to change forever. "It's lovely, thank you Mom, but I would much rather have my *al horeyat*," she said, kissing her on the cheek.

"Believe me dear, if it were within my power, I would give you your freedom."

"I hope that someday women will be liberated."

"*Inshallah* – whatever is God's will."

Inshallah was a word used frequently. It was a response to everything such as, "Are we meeting for lunch tomorrow?" "*Inshallah*." "I need you to get that job done by next month." "*Inshallah*." "Can that lawyer win my case?" "*Inshallah*."

Mother and daughter picked up their abayas at the cloakroom and put them back on. They tipped the clerk 20 riyals – five dollars. "Promise that you'll keep the necklace and not give it away."

"Not even if I needed it to feed a hungry child?"

"Honestly Sahar, you're too much sometimes. C'mon let's go. I'm very hungry. Where should we go eat?"

"How about a juicy American hamburger, fries and soda?" Sahar suggested.

"You don't want to eat in a nice restaurant?"

"No, not really. I'm in the mood for fast food, and I know just the place," she said, getting into the elevator with her mother to meet her *Alkal* Nadim.

They found him sitting in a café, having a friendly chat with a person at the next table. As soon as he saw them, he excused himself and walked toward them. "Finished shopping so fast?"

"Yes, and now we're hungry."

"Where did you have in mind?" Nadim asked.

"Let's get back in the car. Sahar will show us the way."

Ten minutes later, Nadim pulled into the parking lot of an American hamburger chain where women ordered from one side of a divided counter and men from the other. Unrelated men and women were forbidden to be in the same room, not even as a group in a public place. If found together, they'd be harassed by the *mutawan*, arrested and flogged.

Nadim paid for their meals on the other side of the counter and met them in the walled-off family section.

Restaurants were segregated with a "single" section sign meaning single men, and a "family" section sign for women alone or with a *mahram*. In the single section, men sat in plain view of everyone. In the family section each table was blocked off by a curtain. Many restaurants didn't serve women.

"I wish it wasn't *haram* for us to sit in the singles section. What's the purpose of eating out when we don't get to see the outside? "

"Sahar, you're behaving like a foreigner. This is our way of life," her mother said with a reprimanding tone. "I would think you would be accustomed to it by now."

"I'm just getting tired of our way of life. Everything is so much simpler in Europe and America. People never think about these sorts of things," she answered, sipping her strawberry milkshake through her straw.

"Grass is always greener on the other side. I'm sure they have their own issues to deal with," Asima stated.

"I have to agree with Sahar," Nadim replied as he ate his french fries, "It isn't fair that women are forced to sit back here behind a curtain while we get to eat wherever we want."

"Yes, but this is what most women want. They don't want to be bothered with men ogling and harassing them," Asima answered, unwrapping the white paper around her cheeseburger.

"How do you know men would do that? They may go on eating their burgers and not give you guys a second thought," Nadim said.

"I've seen men staring at foreign women who don't have to cover their hair and heard them make lewd remarks."

"That's because they're not used to seeing strangers without their veils. People always want that which is forbidden," Sahar said, eating one of her mother's onion rings. "When you travel through Europe or America, they have so much freedom that no one cares if you walk out in your underwear. People just go on about living their lives."

"Our country isn't ready yet to change and frankly I'm not so sure westernizing our entire culture is such a great thing."

Many Saudis and fundamentalists found the western culture a threat to their Islamic values. This intense fear applied not only to Saudi Arabia but also to all countries that governed according to the laws of Sharia. The more the western countries meddled in their affairs, the more religious and conservative they became, making life impossibly difficult for the modernists.

"We can keep our culture and be free at the same time. Iranians did it before the Islamic revolution," commented Nadim, who had traveled to Iran during Shah's time. "They had no compounds or high walls to separate foreigners from citizens, and they still don't. People were free to practice their religion and still are. Everyone simply blends in. Men and women commingled. Women who wanted to, covered up, and women who didn't want to, didn't."

"And where are these women now? They're back under the *chador*," Asima replied, sipping her Coke.

"That's not true," protested Nadim, who had recently seen pictures of Iranian women. "Many wear the *chador*, but others wear a light, fitted tunic or jacket over their clothes instead of a black, loose garment. They don't cover their faces, and their hair shows through their loosely draped head scarves."

"Unlike here, Iranian women are allowed to vote and many hold positions in the parliament, which is more than I can say for us," Sahar said, wiping the mustard from the corner of her mouth with a napkin. "And they get to participate in the Olympics wearing sportswear. This year, their flag bearer is going to be a woman. Imagine that – a woman representing Iran."

"Our country is the only country in the world that doesn't have female athletes going to the Olympics," Nadim added. "These Iranian women are defiant. They fight for what they believe."

"That's because their government has always been secular until recently. Their women always worked in high positions and were not considered the property of men. Our government has always been governed under Sharia. I don't think that will ever change."

"I guess," Sahar said, wishing that things were different and that she wasn't being forced into marriage.

At least her friend Dawn had married for love. Sahar didn't even like Husam. She remembered keeping in touch with Dawn, visiting her and talking about the good old college days in Barcelona. She had seen the broken arm and bruises on Dawn's body. Dawn never complained until she had had enough. She killed her husband with a kitchen knife and disappeared. No, Sahar would never get married and end up like Dawn.

FIVE

Six weeks after the marriage agreement between the Al-Hijazi and Abdul-Samad families, Sahar had to prepare for her final day before the wedding ceremony and reception. In most cases, the civil and religious contract were signed in an office days before the reception – Muslim wedding ceremonies did not take place in a mosque – and by the time the reception came around, the couple had already consummated the marriage. Sahar had stipulated she would not allow the groom to touch her until after the reception. She had no intention of letting an old man take away her virginity.

In Saudi Arabia, all first-time brides had to be virgins, otherwise they would be considered tainted. With a hostile bride on his hands, Husam pushed to have the reception after the wedding ceremony. Because of enforced segregation of sexes, men and women were not allowed to celebrate together. So, the reception for women took place in a separate room from men. The groom's celebration started earlier than the bride's. The bridal reception started as late as 11 in the evening and ended around three or four in the morning.

In a traditional family, the bride was purified during Henna Night when her body would be rubbed by her maids or family with cleansing and conditioning oils, creams and perfumes. Her hands and feet were tattooed with henna and her hair washed with extracts of amber and jasmine. Henna Night represented the last night before her shift into a life of responsibilities with a husband and future children.

Although Sahar was being forced into marriage, her parents were considered modern in comparison to many Saudi families, especially her mother, who tried to give her anything within her reach. So, when Sahar asked to have estheticians come to her house on the day before her wedding to pamper her, her sisters, cousins and aunts with manicures, massages, facials and body wraps, her mother obliged.

"Smile Sahar, smile. You look as though you're going to your death sentence. You'll be married tomorrow, isn't that wonderful?" one of her cousins told her while she was getting her nails done.

But Sahar's mind was far away. Her body was present but her soul had escaped as it floated above her head, watching her family rejoice in her misery. She was limp and motionless except when one of the estheticians would say, "Lift your arm, so I can wax under there," and she would do as asked like an obedient dog as if someone said, "C'mon go pee. Lift your leg and pee." Without control over her life, she was no more than a puppet manipulated by a man's whim. There wasn't much anyone could do for her or for the plight of any Saudi women, for that matter.

When the estheticians finished, Sahar put on a traditional dress known as *zaboun,* with beautiful silk swirling patterns of light and turquoise blue, fuchsia and white and a matching headdress and *yashmak* – a veil embroidered with silver thread – over her face. It was a commitment to tradition on *ghomra* – the night before the wedding night – that said a bride should not be seen by anyone until her wedding day.

Sahar's *ghomra* took place in the pink and ivory living room of her house. As she entered the room, which was accented with gold moldings, door handles and veneer side tables, she was sprinkled with Riyal coins and small, light .2 ounce silver and gold coins made for weddings. Then all the women began celebrating with Arabic music, dancing, and enough food to make Sahar's stomach turn. Music and dancing were forbidden in the Muslim religion because Islam forbade anything that might lead to lust and fornication. It was believed that music and dancing were used to stimulate thoughts of eroticism and filthy love. Yet in more modern families, these laws were overlooked.

The dinner included *ma'amoul,* also known as *al arous* – the bride, a traditional round cookie made of flour, ghee and dates, dusted with powdered sugar and eaten by the bride before her wedding; *muhallabia,* a custard of sugar, milk, cornstarch and rose water; the sweet *lugaimat* made of flour, cream and black seeds formed into balls, fried and then dipped in sugar syrup; mini date cakes, marmalades, olives and meat dishes, except for ham, which was *haram* in the Muslim religion.

"Have some *ma'amoul,*" her mother said, looking vibrant and young in her spaghetti-strap lavender sequined dress that hugged her curves.

"No, thanks Mom, I'm not hungry." Sahar's hair lacked luster, her complexion looked dull and her eyes were filled with sadness. No amount of pampering could change the deep void she was feeling.

"Please Sahar," her mother begged, "you're embarrassing me in front of everyone."

Sahar loved her mother dearly, so she took a bite. The cookie was delicious but the connotation behind it was not.

"That's better dear. You must make the effort to pretend to be happy even if you're not."

"Yes, Mother."

Asima left her side to dance with her sister-in-law. She could no longer take her daughter's long face.

Rubylin offered Sahar fruit punch. Although some people drank alcohol in the privacy of their homes, if a person was caught in possession of hard liquor, the punishment was severe regardless of one's religion.

"I can't wait to see you all dressed up tomorrow," she smiled, her small red lips fading away, showing off her protruding teeth. "You will be the most beautiful girl in the room."

"Rubilyn, I love you dearly, but could you please not talk about this wedding?"

"Dear child, I wish you were marrying someone you loved, but now you must try to make the best of it." She left to serve punch to the others.

Sahar's mind drifted as she thought of her friend, Dawn. It seemed that she had been thinking a lot about her lately. How horrible her fate had been but at least her marriage was based on love at the beginning. Sahar didn't even have that. How could she sleep with a man she abhorred? She didn't know him very well, and perhaps he wouldn't beat her the way Dawn's husband had beaten her. But she didn't love Husam and knew as soon as the reception ended he would want to consummate the marriage.

"Sahar, c'mon and dance with us," an aunt insisted. "This is your night before you take the final steps."

Sahar got up and started dancing as though she were a ventriloquist's dummy. "Twist this way, yes that's it shake it, very good," her aunt insisted.

After several dances and being force-fed sweets and meats, Sahar was ready to collapse. The guests were wearing out as well, and one by one began to disappear. Once everyone was gone, Sahar went to bed but couldn't sleep. She tossed and turned throughout the night, thinking that tomorrow everything would change forever.

As a newlywed, her friend Dawn had everything she had wanted, a husband she loved, an affluent life, nice clothes, jewelry and a personal servant, Sahar thought. But her destiny had been bitter. Unlike Dawn, had she had a choice, she would have someday married a westerner and lived a simple life.

But Saudi women were not allowed to marry anyone outside of their faith, not even Muslims from a different country unless the king allowed it, which only applied to the royal family and occurred rarely. Even then, the married couple would have to live in exile. Men, on the other hand, were permitted to marry non-Muslims if a potential wife was willing to convert.

Sahar sat up from underneath her covers to get water, when her mother stuck her head in the door.

"Are you asleep?"

"No Mom, come in," she sadly replied and pulled down her tank top, which had gathered above her waist.

"How are you holding up?" she asked with a concerned look.

"I'm afraid not too well."

Her mother hugged her. "I am sorry to see you so unhappy, but soon it will all be over and you'll start your new life."

Sahar cried as never before with her head buried in her mother's arms. "I'm going to miss you. Nothing will ever be the same."

Asima kissed her daughter's forehead. "Did I ever tell you how much I love you, my sweet?"

She nodded her head and stayed quietly in her mother's arms for a few minutes before she spoke again. "I wish *Alab* wasn't forcing me into marriage."

"It's not all your father's doing, you know, but rather your grandfather's."

"*Alab* is weak, and I will never forgive him for this."

"He's weak in many ways and yet strong in other ways. Don't you remember that argument he had with your *Alabalkabir* Kadar over you?"

Sahar looked up and shook her head no.

"Yes, you do. You were 15 and had come home for the summer from your school in Vancouver. Your Grandpa Kadar said you were well past the age of puberty and should not be allowed to go back to school. He said you had to get married."

Sahar started to remember the discussion. "And *Alab* said I was too young to get married and that he was sending me back to finish high school and after that I was going to a university of my choice."

"It was the first time I had seen him stand up to your *Alabalkabir*," she uttered, rocking her daughter to calm her. "I was so proud of him."

Sahar looked at her mother. "But why didn't he protect me this time?"

"Your father is a complicated and stubborn man. You made him angry with all the stunts you pulled with your suitors. He was worried about the family's reputation."

"I'm sorry."

"No, I am. I should have prepared you better for this day, and I didn't. The fact is…" she said looking down at the silk bed cover, brushing her hand against it and looking up, "the fact is, our culture and customs dictate that women must get married and bear children. It has been so for centuries. Unmarried young ladies are frowned upon and single women are pitied."

Sahar started to feel helpless and depressed again. "I'm tired. I think I should go to sleep now. *Ohebbake ya omm* – I love you Mom."

"*Ohebbake kasiran* – I love you more," she replied, kissing her.

SIX

The wedding ceremony took place at an office of a Sharia court official. Since the law required at least two male witnesses or two female and one male – two women's testimony was equivalent to one man's testimony – Sahar's father was there clad in his brown *mishlah* – a cloak – the right side of which was tucked under the left arm. Kadar, his face rigid and venomous, sat in his wheelchair near his granddaughter, intimidating her with his presence at the signing of the marriage contract.

A deadly silence filtered through the room as she endorsed the papers with shaky hands. Sahar thought she was going to faint at any minute but as she looked over to her mother and saw the strength she conveyed with a nod of her head, Sahar straightened her slouched body and thought, *Be resilient; it's almost over. Soon, you will no longer exist and in a month, everyone will forget this day.* But she wished she could go in peace without marrying a man she didn't love.

She couldn't divert her eyes – watching him was like watching a horrible car crash. She didn't want to look yet couldn't help but look. Her husband had thick black eyebrows that connected together over his nose and dark squinty eyes as cold as steel. She imagined his old body, wrinkled like a prune. After all, she was 22 and, to her, someone 46 years her senior seemed like ancient history.

Cool, calm and collected, if Husam felt any worries or tension, he did not show it. However, he did wonder about his wedding night and the rest of his life with Sahar. He knew she didn't want him. If he could not tame the girl and make her succumb to his desires, he would end up divorcing her. His other wives hadn't been in love with him either but they had never denied him anything. Each behaved the way a proper wife should – having his meals ready on time, never defying his authority and willing to have sex whenever he asked – he thought as he watched his bride hidden underneath three layers of veil put her signature on the marriage contract.

Once that was over, a driver took Sahar to an upscale hotel where her family had reserved several suites to prepare for the dreadful eve. The first thing she did was go to one of the rooms, open up her purse and search frantically for a small flask she had kept hidden for the past month. Her thoughts drifted back to a fateful night one month ago.

"Drink this on your wedding night and not any time sooner," the Egyptian chemist had told her, showing her a small purple flask. "First, excuse yourself to use the bathroom and while in there, hum a song."

"What for?"

"It'll take time for the potion to work and if you hum, he'll think you're a happy bride who has finally accepted her fate. Then when you're ready, lie down on the floor of the bathroom and keep humming."

"Why do I have to lie on the floor?" she asked.

"Because if you don't, you'll collapse and the thump of your body will alarm him. He'll rush to save you and he may just be able to do that. And that's not what you want."

"Then what?"

"Soon you will be paralyzed but will still be able to hear voices, especially his when he calls you and you can't answer. He'll ask others to help. Then the emergency service will arrive, but by then it will be too late."

"Will I feel any pain?"

"No, you won't feel a thing. By the time the medics arrive, you will have lost consciousness and all your vital organs will have stopped working."

She must have looked horrified. Alarmed, he warned, "Are you sure you want to do this? It's not too late to change your mind."

She paused for a minute but the thought of living with Husam and his sister brought her back to reality. Many married couples moved in with the groom's family in a villa that housed other siblings and their kin. There was no personal privacy and the tension between relatives often made the living arrangements difficult. "Yes, I am sure." She took the flask.

"C'mon, let's get you dressed. Everybody's waiting downstairs," Rubilyn told her as she walked in the bedroom of one of the suites, shifting the weight of her portly body from one foot to the other to relieve the pain she was feeling in the soles of her feet. "What's that purple thing in your hand?"

"It's nothing really. Just one of my favorite perfumes I was planning to wear tonight."

"Then you'd better give it to me so that I can put it in the honeymoon suite."

"No, I want to keep it close to me."

"Why?"

"It's silly really. This flask has always brought me luck, and I want to keep it close to me. I think I'll put it in my purse," she answered, opening the white purse with the silver handle her mother had bought her and dropping the flask in.

Rubilyn went to the closet, took out Sahar's wedding gown, unzipped it and held it out for her. Sahar stepped into it, slid her hands through the sleeves and Rubilyn zipped it up.

"How do I look?" She offered a forced smile.

"Like an angel. Husam is a very lucky man."

"Thank you Rubilyn," she said, hugging her. "Thank you for taking such a good care of me all these years."

"Miss Sahar, you can let go now. I'm not going to disappear from your life," she said. But Sahar kept hanging on.

"Sorry," she said, releasing her.

Rubilyn helped Sahar put on her tiara and veil. "Are you alright?" she asked, studying her face.

"Yes, I'm fine. I'm just very nervous," she said, slipping on her elbow-length gloves.

"Take a deep breath, and then let it out," Rubilyn suggested.

Sahar did as asked. "Could you give me a minute to myself?"

"Sure, but don't you take long because everybody...."

"I know, everybody is waiting downstairs," she said, watching her maid leave the room.

As soon as the door closed, Sahar removed the flask from her purse and put it in her bra, too scared to let it get too far away from her. The aroma of white roses had taken over the room and the air conditioner gave her goosebumps as she rubbed her arms and looked outside at the murky sky. *You can do this*, she said to herself, feeling an unbearable heaviness. She forced her lead-like body to move away from the window and exit the room. Rubilyn helped her with her train. As they got to the elevator, her two sisters were waiting.

"You look like a princess," her younger sister told her.

One teardrop lingered at the corner of Sahar's eye, contemplating whether or not it should fall, and then at last it rolled down her perfectly made-up face, followed by a second and third. But she didn't budge as it stung her face and felt as sticky and itchy as the rest of her body. She wanted to rip off her gown and crawl out of her skin. *Smile. Smile and be patient. It's almost over*, she told herself.

"You're alright?" her elder sister asked her in Arabic, being only too familiar with a forced marriage. She was 16 when her husband forced himself upon her for the first time. Eight years later, she still hated having sex with him and was glad that he had three other wives. He spent one week with each, giving her a break form the beatings.

Sahar nodded her head and said, "I...I...."

"I understand," her sister empathized, squeezing her hand.

When the elevator reached the lobby, Sahar got out and her sisters held her train. They moved toward the large ballroom. Sahar entered with her hair done up on the crown of her head. Her lovely platinum tiara added a special touch to her long veil when she walked into the room full of women.

Sahar plastered a big smile on her face. "Make sure you look happy on the night of your wedding," the Egyptian chemist had told her.

But her mother, in a mint chiffon gown, noticed the strain in her daughter's smile and silently applauded her for pretending to be happy.

A band played Arabic music as everyone ate and celebrated.

In the upstairs ballroom, Husam looked younger with his salt-and-pepper hair, mustache and beard dyed black. He wore a cream *thobe* and rayon *ghutra* and *bisht*. Saudi men usually dressed in black, white or brown tones because they believed bright colors belonged only to women.

Waiters served roast sheep on a bed of rice; guests ate with their hands. The men did a traditional dance with their arms linked and swords in their right hands as they moved forward and back, raising their swords up and down to the rhythm of Arabic music.

As the night came to an end, Husam went with his relatives to the marriage room and sat and drank coffee for a few minutes. Then all of them left. Sahar went in with her family as well and did the same thing. This was a tradition to ease the bride and groom's stress. When that ended, Asima asked everyone to give her and her daughter time alone as the rest of the family left the room.

"Your hands are as cold as ice," her mother told her, holding them in hers.

Sahar looked at her mother and said, "I'm very nervous."

"I know you are. Do you have any questions for me? Can I do anything to calm you?"

"No, you've been great, but now it's time for you to leave. Husam will come back any minute. *Ohebbake ya omm.*"

"*Ohebbake kasiran,*" she said, kissing her and thinking Sahar looked so much like Saad with her sincere face, dark defiant eyes and perfectly shaped bowed lips. "I love you more, and you're going to be alright. Trust me." She then left the room.

Sahar paced back and forth, wringing her hands when the door opened and the groom entered. As his eyes fell upon her, he salivated. She was a lovely young bride who could make him sexually content, he thought as he approached her, kissed her on the neck and said, "Don't be worried. It will hurt tonight but the pain will not last long."

As he said this, her body stiffened and once again she felt as though she were going to faint. He turned her around, unzipped her dress and moved his beard back and forth against her delicate skin. He noticed a small mole on the right side of her lower back and traced it with his finger. And as his hands moved to the front of her dress, he massaged her breasts and licked the skin of her back. Sahar cringed. Quickly she turned around and told him that she wanted to go and freshen up in the bathroom.

"Don't be long," he said. "I am an impatient man."

"I will try to hurry," she promised.

Behind the locked door, she took out the flask and drank the potion without giving it a second thought, then started to hum like a happy bride and changed into a pair of black pants, a long-sleeve shirt and sweater. She removed her makeup, turned on the faucet, threw a black veil over her face and went to lie on the floor.

"Are you almost ready?" he said, opening a jewelry box and glancing at the emerald bracelet that he was going to give her after they had consummated the marriage. It was a tradition for a husband to give a gift to his wife after their wedding night.

"Yes, almost," was the last thing she said before the potion started to work. A painful flaming sensation took over her entire body. *Damn that Egyptian, he lied about it not being painful*, she thought. But it was too late. She could no longer move as she felt her insides burning.

"I hope you're almost ready," she heard him say but wasn't able to respond.

Minutes later, he pounded on the door. "What're you doing?" When he did not hear an answer, he jiggled the doorknob but realized it was locked. Husam kicked the door as hard as he could, pushed his way in and found her on the floor. "My God," he said. He shook her, but she was lifeless. He removed her veil, checked her pulse – nothing. He called Kadar on his cell phone.

"I'll be right there," Kadar replied. He was with Saad and Asima on their way home. Kadar told the driver to turn the car around and get back to the hotel. He then told his son and daughter-in-law that Sahar wasn't feeling well and that they were needed.

In the Saudi culture, one rarely blurted that someone had died. The news always came slowly to soften the blow – "Oh, your relative is not as strong as he once used to be" and then, "He is a bit under the weather" followed by "Maybe you should come for a visit," and then a few more excuses in between until it was announced that the person had died.

While waiting, Husam checked again for a sign of life by putting his face next to her nose to see if she was breathing – but nothing. He wondered whether she had died from a stroke or heart attack or whether she had committed suicide since she disliked him so much. He replayed the evening in his head. She had hummed like a content bride and then gone into the bathroom. If she incurred a sudden illness and fell to the floor, he would have heard the thump of her body as it hit the ground. If she had been in pain, she would have screamed for help. And why in the world was she dressed in black as though she were going to a funeral instead of wearing the pale peach negligée that was set on the vanity chair? No, she must have planned to kill herself long before entering their suite.

Husam began looking around for an empty bottle of pills but couldn't find any as he searched the counter by the sink, the two drawers beneath it and the cabinets under them. Still, he found nothing. But when he looked inside the wastebasket, he saw the flask. Husam picked it up, unscrewed the lid and smelled it. There was no odor. Curious, he tapped the flask on his palm without thinking that the contents might harm him. A tiny drop of clear liquid fell into his large palm. With the pinkie of his other hand he touched the liquid and then lightly brushed it on his tongue. It had no taste. He then quickly rinsed his mouth with tap water. Odorless, colorless and tasteless, he thought, was it arsenic or some similar poison? He had heard about people committing murder with arsenic. Stupid girl, he said, what a waste. If only he had known, he could have stopped her. Clever of her to hum and let the poison take effect until it was too late to save her.

Time seemed to stand still as he walked back and forth, waiting for his cousin. Finally, Saad and Asima rushed in wheeling Kadar.

"She's in the bathroom," Husam said, his facial muscles as hard as rock.

Asima ran toward Sahar and shook her. "Sahar can you hear me? Can you hear me?"

"She is not breathing," Husam said.

"What do you mean she's not breathing? She was fine when we left her in your hands," Saad yelled.

"Sahar, get up," Asima slapped her daughter lightly on the face. "Get up."

"She has no pulse," Husam offered.

"No pulse? Not breathing. Is she dead?" Kadar said, raising an eyebrow.

"Yes. I'm afraid she's gone," Husam said gravely.

"Are you telling me that my daughter is dead?" Saad yelled as he stared at Husam's swarthy face. Hours ago he was only too happy to give away his daughter and now he was realizing what a big mistake he had made.

"Lower your voice son, we don't need a scene here," said Kadar, who was more worried about what people would say and his business contract with Husam than about the death of his granddaughter. In his eyes, women were precious commodities who bore sons and could be traded to make deals. If they failed to carry out these two obligations, they were worthless.

Kadar wheeled his chair to face Husam and said, "How could you let this happen?"

"How could I? How could you? Who gave her this poison?" he asked, showing the flask.

"We must call the paramedics. They can pump her stomach," Kadar cried.

"She's dead. What's the pumping going to do?" Husam screamed.

"We can't just sit here and do nothing," Saad said, reaching for the phone.

Husam grabbed the phone away from him and hung it up. "Think of the scandal this would cause. No, we must make sure everyone thinks it was a stroke or heart attack."

Committing suicide in Islam was a grave sin because Muslims regarded God to be creator of life and only God was allowed to end life. Suicide bombing, however, was considered a form of martyrdom acceptable by radical fundamentalists and guaranteed one's entrance into paradise.

"Oh my beautiful daughter," Asima said over and over as she held Sahar's limp body in her arms.

"I must get to the bottom of this,' Saad said, delirious. "I must find out what kind of poison she drank. They can save her, you know. They can save her."

Husam smacked him. "Get ahold of yourself, and be a man. She's dead. The only thing we can do is to save face."

So Husam made several phone calls to his connections at a nearby hospital. An emergency crew arrived at the back door of the hotel, went upstairs to pick up the body and put it on a gurney, then discreetly rolled it onto the service elevator. A doctor recorded the time of death at five a.m., stating that it was caused by an aneurysm, and signed off on the death certificate.

For the next few days, there was an uproar in the Al-Hijazi and Abdul Samad families. Neither Sahar nor Husam's relatives could believe her sudden death. Crawford Enterprises major shareholders and Kadar's business partners and employees had been calling to offer the two families their condolences while crossing their fingers that the merger was still going through. Everyone knew that this was not a marriage of love but rather of money, and privately there had been much speculation as to whether her death had been a suicide. Yet in reality, no one cared as long as business went on as usual.

"Excuse me sir, there is a phone call for you from Emad, your translator," a servant told Husam, who was having dinner with his second wife, four sons and two daughters in the dining room of his second villa, which looked identical to his first and third. Since

Sahar's death four days ago, he was starting to get tired of the constant interruptions.

The Muslim religion dictated that a man who took on more than one wife must provide equally for each and spend an equal amount of time with each. Some men, especially the younger generation, didn't take on a second wife and then there were those who couldn't afford to have more than one spouse. Others owned one mansion that housed all their wives. Many liked a separate home for each spouse due to jealousy among wives and siblings. In such cases, all their homes had to look the same with similar furniture.

"Tell him, I'll call back," Husam replied harshly.

"He said it was urgent."

"I'll take it in my study," he answered, as he got up clad in his *dish dash*, a cotton robe buttoned down the front. At home he didn't wear a head cover and neither did his sons.

Head covers were only worn in front of guests as a sign of respect or outside to keep the head from burning in direct sunlight and cover the mouth and nose during sandstorms and cold weather. When male children reached puberty they were taught to wear the head covering as a sign of entering manhood.

Husam picked up the receiver. "What is it?"

"I thought you should know that Jason Crawford called to extend his condolences," Emad said. He was a middle-aged man with a hooked nose, a mustache and a narrow face.

"Thank you, but that's hardly an urgent matter."

"He sounded worried about the merger. He asked if you were still planning your business trip to the U.S. next month." Husam still needed to finalize the signing of some paperwork and was contemplating the purchase of a hospital and an office building he had looked at during his last visit to Los Angeles. He wanted to have another look before he made up his mind.

"No, tell him there are too many things I still have to sort out here. I'll have to get back to him."

"Err...are you sure that's the response you want to give?" Emad was not only an interpreter but also his adviser. He knew that everyone was counting on the merger.

Husam stroked his beard contemplating what to do. He was angry at the Al-Hijazi family for not keeping their end of the bargain. They were supposed give him a pretty young bride, not a dead one. He had hoped that not only their companies would fuse but also their families. Nevertheless, since it was to his advantage to join forces with Kadar, he decided not to pull out of the business deal.

"Are you still there?" Emad asked when he heard silence at the other end of the line.

"Yes. Tell him that he has nothing to worry about, but my trip will have to be delayed due to current circumstances."

"I'll pass along the message, and if there is anything I can…" *do for you,* he wanted to say but before he had a chance to finish his sentence, his employer had already hung up. Emad looked at the receiver for a minute and shook his head. Husam was a difficult man with terrible manners. Emad had been working for him for nine years and only put up with his nastiness since he got paid well.

Back in the U.S., Crawford Enterprises and their investors were relieved that Husam had no intention of backing out of the merger. Although it was Sunday, Jason and Drew stayed at the office until the afternoon in case nervous major shareholders needed to be assured that nothing was going to change. Father and son scheduled an emergency board meeting for Monday to discuss plan B in case Husam decided to back down. Realizing the importance of diversification, they added one detail to their agenda: seek new small investors to balance out larger ones. It was too risky to be so dependent on oversize conglomerates, as they both had witnessed within the past 12 hours.

"I told you that we shouldn't put all our eggs in one basket," Jason said, as he tightly gripped his coffee mug handle with his large masculine hand.

"Yes, you were right, but now we can correct all that," his father replied.

Andrew looked 10 years younger than his age, took good care of himself, eliminated junk food from his diet and played squash after work at a private club on the first floor of the building that he owned.

"We should have never waited this long. It's going to take time to pull in new businesses," Jason answered, staring at his father disappointedly, his jaw muscles tense.

"What choice do we have? We'll all have to put in longer hours."

"I'm already working 70 hours per week. You need to delegate some of my responsibilities to my brothers."

"They're married and need time with their families."

"Just because I'm a bachelor doesn't mean I have nothing better to do with my life. On the contrary, I didn't get married so that I could enjoy my life."

Nominated as the number one bachelor of the year by a famous gossip magazine, Jason had no trouble attracting women. He was stylish, tall and had an athletic build.

"Let's not talk about this today," Drew said looking at his watch, noticing that it was half past five and he was to have dinner with an old friend at six. "I have to go."

"I suppose I'm going to be the only one here in the office on a Sunday."

"No, you should leave as well. I think we've done as much as we could for today," he replied, grabbing his jacket and taking off.

Jason felt the weight of the world on his shoulders. Perhaps if he liked the people he dealt with he would actually enjoy his career, but most of them were shady businessmen who broke the law. Although in the business world one had to bend the rules in order to stay competitive, Jason knew that his father was getting in deeper and deeper with the wrong crowd. Take Husam, for example. He made most of his money by making arms deals with various countries, including countries that had sanctions against them. If two countries were at war, Husam played both sides by openly selling to one and secretly to the other and then sitting back and watching the two annihilate each other. He then turned around and invested the money in real estate. If that wasn't money laundering, he didn't know what was.

He rubbed his face in frustration and after a minute, started dialing Tiffany. He often used sex as a tool to relax his body and mind.

"How about dinner and a night cap?" he asked when she answered.

"I already have dinner plans." She was about to leave the house with her date.

"You want to come over afterwards?"

"That's not going to work for me."

"Have an enjoyable dinner and sleep well. I'll talk to you some other time," he told her and hung up.

She stared at her phone and frowned. He didn't even sound disappointed that she couldn't make it.

"Is everything alright?" her date asked her. He was polite, dark and handsome.

"Yes, everything is fine. Let's go see a movie and have dinner afterwards."

After hanging up with Tiffany, Jason opened up his little black book and went down the list until he was able to contact Madison, his on-and-off-again girlfriend, a brunette with a nice fanny.

"I'd love to have a candlelight dinner with you at your house. What time should I come by?"

"How does seven sound to you?"

"Seven is perfect. See you then." She went to her lingerie drawer to pick out the sexiest thing she could find, grabbing a silk lavender nightie with black lace trim and matching thong, and throwing them in her purse.

SEVEN

On a cold January day, more than four months after Sahar's death, all the commotion about their Saudi investors disappeared in the Crawford mansion and the household had a new staff member named Dawn Parnell. She was a skinny nervous thing with short scarlet hair, dark blue eyes and thick glasses. In the kitchen, Mrs. Beazley, the house manager, introduced her to the employees present at the regular Monday morning meeting. The entire staff had to be there unless they were excused by Mrs. Anderson, the head housekeeper.

Among the staff were the head chef, doormen, laundry supervisor, senior seamstress, the head handyman, stable manager, landscapers, pool man and 25 other servants who rotated around the clock; some were live-ins, others part-timers. After listening to Mrs. Beazley's speech about the week's agenda, what had gone wrong the prior week, the upcoming luncheon, high tea and dinner events, Zoya, a petite and pretty blond maid with honey-colored eyes and braids, showed Dawn to her room located in the servants' quarters, and left to finish her chores.

Dawn took in the stark surroundings: scratched light-gray walls, a small window that overlooked the horse stables and track, the plain furniture that consisted of a twin bed with a faded brown coverlet, a plywood square held up with four wooden sticks to use as a desk, a tiny triangular closet with one shelf, a few white plastic hangers, and a bathroom slightly bigger than the closet. She was glad she didn't own much or she wouldn't have been able to fit it in, she thought wiping the tears welling up in her eyes.

She began removing her folded clothes from her small black suitcase and placed them in a drawer underneath her bed. When finished, she hung up the few items that needed hanging and looked in the bathroom to see if there was a storage place for toiletries when she heard a knock on the door.

"Yes?"

Mrs. Anderson stood at the door. Widowed 10 years ago, she was an unpredictable sort who always felt in competition with younger women and believed that she was as beautiful as any of them if only she could stop eating. The 50-year-old had rust-colored hair parted in the middle and tied into a doughnut behind her head. She was round, and had stubby fingers and narrow eyes. She either liked you or didn't, and Dawn could tell she wasn't on Mrs. Anderson's favorite list because of the way she glared at her.

"Here's your uniform." She handed her a white shirt, skirt and shoes, noticing Dawn's red, tired eyes. "What's the matter with your eyes?"

"Oh, umm, I have allergies."

"Humph." She looked at her skeptically, hoping she didn't have something contagious. "Well, put those on," she said, "and then come downstairs. There's work to do."

Already? But I just got here, she wanted to say. "Yes, of course."

After getting into her uniform and climbing down a flight of cement stairs, she opened a white wooden door, crossed the lawn and headed toward the main house.

Outside, two statues of lions sat majestically on each side of the doorway and inside in the foyer, two very large antique china vases were filled with pale pink belladonna lilies. Two marble spiral staircases inlaid in the center with pricy Oriental rugs led the way to the upstairs rooms. A silver chandelier boasting finely cut crystals divided the foyer in two. On one side was a Victorian old Paris porcelain clock resting on top of a Gothic rosewood console table; on the other a 19th-century rosewood settee highlighted with marquetry and gilding, upholstered in silk.

Dawn turned toward a capacious hallway. The walls were covered with what she presumed were large family portraits; sizable windows overlooked a broad stretch of green shrubbery and a lake. A soft breeze rustled the light translucent curtains and suddenly she felt so carefree that she forgot she was there to work and instead became a visitor admiring the view. She then looked behind her at one of the portraits and saw a handsome young man, with the most beautiful jade eyes, standing in his riding clothes next to a chestnut Arabian thoroughbred, holding a trophy.

"That was me, 15 years ago." A man's voice startled her. He was now 37 and just as attractive but more distinguished looking with his six-foot figure dressed in a dark ash suit, a white shirt and mustard tie. His short curly hair complimented his chiseled jaw and appealing mouth. "Funny how quickly time passes us by, but you probably wouldn't understand," he added, thinking that she was no more than 19.

"Excuse me sir, I didn't mean to...."

"My name is Jason Crawford III," he interrupted, noticing her silver retainer when she spoke. "And you are?"

"Err...my name is...my name is..." her mind went completely blank.

"Don't tell me you have forgotten your own name," he teased.

"No, of course not. My name is Dawn. Dawn Parnell, that is."

"Funny, you don't look like a Dawn. Elizabeth perhaps or Colleen, but definitely not a Dawn." One of Jason's annoying habits was to corner people he didn't know very well, ask them a lot of questions and try to figure out any secrets they may be hiding. In Dawn's case, she seemed very jittery, almost as if the smallest noise would make her jump.

Dawn swallowed nervously. "I didn't know that people had a specific look to go with their names."

"Sure they do. A name should always suit one's personality and features. For example, you can't have a tall athletically built man named Peewee."

"Well, I'm sorry to disappoint you, but my name is Dawn," she responded, completely annoyed by his behavior and forgetting all about the butterflies in her stomach.

"I see that I have offended you, and I'm sorry. It's nice to meet you, Dawn Parnell," he said, extending his hand to shake hers while studying her. She was too skinny for his taste and too plain. And those awful glasses made her eyes look like a cat's, but he thought the few freckles on the bridge of her nose and cheeks were rather cute. "Irish?"

"No," she shook her head. "Scottish."

"You don't have an accent."

"My great-grandmother who moved out here was Scottish," she said unwilling to offer any extra details about her background.

"You must be new here. I haven't seen you around before."

"Yes sir. Today is my first day, and I'm not exactly sure where I'm supposed to be," she said, looking down at the ivory-and-granite floor. His stare made her feel as though she were bacteria being examined under a microscope by a curious scientist.

"I see that Mrs. Anderson is already putting you to work. Come, follow me. I'll show you the way," he replied walking from one room to another with Dawn trailing behind him. He then went down a set of steps that led to offices, a very large laundry room, a sewing room and an immense kitchen where they had their meeting earlier. "Mrs. Anderson? Oh, Mrs. Anderson?" he yelled out.

Mrs. Anderson ran out of Mrs. Beazley's office and into the kitchen. "Yes, Mr. Crawford? Is there something you needed?" she asked, delighted at the sound of his voice. She was infatuated with him and hoped that some day he would notice her.

"I seem to have found your new employee. I have to go now," he said and left.

"Sorry ma'am, I got lost," Dawn said trying not to look at her boss directly, scared of her Medusa glare.

"Humph," she replied with an arched eyebrow. "I hope that you used the service entrance to get into the house instead of bothering the doorman."

"Excuse me, ma'am, but I don't know where that is."

"You have a short memory for such a young person. Ask one of the servants before your shift is over," she answered. "Follow me."

Dawn did as asked and found herself upstairs in the center of a grayish-blue drawing room decorated with a silk, light-blue-and-white floral rug, early American sculptures and paintings. As she glanced around, she noticed a shiny black grand piano in the corner. There was a Regency walnut canapé covered with needlepoint, a graceful recamier with curved feet, a mahogany handcarved center table and several ecru beechwood fauteuils. A large, rectangular mirror bordered by an etched golden frame was situated above a white mantle. Two copper candelabras sat on the mantel and a screen featuring a decorative picture of a foxhunt hid the fireplace.

Fox hunting may have been the game of the rich and royals but it was a barbaric game at that and should have been banned worldwide long ago, Dawn thought. How would the hunters like it if they were the ones being chased and killed as a form of entertainment?

"I want you to vacuum this room and when you're finished, start polishing and dusting," she said as she headed out.

Dawn plugged in the vacuum cleaner behind the recamier and began moving the heavy machine to and fro, but when she got close to the edge of the rug the vacuum made a loud gurgling noise and emitted a burning smell. She checked to see what was wrong and realized that her machine was eating away the decorative threads hanging from the edges of the rug. "Oh, oh, this isn't good," she said, overwhelmed with panic, her face tense and crimson.

Jason happened to pass by, smelled the burning odor and rushed in. He went straight to the socket and unplugged the vacuum.

"Sorry sir," She furrowed her brows, disappointed in herself for being such a klutz. "I don't know what happened. One minute I was vacuuming and the next…."

"Don't worry about it," he replied calmly as he tried to pull out the threads that were caught in between the vacuum bristles. "Next time, just try not to run the machine so close to the edge."

"Are you going to tell Mrs. Anderson?" she asked, afraid that she would be discharged.

"There's no need for her to know. It'll be our little secret. Perhaps you should dust for now and leave the vacuuming to later," he said and left.

With shaky hands, Dawn began dusting. She was scared that she would break something. An expensive vase flew out of her hand and she caught it right before it hit the floor. Her heart stopped for a few seconds and beads of sweat formed on her forehead. *I'm not cut out for this*, she told herself. *I'm not fit to do anything*.

After finishing her chores at the end of the day, the soles of her feet hurt as much as her throbbing head. She collapsed on her tiny bed and passed out until a loud pounding on her door woke her up.

"Go away, I'm trying to sleep."

"Get up, you overslept and missed breakfast," a female voice yelled from behind the door.

"I'm not hungry," she replied, sleepily.

"Not you nitwit, you missed serving breakfast to Mr. Crawford Sr."

"Oh damn!" She jumped up, looking at her old clock. It was nine in the morning and Mr. Crawford liked his breakfast at seven. Dawn opened the door and saw Zoya.

"I'm going to be fired, aren't I?"

She looked at Dawn's disheveled hair and puffy eyes. "You would if Mrs. Anderson ever found out, but thankfully she's in her room sick and I covered your shift."

Zoya came from a poor Russian family and had moved to the U.S. to become a famous model, not realizing that her 5-feet-2-inch-height was a disadvantage even if she did have shapely breasts, a round bottom and fine nose. When her modeling career didn't pan out, she started working as a housekeeper.

Dawn looked at her in surprise. "Why would you help me? You don't even know me."

"We do these sorts of things for each other. One hand always washes the other," she replied with a thick accent, pushing her way in and looking around the bare room. Unlike Dawn's room, Zoya's was bigger, carpeted and had nicer furniture. Zoya once had one of the older, smaller rooms, but when a servant who had worked for the Crawfords for years quit without giving notice because she could no longer handle Mrs. Anderson's erratic temper, Zoya quickly took over the newly remodeled larger room before another maid could stake her claim.

"I don't know what to say," she answered, reaching for her thick glasses and putting them on.

"Just get ready as quickly as you can and go down to the laundry room. I told Fred that you were busy washing clothes and ironing." Fred was always in charge when Mrs. Anderson wasn't present.

"Thank you," she answered gratefully and jumped in the shower as soon as Zoya left. Ten minutes later, she emerged.

The great thing about her short hair was that it was low maintenance, Dawn thought as she threw on her uniform, dried her hair and ran toward the main house. Unfortunately for her, Mrs. Anderson saw her from a first floor window that afforded a perfect view of everyone's comings and goings and made a note of it in a journal she kept of servants misbehaving.

Dawn did one load of laundry after another, running from one machine to the next, taking out the wet contents and dropping them in the dryer while doing hand washables in a large sink. She was so preoccupied that she didn't even notice Zoya entering the room as she tried her hand at ironing and steaming shirts, blouses, trousers, dresses and linens.

"Not like that," Zoya startled her. "Here let me show you. You must make sure that the crease on the trousers falls in the center and not the side. That's how Mr. Crawford Sr. likes them."

"These pants hardly have wrinkles on them," Dawn remarked.

"The Crawfords are meticulous about their clothes and require that everything be pressed after each wearing even when there are no wrinkles."

Dawn nodded and did as she was told. She then moved on to the shirts. Zoya taught her what to do and she ironed six shirts and laid out the seventh. "Whose shirts are these?"

"These belong to Jason Crawford, Mr. Andrew Crawford's son, including the one you're about to iron," she said, grabbing a huge garment bag. "When you're done, hang them in here and then start with the dresses. I'm going to go smoke a cigarette. If anyone asks, tell them I went to the bathroom and will be back in two."

The buzzer on two of the machines rang and Dawn put down the iron and hurried to get the clothes out of the dryers to fold them while they were hot so that they wouldn't wrinkle. A few minutes later, she started to smell something burning and when she looked over, smoke was coming out of Jason's shirt. She hurried to pick up the iron but it was too late. His shirt had a burnt hole in the front. She wrote a note on a yellow Post-it, attached it to his shirt, put it on a hanger and hid it in the middle of the other shirts before covering them with the garment bag.

That night, when Jason returned home, he went upstairs to shower and get ready for his date. When he got out, he dried his fine textured hair, put on aftershave and went to his closet to pick out his clothes. He decided on a pair of dark green pants and the shirt that Tiffany had given him for his birthday a month ago. Jason didn't like it much because it made his skin itch but wanted to wear it at least once so that Tiffany wouldn't be offended. He went through his clothes and pulled out a cream-and-green-striped shirt, noticing a big yellow note on it that said, "I'm so sorry sir. I hope that you forgive me and not tell Mrs. Anderson. I accidentally burned your shirt – Dawn."

He removed the paper, noticed the hole and chuckled at her note, thinking how inept she was for the housekeeping job. He felt sorry for her. She probably needed the money, and he didn't want to terminate her employment. Besides, he was relieved that he now had an excuse not to wear Tiffany's gift. He crumpled the paper and threw it in a wastebasket, grabbed a white shirt instead, put on a tie that matched his trousers and left to pick up his date.

EIGHT

A month went by and Dawn still hadn't adjusted to her job at the Crawford mansion. Today, she was exhausted from cleaning all the toilets – nine downstairs, five upstairs, three at the guesthouses, four at the cottages, his and hers by the indoor and outdoor pools, the tennis courts and the stables. Once done, she mopped the floors, washed the sinks, cleaned the counters and restocked the bathrooms with toilet paper, fresh towels, liquid soap and hand lotion. She then reported to Mrs. Anderson who gave her more work.

"I want you to clean Mr. Crawford's room," Mrs. Anderson told her.

"Which Mr. Crawford?" Dawn asked, looking at her watch. She had been on her feet all day and the last break she had was at one in the afternoon when she had a short lunch. It was now seven in the evening.

"Both."

"But I just finished cleaning 24 toilets."

"Of course if you can't do it, I can give it to someone else but that would mean cutting down your hours starting next week and giving them to someone who can handle the workload."

"No! I can do it," she blurted.

"I thought you could," Mrs. Anderson replied, offering her usual insincere smile.

Dawn dragged her tired body upstairs, starting with Andrew Crawford Sr.'s room. Luckily it was organized and didn't need much tidying up. He and his wife had separate bedrooms. Hers had been cleaned earlier by her personal servant. Dawn changed the Egyptian cotton sheets, fluffed custom-made down pillows, set out clean pajamas, passed the vacuum across the hunter green rug, dusted an African padauk dresser and work desk and finished off by wiping dry the limestone and mosaic tiled bathroom.

But when she got to Jason's room, it was a big mess. Clothes strewn everywhere, a woman's black thong from the prior night's tête-à-tête, condoms stuck in a towel – she could only imagine how often he had done it – a dish filled with oyster shells and empty champagne glasses, one with a red lipstick mark. After picking up his clothes and throwing them in the hamper, she went into the bathroom and noticed the bathtub hadn't been drained, hair and toothpaste in the sink and white goo on the counter, which she hoped wasn't semen. As she cleaned and straightened, she remembered her old home and how hard her housekeeper had worked to keep it clean.

Dawn looked down at her calloused and pruned hands and tears flowed from her eyes. She grabbed a tissue and wiped her face. As she finished up, the bedroom door swung open and Jason came in wearing a business suit, briefcase in hand.

"Oooh! Good-evening sir, I was just leaving."

"Wait a minute," he interrupted her. "Are you feeling okay?"

"Yes," she replied without glancing up. "Just a little tired."

He frowned. "Could you look at me when you're talking?"

Dawn looked up slowly, afraid that he would notice her teary eyes and red, runny nose. "Aaachoo," she sneezed, so that he would think she had a cold.

"Gesundheit," he answered and stared at her. Her eyes were bloodshot and had dark circles under them from a lack of sleep, and her face looked old and weary for a person so young. "How many hours a day do you work?"

"I'm not sure Mr. Crawford. It depends on when Mrs. Anderson dismisses me."

"Just take a guess. Eight hours? Ten hours?" He looked at her inquisitively.

She shook her head no. "More like 15, sir. I work 15 hours a day on average, but I'm not complaining. No sir, I can do it. I'm strong," she assured him, afraid to be fired.

"Any days off?"

"I have Sundays off."

If he was angry, he did not show it. All he said was, "I want you to take the next three days off."

"Is there a problem, sir?" she asked anxiously.

"No, no problem at all."

"Please don't fire me, I'll work harder."

"Relax, girl. I'm not firing you. I'm giving you time off so you can get over your cold," he replied, knowing very well that she didn't have a cold and was too scared to complain about Mrs. Anderson.

"Oh, but I can't, sir. Mrs. Anderson would get very upset with me."

"You let me worry about Mrs. Anderson. You just get better. Then come here, same time, three days from now and we'll talk about your rights."

"But sir...."

"No buts. That's an order," he replied firmly.

She nodded sheepishly and walked away.

"Oh, and Dawn," he yelled after her, waiting for her to turn around and look at him, "don't worry about a thing. Rest up." He smiled and winked.

"Thank you, sir," she answered, heading toward the stairs.

Downstairs in the kitchen, she ate a bowl of chicken noodle soup and afterwards washed her dish. She then went to her room, took a hot shower, and slept till noon of the following day. In fact, she would have slept well into the afternoon had Zoya not knocked on the door with a loud thump that made her jump up and yell, "Damn, I'm late." But she soon realized that she was off for next three days.

"Mrs. Anderson is in an uproar," Zoya said entering the room wearing her white uniform with her hair pulled back, showing off her rhinestone earrings.

"But why?" she asked groggily, wiping her sleepy eyes with her hands and putting on her glasses. "Mr. Crawford said I could take three days off."

"You lucky girl," Zoya replied, plopping down on her bed. "He must like you a whole lot." Although she couldn't imagine why,

Dawn wasn't very attractive, especially when she wore those god-awful glasses.

"I think he pitied me when he saw how tired I was yesterday," she said, straightening strands of her hair that were sticking out.

"Mrs. Anderson does work you the hardest," she remarked, looking at her pink fingernails and thinking it was time for her to change the polish. "Between you and me, I don't think she likes you."

"You don't say," Dawn said, getting off the bed in her long-sleeve T-shirt and flannel pajama pants. She went to the bathroom and started brushing her teeth while trying to carry on a conversation.

"What did you just say?" Zoya asked, wishing that she were as tall and skinny as Dawn. Perhaps then she would have made it as a supermodel instead of a housekeeper.

Dawn spat out the toothpaste. "Everyone else gets two days off and takes breaks when they need to except me."

"That's illegal, you know. You should threaten to file a complaint with the EDD," Zoya told her, noticing that Dawn had no pictures of her family lying around.

"Please don't say anything to anyone. I need the money," she said, rinsing her mouth and then brushing her hair as she came back into the room.

"Don't worry, I won't. I think Mrs. Anderson feels threatened by you because Mr. Crawford is so attentive to you." In a way, Zoya felt a pang of envy toward Dawn. Two years ago Jason had treated Zoya as though she were special but now she was invisible to him. He was still polite to her and said good morning and good afternoon but that was pretty much the extent of their conversation.

"That's not true and even if it were, what's it to her?" she frowned.

"Well, Mrs. Beazley has been thinking about retiring and Mrs. Anderson wants her position."

"Why does that have anything to do with me?" Dawn began fluffing her pillow.

Zoya got off the bed and went to glance outside at the stables. A trainer was taking out one of the horses for a canter. "She's afraid that Mr. Crawford might recommend you instead," she said, turning back and looking at Dawn to see her reaction.

Mrs. Anderson couldn't wait for Mrs. Beazley to retire because she hoped that then Jason would look at her as a manager working in an office instead of a housekeeping supervisor. She would be making more money and be better able to take care of herself. Perhaps she would treat herself to a two-week spa vacation and get a facelift and tummy tuck.

"That's ridiculous." Dawn shook her head as she smoothed the sheets and then straightened up. "I would never want to run a house this size," she answered, gazing at Zoya with candid eyes.

"What can I say? She's just very jealous of you."

"She has no reason to be. Once I've saved up enough money, I'm planning to change jobs and get a place of my own."

"To do what? L.A. is a very expensive city. Do you have any idea how costly it is to rent a place? You'd never be able to afford it unless you're willing to live in a bad neighborhood," Zoya said as she noticed a book of Edgar Allen Poe's poetry sitting on Dawn's desk. Zoya opened it to where it was bookmarked and found the poem, *Alone*.

Alone

From childhood's hour I have not been
As others were; I have not seen
As others saw; I could not bring
My passions from a common spring.
From the same source I have not taken
My sorrow; I could not awaken
My heart to joy at the same tone;
And all I loved, I loved alone.
Then – in my childhood, in the dawn
Of a most stormy life – was drawn
From every depth of good and ill

The mystery which binds me still:
From the torrent, or the fountain,
From the red cliff of the mountain,
From the sun that round me rolled
In its autumn tint of gold,
From the lightning in the sky
As it passed me flying by,
From the thunder and the storm,
And the cloud that took the form
(When the rest of Heaven was blue)
Of a demon in my view.

"You know, this poem is quite depressing."

Dawn ignored her comment. "I don't want to be a housekeeper for the rest of my life."

"Listen to me, you're much better off staying here. You get free room and board, a paycheck and beautiful views. What more could you want?"

"There's nothing wrong with doing an honest day's work as long as you like what you do."

"Who cares as long as it pays the bills?" Zoya set the book back on the desk and looked at her watch. "Well, I'd like to stick around and chat but I'd better get back to work before Mrs. Anderson misses me."

The following day, Saturday, after feeling fully rested, Dawn got up around 10 and decided to walk the grounds. If the 45,000-square-foot mansion with exceptional architectural features, a guardhouse at the main gate, a subterranean parking garage and several guest houses and cottages were magnificent, the 200 acres surrounding it were even more breathtaking. She passed by a library, museum and gymnasium with an indoor pool. The mansion was more like a town that offered everything one needed without ever having to leave. She admired the formal French-style gardens with an expansive lawn, topiary, stained-glass-domed pavilions and romantic rest areas.

There was a secluded pond with a bridge and serene waterfall, enchanting walkways through bamboo and covered arbors, a koi pond, fountains, European-imported statuaries, water gardens, a sparkling heated Grecian-style outdoor pool – which she wondered why no one ever used – and a sports court where volleyball, roller hockey and soccer could be played. When Jason and his brothers were young, the sports court was their playground where they could run, jump rope, play basketball and hopscotch.

As Dawn strolled by the tennis court, she noticed Jason practicing with a machine that spit out balls every few seconds.

"I suppose you wouldn't know how to play tennis, would you?" he asked when he spotted her from the corner of his eye.

"Not very well," she said. She enjoyed watching him move across the court in his polo shirt, which showed off his muscular chest and brawny arms.

He looked at her, surprised, as one of the balls zoomed right toward him as he ducked. He turned the machine off, grabbed an extra racquet and tossed it at her, "Let's see what you can do."

"Oh no. I couldn't...." but still she grabbed the racquet while silently comparing her cheap cotton jerseys and sports shoes to his top-of-the line tennis shoes and designer white shorts, and felt uneasy.

"C'mon, I promise I won't bite." He smiled, showing off two dimples that made him look like a young boy.

She slowly walked to the opposite side of the court, unsure of what to expect.

He threw her two balls and said, "I'll tell you what. I am not going to keep score and will give you five chances to make your serve."

"That's very generous of you," she said tight-lipped, insulted that he presumed she was inept.

"Well, c'mon. Let's go, I don't have all day."

Dawn tossed the ball up in the air and hit it to his backhand. The ball spun away from him so fast that he couldn't get to it.

"Fifteen Love."

"I thought we weren't going to keep score."

"You said we weren't, but I never agreed to it," she answered defiantly.

"I must warn you, I'm very good at this game," he replied, shifting his weight from one foot to the other, trying to be agile and alert.

She served the second ball and this time he barely hit it as they started rallying for a good two minutes until she hit a shot he couldn't return.

"Thirty Love,' she said aloud, knowing that she was starting to get on his nerves.

"You lied to me when you said you don't play very well. Who taught you how to play?" he asked, wiping the sweat off of his forehead with a towel.

"I learned in physical education class at my high school."

He looked at her skeptically, wondering why she was lying. She couldn't possibly be this good just playing during P.E.

"Are you ready?" she asked, wanting to serve again.

"Go on," he grunted in frustration. He hated when his opponent was better than he.

She almost aced the serve, but somehow he managed to return it. They rallied as Dawn made him run from one side of the court to the other, until he found himself completely out of breath.

"Jason dear," he heard his mother calling from where Dawn had once stood watching him.

"Forty Love," Dawn said as he missed the next ball.

"That doesn't count, my mother made me lose my concentration."

"I wonder if an umpire would accept such an excuse at Wimbledon."

"We are not at Wimbledon," he said through gritted teeth. "Could you excuse me for a minute, I need to see what she wants."

"No problem," she said smugly as she watched him trot away. Dawn was suddenly the confident girl she once was, full of life and energy, but when Jason's mother lowered her Marc Jacobs glasses to the bridge of her nose to look at her with disdain, she snapped back to reality, realizing that she had forgotten her place and manners. She should have made every effort to lose to her boss's son.

From nearby she could hear Jason and his mother bickering.

"What is it Cynthia?" he inquired, always calling her by her first name. The only connection he felt he had with her was that she had given birth to him. "What is it that you found so urgent you couldn't put off till later?"

"What are you doing?" Cynthia posed stiffly. Earlier Mrs. Anderson had told her, "It's none of my business, Madam, but I think I saw Mr. Crawford, Jr., playing tennis with the new housekeeper."

Jason peered at his mother and her wide-brimmed straw hat decorated with a jumbo polka-dot sash with long tails. Cynthia loved hats and had several for every occasion stored in beautiful floral boxes, labeled by season and occasion – spring tea, summer garden party, fall church and holidays. She was always petrified to get a wrinkle on that pretty face of hers.

"What does it look like I'm doing? I'm playing tennis, and may I say your interruption made me lose a point."

"I know that you're playing tennis, I'm not an idiot," she hissed. "But why are you playing with the help?"

"Because she's young and plays much better than you."

If there was one thing Cynthia hated, it was to be reminded about how old she was and Jason knew it. She had plastic surgery on most of her body parts, went in for facials and wraps every week and had a trainer, a nutritionist, a masseuse and a psychotherapist who often told her that she suffered from boredom and needed a hobby. "Don't be rude," she said. "I'm only trying to point out the obvious."

"And that would be?" he asked, scowling.

"She doesn't belong in your league."

"Why? Because she's a maid?"

"I'm glad you realize the difference," she gloated.

"No mother, I don't. We were enjoying a game of tennis. Let's just leave it at that."

She uttered, sharply, "Jason, if you don't put a stop to this, then I will have a talk with your father and then get rid of her."

"Good, because once you do that, she will no longer be an employee and I can date her," he said, heading back toward the court.

"Jason Crawford, you get back here this instant. I'm not finished with you." But when she saw that he had no intention of turning around, she stomped her shiny high heels, grunted and stormed away.

From the court, Dawn had been watching Cynthia's body language, her arms crossed in front of her, her nose up in the air as though she were better than everyone else and her tense facial muscles wrinkling her beautifully sculpted face. She could only imagine what they had talked about as Jason approached her.

"I'm sorry, but I have to cut this game short. There is an urgent phone call I have to take. Thank you for a nice game."

"Of course, Mr. Crawford," Dawn said, putting distance between them.

"Mr. Crawford is my father's name. Please call me Jason."

"I don't think that would be wise. Good day, sir," she said as she left the court.

Jason just stood there, forgetting all about his nonexistent phone call.

Minutes later, when Jason left the court and went into the house, he ran into his mother who was complaining to his two brothers in the dinning room. Cynthia's middle son who was spreading wasabi on his sushi, looked up, saw Jason, and said, "Mother is right you know. You shouldn't be hanging out with your housekeeper."

Jason, glowered and replied, "Thanks but I hardly need advice from a person who slept with my high school girlfriend."

"We were kids. I would think that by now you would have gotten over it."

Jason's youngest brother interrupted and said, "Jason never forgives. Isn't that right Jason?"

"Don't you have a wife and children to go home to or have you shipped them off to somewhere so that you would have time to fool around with your married mistress?" Jason said and turned to Mrs. Anderson who had just walked in with a bottle of warm sake, "I will take my lunch in my room."

Sunday, Dawn woke up at five a.m. She was restless. When she had work, she didn't have time to think as much about her future, but now that's all she thought about. She debated whether she should go in the heated pool for a swim but was afraid that someone would see her. Yet she was itching to do something, anything, to burn off the insurmountable energy that was running through her cells and looking for escape. She knew very well that servants weren't allowed to use the pool, but who would know? Her employers wouldn't even be up at that hour. It was Mrs. Anderson's day off and the rest of the household staff wouldn't snitch.

She put on her black one-piece swimsuit, threw on a pair of sweats and a jacket, grabbed a towel and headed toward the pool. She touched the warm water with one foot. The temperature was perfect. Dawn shed her clothes, jumped in, warmed up with the crawl, then switched to the butterfly without a notion that Jason had been watching her from afar.

He, like Dawn, couldn't sleep either and was about to go into the gym for a workout when he saw her. Surprised, he had stood near the gym, observing her remove her sweat pants and jacket. Had it been anyone else, he would have reprimanded them for using the pool but somehow he didn't mind anything that Dawn did. What was happening to him? He was getting too soft, he thought, as he studied her body. It looked curveless like a boy's, and her skin was young and toned. There was nothing special about her except that she played tennis exceptionally well and swam the butterfly flawlessly, two sports that were unusual for an average person to master, let alone a housekeeper. As he eyed her dipping in the water and emerging like a fish that had been just set free, he found himself drawn to the mystery surrounding Dawn. Jason shook his head, reprimanding himself for being so taken by a housekeeper who couldn't possibly offer him any kind of satisfaction. He turned away and went into the gym to ride on his stationary bike.

When Dawn finished with her swim, she dried off, threw her clothes back on and went to have breakfast.

"You're up early," Zoya said when she saw Dawn entering the kitchen.

"And so are you."

"I have to serve breakfast," she said fixing her ponytail and putting on her apron. "What's your excuse?"

"Couldn't sleep," she answered, grabbing a bowl and pouring corn flakes in it.

"Milk and sugar?" Zoya dangled a milk carton and pushed a bowl of sugar toward her.

"Thanks. Why don't I help you, after I finish eating?"

"Don't worry, I have it covered. You deserve your days off. Enjoy them."

"I'm bored out of my mind."

"How can you be bored? You can go for a walk, have a look in the museum or check out a book at the library," she said. Grabbing a set of plates, she whispered, "You might as well take advantage of it before the plump Old Crab comes back."

"Is that what you guys call poor Mrs. Anderson?"

"Poor, my behind, all she does is eat all day and make everyone else do her work," Zoya said, walking toward the sunroom.

Dawn smiled at the nickname and went out the back door to sit on a wooden bench to have her breakfast. The sun was out, shining its rays on her wet hair and cool skin. One of the gardeners was watering the plants a few feet away. A gray rabbit came around briefly with its ears pricked up to graze on the shrubs but when it saw Dawn, it froze.

"Hi beautiful, come here, I'm not going to hurt you."

"He's afraid he'll become stew," said a male voice from behind her.

Dawn turned to see Fred. At 63, he was a hefty energetic man with a wide nose, bald head and chubby face. "Hello, Fred."

He took a seat on the opposite side of the bench and set his coffee mug on a wooden table nearby. "How's the Old Crab treating you these days?"

Dawn looked at him with wide eyes, never expecting him to call her names. After all, both he and Mrs. Anderson were her supervisors.

"You look amazed. Don't be. No one here likes her. She's a conniving person, and I'm the first to admit it."

"But how come she's nicknamed Old Crab when she's clearly younger than some of the servants and Mrs. Beazley."

Mrs. Beazley was 65 years old.

"It's not her age that makes her look old but rather her attitude and nastiness."

"How long has she been working here?" she asked, putting a spoonful of cereal in her mouth.

"About two years or so. Mrs. Beazley was short of help and needed someone to run this house efficiently, so we all got shortchanged." He turned toward the gardener who was watering the plants and called out, "The hedges you cut yesterday were uneven. Would you trim them evenly after you're finished watering?"

"Alright," replied the Vietnamese man with a bamboo hat.

"Mrs. Beazley should have promoted you instead," Dawn said.

"The Old Crab has more experience and education. I didn't even finish high school."

"How come I don't see you in the house much?"

"I'm in charge of the outside employees like the pool man and maintenance staff. I see to it that they show up for work on time and that everything is functioning." He sipped his coffee. "When things break down, I write up a job order along with the estimated cost for the parts and give it to Mrs. Beazley, who reviews it before approving it and releasing the funds to cover the cost."

"Then you have no contact with Mrs. Anderson?"

"I used to work under her before I threatened to quit. I can cook and clean the house. I still have to help out when they're short-staffed."

"Really?"

"Yes, I sometimes go where Mr. Crawford, Jr. needs me. A few months ago, I went with him to his house in Laguna beach. I kept house and cooked for him and his girlfriend, Ashley."

"I thought his girlfriend's name was Tiffany."

"He never stays with any woman for long. Sometimes he rotates them around and then at times, they completely disappear."

"He's not a very affectionate person."

"He's affectionate alright. He buys them flowers, chocolate, jewelry and the usual stuff."

"Those are all material things that don't necessarily come from the heart."

"No, but women seem to like it." Fred stood up. As much as he disapproved of Jason's lifestyle, he didn't like discussing him. "I'd better make my rounds and see to it that everything is working as it should. If the Old Crab drives you crazy, let me know and I'll teach you how to deal with her."

"Thank you," Dawn said, getting up to take her bowl to the kitchen, "Would it be alright if I borrowed a book from the library?"

"Sure, but carry a feather duster with you."

"A feather duster?" she asked, dumbfounded.

"That way if you run into a Crawford, you can pretend you're there to dust."

She smiled. "I'll be sure to remember that."

Dawn took a scenic path back to her room to take a shower and get rid of the smell of chlorine on her skin. A bridge crossed over a creek, on one side of which were a lawn and a bench, on the other horse chestnut, eucalyptus and southern magnolia trees. As she climbed three steps going over the passage, she noticed Jason sitting on the bench, tapping on his cell phone and swearing.

"Excuse me sir, but can I help?" At first, she had wanted to keep her distance but then remembered all the times he had helped her out and treated her with kindness.

He looked up, surprised to see her. "This was working fine yesterday but today, I seem to be out of luck," he replied.

"Mind if I have a look?" she asked, noticing that he had a phone she was quiet familiar with.

"I don't see what you could possibly do to make it work. It is indicating that I have no service, but you're welcome to give it a try," he responded irritably, looking at her short, straight, shapeless red hair pushed back behind her delicate ears. She looked so plain and, at times, homely with her thick spectacles and shiny retainer. Yet, a special beauty radiated through her.

She took his IPhone, turned on a minuscule button on the side and reset the phone by pressing a top and lower button. She returned the phone and said, "Try making your call."

She studied him as he dialed a number – his boyish face, the way he wrinkled his forehead and bunched his lips when he was concentrating and the way he stared at her at times as though he were trying to solve a riddle.

"How did you do it?" he asked after ending his call.

"How did I do what?" she said, embarrassed that he had caught her gazing at him.

"My phone." He held it up, "You fixed it. How did you do it?"

"Oh, that. These phones are bizarre sometimes and shut down for no good reason. All I did was reset it so you can get service." She sat down next to him and showed him how she did it, adding, "We need to set your ringer back on, too." She turned on a tiny orange button and moved from one setting to the next, making sure everything was restored as he looked at her, flabbergasted.

"How do you know how to use the IPhone?" he asked, his ego bruised that his housekeeper knew more about technology than him.

"Oh...um...my ex-boyfriend used to work for Apple as a salesperson. When I would visit him at work, he would teach me all sorts of things," she answered nonchalantly and with assurance. "But I am surprised that you own this instead of a Blackberry. Most executives have a Blackberry."

"This was a belated birthday gift from my friend, George. I only received it late yesterday and haven't had a chance to learn all its functions," he explained as though he were talking to one of his buddies. "I own a Blackberry but I forgot it at...." He stopped talking and suddenly furrowed his brows. "How do you know that most executives own Blackberries?"

"I...I..." she stuttered, wishing that she hadn't shown off in front of him. She couldn't help herself. When she was knowledgeable about a subject, she enjoyed sharing it with other people. "I read an article about it in a business magazine." Dawn shrugged.

"You subscribe to a business magazine?" he asked, tilting his head and gaping at her.

She cleared her throat. "No. Sometimes when I clean your father's room I notice a periodical in his trashcan. I take it out and read it during my break."

"Business interests you, does it?" he inquired, looking at her skeptically. She never failed to amaze him.

"Not particularly," she told him uncomfortably. Now he was asking too many questions she didn't care to answer. "Well, I'd best be going," she said, starting to get up.

"Wait a minute," he said. "Can you tell me if all these phones come without a manual or did they forget to include one in my package?"

"None of them come with one, but if you Google their Web site, you should be able to find a video that shows the basics," she said, taking his cellular, doing a search and showing him the video. "You can also sign up for a workshop at one of their stores," she told him while fidgeting with his phone. She switched over to another site. "And this is how you make the prints bigger with your thumbs if the letters are too small to read. This is how you set up your emails to be downloaded here." She deftly scrolled through the windows. "Also, if your friend bought you a Bluetooth, you'll need to synchronize it with your phone by hooking it up to your PC."

"He got me one but I haven't yet opened the box," he said, hanging on her every word as though she were an expert when he should have been the one teaching her a thing or two. He had been out of the high-tech industry for too long. Half of his time was spent studying market trends and real estate and the other was divided between meetings and his social life.

Dawn sat there with her long legs extended in front of her, her body slouched in a comfortable position and her eyes lowered as she fooled around with his phone. "You can download your schedule from your Outlook in here as well. It's almost like a mini laptop on the go."

"You're an expert!" he remarked, completely impressed and taken with her.

"Not really." She gave him back his phone. "They're just a lot of fun to play with." She then stood up to leave and said, "Well, you have a nice day, sir."

"You as well," he replied, watching her walk away and thinking there was something odd about her that he couldn't quite put his finger on.

Later that afternoon, Dawn went to the library with a feather duster in hand to find a good book to take to her room. When she saw that no one was there, she decided to stay and enjoy the view. The dome-like structure that carried some 30,000 books offered works from Aristotle to modern-day authors. She picked up a copy of *The Canterbury Tales*, sat by a window that overlooked a pond filled with playful red-and-white koi fish and got lost in the stories for a good hour, forgetting all about her glasses that were sitting on top of her head.

"And this is the library," she heard Jason say as he opened the door for a sexy blond who resembled Marilyn Monroe.

Dawn jumped off her seat, and forgot all about reaching for the duster.

"It's gorgeous," the girl said, admiring the American cedar furniture and Brazilian mahogany bookshelves.

"Hello Dawn," Jason said, glancing at her book. "We seem to keep running into each other."

"I…I…It's just that…."

"I see that you're reading Chaucer. How do you like it?" he asked, studying her large indigo eyes and wondering if she felt any attraction toward him.

"I've," *read it before*, she wanted to say, but changed her mind. "I like it so far," she said, admiring his dark purple scarf and whiskey suede jacket, thinking it made him look very bohemian.

"Well, get back to your reading. We weren't planning to stay long."

"Are you sure because…."

He didn't wait for her to finish her sentence when he grabbed the blond's hand, kissed her on the neck and whispered something in her ear that made her blush.

"You are a naughty boy," she said.

"I hope so," he replied as they both darted away. Before the door closed behind them, Jason yelled back at Dawn, "You might try putting on your glasses when you're reading."

Dawn felt the top of her head and quickly put them back on.

NINE

Monday at work, Jason asked his assistant, Yumiko, to get a list of private investigators the Crawford human resources department had used in the past. After observing Dawn play tennis, swim the butterfly, give him pointers about his cell phone and talk about synchronizing, Google, PCs, laptops and Blackberries and later finding her reading Chaucer with her thick glasses sitting on top of her head, he thought she might be a corporate snitch sent over to spy on him and destroy his family's business. He decided to find out who she really was. It had happened to him once long ago when his ex-fiancée had gone through his briefcase to find a bid on a business his company was making. Ever since then Jason had a difficult time trusting people.

"I have Alex Rosenberg on line one for you," Yumiko buzzed him.

"Thank you." He picked up the line. "This is Jason Crawford."

"I was told you were looking for an experienced investigator," a woman with an Israeli accent said.

"You don't sound like an Alex," Jason replied, looking at the list of various P.I.s whose credentials, references and licenses had already been verified by Yumiko. This was the fifth person he was interviewing.

"It's Alexandra, actually. People usually don't like to work with female detectives, so I go by Alex." Born and raised in Israel, Alex had caramel-colored hair and coarse skin from spending too much time in the sun. Her feet, crammed six-inch stiletto heels, were casually propped up on her cluttered desk.

She had come highly recommended by the director of human resources department, but even so, he preferred leaving this type of work to a man. "I'm sorry but…."

"Don't hang up," she said, sitting up erect. Her commanding tone held Jason's attention. "I've been in this business for 25 years and was hired by your company a few years back to investigate one of your employees. If I can't deliver, I won't charge you a dime."

He uncoiled a paper clip and started twisting it into various shapes, a habit he had when he pondered over things. He looked over her résumé on his desk. She had worked for an impressive list of attorneys, had a business degree from University of California, Berkeley, masters of science in criminal justice and had served in the Israeli military and the LAPD, specializing in surveillance. "I see that you haven't had a client for almost a year," Jason remarked, noticing a gap on her résumé."

"I took a year off to take care of my father who was ill," Alex lied. She had a recreational drug problem that had depleted all her savings until Ryan, her love interest who worked as a senior analyst in the clandestine service of the CIA, checked her into a rehab center. She was now fully recovered.

"And is your father better now?"

"Oh yes. He has had a complete turn around," she answered.

"I need a minute to think," he said as he drummed his fingers on his desk. Alex had no criminal history and no complaints had been filed against her. Plus, she had been recommended by the human resources director. And in a way, it touched Jason that she took time out to care for her father.

Alex held her breath, waiting for an answer.

After a long moment he replied, "You are hired. I'll be expecting a report from you at least once a week." He then explained his suspicions about Dawn. "She was sent over to us from an excellent employment agency. I'll get my assistant to fax over her information and a photo."

"Didn't the agency do a background check?"

"Yes they did and so did Mrs. Beazley, who is in charge of employee recruiting, but I just want to make sure they didn't overlook anything."

Employment agencies and employers usually did a statewide check and when, nothing negative would come up, they'd figure the person was clean. However, Jason knew that statewide checks overlook certain details because the search only shows convictions rather than overall suspicious activity. A county background check showed all charges regardless of conviction.

"I'll get right on it," she said, about to hang up.

"Just one more thing before I let you go. Please be discreet. I don't want anyone finding out that you're snooping around."

"Don't worry," she answered, "discretion is my nickname. Oh and my fee is $500 per hour plus expenses."

"Fine. Just include a bill with your weekly report."

"Okay then, I'll be in touch soon."

Jason arrived home at seven that evening. Tossing his tie on his bed, he was about to change out of his Borelli suit and twill French cuffed shirt and take a shower, when he heard a knock on his door. It was Dawn.

"Something you wanted?" he looked at her puzzled, wondering why she had come up to his room.

Wearing her white uniform that had black smudges on it from cleaning screens, she said, "You asked me on Thursday to report to you here after my days off,"

"Oh yes," he replied, trying to recall what he wanted to talk to her about. Then it occurred to him. "Have a seat," he told her pointing at a taupe antique sofa.

Careful not to sully the upholstery, she perched at the edge and watched him pull out a file from his sleek calfskin briefcase. "Didn't Mrs. Anderson go over your rights with you?"

Dawn shook her head. "No. Maybe she forgot."

"Don't try to protect her. She never forgets anything," he said, annoyed at Mrs. Anderson. He knew how systematic and meticulous the Old Crab could be and how nothing ever escaped her scrutiny. "Look, we run our house like a business. Everyone here works 40-hour weeks, eight hours per day maximum and any overtime is compensated either through additional payment or through comp time. You will get two days off each week with the exception of the times when we're short-staffed and, in that case, you will get paid overtime."

Dawn nodded, upset at Mrs. Anderson for abusing her and glad that now she knew her rights. She had always thought that the rules that applied to white-collar employees couldn't possibly apply to servants.

"It's all in here," he said, handing her a folder. "Sick days, personal days and vacation time. Stand up for yourself, and don't let Mrs. Anderson take advantage of you."

She stared at him, baffled that he was so nice to her.

"Why are you looking at me like that?"

"It just that...that you're very kind."

He passed her a big smile. "I try. I sure do try."

His gaze upon her made her nervous as she got up. "Thank you," she said, started to leave, then turned around and asked, "I know you have been more than generous with me, but do you think you can ask Mrs. Anderson to give me this weekend off?" When she saw his look of disapproval, she added. "I wouldn't ask if it weren't important."

"Very well then, but next time you should ask her yourself. She doesn't like me to go over her head."

"I understand. Thank you again."

The weekend came and went. Jason instructed Alex to follow Dawn and find out where she was going. In fact, that was one of the reasons he had agreed to give her time off before speaking to Mrs. Anderson. The last time he had told Dawn to rest for few days, Mrs. Anderson had been quite upset with him and complained to his mother about being short-staffed because her son favored one of the housekeepers.

To find more about Dawn, Alex got to work immediately by using her connections – other investigators, people she had befriended in the police force and investigative databases to find information such as aliases, prior addresses, telephone numbers, social security numbers, previous employers, schools attended, criminal convictions, civil litigation history, credit history, assets, liabilities and bank accounts. She conducted county and statewide checks for arrests and disposition records and looked into her travel history. Nothing negative surfaced except for one matter that she needed to discuss with Jason.

"Hi Alex, did you find out anything?" Jason asked while talking to her from his headset as he put his elbows on his neat glass desk, gazing mindlessly at a black-and-white abstract photo on the wall.

At age 53, Alex looked and felt 15 years younger thanks to her regular Krav Maga workouts – an Israeli system of fighting skills. She dressed youthfully, owned 50 pairs of jeans and a large collection of tennis shoes and stiletto heels. Today she wore faded Levis and a red, cotton knit sweater as she sat on her ruby leather chair, looked at her disorganized office and repeated the same phrase in her head that she had for the past 20 years: *Someday I will pay someone to put things away for me.* "I'm afraid she is who she says she is."

"Can you be more specific?" Jason asked.

"Well, last week I took a flight to Salt Lake City, Utah, and then drove to Huntsville."

"Whatever for?"

"I went to University of Utah's library in Salt Lake, checking old yearbooks, looking for pictures of her and comparing them to the information and ID photo you gave me."

"And?"

"And, like I said. She is Dawn Parnell."

He started drawing a flow chart on his PC – Dawn…U of U…Huntsville.

Alex popped a hard candy into her mouth. "While I was in Utah, the investigator I had on Dawn's tail followed her to the office of a travel agent. He had gone in and pretended to be a customer while waiting for Dawn to finish her transaction. He had listened to Dawn's request as she made her travel plans."

"Where was she going?"

"To Huntsville. When her flight arrived in Salt Lake, I followed her. She took a cab ride to a small diner on a street near a highway filled with knickknack shops, bed and breakfast places and inns."

The clacking of the candy against her teeth as she spoke was starting to get on Jason's nerves. "Would you mind not eating while we're talking?"

"Sorry," she said and spit out her candy into a trashcan.

After Dawn left Utah, Alex had hung around her father's diner and at a nearby hair salon, striking casual conversation with the locals while hoping to gather information.

"Dawn met a middle-age woman at the diner, which I found out later was her mother. They sat down in a booth, and Dawn gave her a large manila envelope and said something to her that made her start sobbing," Alex told Jason.

At a hair salon two doors down from the diner, Alex had her nails done while listening to some ladies talk about poor Selma Parnell crying after a visit from her daughter. One of the ladies had pouffy hair, the other dressed in pink-and-white polka dots and the third had neck of a giraffe.

"Poor Selma," the pouffy haired lady said, "She keeps everything to herself and doesn't like to talk about her troubles."

"Yes, but we all know that daughter of hers has always been up to no good," the long-necked lady had said. "What was she thinking, surprising her mother like that?"

"Did you happen to hear any part of their conversation?" Jason found himself wondering what kind of relationship Dawn had with her parents and what she could have possibly said to make her mother cry.

"No, I was too busy taking pictures of them from outside," she told him, as her stomach growled. Alex looked around to see if she could find something less noisy to eat. She settled on a banana.

"Why didn't you listen in?"

"Look, you wanted me to be discreet. I couldn't very well go around town, listening in on everyone's conversations and asking questions. In a small place like Huntsville, people talk and I had to be careful how I got my information."

"You're eating again aren't you?"

Alex ignored him this time. "The man whom I found out later was her father came out of the kitchen to serve a customer and saw his wife crying. He went to Dawn and his wife and as soon as he saw her, the plate full of eggs and bacon fell out of his hand and hit the floor. He exchanged a few words with Dawn and then threw her out."

"I heard her father kicked her out of his diner," Alex recalled the pink-and-white polka dot lady say.

"My God!" Jason started to feel bad for Dawn having such a strained relationship with her parents but, then again, his own relationship with his parents was no better, he thought.

"After she left them, she went to a nearby park, sat on a swing and had herself a good cry," Alex said finishing off her banana and throwing the peel in the trash. "She then went back to her motel and didn't come out until the next day."

"She has miserable parents," he said sadly as he remembered how he had felt when he was 14, catching his mother with a stranger, whose hand was inside her blouse as he fondled her breasts. Jason fled for his room and cried the rest of the day. It was the first time he knew that his mother had cheated on his father and the last time he ever cried over a woman.

"Apparently they disowned her when she changed her religion from Mormon to Muslim," Alex said, looking down at her notes and recalling a conversation she had with a girl named Jenna, who was Dawn's friend.

"I'm sorry, what did you say your name was again?" Jenna asked as she pushed a library cart filled with books she had to file.

"My name is Tracy Milford," Alex said in a nasal voice. Alex found out about Jenna at a local Mormon temple when she had pretended to be an old friend of Dawn's who had lost touch. One of the bishops told Alex that the last time he talked to Dawn was right before she decided to go to school in Barcelona, but he did hear from a friend of hers named Jenna that Alex had decided to convert to Muslim, get married and move to Saudi Arabia.

"Is there any way I can get in touch with Jenna?" Alex had asked.

"She works at the Ogden Valley Library," the bishop told her.

Alex headed straight to the library, courtesy of her GPS.

"I don't remember Dawn ever mentioning you," Jenna said, looking at Alex inquisitively when she dropped by her work.

"We met at the university in Barcelona about three years ago."

"That figures."

"What figures?"

"Dawn didn't tell me much about her friends in Barcelona, and then she really changed when she fell in love with Youssef something. Can't remember his last name," Jenna said as she shelved books.

"I can't recall his last name either, but I do remember seeing her going out with him all the time," Alex said, picking up the cue to get more information.

"Then you know more than I do. I never got to see her boyfriend, and I lost touch with her about two years ago when she married Youssef and moved to Riyadh."

"That's too bad. I was hoping to get ahold of her. You see I was an exchange student there when I met her, but I had to leave to go back home to Seattle," Alex fibbed. "After that, I never heard from Dawn again. I kind of miss her."

"I miss her too. I still remember when she converted from Mormon to Muslim. She said she had to because her husband was a Salafi Sunni – an ultra conservative Sunni. Her parents were furious."

"I had no idea her parents didn't approve," Alex poked.

"Didn't approve? They told her to never come back home," Jenna said.

"Alex?" Jason shouted when she had stopped talking.

"I'm here. I was having a flashback of my conversation with Dawn's friend."

"Who is her friend?"

"Jenna. She's the one who told me quite a bit about Dawn."

"Did she tell you why she changed her religion?'"

"She fell in love and married a Saudi man named Youssef and Saudi Sunni Muslims are supposed to marry other Saudi Sunni Muslims."

"And if they don't?"

"There are exceptions. Men are allowed to marry any woman as long as she converts. A woman isn't granted the same rights unless she's a member of the royal family. In that case, the King may make an exception but the husband has to convert to Muslim and both husband and wife will have to live in exile forever."

"How do you know all this?" he asked with tremendous curiosity. Although he had many Arab clients, he had never traveled to any of their countries and his knowledge of their culture only pertained to the business environment.

"I'm from Israel and my cousin was once in love with a Saudi," Alex said. "I found out that no Saudi Muslim is allowed to marry a Jewish person even if that person is willing to convert."

"Tell me, where did Dawn meet her husband?" he asked thinking Dawn seemed so naïve and yet had lived such a complex life.

"She met him in Barcelona."

"Where did she get the money to go there?"

"After high school, she spent a year taking care of celebrity-owned homes in Salt Lake City when they were away. You know, watering their plants, taking their pets for walks and feeding them, opening the gates for the service people and duties like that."

"Hang on," he told her and buzzed Yumiko, noticing a call on one of his lines. "Hold all my calls."

"Sorry sir, but your mother insists on speaking with you."

"Tell her that I'm going to be in meetings all day and can't be interrupted. I'll talk to her when I get home." He picked up Alex's line again. "Continue."

"Dawn attended the University of Utah, majoring in linguistics. She's actually quite smart, has a 4.0 GPA and got in on a scholarship."

Alex had a friend hack into the University database and found out about her major, GPA and address.

"You still haven't told me how she wound up in Barcelona."

"She went there on an exchange program for a year and that's where she fell in love, got engaged, converted and got married."

"So, how did she end up as a housekeeper?"

"Well, that's what we need to talk about."

"Why do I get the feeling that I'm not going to like what I'm about to hear?" he said, getting up to get a bottle of orange juice from a mini fridge. He twisted the cap, popped his blood pressure medication in his mouth and took a swig.

"After she married, she moved to Riyadh with her husband and then she sort of fell off the radar. I couldn't find any record of her entering the country besides the fact that she showed up one day at Kate's Housekeeping Agency in L.A., turned in her application and résumé and got hired a few weeks later at your household."

He didn't know what to think as he fell into silence.

"Jason, are you still there?"

"Yes, I'm still here."

"If you want, I can continue digging into her past, but it could get her into trouble with the department of immigration."

He made a fist and began tapping his thumb on his keyboard. He didn't want to ask his business connections for help because that's all they were – business connections. He wasn't close to any of them the way he was to his friend George and didn't know whom to trust.

"Look, I've been doing this job for too long and I can smell shady characters from miles away, but this girl is not one of them. She may be hiding something, yes, but I doubt it has anything to do with you."

"What do you mean?"

"You know how the Arab culture works. For all you know, she might have had a husband who beat her and she might have arranged an escape. I mean the man she married had powerful ties to the religious police and the business world. Maybe she tried to get out of the country legally and was prevented," she said, closing her folder.

"But even if she did escape, why not expose the man who abused her and ask the U.S. government to hold him accountable?"

Alex got into her usual relaxed stance as she leaned back on her chair and extended her legs on her desk. "Our government doesn't like to get involved in matters that concern the Saudis. We have a president who worships Saudi Arabia and whose family has become insanely rich through their dealings with the royal family."

He frowned. "I guess what baffles me is why an A student would take on a job as a housekeeper?"

"Abused women have low self-esteem. Their husbands usually abuse them physically and mentally by telling them that they're good for nothing and would never survive on their own," Alex said, twirling a pen in her hand, "That's probably why many of them are so dependent and afraid to leave their spouses. Well, that and the fact that they're afraid if they leave their husbands will find them and eventually kill them."

"And you know this because…."

"I volunteer for an abused women's shelter in my spare time. And I read a lot.'"

"You're just a wealth of information, aren't you?" he said, drinking the rest of his juice.

"I have to be in my line of work or I wouldn't be any good. My friends call me the walking encyclopedia."

He chuckled.

"Anyway, getting back to the matter at hand, if you want, I can continue digging but be prepared to get her into a whole lot of trouble, especially since Homeland Security is suffering from paranoia."

He rubbed his face, sighed and thought for a moment. Dawn had never done anything wrong with the exception of burning his shirt and pulling the threads on the carpet, but those weren't reasons to ruin this girl's life. "No, you can stop your search for now, but send me the information you got. I have some thinking to do before I make a final decision," he said, realizing that Dawn's return on Sunday was from Huntsville. She was listless and somber as she had passed right by without noticing him.

Dawn climbed up the stairs of the employees' quarters to her room and crashed on her bed. Despair was a funny thing, it could even knock an elephant down, she thought, closing her eyes and hoping that her pain would go away. Soon she fell into a deep sleep and her subconscious took over, looking for a way to release the stress of the past two days.

He slapped her hard across the face, her frame small and his twice her size. She flew across the room and hit her head against the door. Then he came after her, using her as a punching bag and choking her as her arms flailed up and down the way an animal wiggled when it had just been trapped. When at last he thought she could possibly die, he let her go as she collapsed to the floor and fainted. The next time she got up, it was dark outside and he was gone, probably visiting his other wife. "You must leave him, you must find a way to escape," a voice in her head had said. Dawn had laughed like an idiot in an insane asylum. "You don't get it do you? Don't you think I have tried? There is no escape from Riyadh."

Dawn woke up with beads of sweat running down her body. A nightmare, that was all. It was all a nightmare, she kept on repeating as she got up, her body caught between sleep and reality. Turning the lights on to ascertain that she was now living in the U.S., she looked out over the stables, taking in the cool night air and pinching herself to make sure she wasn't dreaming. *I'm here, I'm alive, I feel liberated.* At last she smiled and stayed up for a while before going back to sleep. This time around, her mind was free and she dreamt she was running on the beach, her sheer *abaya* covering her from head to ankle as the wind blew in her direction, making her feel completely uninhibited and delightful inside.

After her dream, and for the next few weeks, Dawn's life was rather quiet and serene. She worked the hours she was assigned, took two 15-minute breaks and a 30-minute lunch. When Mrs. Anderson gave her a hard time, she pointed to her employee rights in the manual.

Unfortunately, not even a manual could help the fact that all new workers always got the jobs nobody wanted. At a meeting right before Easter, Mrs. Anderson announced that Dawn and Fred were to fly out to Zematt, a year-round ski resort in Switzerland, to prepare Jason's large house for him and Tiffany, who were planning to ski there.

"You don't mind dear, do you? Fred will be there as well to help out with your chores." Mrs. Anderson said.

"Well, I was hoping to have some free time to...." Dawn started to say, but when she noticed Mrs. Anderson's stern face, she said, "No. I don't mind. I'll help Fred out." She was scared of traveling outside the country and passing through immigration. The thought of spending an entire week under Jason's scrutiny didn't appeal to her either. The last time she had spoken to him was when he had told her she needed to learn to stand up for herself. After that, she pretty much stayed out of his way.

"Trust me, you will have plenty of time to yourself, and the chalet in Zermatt has magnificent views. None like you could have possibly seen before."

"Presumptuous witch," Dawn muttered.

"Sorry dear, you're going have to have to speak louder because I can barely hear you."

Zoya, who was standing next to Dawn, put her hand over her mouth so that Mrs. Anderson wouldn't see or hear her snigger.

"I said I'm sure it will be lovely. Now, if you'll pardon me, I have to iron," she answered with a hint of irritation that did not go unnoticed by Mrs. Anderson, who felt triumph angering the girl she disliked so much.

Mrs. Anderson had seen Jason display favoritism toward Dawn and didn't like it. She also knew how snooty Tiffany was and how she treated housekeepers with disrespect. This trip would be a good lesson both for Dawn and Jason. Tiffany would teach him how to treat a maid and Dawn would realize that she was no more special than the other housekeepers.

How dare a low-level maid dig her claws into someone as fine as her boss, Mrs. Anderson thought as she made a few changes to the new schedule when the meeting was over. No, he belonged to her and it was only a matter of time before she could make him see how wonderful she was. As soon as Mrs. Beazley retired, all would change for her. She would use up her personal and sick days and her one-month vacation to have her eyelids and saggy cheeks lifted and have gastric bypass surgery to lose her excess weight. She would hire a personal trainer who would help firm up her body and get an expensive haircut and makeup lessons from a professional. Once Jason saw the makeover, he would not be able to resist her. Yes, Mrs. Anderson had it all planned and wasn't about to let some girl from nowhere ruin her dreams.

TEN

Dawn and Fred passed through immigration without a problem and took a 12-hour Los Angeles-Frankfurt-Geneva flight with a layover of two hours in Frankfurt followed by a two-hour train ride to the romantic Visp valley known for its vineyards and saffron. Fred had reserved two rooms in a cheap lodge – single beds, tiny sinks, no showers and small bathtubs. He knew they would be arriving in Visp around midnight and there would be no available trains to take them into Zermatt.

The following morning they took the Glacier Express – a scenic train on a cogwheel track with spectacular panoramic views of the rugged cleft through which the Rhone River descended to Rhone Valley, overlooking rows of weathered farmhouses and huts clustered on the mountainside, sheep, cattle and goats in the fields, and glaciers and Alps.

"What a stunning scenery," uttered Dawn, who had skied in St Moritz long ago. Although St. Moritz was posh, it lacked Zermatt's unparalleled charm and character.

"Isn't it?" said Fred. "No matter how many times I come here, I can never get used to the beauty of this place."

"You've been coming here regularly, then?"

"Oh yes, at least once a year for the past seven years. Mr. Crawford, Jr. loves it here."

"Mr. Crawford, Jr. is a lucky man. He is free to live his life anyway he desires," Dawn sighed.

"Yes, he is lucky, although I doubt he realizes exactly how lucky he is," replied Fred.

"What do you mean?" Dawn looked at him inquisitively.

"Well, you know…People who are wealthy, always take things for granted."

"True," replied Dawn, looking out the window at the fields and feeling completely relaxed and content.

Soon, Fred and Dawn arrived at the riverside, a place where electric taxis took passengers into Zermatt. A car-free district, Zermatt was a tiny village with only 6,000 residents and one of the country's most popular ski resorts. Solar-electric ski buses picked up patrons to the Matterhorn departure and two inclined elevators carried groups up to their chalets. All those who had driven their oil-guzzling cars had to park at the village of Täsch and either walk or take a train shuttle into Zermatt. Dawn and Fred took an electric taxi to Jason's home with a 15-minute drive from the center of the village.

Perched on a mountaintop in Valais, one of the 26 cantons of Switzerland, Jason's 7000-square-foot three-story larch chalet was located in a quiet and sunny location with the utmost privacy. The frosted, slanted roof gave it a homey feeling and the floor-to-ceiling windows displayed stunning views of the Matterhorn. Fred and Dawn had arrived early to make sure the fridge and the bar would be stocked and the house was clean. Fred had faxed ahead to a local grocery store and had them deliver food, drinks and fresh flowers upon their arrival.

The front entryway led to the ground floor with a semi-circular bar and a cozy living room with a stone fireplace. On the opposite side of the living room were the formal dining room and spacious modern kitchen. Pool and chess tables separated the living room from the dining area. A back entry opened to an all-glass ski room with heated boot racks where gear was placed before entering the house.

Dawn looked at the beige sheets covering the furniture and then outside at the balcony, carpeted with snow. Inside, a stairway led to the basement, which opened up to a hallway. She followed Fred, luggage in hand, down the stairs.

"That's where you'll be staying," Fred said, pointing to a room next to the laundry room, "My bedroom is the one next to the kitchenette."

"What's in the room at the end of the hallway?" she asked, thinking that Fred wasn't looking well. His face was tired and gloomy.

"Oh, that's just a storage closet."

"Hmmm," she replied and went into her bedroom with a slanted roof. There was a single bed with a white comforter and two pillows, a desk lamp sat atop a nightstand and a picture of a horse carriage on a cobblestone street framed in red hung above it. Dawn unpacked, freshened up and went upstairs to help Fred who was putting away the groceries.

"Why don't you remove the sheets from the furniture and throw them in the washing machine. Then run the vacuum and dust," Fred told her. "When you're finished, you can help me with the upstairs rooms." He then looked at his watch that his wife had given him for their 25th anniversary and said, "We have five hours before Mr. Crawford gets here."

Dawn looked at Fred's chalky complexion and said, "Are you alright?"

It was April 11 and Fred wasn't feeling all that great. He would have been celebrating his daughter's birthday today had she and his wife not died in an accident a year ago. "I'm fine. Just a bit jet-lagged."

"Why don't you go rest? I can clean up by myself," she said, looking concerned.

"No, there is much to do. I'll take a nap when I'm finished."

Fred organized the kitchen, went upstairs and tidied the rooms and started cooking. Once finished, he gave instructions as to what Dawn needed to do, went downstairs, took two aspirins and went to lie down on his bed, hoping that his migraine would go away.

After placing mint chocolates on eiderdown pillows in the upstairs master bedroom along with a fresh fruit basket on a long maple table, chilled champagne in a silver ice bucket and two long-stemmed glasses, Dawn left to check on dinner before her employer arrived. She took the stuffed crab mushrooms, halibut and roasted potatoes out of the oven. Had they baked any longer, they would have lost all flavor. As she did this, she heard Jason swearing and yanking the front doorknob. Dawn opened the door, only to find a very upset but handsome face staring at her and, at that particular moment, she found herself attracted to him. As she looked into his tired green eyes, her heart skipped a beat.

"This day just keeps getting better and better," he yelled in anger more to himself than her. "The airline lost one of my bags and I left my damn keys at home and brought the wrong ones. Good thing you're here or I would have had to call a locksmith or broken a window to get in."

Jason actually had no idea how easy he had it. Unlike Dawn and Fred's long, tiring ride, he had a nonstop flight, sat in first class on a wide, cushy seat that turned into a bed, and taken a chopper to Zermatt.

"Please come in and relax. Dinner is ready, and there's a nice fire burning in the fireplace."

"Don't bother trying to cheer me up and get rid of the extra plate on the dinner table," he said, glancing over at the colorful orchids and two ivory candles in crystal holders. "My date canceled out on me the last minute. Apparently she didn't want to be in the cold and decided to stay at her parents' villa in Liguria."

"I can see why she wouldn't want to trade the beautiful beaches of the Italian Riviera for the snow. Why didn't you join her?" she said, pushing back her hair, which was in need of a trim behind her ears.

"Because I wanted to ski," he replied with frustration, "and now I have no one to ski with."

Dawn, who was an apt skier, kept quiet. "Perhaps you would like a glass of brandy," she said, remembering how Fred always poured Jason one when he came home from work. "Won't you have a seat by the fire? I'll pour you some."

"That's not necessary. I haven't eaten all day. If you don't mind, I'd like to have my dinner in my room."

"Of course. There is champagne in your room unless...."

"Get rid of it along with anything that would remind me of how much fun I could be having at this very moment," he told her, thinking that it wasn't Tiffany that he longed for but rather that he had been looking forward to sharing his vacation with someone, anyone, as long as the person wasn't a family member.

Dawn nodded and went to his room, removing everything she had placed there earlier. She was about to go into the kitchen when he interrupted her.

"Where is Fred? Didn't he come up here with you?"

"He prepared your meal and went downstairs to rest. He's not feeling well."

"Who is going to draw my bath before I go to bed?" He furrowed his brows.

"I'll take care of it."

He grunted, walked to the bar and poured himself a glass of wine. Dawn went into the kitchen, put his meal and utensils on a tray and brought them up to his room, which had a balcony and perfect view of naked oak, beech trees and snow-laden grounds. He was seated on his bed with his legs extended in front of him, watching the news. She set his tray down.

"Will there be anything else?"

"No, I have everything I need. Thank you," he forced himself to say even if he was in no mood to thank anyone.

Several hours later, he buzzed Dawn on the intercom and told her he was now ready for his bath. Dawn found him in the bathroom, sitting in the dry sauna with a towel wrapped around him. She poured oak-scented bubble bath into the oversize tub and turned on the faucet, noticing his well-defined body getting out of the sauna and going into the Jacuzzi. She couldn't stop staring, but when he caught her eyes, she quickly turned away.

"I'll be back to turn off the faucet," she said and left to clear his tray. When she returned, the tub was more than half full. She turned off the water, and laid his terrycloth robe on a nearby table along with extra towels within his reach. "May I get you anything else?"

He came toward her with nothing covering him. "Will you scrub my back with a loofah and wash my hair before you go?" he asked, noticing her crimson face and wide eyes. "What's the matter? Haven't you seen a naked man before? I suppose I should've covered myself before leaving the Jacuzzi. I'm so used to Fred preparing my bath and wasn't thinking."

Her eyes traced his well-defined arms and chest, his tight torso and flat abs and shifted to his well-endowed masculinity and strong thighs. He looked like a Greek god, Dawn thought. With speechless admiration, she picked up the loofah and put one hand on his shoulder to steady herself while the other scrubbed his back.

Her touch against his skin felt warm and soothing and her strokes were so much gentler than Fred's. "Could you wash a bit lower?"

"My sleeves will get all wet," she complained.

"Then pull them up."

She did as he asked, but as she stroked his lower back, her breasts accidentally brushed against him and she felt embarrassed.

"That's good, thank you," he cleared his throat. "You can now wash my hair."

As Dawn gently massaged his scalp, he felt the stress of the day escaping his body and wished she were his girl so he could have his way with her right then and there. After shampooing and rinsing his hair, Dawn quickly left without asking if there was anything else she could do for him. The whole experience had been foreign to her and she didn't quite know how to react. All she knew was she wouldn't have minded if he had kissed her nor would she have minded if he had pulled her into the tub with him. She splashed cold water on her face and wished that Fred would be better by tomorrow so she would never have to draw Jason another bath.

Dawn made herself a cup of hot milk, grabbed a book she had thrown in her bag – *Jane Eyre* – and went to sit by the fire. She read for an hour and was so absorbed in her novel that she didn't hear Jason's footsteps when he walked into the kitchen to get a glass of water. He called her name. She jumped up and shut her book.

"Are you always this jittery?" Jason asked, looking at the mug she was using. He had bought it long ago on one of his trips to Madrid.

"No, no I am not. I was deeply focused and you caught me by surprise. I'm sorry for sitting here, but I thought you were asleep."

"I see you're drinking out of my favorite mug," he teased.

"Forgive me. I had no idea," she said, her face turning scarlet. "I saw it up in one of the cabinets and really liked it." It had a picture of a large dilapidated building in Spain.

"Then it's yours."

"Oh, but I couldn't."

"Please, I insist. I behaved terribly by taking out my anger on you, and it's my way of saying thanks for putting up with my bad temper."

"Thank you. And don't worry, your temper is nothing compared to...." and then she stopped herself.

"Compared to?"

"Nothing. It's not important. Too bad about your date disappointing you, but life never goes the way we want, does it?"

"Suppose you're right," he said, studying her and feeling sorry that someone so young should know about life and disappointments.

She felt uncomfortable under his scrutiny and wondered why he took such a strong interest in her. "If Fred and I can do anything to make your stay more comfortable, please let us know."

"No, there isn't a thing either of you can do for me," he answered, continuing to look directly at her, watching her fidget and then divert her eyes from him, "not unless one of you knows how to ski."

She was the help and he, a man who had everything. Surely someone in his position would find her far beneath him, but then again, he did play tennis with her before his mother had interrupted them. And how much more fun it would be to ski than to stay cooped up in a house. "I...I...nevermind," she said, starting to move away toward the kitchen.

"Nevermind? Nevermind what, Dawn?" he insisted, waiting impatiently for her answer.

She turned around and after hesitating for an uncomfortable moment, blurted, "I know how to ski, but I don't think it would be appropriate for us to ski together."

"You know how to ski?" he said in surprise, but then remembered that she was from Utah.

"It's one of my favorite sports, except that...."

Overjoyed that he now had a ski partner, Jason grabbed a pen and cocktail napkin from the bar. "I'm going to leave Fred a note about us going skiing early tomorrow or he might panic and file a missing person's report."

"But...."

"Let's meet at seven, have coffee and then head out to the lifts."

Never wish for what you want or you might just get it, a friend of hers had told her long ago.

"I don't have the right clothes or equipment," she protested, suddenly unsure that fraternizing with the boss was the right thing to do.

"There are several ski hats, gloves, jackets, pants and glasses in one of the downstairs closets," he told her. "I always keep extra ones in case someone forgets. I'm sure you'll find something in there that will fit you."

"What about shoes?" she said, a part of her hoping that he would change his mind and decide not to go with her and the other hoping that he would insist on it.

"There's a shop in the area that opens up early. We'll rent you something there," he offered and went into the kitchen to stick the note on the fridge.

Dawn followed him. "I can't leave all the housework to Fred. He would never forgive me."

"I explained in the note that I stole you away, and we'll be having lunch at a nearby café. I'm sure Fred can whip up something for himself without needing your help. Now, get some rest. I want to get there before the crowds, and you need extra time to have your skis fitted."

She nodded and went off to bed but still had a hard time believing he would want to ski with her as she tossed and turned with excitement all night long. When morning finally arrived, coffee was ready at exactly seven.

Dawn had been so excited that she had risen at five, taken a shower, picked out her ski clothes: purple down jacket, windproof soft polyester pants, ski hat and goggles. From her own wardrobe, she chose a taupe turtleneck. After preparing eggs and sausage for Jason, she went downstairs and made herself a bowl of muesli in the kitchenette. Jason ate his breakfast while reading the paper and when finished, he called on Dawn. Before nine o'clock they were on the slopes.

Zermatt had enormous ski areas with plenty of off-trail skiing and three main piste – the Klein Matterhorn, the Sunnegga and the Gornergrat – from which adventure-seekers could glide back into Zermatt or to the Italian side, Cervinia. Jason chose the longest run – the Klein Matterhorn at 12,500 feet above sea level and eight miles of joyous run back to the village. They took a lift to the highest sightseeing platform in Europe as their car stepped out of a tunnel to overlook the uninterrupted dazzling glaciers with astounding 360-degree views of the Swiss, Italian and French Alps.

"I feel like I have died and gone to heaven," Dawn exclaimed. During much of the ride she stood still, in awe of the mysterious Alps piercing through the heavy fog. Signs cautioned passengers to refrain from exertion so they could acclimate themselves to the thin air.

Jason smiled. "I know what you mean. I feel the same way each time I come up here."

"At the gondola station, before we left, I read in a brochure that this cable car didn't even exist before 1976."

"That's absolutely correct. Zermatt used to be a quiet hidden treasure until tourists discovered it. When I was a kid and came here for the first time, I took a cable car, switched to a T-bar and changed again to a chair lift to get to a trail. Nowadays they have abundant transportation to get up the mountains at the speed of light."

Dawn tried to imagine what he was like as a child and wished that they had known each other when they were younger.

"Come, I want to show you something," he said, walking down about 50 feet in his ski boots toward a tunnel.

Dawn followed him and entered into a long, steep slippery ice tunnel carpeted with rubber as she hung onto a rope so she wouldn't slide down. Several minutes later, the corridor opened up to a large room filled with ice sculptures. "I read about this in the brochure; I just never imagined myself being in it," she remarked.

"This is called Glacier Grotto or the Ice Palace."

"I cannot believe that people actually carved this tunnel. It must have taken months," she said as she walked past sculptures of a goat, bear, horse and an eagle.

"It is pretty amazing; isn't it?" he said admiring the blue hues created by florescent lighting and natural light.

"It is as amazing as..." she cleared her throat. "I have never seen something so incredible."

"It is as amazing as what, Dawn?" he asked, staring at her and then looking at a sculpture carved in the shape of a heart and another of a flower.

It is as amazing as Cuevas del Drach limestone caves on the island of Mallorca, she wanted to say. "Nothing. That's a beautiful carving," she said, changing the subject and pointing at a Buddha.

"Yes, it is," he sighed, wishing that she would talk to him about her past.

When they finished their tour of the palace, they ascended the same way they entered.

Once outside, Jason snapped his boots into his skis and said, "You're ready to have fun?"

Dawn nodded, put on her skis, and soon the two switched from being spectators to participants.

Jason was impressed by Dawn's grace and effortless manner as she glided down the mountain. Sometimes they'd race each other and other times they'd move together in harmony. A few times the two stopped to people-watch and take in the scenery – the vivid blue sky with patches of white clouds, sun that shone warmly above their heads and snow-covered trees – but mostly they coasted on the slippery surface, enjoying each other's silent company. At noon they stopped for lunch.

"Where did you learn how to ski?" he asked her at a cozy family-run mountaintop restaurant with an unobstructed view of the glaciers.

"When I was six, my mother used to keep house for a couple who liked to travel with their two boys. Every winter we'd go skiing, and I was invited to take lessons with the boys while my mother stayed back and took care of their home," she said, sampling her *pastetli* – a Swiss dish of meat pie with curry and Worcestershire sauce. They were seated outside behind a square, pine table. German-, Italian- and French-speaking customers took up the other four tables. Inside, a woman yodeled, entertaining the guests.

"How long did your mother work for them?"

She shrugged nonchalantly, "I don't know. About 10 years."

"No wonder you ski so well," he said, eating his *zürcher geschnetzeltes* – a stew of veal, mushroom and potatoes. "Did you continue skiing after that?"

"Oh yes, here and there when opportunities presented themselves."

There were plenty more questions he wanted to ask – like whatever possessed her to change her religion and alienate her parents? What happened to her after she moved to Saudi Arabia? How did she get out without any evidence of her exit? And why were her parents so unforgiving? He hoped that someday he would gain her trust enough to get answers.

"What are you thinking about?" she asked, noticing that his attention was elsewhere.

"Nothing in particular."

"You seemed to be deep in thought," she said, looking at the crease on his forehead. He was a nice person and had her circumstances been different, she would've befriended him. "There must have been something important occupying your mind."

"It's work stuff; I don't want to bother you with it," he replied, giving her an amiable smile and patting her hand lightly.

"Do you like what you do?" she asked, pulling her hand away and moving it toward her face to make sure she was still wearing her glasses. *What in the world did he see in her?* She had made every effort possible to appear homely, and yet she could tell he was drawn to her.

He found it odd that she was repulsed by his touch and hoped that they could have a short affair, since Tiffany wasn't around. "Long ago, I wanted to design virtual reality games," he told her and moved his feet so that they touched hers.

She pulled back. "Really? That's quite different from real estate."

"Yes, my friend George and I were going to open up our own business but, like you said, life never goes the way we want it." He appeared regretful.

"What stopped you?" she prodded, taking a sip of her *glüwein* – spiced warm wine.

"Andrew had a heart attack and had to take a break from work. My family needed me to help run the business. When Andrew recovered, he couldn't work as much and asked me to stay on," he answered, wondering why he was confiding in her. He was the one who always asked the questions while others exposed their vulnerability to him.

"Isn't the Crawford Enterprises a publicly held company?"

"We used to be a privately held company until 10 years ago when we went public and did an initial public offering."

"Do you ever wish that you had followed your dreams?"

"Sometimes, when things go wrong at work. But it's too late to change," he stated, breaking off a piece of his baguette.

"It's never too late to change," she answered, thinking of her own past and how far along she had come.

"That's a bit too optimistic, isn't it? Besides, my family needs me," he told her. "What about you? What are your dreams?"

"I would have liked to have a job where I could help people and make a difference."

"You mean like being a doctor," he said. Ever since Alex had told him that Dawn had a 4.0 GPA, he had been thinking about how Dawn was wasting her time working as his housekeeper. He had been toying with the idea of offering her an entry-level position at his firm. Except that he still didn't know what happened in Riyadh and after she got back to the U.S. He needed those gaps filled before he could trust her.

"No, like being a social worker."

"A noble dream but it's hard to live on a salary of a do-gooder," he said, as a true capitalist. Owning a business and accumulating wealth were of utmost importance to him.

"I don't need a lot – just a small place of my own, a simple environmental-friendly car and money to pay my bills and live comfortably in my old age. That's why I'm putting away as much as I can." Her first goal was to save enough so that she could leave her current job, but she couldn't very well tell him that.

"Your needs are small compared to mine, I suppose," he replied finishing off his stew. "How would you like to go paragliding this afternoon?"

"Paragliding?" she asked with surprise. "I don't know how."

"That's not a problem. I have given tandem rides to many of my friends."

Dawn looked at him with uncertainty. Although she didn't have a fear of heights, paragliding was a bit too adventurous for her.

He noticed her worried expression. "I have been doing this for years and have an advanced piloting license recognized internationally. But if you don't feel comfortable…."

"No, I would love to go," she said, never turning down a challenge. She looked forward to being suspended in air and feeling a sense of complete freedom.

During this time of year, Jason usually glided from Rothorn to Zermatt, a convenient spot to lift off and land but, because he didn't want to overwhelm his guest, he decided to cut the flight shorter and land in Sunnegga instead. "Great. We'll take a shorter route and hike the rest of the way into Zermatt."

She smiled, showing off her metal retainer. He was treating her like one of his friends and she was enjoying every minute of it. "What about Fred?"

"What about him? He doesn't know how to paraglide," he said, noticing her braces and wondering why she didn't wear those new clear plastic ones that dentists offered.

"No, what I mean is, won't he be mad? I haven't been much help to him all day."

"Don't worry about Fred. There isn't much for him to do anyway. We'll go gliding after I take a shower and nap. Later we'll have dinner in the village," he said, not believing the words that had just escaped his mouth. What the hell was he doing? Was he so desperate for a date that now he was hanging out with one of his servants? He felt a deep loneliness, and this scrawny girl sitting in front of him somehow filled that void.

"Are you sure? Are you sure you want to spend all of your free time with me?" she replied as though reading his mind. Why was he so nice to her and what did he want from her? Nothing, he must have wanted nothing, because what could she possibly offer him?

"Yes, I'm sure or I wouldn't have asked."

"In that case, thanks for inviting me."

When they got back to the house, Fred was outfitted in a green apron, chopping up vegetables in the kitchen. He greeted Jason but didn't say anything to Dawn except to give her a disapproving glance.

"Fred, I want you to take the day off and enjoy yourself. Don't worry about making up my room, I can do it myself."

"Sir?" he looked bewildered.

"You heard me. Dawn and I are going paragliding and will be eating out tonight."

"What about your afternoon tea?"

"Let's skip it for today. You're free to do as you like."

"Very well sir." Fred stopped chopping. No use in making dinner if no one was going to eat it.

When Jason went to his room, Dawn asked Fred, "Are you angry with me?"

"No," he answered abruptly.

"You're sure acting like it. You didn't even say hi to me when I got back."

"My apologies madam," he said sarcastically. "Shall I go draw you a bath?"

"Draw me a bath? What the hell are you talking about? I never asked you to do anything for me. In fact, didn't I help out last night when you weren't feeling well?" she asked, picking up a piece of carrot and munching on it.

Her munching irritated him to the core. "Look at you sauntering in here and acting as though you're the mistress of the house."

"I don't behave that way, and you know it," she quietly insisted.

"You know you're just someone to keep him company for tonight. Tomorrow, he'll be with somebody else." Fred liked Dawn and didn't want to see her get hurt. In a way, she reminded him of his daughter – athletic, vivacious and kind.

"I have no intention of going to bed with him; not that it's any of your business."

"Do whatever you want. You're a big girl," he huffed, putting the vegetables in a plastic bag and sticking them in the fridge.

"I don't have to take this," she said and went downstairs. She couldn't figure out for the life of her why Fred was so resentful unless he wanted her to stay home and help him out. She took a short nap and then went up to brew Jason's tea before Fred would come upstairs. She knew Fred was a creature of habit and liked to keep a schedule. This whole thing about skipping tea and Jason making his own bed must have bothered him immensely. Since Dawn wanted Fred to be content with her work, when Jason was having his tea out on the patio, she went to his room and tidied everything. As she left the room, she ran into Fred.

"I took care of everything," she said. You just go and relax. I even have tea ready for you downstairs."

Fred just shook his head with disapproval and left. If she were his daughter, he would never allow her to date someone like Jason. She was too sweet of a person and deserved someone who truly cared about her.

Dawn and Jason took the Sunnegga-Rothorn path, one of the favorites with local skiers due to its diversity. They started with the express underground funicular to Sunnegga and switched to a high-speed chair lift up to Blauherd, a paragliding takeoff site used during spring and summer. From there, they boarded a 150-person cable car to Rothorn. When at last they reached their destination, Dawn noticed a glider taking off the mountain top and her heart pitter-pattered. *Too late to change your mind* — she told herself — *you already told him you would do it. Be brave and bite the bullet.*

"Something is different about you," he said, looking at her intently, trying to figure out what it was.

"Maybe I look rested after my nap. I didn't sleep well last night."

"That's too bad." Suddenly he realized why she looked different. "You're not wearing your retainers."

"Oh...umm...they were...my gums felt irritated earlier, so I removed them to give my mouth a break."

"I checked the wind conditions before we left. It looks like we'll have mild winds – only 12 miles per hour," Jason told her as he unloaded his gear and began to set up his parafoil. He had on a black-and-white jumpsuit over his clothes and lent Dawn a yellow one.

"I heard it stopped snowing the night before Fred and I got into Zermatt."

"Lucky us. We get to enjoy nice weather. Nothing is worse than getting the parafoil wet."

Oh dear God. Please don't let it snow or rain and above all, don't increase the speed of wind, Dawn begged silently.

"But don't worry," he said as though reading her mind. "I have a high-performance canopy made of nonporous fabric."

"What is that for?" Dawn asked pointing to what looked like a transmitter.

"It signals us with increased pitch in beeps as we gain height and with droning when we lose altitude. You see, birds have a keen awareness of atmospheric pressure but humans cannot perceive the ongoing rising and sinking air."

The Dawn of Saudi   115

"Do you need help getting set up?" she asked in order to preoccupy her mind.

"No, thanks, I think I've got it under control." He pulled out his parafoil from his backpack, unfolded it and spread it flat on the ground. "On its own, this canopy is lifeless. It's the incoming air that keeps the wings inflated, helping to maintain its shape," he explained to Dawn.

She was so nervous that all she heard was "Blah, blah, blah...."

"Here," he said, handing her a helmet and a pair of large dark goggles, "Go ahead and put those on. I turned on the microphone in your helmet. You can talk to me through it once we take off."

He laid a network of lines that connected to the parafoil, making sure they were arranged properly. "These lines you see here are connected to left and right risers and the risers are linked to my harness by two carabiners," he said, pointing at them.

"I hope you have a reserve parachute," Dawn said, looking worried.

"Yes I have one. It's attached to my harness and is strong enough to hold both of us," he said. "But don't worry, we won't be needing it. I have done this a thousand times and have only ended up with broken bones once." When he saw her gaping at him, he added, "I'm only joking. I have never had a problem."

"There's always a first time," Dawn mumbled under her breath, afraid to crash.

He put on his knapsack and helped Dawn with her equipment. There were two conjoined parts – the first went around her shoulders, and resembled a backpack that supported her spine; the second supported her thighs with a belt going through her crotch. Jason fastened her belt, connected his backpack to the parafoil and connected his gear to Dawn's.

He spread his arms up and open, and ran forward down a mountain with his body leaning against Dawn's back. Dawn felt his hard, taut body against hers as she dragged her heels, afraid to take off. She leaned back against him and yelped.

"Don't be scared, it's a lot safer than it looks. Just give up control and let me lead the way," he told her as he darted forward and the two lifted off as Dawn let out a scream.

From down below, they looked like they were both seated on a chair, as a ribbed canopy spun them around. But it was Jason who was pulling all the strings as he turned and twirled in a semicircular motion, showing Dawn the snow-covered Matterhorn and the skiers below them who resembled miniature toys. It was a beautiful and cloudless sunny afternoon. They sailed smoothly with their legs dangling in the air and the world beneath them. An hour later, Jason said, "Shift left."

"What?"

"Shift your weight left," he demanded.

As she did, Jason made a 360-degree turn in midair. Dawn let out a loud cry, and when at last they were in an upright position, she yelled, "I'm going to kill you when we land."

"C'mon admit it, aren't you enjoying this just a tad?"

"I was until you flipped us over. Are you out of your mind?"

"I was simply having a little fun. After all you did beat me in tennis. This is my way of getting back at you," he bantered.

"That's very different. I wasn't trying to give you a heart attack," she said.

Jason chuckled. "I'm sorry, I won't do it again." He steered their airfoil away from the Matterhorn toward an area in Sunnega where several hikers had stopped near a bench to enjoy the scenery. "We're going to land soon and hike the rest of the way," he told her, as he lowered the parafoil. The two soon came close to the ground as Jason stood up from a seated position and Dawn followed suit. He let go of the controls and the parafoil yanked them backward. Jason grabbed Dawn around the waist so she wouldn't fall back. When at last he let go of her, she said, "That was incredible. Can we do it again?"

"I think that's enough excitement for one day, young lady. We'll give it a go again tomorrow afternoon." They packed up his gear, shed their jumpsuits and began hiking in their jeans and sweaters.

In Zermatt, many paths were cleared of snow for hikers. Of course, some preferred climbing up the glaciers as they used their climbing gear, crampons, ice ax and rope to advance up. But Jason had a different plan. They climbed up a snow-free trail for an hour through marmot country toward Stellisee and stopped there to enjoy a lake where the water was transparent as teardrops. The Matterhorn and the cobalt sky reflected in the water.

"Words cannot possibly describe the beauty of this lake," Dawn remarked.

"My favorite thing is the tranquility."

They sat there for a while, each silently reflecting on their lives – Jason about his lonely childhood and lukewarm parents; Dawn about the past she left behind and the uncertainty of her future.

Then Jason broke the silence. "Do you prefer heliskiing or airboarding tomorrow?"

"I know heliskiing is when a helicopter drops you off with a guide at an off-piste run, but what in the world is airboarding?"

"Airboarding is similar to riding a body board in the ocean except that you're gliding down the mountain, head first. Expert airboarders sometimes reach a speed of 80 miles per hour or more."

"Jason, if you're planning to get rid of me, all you have to do is fire me."

Jason laughed at her remark. "Don't worry. We won't be going that fast. Our guide will tell us what to do."

"You mean to tell me that that this is the first time you'll be doing this?" she raised her brows.

"Yes, it's a fairly new sport and I thought it would be fun. But if you're not comfortable…." he taunted her.

"Are you challenging me?"

"No such thought entered my mind," he teased.

"Fine, you have yourself a deal," she said, planning to outperform him the next day.

"Great," Jason replied. "I made reservations for two long ago, and I'm glad that I won't have to cancel it."

"You mean if I had said no, you wouldn't have gone by yourself?"

"No, I don't like doing things by myself," he admitted, glancing at his watch. "We should go."

"Is there somewhere you have to be?" Dawn asked disappointedly.

"You will find out soon enough," he said and got up.

They returned to their walking path until they reached the last junction. From there, they began descending. Dawn was glad, because she was tired from all the climbing. The two walked down to Grindjisee, a broad, gently descending track. After an hour they reached Grünsee Lake, also known as the Green Lake, filled with glacier water that came directly from Findel glacier. And when the sun started setting, it descended behind the majestic mountains, splashing the most beautiful hues across the smog-free sky. A bottle of wine, a loaf of bread and cheese would have been a perfect end to this very perfect day.

"Let's stop here," Jason told her.

They were near a picnic site. A big man with a rugged face and a dark windbreaker had been waiting for them.

"What's that?" she asked, pointing at a basket, several olive-and-white checkered blankets and an inflated rubber mattress.

"I called in ahead and asked for someone to bring those out for us. I thought perhaps we could have an early dinner here," he replied.

She was surprised by his sweet gesture but then it occurred to her that perhaps he was too embarrassed to take her to a fancy restaurant in the village since she didn't have the right clothes and breeding. "Thoughtful," was all she could say.

"I hope this is okay," when he heard a note of sadness in her voice. "I mean, we can go to the village instead, if you like. I just thought that this is nicer than eating in a restaurant. Later we can go in and catch a movie at Vernissage, an entertainment center."

No, he did like her. Otherwise why would he want to take her to the movies? "This is great. You just took me by surprise, that's all."

She unfolded one of the blankets, spread it over the mattress and looked inside the basket. There was Camembert, mixed green salad laced with balsamic vinaigrette, roast beef and ham, assorted warm rolls, chocolate mousse and a bottle of Bordeaux with wine glasses. He was definitely interested in her, but she wasn't sure of her feelings toward him. He had everything going for him except that he was a ladies' man, so Dawn knew she had to be careful.

"I have to thank the shop. They really outdid themselves this time."

"You've done this before?"

"Yes, every time I come up here," he said, regretting it as soon as he said it. For some odd reason, he really liked this girl. He felt that he could talk to her with ease and wasn't worried about impressing her.

"I'm glad to hear that, because I sure would hate to think that you went through all this trouble just for me," she said with a pinch in her voice. She uncorked the wine and poured.

"What do you mean?"

"Well, I am your housekeeper, and I should be the one going out of my way to please you. Besides, soon this Cinderella will have to go back to her chores."

"Why do you do that?" he asked, frustrated by her sarcasm.

"Do what?"

"Create such a big space between us by constantly putting yourself down?"

"Jason, there is no us. You and Tiffany are an us. You and I can never be an us."

He looked irritated by her remarks and started digging into his salad. Dawn picked up a roll. But somehow her perfect day had been stained by their differences. She wished she had money, power and influence, all the things she had been hating for such a long time. They ate quietly for a while, enjoying the atmosphere around them.

"Thank you. I've been having a great time," Dawn admitted.

"You're welcome," he said with a surprised expression on his face. He then raised his glass and clinked it with hers. "A toast to staying in the moment and forgetting about all else."

"Cheers," she said, taking a sip. "But how can you do it?"

"Do what?"

"You know, stay in the moment and not let your thoughts drive you mad," she said, throwing one of the extra blankets over her legs to keep warm.

"It's hard and takes practice but somehow when I come to this spot, it all becomes effortless," he told her, putting one arm around her. "Can you see that over there?" he said pointing toward a far away tree.

"You mean the tree?"

"No," he answered, reaching in his knapsack and handing a small pair of binoculars to her.

She put her hands around the apparatus and he reached around her shoulder, putting his hands over hers and guiding her eyes toward the direction of where he wanted her to look. "Is it a goat?" Dawn uttered, looking at the four-legged animal with a pair of upright close-set horns and prickly ears.

"Almost, but not quite. It's a chamois. They are indigenous to the mountainous areas, especially the Alps. Their hooves can cling to rocky surfaces due to their elasticity."

Dawn gazed at it for a long time. It had brown fur, an inky tail and a white face with black markings. She noticed that its horns had a sharp backward curve.

"Now, look up there," he said, shifting her hands to a nearby pine.

"What kind of bird is it?" she asked staring at a colorful species with a black-and-yellow beak, gray head, gray-brown back and red-brown flanks.

"That's an alpine accentor also known as a mountain sparrow. They lay their light blue eggs in a rock crevice. The females are polyandrous; the male takes care of the chicks only if he thinks he's the father."

"Really?" Dawn grinned with amazement.

"Yes, they don't care much for raising some other bird's offspring. Listen," he said as the bird started to sing melodiously.

"He has a beautiful voice."

"You see, this is why I come to this spot every year. I want to get away from work and from unscrupulous married investors who have to be wined and dined as they ogle over young girls and take them back to their hotels."

Among Jason's many responsibilities was to make sure his clients were sexually content. His company had covert ties to a discreet call girl service under the leadership of Madam B, who handpicked and trained each one with care.

"Doesn't it bother you to cater to them?"

"I try not to think about it," he said, putting his hand through his hair, "especially when I know how much money our firm will make by doing business with them."

The fact that he would do just about anything for money didn't sit well with her, but she decided to hold her tongue.

"I can tell you don't approve by the look of disgust on your face," he said, reaching for a wedge of Camembert.

"It doesn't matter what I think, what matters is how you feel after each transaction."

"I don't expect you to understand."

"Try me," she said, eating a slice of ham.

"This is the only life I know. I grew up with a certain lifestyle, and it's hard to give it all up and live a modest life."

"I understand," she replied calmly.

"What do you understand?"

"That you're afraid of taking risks and that status is more important to you than your own happiness." She started to pack up.

"You're angry with me?"

"No, but I do think we should leave. It's starting to get dark and we may not find our way back." The sun was now completely gone and soon it would be dusk.

"You still want to go see a movie?"

"Of course, I haven't been to the movies in quite a long time."

He sighed in relief and used his cell to call the shop where he had ordered his food. "This is Jason Crawford; we're leaving the trail now. You may want to send someone down to pick up the basket," he offered.

After they got back from their hike, they changed at the house. Fred was nowhere in sight. He had left them a note that he had gone to a bar to shoot pool. Dawn felt less guilty, thinking that he was at least going out to enjoy himself.

"You're ready to go?" Jason asked her as he climbed down the stairs, noticing that she had traded her jeans for a pair of light-blue corduroy pants, had thrown on a pink sweater, a long scarf and boots. He thought she looked pretty but too young to be his date.

She thought his ebony dress pants, bone-colored turtleneck and tailored wool coat made him seem more sophisticated and older but Dawn didn't care. She had fun when she was around him and that's all that mattered. "I sure am. What're we going to see?"

"A mystery; Do you like mysteries?"

"Yes, very much."

They took a taxi to Vernissage and entered a building designed by Heinz Julen – a well-known Swiss artist named after the creator of Heinz ketchup. A fascinating spiral staircase wound itself up to a stark white art gallery displaying modern art, a British-style pub, another bar with a fireplace and soothing music, a club with a live band, and a movie theater where one could order dinner or sit at a bar while watching the movie.

Jason asked for Eter Poire – a pear brandy grown in southwest canton of Wallis. Dawn requested kirsch. Then they sat down on large, comfortable leather chairs waiting for the movie to start. The theater crowd was a mix of young and old.

"This place is really something," Dawn said, staring at the theater. which resembled a private screening room. Metals and weathered wood created a modern-looking structure.

"Does that mean you like it?" he asked. The entire day he had tried to show off Zermatt, one of his favorite places in the world. When he was with Dawn, he felt as though he was seeing everything through her eyes for the first time and sensed an immense pleasure and appreciation of all that he took for granted. At that moment, he realized he truly was a lucky man.

Dawn nodded her head and looked around at the eclectic decor and large crystal chandeliers and said, "It's different and rather interesting." She, in the short time she had spent with him, had been feeling as though she was living a dream and was afraid to wake up.

"Do you like to dance?" he asked, hoping she would.

"I do, but I'm not really good at it."

"You know what they say – practice makes perfect." He gave her a naughty look.

She knew he was trying to woo her and was finding it more and more difficult to resist him. "If you're suggesting that we should go dancing after this. I'm going to have to decline. I have no energy left in me."

"No, I was thinking about tomorrow night. We'll paraglide in the afternoon, this time all the way down to Zermatt, rest up and then go dancing. The village has fantastic après-ski nightlife."

"In that case, I accept," she said, as the lights dimmed and the movie started. Forty minutes into the movie, Jason slouched in his chair and passed out. Dawn glanced over and was tempted to wake him but decided to wait until the show ended.

ELEVEN

The next morning Jason and Dawn rose before Fred, and after eating a light breakfast, they headed for the heliport where Jason's hired pilot and guide picked them up. The chopper dropped them at an off-piste run at a modern resort called Cervinia, on the Italian side of the Matterhorn, where the ride down was gentler than the day before.

Their guide, Ulrich, a 28-year-old athletic Dane with a slight accent, helped them inflate their limp bullet-shaped body boards with high-compression pumps, while explaining. "What is wonderful about airboarding is it doesn't require a lot of equipment, and you can easily fold and fit it into your small light rucksack." An airboard, also referred to as a tube, float, sledge, floating rubber tarp and vehicle, turned out to be an inflatable body-board used on snow with hand-holds and grooves on the underside that allowed riders to make sharp turns and stop quickly in snow.

"How hard is it to learn?" Dawn asked.

"I heard it's quite easy, and no experience is necessary," Jason said.

Ulrich smiled at his naïveté. "As long as you follow the rules, you'll have no trouble getting down. I particularly chose this terrain because there aren't too many trees or cliffs."

"You mean to tell me that people actually go through trees and jump off cliffs with these floating rubber tarps?" Dawn queried.

"Yes, especially those who plan to participate in races, but I don't recommend it on your first day," he said, staring at Dawn as though he was interested in her. "Now let's get started."

Jason and Dawn listened to every word their guide taught them. Dawn decided to glide down slowly so she could get a feel for the tube. Jason thought it was going to be a piece of cake and was planning to fearlessly go for it.

"Your airboard has grips and a hard rubber bottom for going over ground irregularities such as jutting rocks and ice jags."

"How safe is this sport, anyway?" Dawn asked, putting on her silver helmet and shin guards.

"It's safer than skiing since you're only inches away from the ground. When you go down, keep your head low and toes off the ground."

Jason recalled his first ski lesson in Zermatt. His Swiss-German instructor who sounded as though she were speaking Swiss-German instead of English insisted he catch a T-bar to go uphill to an intermediate slope, which was difficult for a beginner. She then had taken Jason's poles away and told him to go down the mountain. It hadn't been a pleasant experience because it was hard to balance without poles and he kept on falling. Luckily, this teacher spoke English flawlessly and his instructions were easy to follow.

"Your airboard acts like an airbag upon impact and is designed to protect you on rough terrain," he explained. "If you make too sharp of a turn, you will turn over. When making turns, try to shift your body weight evenly."

"What about our arm position? Jason inquired, reaching in his backpack for his dark purple goggles.

"Keep your arms tucked in and your elbows pointed back as though you're about to do tricep push-ups and always lean your body in the direction you want to turn."

"Once we get going, should we head all the way down to Cervinia?" Dawn asked.

"I'll be skiing right behind you to make sure you're doing okay. At some point, I will ski in front of you. That's when you and your boyfriend should slow down and come to a stop by turning your airboard at a 90-degree angle to your downhill direction."

Jason said, "Oh, we're not…"

"We're just friends," Dawn interrupted.

"In that case, may I take you out for a drink tonight?" asked Ulrich.

Dawn, surprised and flattered, looked over at Jason, noticing his stern face and replied, "Thank you but no. I have plans tonight."

"If your plans don't pan out, call me. Here's my number," he said, handing her his business card.

Dawn put his card in her pocket.

"Well, I don't know about you," Jason said, looking at Dawn and trying hard to hide his jealousy, "but I'm ready to go."

"Okay then," said Ulrich, "let's see what you can do."

Jason belly-flopped on his sledge and took off at a fast pace.

"You're next," her guide told her.

Dawn glanced at him hesitantly and then lowered her body to the gray airboard as she glided down the mountain and picked up speed to catch up with Jason.

They rode for two hours until their instructor skied on ahead of them but Jason increased his speed, making fancy turns and showing off. Soon he hit a hard bump, lost all control, flew off his airboard and crashed into deep snow with his sledge landing on top of him.

Dawn gradually halted by turning her float sideways.

Ulrich swooshed in front of Jason who was pushing the six-pound vehicle off his body. "Are you alright?" he asked.

"Yes, I'm fine. It's my ego that's bruised," he replied shaking the snow off his ski clothes.

Dawn turned her face away, bit her lips and tried hard not to laugh.

"Well," said Ulrich, "you guys did well for your first time. Let's break for 10 and catch our breath. We'll then continue on all the way down."

Their guide used his airboard as a bench and relaxed. Jason sat next to Dawn on her rubber tarp so that his body touched hers. Dawn enjoyed their closeness but couldn't help feeling uneasy.

"So, who invented these things anyway?" Jason asked bitterly, his derriere sore from the hard fall.

"The airboard is based on a similar concept as the sled. The North American Indians used to build sleds made of birch for transportation of their teepees, tools and food. By the mid-19th

century, sled races were being held in Canada, the U.S and Russia. Later the alpine patrols came up with their own version for carrying the injured through tight woods," their guide explained, snacking on an energy bar from his pocket. Would you like some?" he offered.

"No, thank you," Dawn replied.

"Me neither," Jason added and put his arm around Dawn's waist, "We'll be lunching in Cervinia once we get down."

Dawn couldn't understand why suddenly Jason was so possessive of her, unless he was jealous. But why would he be when he already had so many girlfriends?

Ulrich bit into his bar and continued, "Around 1948, Sevylor, a French company, invented portable inflatable tubs named Dou Dou. Later the company expanded on the concept, inventing blowup kayaks."

"Dou Dou?" Jason chuckled.

"Yes, I know. My thoughts exactly," Ulrich said. "Anyway, Joe Steiner, a Swiss skier from Zug injured for two years from a snowboarding accident was no longer able to stand on his ankles due to torn ligaments. So, he hooks up with the maker of inflatable hospital mattresses and 10 years later perfects the design of the airboard."

"Fascinating and clever," Dawn said.

"I thought the same thing," Ulrich replied. "Well, let's finish up this ride." He then got up, grabbed his poles, slipped his goggles on and snapped into his ski.

Jason and Dawn lay on their boards.

"Remember Jason, not to panic and not to turn too sharp when you pick up speed. Had you hung onto your airboard last time, you would have flown off into air and landed right back onto the snow because your board is designed to protect you on rough terrain."

Jason nodded sheepishly before he took off cautiously.

Dawn on the other hand who was getting the hang of the sport, whizzed right by Jason, slid down in an S-shape as she handled each turn with perfection. She felt as though she were on top of the world and nothing could possibly hurt her.

Two hours later, they were all the way down in Cervinia, where they thanked their guide.

"Dawn, you're a pro," said Ulrich, noticing Jason's long face. "Jason you did much better than the first time around. Your turns were a lot smoother."

"Thank you," he replied with a half-smile.

They ate at a kitsch eatery with rustic décor, wood beams and plastic tablecloths. Dawn stayed alert, making sure that she didn't blunder in her answers.

"Have you ever been married before?" Jason asked her, drinking his mineral water and studying her reaction.

"No, never," she responded, digging her fork into her pasta and chewing it nervously.

How odd, he thought, for her to be hiding the truth. What was she so afraid of? He decided to play along to see how far she would go with her deception. "Have you traveled outside the country?"

She hesitated for a moment and then fibbed, "No, this trip is my first journey outside the states."

"Do you spend time with your parents often?" he asked, noticing her eyes twitch as he ate his polenta and porcini mushrooms.

She flicked her eyes from side to side, looking for a way out. "I try to spend time with them as often as I can." One day she would tell him the truth but today wasn't going to be that day.

The more she hid from him, the more he wanted to know. She was a puzzle waiting to be solved and someday he hoped to put together all the pieces.

"What religion do you practice?" he said, tilting his head to one side and watching her knock a spoon to the floor.

"Excuse me," she said and bent down to pick it up but it had slid all the way to the next table. She straightened her body and said, "I'm Mormon. Haven't been to temple in a while, though. Suppose I should plan to go one of these days." She felt guilty for being dishonest with him.

Jason realized he was making her feel uncomfortable and decided to stop quizzing her. "You know, I have been really enjoying our two days together."

"Me too," she replied with a sigh of relief, grateful that he had changed subjects. "I could stay here forever and never miss living in a big city."

"Are you still up for paragliding and dancing later?" he asked, leaning forward, holding her hand and caressing it.

"You bet," she said, blushing at his gesture but not pulling away from him this time. She knew she shouldn't get involved and yet, she felt a strong attraction toward him, which made her lose all common sense.

When they finished eating, they took a chairlift and gondola back into Zermatt. Jason stood close to Dawn as he looked outside the gondola, confused about his feelings toward her. She wasn't like any girl he had dated and he wasn't sure pursuing her was such a good idea. Unlike his other girlfriends, Dawn was sweet, sincere and vulnerable and Jason didn't want to hurt her. Yet, he didn't want anyone else to date her either. *You're crazy Jason Crawford; you know that,* he told himself.

When Dawn and Jason arrived at his chalet, they were joking and laughing as they walked into the living room.

"There you are. Fred told me you had gone skiing, and here I was worried that you were all alone," Tiffany said, looking haughty in her cashmere cardigan, a pearl necklace and a pair of dark, burgundy wool slacks. Her shiny brown hair lay softly in front of her big bosoms.

Speechless, Jason stared at her, and then at the two friends Tiffany had brought along. The smile on Dawn's face faded.

"Honey, you look as though you have seen a ghost. Where are your manners? Aren't you supposed to kiss me and greet your guests?"

"Forgive me," Jason replied, kissing her on the lips, not bothering to explain that he had gone airboarding and not skiing. He then turned to his friends and said, "Hello Travis, Vanessa. "

Travis and Vanessa, who looked like Ken and Barbie, were two of the richest trust-fund babies in the U.S. Vanessa's parents owned a series of television and radio stations. Travis' father was a multibillionaire whose company, now diverse, had once specialized in making doorknobs.

"You sounded so upset with me when we spoke two days ago that I decided to pack up and bring along our friends. I hope that's alright."

"Yes that's fine." He forced a smile. "Did Fred show you to your rooms?"

"He certainly did, and we're all settled in. Why don't we go sit by the fire, have a drink and then go into the village for a nice stroll." She then turned to Dawn, wiggled the glass in her hand and said, "Could you get me another sherry?"

Embarrassed, Jason took the glass from Tiffany. "I'll get you some. Does anybody else need to have their drinks refreshed?"

They all looked at each other and then at Jason with baffled expressions. "No, Vanessa and I are still nursing the ones we have," Travis said, sitting down on the living room sofa. Tiffany and Vanessa settled into the chairs. Dawn, pushing back tears, went into the kitchen to help Fred make a cheese plate, but it was all ready to go.

"You don't have to serve them you know. Let me," Fred told her when he saw all color drained from Dawn's face.

"Thanks, but no thanks. Let me face reality," she said, picking up the silver platter.

Relaxing near the fireplace, Travis lay back against the sofa, with one ankle crossed over his knee and said, "It's a bummer you had to go skiing by yourself."

"Actually I didn't go by myself," Jason replied from the bar as he poured the sherry. "Dawn went with me."

"Who is Dawn?" Vanessa asked, looking at Jason with her baby-blue eyes through her thick, fake eyelashes.

Jason handed Tiffany her drink.

"She's the maid." Tiffany suppressed a giggle.

"You went skiing with your maid?" Travis said as Dawn walked in and offered cheese to everyone with shaky hands.

Jason took the plate from her and set it down.

Travis traced Dawn's figure with his eyes and wet his lips. He had an Ivy League haircut, short in the back and long on top of the head with bangs swiped to one side, and a family crest stitched on the front pocket of his gold-buttoned blazer.

"We can help ourselves, and then we'll be leaving shortly," Jason said, "Don't worry about serving anything else or waiting up tonight. We'll be dining out." He nervously took a seat next to Travis.

"Of course, sir," she said, sounding hurt and left to go to her room.

He heard the pain in her voice but didn't quite know how to react. He couldn't apologize to her for what Travis had said. He couldn't show any affection toward her or they would think there was something going on between them. He and Dawn had a wonderful time and enjoyed being in each other's company, but now it was time to move on. Yet, he couldn't help but wish that she were one of them. The reality was that she was the help and nothing he could do at that moment could change that. But why did he prefer to be with her?

"You're very quiet Jason, is something bothering you?" Tiffany asked, thinking that perhaps her boyfriend had a thing for Dawn. Tiffany had noticed how awfully chummy the two were when they entered the house and the flabbergasted frozen look on Jason's face.

"No, nothing's bothering me. I'm just a little tired and my body's a bit sore from paragliding and hiking yesterday."

"You went paragliding without me?"

"As I remember correctly, I asked you to come to Zermatt and you said you wanted to stay in Liguria. So, I went paragliding with Dawn instead."

"You don't say," Vanessa said, widening her eyes. Since when did a maid replace her best friend Tiffany?

"You dog," Travis whispered in Jason's ear. "Does she perform other services?"

Jason got up in anger. "Apologize right now or I'll have you thrown out."

"Calm down Jason," Tiffany said. "I don't know what Travis whispered in your ear but I do know that you have been under a lot of pressure at work and you're not yourself. But you must admit hanging around the help is not one of the wisest decisions you've ever made."

Jason gritted his teeth.

"Sorry, if I upset you old man," Travis said, raising an eyebrow.

"Consider it forgotten," Jason replied. What else could he say? Travis' father did a lot of business with Crawford Enterprises and Jason wasn't about to jeopardize it over a girl who hadn't been exactly honest with him. "If you don't mind, I'll go clean up and we can go into the village."

Thirty minutes later when they left the house, Jason wasn't happy. He felt terrible about Dawn but decided to make it up to her by buying her a gift when he got back to Pasadena. The four walked around, savoring the fresh clean air and going into delightful small shops. Tiffany remarked that the stores didn't offer as many quality items as the stores in Gstaad. Vanessa found a pair of ski pants she liked and Travis a book on the art of fishing with finesse. Later, they dined at Mood's, a gourmet restaurant in a three-story building, with two cozy bars and a yacht club. After dinner, they went downstairs and enjoyed drinks at Pink Elephant's Jazz and Piano Bar and talked about their travels, playing golf and the thrill of riding one's own plane.

At home, Dawn cried until her eyes were swollen. Fred heard her, knocked on her door and went in.

"Go away and let me be, please," she said.

He ignored her plea and went to sit next to her on the bed. "I'm deeply sorry about what happened earlier. They're nothing but a bunch of tactless rich folks."

"It's my own damn fault," she wept. "You tried to warn me but I didn't listen."

"I just didn't want you to get hurt, that's all. I've been working for him for a long time and though I've never heard a cross word from him, I've seen women come and go through a revolving door. He's just not a commitment kind of guy."

"That's not what I wanted from him." She sat up, wiping her tears with her sleeve.

Fred reached in his pocket, pulled out a handkerchief and gave it to her.

She wiped her face and said, "For the first time in a long time, I found someone with whom I had things in common. You know, like one would with a good friend."

"Yes, I know. He can be a charming gentleman when he wants to be, but it never lasts."

"I suppose there was nothing he could do in front of them. I mean, he couldn't very well invite me to join them, could he?" she asked, thinking that had their roles been reversed, she would have never treated him that way.

"No, he couldn't have."

"I just felt so inferior, like I was nothing," she sniffed. "What's ironic is that I was once one of them. You know wearing the right clothes and jewelry."

"Sure you were. Sure you were," Fred replied not having a clue as to what she was talking about. He thought for a moment that she was delusional.

"I don't expect you to believe me," she said as though reading his thoughts, "but none of it matters. My past is my past, and I have to now focus on the present."

"I have an idea. Let's go upstairs and have dinner in front of the TV. There are lots of DVDs you can choose from," he offered as though he was speaking to a blubbering child. "I made dinner and there's plenty for two. I even bought ice cream for dessert."

She wiped her nose. "No, I don't want to go upstairs. If they come back, I can't face them."

"I heard them say they're going dancing and drinking after dinner. So, they won't be back for a while."

"I am hungry," she replied. Her stomach rumbled to agree.

"That's a girl. Go splash some water on your face, and I'll get dinner going."

"Thanks for not saying I told you so," she said, kissing him on the cheek.

Upstairs, the two sat behind the bar, ate a delicious meal of quiche and mixed green salad tossed with pine nuts followed by chocolate-cherry ice cream. They watched *Jump 'n Jack Flash*, a comedy starring Whoopi Goldberg, and Dawn, who couldn't stop laughing, soon forgot all about Jason and his friends. "Thank you Fred," she said when the movie ended. "I will never forget what you did for me tonight. If I can ever repay you, please let me know."

"I'm only glad that I could cheer you up." The two cleaned up, said goodnight and went to bed.

When they returned from their night out, Jason and Tiffany had sex, but he couldn't stop thinking about Dawn. The next morning, he wanted to find a way to apologize to her. As she served him and his friends breakfast, he watched Dawn move back and forth from the kitchen to the dining room and noticed that she seemed to have no animosity toward him. If she did, she was doing a great job of covering it up. Dawn had gone back to exactly the way she had been at his home in Pasadena. It was as though they had never skied together, shared a meal or conversation. Her professional behavior had put miles of distance between them and he wasn't sure if he liked it. How could anyone just turn their emotions on and off in such a quick manner?

"Would you like some milk with your coffee, sir?" she asked him.

"You know very well that I like my coffee black," he said irritably.

"Forgive me sir, sometimes it's difficult to remember everyone's likes and dislikes," she lied.

Fred quietly sniggered at her answer and admired her for being strong.

Jason grunted.

Tiffany said, "I take milk in mine."

"Yes, ma'am," she said pouring milk in her coffee. She continued going around the table "sir"-ing" and "ma'am"-ing everyone until breakfast was over and they all picked up their ski gear and left. As soon as they were gone, Dawn felt a sudden sadness come over her. She couldn't help wishing that Tiffany and her friends had never arrived. Had they not shown up, she could have been skiing at this very moment. Perhaps it was all for the best. Although she once had lived a good life, she and Jason were worlds apart in their ways of thinking and behaving. She had no problem telling off people and standing up for her friends, whereas Jason always had to do the proper thing. Had their situations been reversed yesterday, she would have stuck up for him. But Jason was too weak to do the same for her and for that reason she couldn't find it in her heart to forgive him. From now on, she would put up her guard, she thought, as she cleared the table and then helped Fred make the beds and clean the bathrooms. When finished, the two went for a walk and Fred treated her to a late lunch, which made her happy. Jason had told them that they were going to ski all day and then have dinner out.

After she and Fred returned to the house, they found Jason at the bar all by himself, nursing a glass of brandy and frowning. "Sorry sir, but we thought you'd be out with your guests and being that we had our work done...."

"No need to explain Fred. I came back early because I twisted my ankle. I told the others to stay on and ski. We're all going back home tomorrow."

"I suppose that makes sense. No use in staying here if you can't ski."

"Yes, well, could you have Dawn bring me an ice pack?" he said, limping toward his room.

She wanted to kill him. He was pretending that she wasn't even in the room with them. Why didn't he just ask her directly? If she had a place of her own and didn't need this damned job, she would tell him off. So, before Fred could get the ice pack, she went looking for it and took it to Jason's room. She placed it over his ankle, but it didn't look swollen or bruised. Was he faking it? And if so, why? "Can I get you something for your pain, sir?"

He grabbed her by the forearm and pushed her down on his bed. "Cut it out, will you?"

"I don't know what you mean, sir," she replied defiantly.

"You know exactly what I mean. You were calling me Jason yesterday and today I'm back to 'sir.' "

"I have to be very careful of my station and not insult anyone. You will always be the master's son and I the servant."

"And this has nothing to do with the fact that I went skiing with my girlfriend instead of you?"

"Why should it? I never expected you to think of me as your equal," she answered, obviously hurt.

"Is that what you think? You think that Tiffany is my equal?" he asked, looking at her with narrowed eyes.

"She has the right background and career and you can take her out without worrying about your image," she replied, a lump forming in her throat.

"Let me tell you something – there have been and will always be many Tiffanies in my life. Is that how you want me to treat you?"

"I don't want you to treat me like anything. I am a maid in your household and I'd like to keep it that way. I have no intention of getting involved with you as friends or otherwise," she said, yanking her arm out of his grip and leaving.

Jason sat still for a long time, uncoiling a paperclip and toying with it. He then picked up the phone and called his friend. "George, how's it going old buddy?"

"I'm just dandy as I ever could be. How about you?"

George Maloney, Jason's age, had dark curly hair, a small gap between his two front teeth when he smiled and an irresistible personality.

"Great. Really great," Jason answered trying to sound chipper.

George knew his friend since childhood and could tell he sounded glum. "Alright, what's bugging you?"

"Nothing. Can't a friend call his buddy to see how he's doing?"

"Yes, but the last time we spoke, you were going to spend your time up by the glaciers. How did you put it? Oh, yes, I remember now, 'All I want to do is ski, paraglide and have sex for a whole week'," he said, muting his TV. It was near the end of basketball season and he was seated in his den in South Beach, eating pepperoni pizza and drinking beer while watching the Miami Heat struggle against the Detroit Pistons.

"You know for someone who has a bad memory, you certainly can remember ridiculous details about my love life," he replied, drinking his brandy.

Always forgetful about birthdays and anniversaries, George often got into trouble for it. "What love life? I've never seen you commit to anyone," he chuckled.

"Commitment is a waste of time," he answered readjusting the pillows on his bed and resting his back against it. "I pick a flower wherever I go and move on."

"Yes, but I doubt your dates know that."

"I've never pretended otherwise. I can't help it if they become clingy."

"I take it it's not going well with what's her name – Terry? Tammy?" he asked taking a bite of pizza.

"Never mind that. Listen, are you going out of town or staying in Miami?"

"No, I'm staying put in South Beach for at least a month. Want to come down? I have plenty of room here. We can hang and maybe pick us up some eye-candy. What do you say?"

"I'm hoping to be back in L.A. by tomorrow night. I'll fly over to Miami the day after. You think you can meet me in the evening at Miami Airport day after tomorrow?"

"Why don't you call me before your flight takes off and let me know the time."

"Talk to you then," Jason said. He then called Swiss Air to reserve a seat and buzzed Fred.

"Sir?"

"Will you please come into my room?"

"Right away, sir," he said and headed upstairs.

A few minutes later, Fred showed up at Jason's room.

"Listen, could you make sure my belongings are packed by tonight? I'd like to get an early start. I'm planning to leave at 5:30 tomorrow morning."

"Certainly sir. Are your guests leaving with you as well?"

"No, they can stay behind and ski. They'll probably leave in the afternoon. I hope you don't mind."

"Certainly not, sir," he said, studying his boss. In all the years he had worked for him, Jason always stayed on with his guests. Maybe his ankle was really bothering him, in which case he shouldn't be traveling alone. "Are you sure you're up to traveling all by yourself? I mean with the hurt ankle and all."

"Don't fret, Fred. I'm fine. I just have to get back. Have some business to take care of."

"Very well, sir. I'll have breakfast ready for you at five."

"Thanks Fred. You're a good man. Oh, and call and reserve a car to pick me up and drop me off at the heliport. Then arrange for a chopper to fly me over to Geneva."

"Certainly sir," he said. He did as requested and also made reservations for himself and Dawn.

The next day Jason left early in the morning, leaving Dawn to wonder why he had left in such a rush and worrying about whether he was going to replace her. Fred made breakfast for the guests and after they went skiing, he and Dawn cleaned up. Where she once had her own housekeeper to clean up after her, Dawn was now the servant. But she knew that no matter how long she was at this job, she could never get used to serving people. She had to save every penny she had to get out of her situation, she thought as she changed the sheets where Tiffany and Jason had slept. She pictured them together, eating strawberries, drinking champagne and having sex. Dawn shook her head to get the image out of her mind.

After she and Fred were finished with their work, they packed their own belongings as well. Fred made a steaming asparagus soup and tuna sandwich and had lunch with Dawn on the birch balcony, overlooking a vast spread of mountains and frosted pines.

He knew no one was going to be back anytime soon as the two ate without conversing until Fred broke the silence.

"Don't look so sad. He's not worth it, you know," he said, turning on the heated lamp above their heads. Patches of snow covered the slopes around them and the sun was starting to push its way through the clouds.

"Who?"

"You know who I'm talking about."

"I never expected anything from him," she said finishing her soup, feeling it warming her insides. "I guess I just enjoyed his company, and that's probably what I will miss the most."

"You know, his parents had a bad marriage," Fred offered, biting into his tuna. "His mother cheated on his father all the time."

"And yet they live in the same house, pretending to be happily married."

"Till death do us part is the Crawford family motto. I think that's why Jason doesn't want to marry."

She wrinkled her forehead and gave him a puzzled look. "But doesn't his father mind that his wife is unfaithful?"

"He did at first, but I think as time passed he got over it. He has a mistress or two kept somewhere but never brings them home," he said, finishing off his sandwich.

"That's quite sad. My parents have problems – no marriage is ever perfect. But I know they love each other."

"You never talk much about your family."

"There isn't much to tell. I never got along with my father and mother…well…my father has a lot of influence over my mom."

"Do you have any siblings?"

"No."

"What about aunts and uncles?" Fred enjoyed listening to people and asking a lot of questions but he didn't much care to talk about his own life. It was too painful to talk about how he had lost his beloved wife and daughter in a car accident when a driver who had fallen asleep at the wheel, knocked their car over a cliff in Malibu Canyon.

"No, I don't come from a large family," she said and started cleaning up. Dawn, like Fred, didn't like talking about her relations or the past.

He stared at her, perplexed. "Why are you in such a rush to leave? They're not going to be back anytime soon and you still haven't finished your sandwich."

"I'll save it for later. It's chilly out here. I want to go in and make us a cup of hot cocoa. Maybe we can have it in front of the TV." She preferred it when they watched TV because they could talk about the actors and the focus wouldn't be so much on her. This whole trip had been a mistake and she should have avoided it at all costs. She shouldn't have become close to anyone.

"I'll come in a minute," Fred said. "I want to enjoy the fresh air."

So their closeness ended just like that. They talked about this and that but nothing personal while they watched TV.

When the guests returned, Fred opened the door and greeted them.

"Can I get you something to eat or drink?" Dawn asked.

"No, thank you," Tiffany responded dryly. "We had spaghetti with caviar at Elsie's bar and will be going back to my parents' villa soon."

"Actually I'm parched from drinking too much champagne. I wouldn't mind a glass of water," Vanessa said and watched Dawn disappear into the kitchen and come back with one.

Vanessa took it and followed Tiffany upstairs to freshen up before they got ready to leave. Fred went downstairs to use the bathroom. Travis walked over to the patio to take in the view and when he came back inside, he went to the kitchen to get a soda and found Dawn cleaning the stove. He began massaging her shoulders.

"Please sir, I have work to do," she said.

"I can make it worth your while," he told her, turning her around and forcing himself on her and kissing her neck.

"What is going on here?" Fred happened upon them in the kitchen and witnessed Travis taking advantage of Dawn.

"Nothing that's any of your business," Travis replied rudely.

"Dawn, why don't you go pack your things? We'll be leaving shortly," Fred demanded.

Relieved, Dawn did as he asked.

Fred turned to Travis with a tight face and warned, "I'm going to pretend this didn't happen and if you were smart, you would march yourself right upstairs, pack your things and leave as quickly as possible."

"Okay, old man. No need to be so touchy," he answered with his hands up in the air.

"Stupid jerk," Fred mumbled after he was gone.

When the guests left and Fred shut the door behind them, he said, "Good riddance. Don't ever come back again." He then went downstairs into Dawn's room and said, "Are you alright?

Dawn nodded. "I'm not sure what would have happened had you not walked in there," she said, putting a sweater in her suitcase. "I mean, it would have been my word against his and who would have believed me?"

"I would have. If anyone ever touches you inappropriately, you let me know right away and I'll take care of them," he told her with a serious face.

"Thank you." She looked at him appreciatively.

Dawn helped Fred tidy the upstairs bathrooms once again and covered the furniture with sheets to protect them from dust.

Afterwards, they grabbed their luggage and took a taxi to the train station. Fred wished to get to know Dawn better but he also knew his boundaries and when to quit asking questions people didn't like to answer. He thought of Dawn as his own daughter and though Dawn kept her distance, in the short time he had spent with her in Zermatt, he decided that she was a good person even if she did have a past she tried to hide.

"Fred?" she blurted as they got closer to Visp to exchange trains for Geneva airport. For the entire train ride she thought about Fred and how he had tried to protect her, help boost her confidence and control her feelings toward Jason.

"Yes?"

"If I could choose my father, I would want him to be just like you."

"Thank you." He smiled in surprise, thinking that for the first time in a long time he had not been severely depressed. "I tell you what, why don't you think of me as your adopted dad and feel free to come to me whenever you need anything?"

"Okay then, Papa Fred," she said, kissing him on the cheek. "You too can always count on me."

TWELVE

The day Fred and Dawn returned from Zermatt, Jason left for Miami and life returned to normal. Mrs. Anderson was her usual self, dishing out orders left and right. Dawn kept to herself and spent her free time reading in the garden if the sun was out, and in the library when Mrs. Anderson was too busy to notice. At times she'd pass by the stables, wishing she could ride one of the horses.

"Hello there," an elderly man with tartar-stained teeth said, startling her. He was standing outside the stables on an overcast afternoon, finishing off his cigarette. Dawn was savoring a Granny Smith apple on her lunch break.

"Hi yourself," she answered, wanting to shake his hand but hers was sticky from the apple's juice and his was dirty, so she decided against it. "My name is Dawn."

"Nice to meet you Dawn," he said, dropping his handmade cigarette to the ground and extinguishing it with his foot. "I'm Jake. I've been watching you pass here often, admiring the horses. Do you ride?" he asked, pulling up his baggy jeans, which were gliding down his thin frame.

"I used to but not so much anymore," she told him, walking into the stables and examining the 14 stalls housing a nice selection of horses – Arabian, American quarter, Spanish Barb and Hungarian Warmblood.

"Why did you stop?" he asked, following her.

"I don't have the money to indulge in horseback riding," she said, taking another bite of her apple.

"I'll give you a horse to ride," he offered.

"Mrs. Anderson would never allow it," Dawn told him, looking in the direction of the house and hoping she hadn't seen her go into the stables.

"Forget Mrs. Anderson. I'm in charge of the horses. You just tell me when you want to ride and I'll saddle one up for you."

"I can ride any of the horses?" she asked, eyeing an Arabian.

"No, only the ones meant for the guests, which are the Spanish Barbs," he replied, pointing to a deep-brown one. "They're quite friendly, comfortable to ride and make great trail horses."

"What about the Egyptian Arabian?" she asked, pointing at a white horse.

"Her name is Mystery, but you can't ride her. She doesn't let anyone near her except Mr. Crawford, Jr. But even he gets mad at her sometimes. She's quite temperamental," he said, coughing thickly from the tobacco that was still sitting in his throat.

"I wonder why he would keep her around, then."

"Because he likes her the most when she gives him a hard time. I suppose he likes the fact that he can never figure her out."

"What do you mean?"

"Sometimes she lets him ride her and they get along fine, but other times, when she isn't in a good mood, she tries to throw him off."

"That's because he doesn't know how to handle her," Dawn said, walking over to the horse before the man could stop her and offered the mare the remainder of her apple. Mystery ate it with delight and then rubbed her face against Dawn's arm. "You're not so bad, are you? You just want to be loved."

"Well, I'll be damned," the man said, looking at Dawn and then at Mystery with wide eyes. "She seems to like you, but I still wouldn't try to ride her if I were you."

"I couldn't right now, anyway," Dawn admitted, glancing at her watch. "My break is over, and I have to get back. It's been nice chatting with you," she said and scurried off.

While Dawn was working hard to make ends meet, Jason was in Miami lying on the beach, eyeing girls in their bikinis, getting massages and going to nightclubs with his friend George. Today, he was seated on a chaise longue on the balcony of George's condo which had a waterfront ocean view.

"You know, I'm tired of traveling and have been thinking about selling this condo and moving to L.A. permanently." George said, drinking a gin cocktail early in the afternoon.

His Complex was situated on 15 acres of lush private gardens. George's condo had five bedrooms with high ceilings and glass sliding doors. The facility offered several pools including a lap pool on the roof, two floors of fitness center, a tennis club and a spa. It was a short walk to South Beach and a brief ride to downtown Miami.

"What about your work?" Jason asked, wearing nothing but his purple trunks.

"I can always move to a different department that doesn't require traveling." George was a senior computer programmer.

"It would be great if you came to L.A," he answered with excitement. "We can hang out more often."

"Do you ever think about the computer game business we planned when we were in college?" George asked, reminiscing about the past.

"Once in awhile I think about our old dreams," Jason chuckled. "I still have our business plan in a drawer somewhere at home – C&M Games, a computer games and virtual reality company."

"C for Jason Crawford and M for George Maloney. What a great pair of businessmen we would have made," he said, relaxing in his seat, basking in the sun. "Sometimes I think about quitting my job and opening up my own computer business."

"Do you?" Jason asked lifting his head from his chair and staring at his friend. "And would you continue designing computer games and virtual reality?"

"Sure would, except that instead of working for someone else, I would be my own boss," he said, "But then I wake up from my dream and realize that I need my regular paychecks. Ladan thinks I should just go for it. She thinks I can pull it off."

Ladan, George's ex-girlfriend, met George and Jason while attending Carnegie Mellon University. George and Jason were double majoring in computers and business, and Ladan in physics and chemistry. They hung out together studying, playing tennis and going to parties. A year before finishing their undergraduate degree, Ladan, an Iranian, fell in love with a Cuban who owned an upscale hotel in South Beach. She broke it off with George, got married and moved to Miami. George continued with his studies and received his master's in entertainment technology and a Ph.D. in robotics.

"I saw her picture on the dresser next to your bathroom. I didn't know you were still talking to her," Jason said, remembering her photo and thinking how exotic she looked with her cropped black wavy hair, onyx eyes and olive complexion.

"What were you doing in my room?" George asked, irritably. The truth was that he still loved Ladan, but didn't want to admit it.

"My electric razor stopped working this morning and I needed to borrow yours while you were up on the roof swimming. I didn't think you minded," he said, applying sunscreen on his face and arms.

"No, I don't mind."

"So, what's the deal between you two? I thought she was married."

"She got a divorce a year ago. Her husband told her he wasn't in love with her anymore." He gazed at the ocean with somber eyes, wishing that Ladan and the Cuban had never met.

"Does she have any children with him?" Jason inquired, remembering how much Ladan loved kids.

"No. She said he already had a boy and a girl from his prior marriage and didn't want to have anymore."

"Did she ever go back to school and finish her degree?" Jason asked, thinking what a big mistake Ladan made when she dropped out of college.

"Yes, she not only finished her undergrad, but she continued with her education. She now has a Ph.D. and teaches chemistry and physics at the University of Miami. She's been talking a lot lately about moving to L.A. I think she recently sent out her résumé to USC.

Jason cocked an eyebrow and said, "So, that's why you want to move to L.A. You want to be where she is?"

"No, we're just friends," George cleared his throat. "We have dinner or go to the movies sometimes." He started playing with the straw in his drink.

"Then how come you keep a picture of her on your dresser?" Jason inquired, observing his friend's reaction.

"It's just a picture. It doesn't mean anything." George shifted uncomfortably in his chair.

"You feel nothing toward her, then?" he asked, teasingly.

"She broke my heart when she dumped me for the Cuban," he yelled, "I'm not going to fall for her again. We're just friends now."

"If you say so," Jason smirked and shook his head, thinking how he was no different than his friend George because he, too, didn't like to admit that he had feelings for Dawn.

Jason came home from South Beach. Dawn hadn't seen him for a week when she returned to the stables on her day off. Mrs. Anderson was out of town, visiting her sister, who lived an hour away. The household was ecstatic due to her absence, and everyone took it easy.

"Ready to ride today, Miss?" Jake said when he saw her in her dark blue jeans, white sweatshirt and tennis shoes.

"I'm tempted but don't want to get into trouble," Dawn replied. Her hair was longer since she had started working at the Crawford mansion, and she was actually able to pull it up into a short ponytail.

"C'mon go for it. No one's around. I'll settle up Serenity for you," he encouraged her, going toward one of the Spanish Barbs.

"No, if I'm going to do this, I'd prefer riding Mystery."

"I know you said you know how to ride, and sometimes I bend the rules for the experienced guests and let them ride their favorite, but Mystery would never allow you to ride her."

"I bet you five dollars she will."

A gambler by nature, Jake never could say no to a sure bet. "You're on, but don't be mad if she throws you off," he told her and saddled Mystery up.

As soon as Dawn mounted, the horse lifted its hooves up in the air and shrieked. "Settle down you miserable beast," he yelled out.

"Does everyone talk to her like that? It's no wonder she doesn't let people ride her," she replied, trying hard not to fall off.

"Pardon my manners," he answered sarcastically and turned to the horse. "Excuse me your grace, it isn't ladylike for you to raise your legs up like that." He then looked at Dawn. "How's that? You think that'll work?"

"Oh, never mind," Dawn replied, ignoring him. "C'mon baby, I'm not going to hurt you," she repeated with a firm voice several times, tightening her grip on the reins. And when at last, the horse calmed down, it took off at a lightning pace around the track. Dawn felt the cool air against her cheeks and the excitement of the ride. As she guided the horse around the corners, she knew she and the horse were starting to bond.

From across the track, Jason, who had come home a day early from Chicago, watched her riding his favorite horse and once again wondered about the enigmatic Dawn. How in the world she was able to handle his temperamental pet was beyond him. He approached the track with a girl in tow and whistled for Mystery, but the horse ignored him. She had found herself a new owner and was having too much fun to stop.

Dawn looked over to see who was whistling and her heart dropped. "Oh damn," was all she could say as she headed toward her boss, regretting having taken Mystery for a ride. She dismounted, afraid that Jason would reprimand her. "Jason! I mean Mr. Crawford. We didn't expect to see you till tomorrow. Mrs. Anderson...."

"I came back early," he answered curtly. "I see you're riding my favorite horse. What I don't understand is who taught you how to ride and where did you learn to tame a horse like that?"

"Well, one of the families...."

"Yes, one of the families your mother worked for taught you how to do it," he finished her sentence irritably. He was upset with her but unsure why. Perhaps he had a hard time believing her. Perhaps he was mad at himself for dumping Tiffany and picking up a girl in South Beach who looked like Dawn in the hopes that he would stop thinking about her.

Dawn didn't know what else to say. He had caught her at a bad moment, and she was a terrible liar. She wondered what happened to Tiffany. This new girl had red hair and blue eyes like her own except that she looked much prettier. Her hair was silky, her bangs were cut to perfection, and her nails were nicely manicured, and she wore a Dolce & Gabbana dress. Dawn had recognized the style as soon as she had seen it. Dawn's hair was frizzier than usual from the ride, her body was sweaty and she had broken two nails when she struggled with Mystery to bring her hooves to the ground.

Jason didn't introduce the girl but simply said, "Have Fred bring us tea to my room, and tell him we'll be dining out."

I'm off today, ask someone else, she wanted to say. "Of course, sir. Anything else?" she asked, still expecting him to introduce the girl out of politeness. But he just walked away holding her hand. Dawn later found out from Fred that her name was Johanna and that she was the editor of a fashion magazine. Jason had met her at an exclusive club in Miami.

However, two weeks later, the girl disappeared from Jason's life and was replaced by Madison, his on-and-off again girlfriend, who was a noted part of a wealthy business family. Dawn met her one night when she was ready to turn in as she walked toward the servants' quarters. She and Jason were returning from the theater.

"Could you tell the cook to make us a late breakfast, say about 11? We're tired and want to get some rest," he said.

"No problem," she replied and went back to the kitchen to write a note.

Jason told his date that he'd be right up, he just needed to grab a glass of water. "Will you get me one too?" Madison said, taking the stairs up to his room.

Dawn, who had just finished her note, posted it on top of the cook's schedule book and turned around to leave when she bumped into Jason and lost her balance. He automatically grabbed her around the waist.

"Excuse me sir, I didn't hear you come in," she said.

"Are you ever going to stop calling me sir, or are we going to go through this every time?"

"Mr. Crawford…."

"Mr. Crawford is my father, my name is Jason," he teased, staring at her defiant eyes, his hands still on her waist.

"Please stop manipulating me," she told him, but he tightened his grip around her and brought her close to him, brushing his lips against hers.

"Don't, don't kiss me and then go upstairs and make love to someone else. This isn't right," she pleaded.

"Would you rather that I made love to you?"

"No, I would prefer it if you ceased taunting me. I would prefer it if you respected me."

As soon as she said this, he let her go and regretted his action. "I may not show it, but I do respect you," he told her and went to the fridge to get two bottles of water. She tearfully walked away, hating him for treating her as though she were dirt. Yes, he said he respected her, but his actions didn't match his words.

The next day, Jason sat in the sunroom eating his breakfast. Madison was still in the bathroom, primping. He expected Dawn to be serving him, but it was Mrs. Anderson who had come in with a hot pot of coffee and the morning paper. He noticed that she had lost some weight, let her hair down and was wearing makeup. "Where's Dawn?" he asked.

"I sent her to clean the lavatories by the pool," she said, gloating that she had at last been able to point out the obvious – that Dawn was a maid in a low position in his household and he should stop paying her so much attention.

If he didn't like Mrs. Anderson, he liked her even less after hearing what she had to say: "Didn't you hire a new girl who was supposed to be in charge of the lavatories?"

"Yes, but she is so talented that I have decided to give her kitchen duties."

"Really?" he said, staring at Mrs. Anderson as though seeing through her for the first time. He finally realized that she was interested in him. She was looking at him with desire. How could he have missed it before? And more importantly why was she so infatuated with him when he had never given her a reason? The woman clearly had a distorted view of reality. "I want you to have the new girl clean the toilets and give Dawn time off to do as she pleases."

"B...b...but sir," she stammered, turning red, "we would be short of help."

"No, you won't. We're well staffed, and I'm sure you know how to delegate," he answered firmly.

"What about tonight's dinner? Will she be helping us out?" she asked, her facial muscles as tense as a rock.

There was going to be a family dinner with his two brothers, their wives and children, and his parents, but Jason had no patience for any of them. "Take away one plate; I have other plans. As far as Dawn's concerned, I expect her to serve the cocktails and hors d'oeuvres."

"But she was supposed to be on cleaning duty."

"Then change the schedule," he replied, dismissing her with a flick of his hand to show how it felt to treat people as though they were beneath him.

"Excuse me sir," she answered, leaving in a fury. She had to find a way to get rid of Dawn. Ever since Dawn had started there, the household had become unruly. Once she was in charge of everything, now she was losing control.

Jason started reading the paper when the door reopened. It was his father, looking displeased. "Have you seen the tabloids?"

"The tabloids?" Jason wrinkled his forehead. "Since when do you read the tabloids?"

"Since this morning when your mother pointed out that you were getting married to Madison and didn't have the decency to tell us."

"What are you talking about?"

"This." He smacked the paper in front of him. "Are you out of your mind to be marrying this girl when she has been very open about her dislike of the Muslim community?"

Madison was a big supporter of Jerry Falwell, who believed that Muslims and Jews couldn't go to heaven. Jason had known this all along but didn't care because she satisfied him in bed and, up until now, had managed to keep her name out of the papers by assuring interviewers that he had no intention of settling down.

Jason took the paper and read the front-page headline: "Jason Crawford, Eligible California Bachelor Will Marry Madison Harper of Harper Corp." The article reported that Madison admitted she and Jason had finally decided to tie the knot and were soon getting engaged. The wedding was to be held on the Crawford estate. Furious, Jason picked up the phone. "I will sue their behinds for slander," he replied as he dialed the publication. "Jack, please," he told the receptionist when she answered the phone.

"May I ask who is calling?" a soft-spoken girl asked.

"This is Jason Crawford."

"I'm sorry Mr. Crawford, but Mr. Mitchell is in a meeting. May I take a message?"

"Unless he wants a big lawsuit on his hands, tell him to take this call or he'll have to face the consequences."

"Just a moment, please," the receptionist said, putting him on hold and buzzing her boss. "I have Jason Crawford on line one."

"Take a message, I'm in a meeting."

"I think you should take his call. He is threatening to sue the paper."

"Thank you," he frowned, picking up the line, "Jack here. What's all this about a lawsuit, Jason?"

"Look Jack, I've been tolerant up to now, having you guys twist the truth about my personal life, but this time you've gone too far."

"What are you talking about?"

"You know exactly what I mean. Why did you print that I was getting married? Do you have any idea what kind of damage this is going to do to my father's business?"

"The story about your engagement to Madison came from the horse's mouth."

"And that would be?"

"Madison! She was interviewed at lunch yesterday by one of our gossip columnists and when asked about her on-again, off-again relationship with you, Madison said, and I quote, 'We have been talking about getting engaged for some time now. We were thinking about having the reception at the house,' end quote."

"Madison would never say that. She knows I would never marry her."

"I'm sorry Jason, but that's what she told us."

"Then print a retraction, saying that there was never a proposal to begin with and that your source had misled you."

"Fine, fine. Can I go back to my meeting now?"

"Yes, but before I let you go, the next time you hear a story like that, you'd better confirm it with me. Goodbye," he said, slamming down the receiver.

"Well," said his father, "what are you going to do about this nonsense?"

"Please Andrew, would you just let me handle it?"

"I'm going, but I'm warning you, take care of it ASAP before our Arab investors get a whiff of it."

Madison walked in just as Drew was leaving. He gave her a hostile look when he passed by. "What's going on?" she asked Jason. "I could hear you guys arguing all the way down the hall."

"Madison,' he said with a strained voice, trying hard to control his anger, "did you or did you not tell the *Community Press* that we were getting married?"

"Oh that. That's what you're all so upset about?"

"Just answer the question," he ordered, looking at her with eyes that could kill.

"I might have mentioned something the other day," she said, taking a croissant, "but you said yourself that you wouldn't mind marrying me." She took a seat next to him and acted as though nothing were wrong.

"When? When did I ever say that?" he yelled.

"Several nights ago when we were in bed. You know, after the Emerson party. You were at my place or don't you remember?"

"We had both been drinking and taking Ecstasy. God knows what else I might have said. I would've proposed to Mrs. Anderson for all I know had she been in the room. What's the matter with you? Your statement to the press was completely irresponsible."

"Why don't you want to marry me, Jason? Am I not good enough for you?" she asked, playfully pushing his hair away from his face.

"Madison, I'm not going to allow you or anyone to manipulate me into marriage," he said, slapping her hand away, "And since you're so keen on settling down, I think we should break up."

"For how long?"

"Oh, I don't know. Forever?"

"What?'

"You heard me. I want you out of this house, and I never want to lay eyes on you again.

"Jason, I'm sorry." She began sobbing. "I just thought you needed a push. I promise I will never...."

He got up and threw his napkin on the table. "We had a nice time while it lasted and now you're just wasting you tears on me. I have no intention of marrying you or anyone else for that matter. I expect you packed and out of this house before this afternoon." He stormed out.

An hour later, Madison was gone and the entire staff knew what had happened. Dawn, who had heard the story from Fred, felt sorry for her. She saw her crying from the garden and disliked Jason more than ever. The way he treated women was cruel, and she was glad that nothing had happened between the two of them while they were up in Zermatt. He was a man not to be trusted with her feelings.

THIRTEEN

At the end of May, in honor of their company's 60th anniversary, the Crawfords threw a large party at their estate. Fresh flowers and candles were set as centerpieces on a highly polished dinner table that seated 100 guests in the long, rectangular dining room. Italian fine china with gold trim, Prussian water goblets, Waterford Bordeaux wine glasses and Tiffany silverware dressed the table. In the kitchen, a French chef hired from outside for special occasions was issuing orders to the kitchen staff and the cook didn't like it one bit. "He thinks he's so great," he mumbled under his breath. "Why, you need a microscope to see the small portions he serves."

"Did you say something?" the chef asked.

"I was just complimenting you on the splendid job you were doing."

"Merci," he said with his thick, French accent. "Could you go to the wine cellar and get me a nice bottle of sherry? Then come back, and I'll teach to you how to make the meat sauce."

"Why certainly," the cook answered with a plastered smile, grunting as he walked off. "Damn French fool, pushing me around. That's my kitchen he's working in."

Out in the hallway, two workers finished waxing the floors. A couple of maids stocked the bathrooms, making sure the mirrors and the sink areas sparkled. Mrs. Anderson supervised by walking around with her to-do list, checking to see if the work was done to her satisfaction. Hired bartenders wiped all the glasses and double-checked to make sure that the bar was fully stocked.

In her room, Dawn prepared for the big night. She was one of the servers and wanted to make sure she looked professional and fit the part. Mrs. Anderson, who wasn't happy about Dawn having one of the easier tasks, sent over a freshly ironed black pantsuit to her room. After buttoning her jacket, Dawn wished she could keep the suit. It fitted her perfectly and complimented her red hair.

The guests were to arrive any minute and she was to take their drink orders and serve appetizers. As she walked through the drawing room toward the kitchen, Jason's eyes traced her boyish figure from head to toe. If only she would put an extra 20 pounds and get a nice haircut instead of pinning it back, she would look very sexy, he thought as he approached her.

"Hello, Dawn," he said, thinking how much he missed talking with her. Ever since he made a pass at her two weeks ago in the kitchen, he stayed away from her. He liked her but was afraid to get involved. She was nothing like Zoya and he knew he would eventually have a difficult time breaking it off. Women like Dawn were the marrying type whereas women like Zoya were out to have a good time. For now he was just looking to have a good time.

Dawn was glad that she hadn't run into him much lately. He had been out of town on business several times and when he came back, he often dined out. She was worried about her feelings toward him and had to make sure to keep it under control. "Good evening, Mr. Crawford," she answered politely, and before he could engage her in a longer conversation or make a pass, she headed for the kitchen.

Soon, guests made their way in as they handed their coats and wraps to the butlers. Jason, his father, mother, brothers and their wives began greeting everyone. Among the guests were politicians in their pricy tuxes and extravagant gowns, lawyers, investors and business associates – all of whom enjoyed rubbing shoulders with the crème de la crème. Dawn, Zoya and other servers walked around with trays of hors d'oeuvres. Husam was there as well as Emad, his translator, wearing their *ghutra*. Their beige *bishts* were worn over their suits as they were ushered to a separate room along with some of the other male guests who were either unmarried or had attended without their wives.

The private room had a Moroccan atmosphere. It was set up with embroidered, geometrically patterned velvet cushions with turquoise throw pillows, beaded drapery of bright gold, eye-catching red, vibrant purple and emerald silk. Dawn, who was supposed to only serve the drawing room guests, upon Zoya's insistence, made the mistake of following her into the private room and was jolted when she entered but tried to keep her composure nonetheless.

There were 22 Call girls and 11 male guests in the room. Some women in short seductive dresses had their arms around some of the Arab men, others sat on the laps of well-known American politicians and businessmen and the rest circulated the room, making sure the guests were satisfied and later accompanied them to their hotel rooms.

"Go on and serve their drinks, don't be afraid." Zoya poked Dawn.

Dawn moved about reluctantly, not liking what she saw. One of the Arabs had his hand slid between a blonde's legs as he flirted with her. A politician was nuzzling a brunette's neck. Against a wall, a man had his hand inside a woman's bra as he kissed her. But when Husam, who had a taste for red hair and blue eyes, spotted her, he told his translator to take the tray away from Dawn. Then he grabbed her and pushed her down on his lap. He had dyed his hair black and trimmed his beard and mustache.

From afar Zoya saw him trying to kiss Dawn as she pushed his face away.

"You're a feisty skinny thing, aren't you?" he said in Arabic. "You'd be great to toss around in bed. You are so wetting my appetite."

Zoya flew out of the room to get help. She went straight to Jason, who was talking to Arnold Reef. Awhile back, Jason's father had helped Arnold escape an SEC investigation when he was charged with insider trading. It involved the stock of a drug company. Arnold along with many politicians and businessmen, made obscene amounts of money by playing on people's fear of a bogus bird flu virus that was created in a lab by scientists whose palms were greased by powerful players.

"There's a phone call for you in your office," she lied.

"Take a message. Can't you see I'm busy talking?"

"He said it's important."

"Excuse me, Arnie," Jason said, heading toward his office.

"This way," Zoya said to him, pointing to the private room.

"But my office is in the other direction," he protested, thinking she had lost her faculties.

"Dawn's in trouble. One of your guests is all over her in the private room."

"What the hell is she doing there? She was not supposed to be working in that room," he blurted angrily.

"It was my fault. I asked her to help me out in there. I am sorry."

Jason shot Zoya an angry glance. When Zoya had started working there, Jason had a short fling with her. She was bold and liked living on the edge. That's what had turned him on at first. But later he tired of her and dropped her. He followed Zoya in the room and saw Dawn struggling with her captor. "La tamosunni ayyoha ellahjouzo al nazif," get your hands off of me, you dirty old man she warned him in Arabic.

"You speak Arabic? I like that. I promise we'll have fun tonight," he said grabbing her wrist and telling Emad to get the car.

Jason stood in the way of the door and the translator. "Please tell your boss that he cannot take the girl with him."

"Why not?" Emad asked, looking like Julius Caesar with his inky hair combed forward. He stared at Jason with his bulging eyes, waiting for a good explanation. To him, American women were all easy and fair game.

"Because she's not for sale. He can have any woman he wants in this room except the servers."

The translator relayed the message to Husam, who was drunk and beyond reason.

Jason looked at Dawn's horrified face and shaking body. "Please let her go, and I will find you another girl." He tried to loosen Husam's grip around Dawn's wrist.

The guests and call girls started to look in their direction, wondering what was going on.

"He doesn't want another girl. He likes this one, especially since she speaks Arabic and is very shy," Emad interpreted.

"Tell him I will give him someone very experienced. She can act very shy, has the same hair color and eyes, big breasts and a curvy bottom."

Husam shook his head no.

A silver-haired gentleman in a dusky gray suit moved toward Jason. "Can I help?"

"Thank you Congressman, but I have it under control. Everything is fine," Jason assured him. Jason turned his attention to Husam. "Look, the girl you're holding is to be engaged soon," he lied. "You cannot take her with you."

Emad tried to convince Husam to accept Jason's offer and take another girl. Husam finally agreed and released Dawn.

"Go to your room and stay there," Jason told Dawn angrily.

Zoya jumped in. "But she didn't do anything wrong."

"Haven't you caused enough problems for one night? Go do your job and let me handle it," he yelled.

Zoya moved away and did as he requested. Dawn left the room as well.

Jason noticed that some of the guests were still staring. "Please don't be alarmed, people. There was a simple misunderstanding. Go ahead and enjoy yourselves." He then called Madam B, who ran a top-notch prostitution business, and told her to meet Husam in his hotel room.

"You know I don't turn tricks anymore." The former pro now ran a lucrative business.

"Yes, you do. Weren't you at Senator J.C.'s house a few nights ago?"

"That's different. J.C. and I have been dating for a while now."

"That's not what he told me. He said you were a great lay and that I should give you a test drive." Jason, well acquainted with J.C., knew he would never leave his society wife for an ex-call girl.

"That bastard used me," B said, clearly hurt. "Tell your guest I'll be in his room in an hour; I want double my usual fee and nothing less. If he wants to throw in a necklace or bracelet, I'd be much obliged."

"Don't worry B. I'll take good care of you," Jason promised, relaying the message to Emad.

Husam left the party right away, eager to have sex. Jason snuck out of the house and walked toward Dawn's room. He opened her door without knocking, slammed his hand on her desk, which made her jump and yelled, "Who the hell are you and how do you know how to speak Arabic?"

She immediately pulled out her suitcase and started packing.

Jason grabbed her arm and pushed her down on a chair. "Look, I know your parents abandoned you when you decided to marry a Saudi man and change your religion."

Her jaw dropped open. "You had me investigated?"

"What did you expect? You've been lying to me from the first day. I had to be sure you weren't a corporate spy out to ruin us."

"A spy?" She started laughing. "Is that what you think I am?"

"I don't know who or what you are. You're a housekeeper who is knowledgeable about search engines, emails, Blackberries and Iphones, who reads business magazines, speaks Arabic and knows how to play tennis, horseback ride and ski. You don't exactly fit the profile of a maid."

"I've had enough of this," she said, resuming her packing. "I don't owe you or anyone an explanation. My private life is none of your god-damned business."

"Then perhaps you would like to explain to the authorities how you entered this country without a single trace of your existence."

Dawn let go of the shirt in her hand and, for the first time in a long time, felt completely defeated.

"Well?" he said, picking up the phone, "you either tell me the truth or I'm going to make a call I should have made long ago."

"Put the phone down," she told him, all color drained from her face as she collapsed on her bed. "What did your investigator tell you?"

"Everything up to the point when you left Barcelona. I know that you met a wealthy businessman there and got engaged," Jason said, taking a seat facing her bed.

"Oh god," she said covering her face with her hands and not saying anything for a long time. She couldn't tell him the entire truth.

He waited anxiously, hoping that whatever she was hiding was something he could handle.

She looked at him for a moment, still debating what she should hide and what she should tell. "The thing that you must understand is that my husband was very charming at first. He gave me more money than I could ever imagine. He was my first love, you see."

Jason felt a pang of jealousy and suddenly found himself competing with a man he knew nothing about. "What was your husband's name?"

"Youssef Al-Nassar."

Jason didn't recognize the name.

"He bought me expensive gifts and took me to nice places. For the first time in my life I was able to do things I wanted without being on a budget. I know you think it's weird how a poor girl like me would know how to do so many things, but I had always been very athletic, got into school on a tennis scholarship, majored in linguistics and Arabic and minored in Spanish."

"What happened after Barcelona?" he asked impatiently.

"Before I tell you that, there is something you should know. Husam knows me and I hope he didn't recognized me."

"How? How does he know you?"

"He was friends with Youssef. The first time I saw Husam was at a dinner in Barcelona. It was a long time ago, before I was married. He was there with some young girl, and I was with my fiancé. He was friendly enough and made jokes but I disliked him then just as much as I dislike him now. He leered at me the entire night and made chauvinistic jokes."

"Isn't that part of the Saudi culture?"

"No, not all Saudis are that way. There're many liberal Saudis, especially the younger generation. The fundamentalists, religious leaders and older generation are the ones who hold on tightly to tradition and old value systems."

"Then what happened?" he asked, leaning forward, giving her his full attention.

"Well, despite my friend's warning, I changed my religion, got married and moved to Riyadh."

"Who was your friend?"

"Sahar Al-Hijazi."

"The girl who married Husam and died on her wedding night?" he asked with wide eyes.

"You know her?" she gaped at him.

"Not personally, no. But I did a lot of business with her grandfather Kadar and later with her father, Saad, quite an agreeable man. Then Kadar's company joined with Husam's right around the time Sahar got married."

Goose bumps rose all over Dawn's body as she stared at him speechless for a long time before she said, "This all feels extremely strange."

"I agree," he replied, tapping his fingers on her desk, trying to make sense of it all. "Did you meet Sahar through Husam in Barcelona?"

"No; the first time Sahar and Husam met was in Riyadh. I met Sahar while attending school in Spain." She changed position and sat cross-legged against the wall behind her bed.

"Her death must have been hard for you."

"Yes, very hard, we were extremely close," she told him, tears welling up. "We kept in touch even when I began my married life. My Arabic improved through time and I learned how to cook. I had a maid and a large house but wasn't allowed to leave it without my husband."

"And that didn't bother you?" he asked, feeling sudden compassion for her.

"What choice did I have? It's a life I chose for myself. When I look back, I realize now how stupid and naïve I was," she said wiping her eyes. "You see, he promised me that we would live in a compound when we got to Riyadh."

"A compound?" he questioned her, never having traveled to Saudi Arabia.

"Compounds are like apartments where westerners live. The structures are walled off from Arab citizens so that they can't see inside. Guards with machine guns keep intruders out and check your ID when you try to get back in."

"Sounds more like a prison to me."

"In a way it is, but living there is easier than living in an Arab neighborhood. Men and women mingle, play games like baseball, swim and lay out in their bathing suits and watch movies."

"And if you're not in the compound?"

"Men are not allowed to see, talk to or walk with women who are unrelated to them."

"Suppose that's normal over there."

"Yes, but it's not what I had agreed to when I got married. He told me that we wouldn't be living in Riyadh all the time and that we'd be traveling to Europe often. I figured I could live with that."

"When you found out he lied to you, why didn't you divorce him?"

"I tried many times, but the court denied my requests. You see, my husband's business wasn't doing well, so he started picking on me," she said. "At first, he verbally abused me: Why couldn't I cook the meal to his specifications? Why did I wear my hair a certain way? Why did I answer him back instead of just shutting up? But the worse his business got, the more he abused me and then the beatings started."

"He beat you?" he asked with obvious pity.

"In the beginning, he beat me in areas where no one could see. You know, on my back or legs, but after awhile he became careless. I had bruises on my face, and he broke my arm two times."

"Good heavens!" he said, horrified.

"Then one day he came at me, choking me like this" she said, making a circling gesture with her hands around her neck, "just because I had made the wrong dish. I thought I was going to die and then I must have fainted. When I finally woke up, I knew I had to escape."

He tensed and his hands turned into fists as though her husband was in the room and he was about to beat him to a pulp. "But how? He didn't let you go anywhere without him."

"I communicated through my maid. She knew someone who could get me a fake I.D., passport and papers to leave the country. In return, I gave her most of my savings," she said, hearing a noise outside. Dawn got up and opened the door, but no one was there. She wondered whether someone had been eavesdropping or whether she was simply going mad.

"Is everything alright?" Jason asked, following her to the door.

"Yes, I thought I heard...nevermind."

"You were fortunate, you know," he said, returning to his chair, "Your maid could have squealed or taken your money and left."

"I had to risk it. I couldn't live in that country anymore," she said, back on her bed. "I needed my freedom. I needed to be able to walk out without being covered from head to toe. I felt suffocated under my *abaya*. Sometimes, it would get excruciatingly hot under there when my husband would take me to the *souk* to do my shopping."

"What name did you travel under?"

"Hope, Hope Patterson. I laid low for a long time and worked under that name in fast-food restaurants, but I wasn't making enough to make ends meet. I needed a job with free room and board.

"What did you do?"

"I switched back to my real name, Dawn Parnell. I had house-sitting experience with references so when I turned up at Kate's Domestic Agency, they hired me."

"I suppose when you got back, you couldn't have reported your mistreatment to the U.S. government, could you?"

"The U.S. government has strong ties with the Saudi government and they look the other way when there is any kind of human rights violations. Besides, the American government lays out everything a woman needs to know before marrying a Saudi on their U.S. Department of State Web site."

"I didn't know that."

"I didn't either. I found out when it was too late. I learned that unless a marriage contract states otherwise, when a woman marries a Saudi man in the U.S., has his children, and decides to go visit Saudi Arabia, the husband may keep the children there forever without the mother's consent."

"Forever?"

"Well, if the child is a boy, he can leave after age of 18, but if it's a girl, she may never be allowed to leave by the father, can be forced into marriage and be oppressed like a Saudi woman for the rest of her life."

"Do children wear *abayas*?"

"Right after they get their menses, sometimes sooner. The American mother can leave with the help of the U.S. government if she has registered with the U.S. embassy, but the children may be forced to stay."

"And you didn't register with the embassy before you left, did you?"

"No, I didn't. Besides, my husband would have killed me if word got to him that I was trying to escape. No, I had to hide my departure from him."

"Did you have any children with this man?" he asked, hoping that she didn't.

"No, and he blamed me for it. That's another reason why he'd kick me and call me a good for nothing wife."

He held her hands in his and said, "You're lucky to get out of there alive. But how did you pass through immigration when we went to Switzerland? Didn't the person who gave you a boarding pass ask why there was no record of your entry into U.S.?"

"Oh yeah...I was petrified when Mrs. Anderson volunteered me to work for you in Zermatt. I put a call through to the people who had helped me escape. They said when I go to the terminal, look for a Sri Lankan girl who works behind the Swiss Air ticketing counter and she would take care of me."

"What was her name?"

"I'm sorry but I cannot tell you that."

"Who are these people who helped you?"

"I don't know anything about them and they told me never to discus them with anyone. I have already said too much."

Sitting back and crossing his leg over his thigh, he put his elbow on the arm of the chair and rubbed his chin.

"Are you still going to report me to the authorities for getting into the country under a false name?" she asked, worried about what the Saudis would do to her if she were sent back.

"No," he said, falling into deep thought. Ever since Alex had told him that Dawn was well educated, he had been thinking about giving her a position as an assistant in his firm or perhaps even a position as an interpreter except that he didn't know how well she spoke Arabic or if she spoke any other languages.

"Can you read and write in Arabic?"

"Yes, Arabic was one of the languages I specialized in."

"And do you speak any other languages?"

"I'm fluent in Spanish as well," she said, wondering why he was asking her such questions.

He didn't know why but he wanted to protect her and give her a better life. She had been treated with cruelty and here was an opportunity for him to reach out and help someone who needed it.

"I'm going to give you a try as an interpreter but you'll be on three months probation."

"I'm confused. I'm on probation?" she asked, not digesting the first part of his sentence and only hearing the last.

"All employees of our firm are on probation for the first 90 days until they prove themselves. It's standard procedure."

"But I don't work for your firm, I'm part of your house…," she said, tilting her head. "I'm sorry, can you repeat what you said?"

"That you'll be on probation for three months?"

"No, the other part of your sentence."

"That you'll be working for me as an interpreter?"

"Truly?" she asked, her face glowing like a full moon. "Do you truly mean it?"

"Well now, don't get too excited. It's only a tryout. If you're as good as you say you are, then you'll be working for my firm permanently."

She jumped up and hugged him.

He smiled at her gesture and was glad that he was able to make her happy.

She let go of him, suddenly realizing that hugging one's boss wasn't a good idea. "Excuse me Jas...I mean Mr. Crawford...I just...I just...."

"Now listen here, if you're going to work for me, you're going to have to start calling me Jason."

"Jason, is this for real? You're hiring me? What about Mrs. Anderson and Mrs. Beazley?"

"Don't worry about them. I'll take care of it. Now, let's see," he said, and began pacing the room. "You can work from your room. We have a lot of documents and contracts that we send out for interpretation but now that I know you speak Arabic, I can give them to you."

"I'm going to need a computer and good dictionaries to use as references," she said, suddenly feeling excited and energetic.

"I'll give you a laptop and an expense account to buy things you need. Just keep all of your receipts."

"Thank you," she said, feeling guilty for not telling him everything.

"You may have to travel with me from time to time as my assistant. Would that be okay?" he asked, hoping that he could get to know her better.

"Yes, as long as you keep Husam away. I'm really scared that he may have recognized me."

"Don't worry, he has his own translator. I doubt you'll be seeing much of him anyway." Jason had been meaning to transfer his dealings with Husam to his brother for a long time. Husam's behavior tonight was the push Jason needed.

"You would do all this for me?"

"Well, I never really liked Husam."

"Why do you do business with him then?"

"I used to work with his business partner, Saad, you know, Sahar's father. A really nice man but ever since his father's company merged with Husam's, Husam is the one who travels out here."

"I've never met them. Is Sahar's grandfather a kind man?"

"No, I'm afraid he's a lot like Husam. I hear that he's now a paraplegic and can no longer travel."

"Hmmm. I wouldn't know."

"I have to say that this night has been one of the most interesting and eye-opening of my life, but it's getting late and I'd better get back to my guests," he said, glancing at his watch. It was 10 o'clock. He had been in her room for the past two hours. "I'll sneak back in. I don't want anyone to know I was absent from my own party."

From the kitchen window, Mrs. Anderson seethed as she watched Jason run back to the main house. Earlier, she had found out from one of the workers about what had had happened between Husam and Dawn, about Dawn being sent to her room and Jason checking on her. What Mrs. Anderson couldn't figure out was why someone like Jason would care so much about a poor nobody instead of her. She had seen women enter and depart from Jason's life and never found any a threat. But Dawn was different. Every time she was unhappy, Jason was rescuing her. What did Dawn have that she didn't? Granted she was older than him but she had read many articles about younger men being attracted to older women. Besides, she was much better looking than Dawn and had much more potential. Soon, she would take over Mrs. Beazley's position and become manager. She had already lost 20 pounds, was working on losing the rest and recently spent a lot of money on new makeup and a hairdo. Why didn't Jason notice her the way he noticed Dawn?

Meanwhile in the hotel's presidential suite, Husam relaxed on a king-size mahogany bed underneath silk sheets with Madam B, wondering where had he seen Dawn. Her face and the way she moved looked so familiar to him, he thought, as he contemplated taking a swig of a 50-year-old bottle of cognac sitting on the nightstand. Could she have been one of the many girls he had had sex with in the past three years on his trips abroad? If so, why would she hide it? Maybe she didn't want her present employer to find out. And the way Jason had protected the girl infuriated him. After all, she was nothing but the help and, in Husam's country, men did as they pleased with their housekeepers. Yet here in America, they had all these stupid rules. As these thoughts ran through his mind, he dozed off.

He began dreaming that he was a guest at a house in Riyadh where unrelated men and women without veils mingled in a room. Dawn was there as well, speaking to one of the men with whom he did business. The man whispered something in Dawn's ear. She turned, passed Husam a smirk and left with the man. Husam snapped out of his dream, jumped off his bed and turned on the lights. Madam B pulled the covers over her head, bothered by the bright lights.

He picked up a phone and dialed Emad, who was resting in a standard room, several floors below Husam's suite.

"Hello?' his translator answered sleepily a few rings later from his double bed.

"I want you to find out who the girl at the party was," Husam said in Arabic, hoping that the woman in his bed wasn't able to understand.

"Which girl?"

"The girl Jason was protecting so closely."

"It's three in the morning. Don't you ever rest?"

"You must locate a private investigator in Los Angeles and put him in touch with an investigator in Riyadh. Between the two of them, they should be able to sort out who this girl is."

"Riyadh? I thought the girl was an American."

"Just do as I say, and don't question me."

"I don't know any detectives out here."

"Be resourceful and ask around. But whatever you do, do not ask for Jason's help."

"I'll figure out something. Can I go back to sleep now?"

"No, I need you to get on it right away."

Peeved that his boss had woken him up for no good reason, Emad said, "It's closed everywhere right now. I'll deal with it in a few hours when businesses open." He then hung up before Husam could protest and tried to fall sleep again.

FOURTEEN

Dawn began working as an interpreter, in one of the guest houses that the Crawfords rarely used. The exterior had a granite tile hallway behind arched columns. An elliptical walnut door opened to heated limestone floors, gamboge plaster walls and mahogany cabinetry.

She could still remember the look of disapproval on his face when he caught her with a checkered aqua handkerchief tied around her head, a raggedy T-shirt and capris while standing on a ladder wiping the windows with a towel.

"What are you doing?" he asked her. "I thought I told Mrs. Anderson to send over someone to clean this place."

"I can manage," she said climbing down the ladder and starting to dust.

"I know you can manage, but that's no longer your job. Dawn, if you want to move up in society, you must stop behaving like a housekeeper."

"Housekeepers are people too, and there's nothing wrong with putting in a good day's work. Besides, the only difference between housekeepers and their bosses is the family they're born into."

"What do you mean?"

"Take yourself for example, if you were from a poor family where you had to work at a young age to support your brothers and sisters, you might have ended up a gardener."

"I see what you mean, but I have no time to get into a debate with you over hypothetical situations. I would rather you concentrate on the documents I gave you than clean."

"You forget that I'm young and full of energy. I can do both."

"I mean it Dawn. I'm not asking you, it's an order. I don't want the other maids to look at you as though you're one of them."

"I am one of them. And since you're so persistent on this point, then perhaps you should ask Mrs. Anderson to send over someone I'm unfamiliar with instead of Zoya, who is my friend. I can't very well extend my legs on the coffee table while she vacuums the carpet underneath me."

The modest-size guesthouse with vaulted ceilings had a small kitchen and large French windows that overlooked a pretty garden. Two amber-and-saffron upholstered chairs and a comfortable sofa sat in the main room along with a large desk with a laptop and printer/fax, and a shelf filled with reference books. A back room housed a queen-size bed framed in wrought iron as well as a vanity table, bathroom with decorative ceramic tiles and large glass shower.

"I'll ask her to send one of the newer girls. The Old Crab probably sent Zoya on purpose."

"You call her the Old Crab too?"

"It's Fred's fault, really. He gave her the nickname," he chuckled.

"If no one likes her, why do you keep her?"

"Cynthia likes her, and whoever Cynthia likes, stays. Besides, Mrs. Anderson always gets the work done," he said, dropping documents on her kitchenette counter. "I need these translated by Monday." It was Thursday.

"No problem," she told him. But looking back she could still remember how hard she had labored over them and the few hours of sleep she got. Yet she still felt fortunate. It was actually all thanks to Husam, who made a move on her.

Her job as a translator was a breath of fresh air compared to being a housekeeper. The shorter documents were emailed and the larger ones with attachments, details and explanations were messengered to her. The technical ones, which required knowledge of real estate law, were the most difficult, but Dawn never complained. She used dictionaries, grammar books and the internet to finish each project before the deadline. Once in awhile, she would call Jason's assistant with questions. A great teacher, Yumiko, explained the company's various dealings with utmost patience. Over time, she and Dawn were starting to form a special friendship, Dawn thought as her phone rang.

"Hello?"

"Hi, it's Yumiko. Are you doing anything after work?"

"Nothing important, why?" she asked, as she made notes in Arabic on a new contract she was translating.

"How would you like to go to happy hour and have a girls' night out? There's a Mexican restaurant with great appetizers and tasty margaritas."

Dawn dropped her pencil, sat back in her chair and said, "That sounds like fun; Is it going to be just the two of us?"

"No, Zoya is coming too," Yumiko answered, as she sifted through the mail.

"Are we talking about the Zoya who works for Jason at his house?"

"The very one."

"I didn't know you were acquainted with her."

"I met her through my husband who is friends with her boyfriend. Listen I have to go. I'll pick you guys up at six at the employee entrance."

"See you then," Dawn said, going back to her work.

Two hours later, Yumiko pulled up in her dark blue Mazda and drove them to Mi Casa es su Casa located in the charming neighborhood of Montrose near Pasadena. The family owned restaurant was lit with straw lanterns and the walls were covered with murals of quaint homes and villagers in Mexico.

"This place is packed," Dawn remarked, dressed in a loosely fitted short-sleeve cyan dress.

"You have to be aggressive here and push to get to the hors d'oeuvres," Zoya said as she eyed an empty table and claimed it.

As soon as they sat, a waitress in an embroidered floral dress came over to take their orders.

"Three blended margaritas with lots of salt," Zoya ordered. Her hair was curled and she was wearing bright red lipstick.

The waitress nodded and left.

"What if Dawn doesn't like salt or her margarita blended?" Yumiko looked at Zoya flabbergasted. "Honestly Zoya, you're too much sometimes."

"You like blended margaritas, don't you Dawn?" Zoya asked her.

"Anything is fine. I'm only glad that we get to spend time with each other."

"You see, she doesn't mind," Zoya said, leaving the table and returning with taquitos and quesadillas for everyone. A bunch of young guys at the next table prowled the crowd for single girls, drank Tequilas and laughed obnoxiously loud.

Their waitress came back with their drinks, a basket of chips and salsa.

"How do you like your new job, you lucky devil?" Zoya asked Dawn.

"It's work. Lots of work but much better than working for Mrs. Anderson."

"Jason is a great boss, isn't he?" Yumiko added, licking the salt on her glass and gulping her drink. She had a heart-shaped face, small lips and black silky shoulder-length hair.

"I have to admit, he's easy to work for," Dawn said. Afraid to lose control and blab about her past, she sipped her margarita and ate a taquito to dilute the effects of the alcohol.

"I have known him for five years now, and he has always treated me with respect."

"That's because he knows you're married," Zoya said, downing her drink and ordering another.

"Slow down and let us catch up, will you?" Yumiko pushed to finish hers and then ordered another.

"You sound bitter about Jason. May I ask why?" Dawn inquired.

"I'm not bitter," Zoya responded, "I'm just making an astute observation. He's a player. We all know it. But here is Yumiko trying to make it seem as though he's a saint."

"I didn't say he's saint, you did. I was just trying to say that he has always been nice to me."

"Maybe you're right. He does have a good heart," Zoya raised her glass, "To our boss Jason without whom we would all be out of jobs."

"Here, here," Yumiko said as they clinked their glasses.

"How is that husband of yours?" Zoya asked.

"Oh fine. He's in Hawaii on a business trip."

One of the guys at the next table slurred to Yumiko, "Would you and your friends like to join our table?"

Yumiko raised her left hand, shook her diamond band and said, "Married." She then pointed at Zoya and said, "Boyfriend, but my friend Dawn is single."

"How about it? Would you like to join us?" he said, smiling crookedly.

"No thank you," Dawn answered as the mariachi band started up.

"You should go have a drink with him," Zoya said, biting into a taquito.

She shook her head, crinkled her nose and said, "He's too drunk. I like my men sober."

"Wish I wasn't married and could join them. The one with the blue-jean jacket is yummy," Yumiko said glumly. "Marriage sometimes feels like a life sentence."

"I can understand that," Dawn said.

"How would you know? You've never been married," she replied, drinking half of her margarita.

Dawn cleared her throat, dipped a chip and said, "I have seen enough unhappily married couples in my lifetime. Some pretend to be happy, but I can see right through them."

"I would rather be unhappily married than not married."

"Really?" Dawn asked with surprise.

"When you're single, people feel sorry for you. Who needs that?"

"Surely you can't be serious," Zoya said. "I certainly would hate to think that's how you feel about us."

"That is not how I look at you, but others who conform to society's rules will never understand you."

"Didn't you marry to conform to the norm?" Dawn asked.

"No. I fell in love with my husband, but when the sparks went away, it got stale. If I have sex once a month, I consider myself lucky."

"How long have you been married?" Zoya asked, curiously.

"Seven years, three months, five days and 16 hours, but who is counting?" She burped. "Oops. Excuse me."

Zoya glanced over at Dawn and raised an eyebrow.

"I don't expect you guys to comprehend. In a way, I envy you two."

"Hey, c'mon," Zoya said. "We're supposed to be having fun. Let it go, and let's all get drunk."

I think Yumiko is already drunk, Dawn wanted to say but kept quiet. And so the three ate, listened to music and relaxed. Dawn, who had planned to stay sober, was starting to feel tipsy as well. When they were ready to go home, Dawn took away Yumiko's keys and asked the hostess at the door to call a taxi.

"I tell you I'm fine," Yumiko said, staggering out.

"Yeah, she's fine," Zoya giggled, followed by a hiccup.

"Neither of you are fit to go anywhere. We'll all sleep at the guesthouse. Yumiko can pick up her car here tomorrow."

"Why don't you drive us?" Zoya suggested.

"Because, I don't want to get pulled over by a cop," Dawn replied.

When their taxi arrived, Zoya and Yumiko got in the back. Dawn sat in front and gave the driver directions as she listened to Yumiko and Zoya sing all the way home, "hundred bottles of margaritas on the wall...hundred bottles of margaritas...you take one down and pass it around and there's 99 bottles of margaritas on the wall...Hey...99 bottles of margaritas on the wall...."

The following morning Yumiko and Zoya had horrible hangovers and both called in sick. Dawn had risen after eight, taken a shower and threw on a pair of jeans and a violet shirt. She made a strong pot of coffee, prepared bacon and eggs and placed them on the kitchenette counter as she stood on the opposite side of it, taking a bite of toast.

"None for me, thanks," Yumiko said as she sat on the bar stool with puffy eyes. "Not much of a breakfast person. But I will have some of your black brew."

"Thanks for making breakfast," Zoya said, taking a seat next to Yumiko. They were both wearing long nightshirts Dawn lent them. "Sorry that you had to sleep on the sofa last night. I should have stopped drinking after the fourth margarita."

"If there's anything I can ever do for you," Yumiko added, "let me know. I really appreciate you taking care of us last night."

"Same here," Zoya said, "I'm there for you if you need me."

"Thanks. I may just have to take you up on your offer someday."

"By the way, where's my car?" Yumiko asked.

"I left it at the restaurant's parking lot."

"I'll give you a ride there," Zoya said, eating her eggs.

The phone rang and Dawn picked it up. "Hello?"

"It's me Jason."

"Is that my husband?" Yumiko yelled. She had left him a message on his cell phone while Dawn was in the shower and Zoya was still asleep.

Dawn put her finger to her lips to stop Yumiko from talking.

"Can I have your bacon if you're not going to eat it?" Zoya asked Yumiko.

"Go ahead," Yumiko said.

"Is that Yumiko and Zoya I hear in the background?" Jason asked.

"No, it's the TV," Dawn said, turning it on and increasing the volume.

Zoya rushed to get the remote out of Dawn's hand. The volume was killing her head, "Are you crazy girl?"

"I know that was Zoya's voice," Jason said. "I thought she was sick."

"Please don't get mad." Dawn wrinkled her forehead. "The three of us went out for drinks and they had a little too much. They spent the night over."

Jason laughed and recalled his college days hanging over the toilet after a night out with his friend George. "I'm not mad. I called to tell you to get your things ready for the weekend. We're going to Dearborn, Michigan," he told her, seated on a black leather chair in his office.

"Dearborn? What on earth for?"

"I have clients from the UAE who are in the country for a short period and want to meet...ah, here it is," he said, shuffling through his files.

"Here what is?"

"A file I've been looking for."

"But you're not giving me much time. The weekend is two days away, I still have to finish translating the Spanish paperwork you gave me and don't own a single business suit." She grabbed her coffee mug and went to sit on the couch.

"Why not? You're a businesswoman aren't you?"

"Yes Jason, but I work out of your guesthouse. Up until now, I had no need to purchase a suit," she told him, looking out the French windows at her quaint garden with colorful roses, lamb's ears, eucalyptus, heather and wax flowers.

"Then I recommend you go buy clothes. Forget about the documents that the messenger brought over yesterday. This is more important," he warned her, getting off his chair and throwing on his jacket.

"Very well," she said.

"Oh, Dawn?"

"Yes?"

"I got us a suite. I hope that's alright with you."

For a second she thought he was expecting much more than business. What did he mean getting one place for the both of them when he had made numerous advances at her?

When Jason heard silence on the other end of receiver, he explained, "All the rooms in the hotels were booked. There are several conventions going on at the same time as well as the Arab Festival, which brings in some 300,000 people."

"Ummm," she shifted uncomfortably in her seat. "Are there separate beds in the suite?"

"Of course. You'll have your own room and shower facilities and I'll have mine. If this arrangement makes you feel uneasy, please let me know."

Well, at least we'll be sleeping in separate rooms, she thought. "It's fine Jason. We're both professionals who are there to do a job."

"Great then, I'll meet you at the front entrance, say about 8 a.m. on Saturday."

"See you then."

FIFTEEN

Dawn soon found out that Dearborn, a Detroit suburb, was home to the largest Arab population outside of the Middle East. Considered a sister city to Dubai, Detroit solidified its relationship in 2003 during the Arab economic summit. No wonder Jason's UAE clients were more comfortable meeting in Dearborn, Dawn thought, as their flight arrived early Friday afternoon and a limousine driver took them to their hotel.

"Let's clean up and go check out the Arab Festival since we're not meeting our clients until tomorrow," Jason suggested on their way up to their room.

At first, this idea didn't interest Dawn, but she decided to go with the flow and please him. As she entered, Dawn looked around their spacious luxury suite. The entrance opened to a seating area with ebony porcelain floors, sofas and chairs upholstered in woven gold-and-platinum-color fabric, a wet bar and a faux fireplace. On the glass balcony, set beneath a 22-foot-high cathedral ceiling was a bronze oval table with six chairs overlooking the city of Detroit. Dawn's quarters had a wide sliding door, contemporary canopy bed, black lacquered cabinets, walls inlaid with mother of pearl, and a marble shower and bath. Jason's bedroom, similar to Dawn's, was right across from hers.

They unpacked, got ready and went to the elevator to go down to the lobby when a tall figure emerged. It appeared to be a woman, dressed in black from the top of her head to the floor, her face and eyes hidden underneath a veil and mesh grid, making Dawn feel as though someone had stuck a hand inside her and was squeezing her heart as hard as possible. She froze in her steps and watched the woman exit with her husband.

"You can go in now," Jason repeated a few times, holding the elevator door open, but Dawn hadn't heard a word. Finally, he yelled, "Dawn!"

"Yes?" She snapped out of her shock.

"Are you alright? Do you want to go back to your room and rest?" He noticed her terrified face and thought she was going to faint at any minute.

"No," she said, as she boarded the elevator and pushed the button.

"It's not important for us to go to the festival, you know. Let's go get you a drink at the bar."

Dawn nodded as the two went to sit on a semicircular velvet booth behind a small round table. The atmosphere was serene with dim lights. A young waitress with a friendly smile took their orders and left.

"I'm sorry about my behavior earlier," Dawn meekly offered, still shaken by the woman in her *burqa*. Ever since she left Saudi Arabia, she hadn't seen anyone dressed that way.

"Don't worry about it," he told her, noticing two dark-skinned men with long beards come in and take a table.

The waitress returned with two glasses of shiraz, pâté and crackers, and a bowl of nuts.

"Have some, it'll relax you," Jason suggested.

Dawn did as he asked as she listened to the men speak in Arabic. She was astute and knew which accent was from what region and which was a Saudi Muslim as opposed to a Jordanian or Iraqi Muslim. "Look at them, if that's not hypocrisy at its best, I don't know what is."

Jason looked confused. "I'm not sure what you mean."

"See those men over there," she said, glancing discreetly in their direction. "They're what you call the *mutawan,* who are probably out here to snoop and see what everyone's doing."

"Who are the *mutawan?*"

"They're the religious police in Saudi Arabia in charge of protecting vice and virtue," she explained, wondering what they were doing all the way in Dearborn.

"And yet they're drinking," he stated with raised eyebrows.

"They break all the rules they preach while they walk around and grab unrelated boys and girls to be flogged because they are not allowed to be together. Other times, they go after people who don't pray during prayer times and beat them publicly with sticks," she said, spreading pâté on a cracker. The wine was making her woozy.

"Out here?"

"No, back in Riyadh, but believe me if they had any power in the U.S., they'd enforce their laws, segregating men and women and forcing everyone to pray." She took a bite of her hors d'oeuvre and savored it.

What Dawn didn't know was that the *mutawan* weren't in Dearborn by accident. They were there to follow her.

"I feel bad for you, what you had to live with. It's no wonder you reacted so strongly to the lady in her *abaya*."

"You mean a *burqa*. An *abaya* is an overdress but a *burqa* is a head-to-toe covering with a mesh grid over the eyes," she answered, swirling her wine. "The funny thing is, if she were told that she was free to take it off, she wouldn't do it because it would make her feel uncomfortable."

"How so?" he asked.

"When it's repeatedly ingrained in you that a wholesome girl must cover up, you start believing it. I remember when I first removed my cloak and veil after my escape. I felt completely naked and thought everybody was staring at me, but they weren't. It was all in my head."

Jason just listened. He knew about women in that country but up until now never thought about it much. He drank his wine and tried the nuts.

"When they instill in your mind that a woman who shows her hair or skin is nothing but a whore, you begin accepting it as the truth. And worse, their teachings of vice and virtue taint the way you perceive men and women everywhere."

"I suppose it would be taboo for you and me to be sitting here, drinking alcohol."

"Muslims and Mormons are not allowed to drink alcohol but some do. What's interesting is that we wouldn't even be allowed to drink coffee together in Saudi Arabia," she said, watching the bartender shake a silver martini flask and pour the green drink in a glass.

"One of the business protocols I learned early on was to never ask about the health of a Saudi man's wife," he said.

"Yes, otherwise they'd think you're interested in their wives and get angry with you."

"Tell me, what would I do if I were there with a female coworker and wanted to get a cup of coffee?" Jason asked watching their server walk away as she swayed her hips from side to side.

"It's recommended that foreigners stay within their compounds and not move into Arab neighborhoods. You see, it's *haram* – forbidden – to parade around with a female coworker even if you are an American. Men enter the front door of a coffee shop but women have to enter from the back. Some places refuse service to women," she told him, looking at a woman in a business suit who entered and went to sit at the bar.

"Are there signs indicating the refusal of service?"

"Not always, and if a foreigner who doesn't know better tries to order by herself or with a male coworker, she will get arrested by the religious police."

"Talk about ruining the pleasure of drinking an afternoon coffee," Jason said, noticing the Saudi men stare at the woman at the bar and saying something to one another.

"Everything is segregated, the way it used to be in the south during the times of slavery, except that women are the slaves in this case," she said, watching Jason stare at the religious police. "They think she's a prostitute," Dawn told him.

"Why would they think that?"

"In the eyes of conservative Saudis, a woman sitting alone at a bar is a prostitute."

Jason shook his head at their stupidity and returned his attention to Dawn. "I've read a few interviews with Saudi women who said they were content with their way of life."

"Many love their country and hate it when the western countries criticize them. They think western women are loose because many sleep with one man after another. Then there are those who are dying to break the taboos and get their freedom but are afraid. They write blogs, books and poems under false names to express themselves without getting caught."

Jason noticed that the *mutawan* were now gazing at them, analyzing their every move. "C'mon, let's go outside for a walk."

"I wouldn't mind if we went to the festival, now. I feel much better."

There was much she missed about Riyadh – the bazaars, the strong coffee with cardamom, the famous Arab hospitality and the Middle-Eastern merchandise.

"In that case, let's go."

They walked for 30 minutes to Schaefer Road where Arab musicians played their songs outdoors and food booths served regional delicacies. Women drew henna art on the hands of tourists; others offered coffee-cup readings. Tables displayed arts and crafts, and a giant Ferris wheel overlooked east Dearborn.

"I had no idea that something like this even existed in the U.S.," Dawn commented, ordering two *samboosaks*.

"What is it?" Jason asked, looking at the puff pastries the vendor handed him.

"Try it, you'll like it. It's made with flour, ground beef, onion and parsley."

Jason took a bite. "Ummm…it's delicious."

"I told you, you'd like it."

They continued their stroll. Jason noticed women in their *hijabs* – any type of clothing that concealed the body. By covering up in the presence of men who weren't their relatives, women would deflect the desires and gazes of the opposite sex. The degree of *hijab* depended on one's culture and religious beliefs. Some wore formal *abayas* and *burqas*, others with just headscarves and long oversize jackets hiding their figures, and others in long-sleeve tunics and pants as well as modernists who blended in with their western outfits. There were children running around, wives with their husbands, grandparents, aunts and uncles. In a way, he envied them for having such close family ties unlike his own. Dawn bought a ceramic vase with a white, yellow and blue floral pattern and a large, royal-blue scarf. She asked one of the vendors where she could find a mosque so she could show Jason what the inside looked like. It turned out that finding a mosque in Dearborn was as easy as finding a church in Rome. It was only matter of finding the closest one.

Several blocks away they found a mosque with a dome-like structure and two long pillars. Since it wasn't prayer time, they were allowed in. They removed their shoes before entering a carpeted area, and Dawn threw on the scarf she bought. It covered her hair, neck and bosom, as those were the rules.

"This is my first time inside a mosque," Jason commented, looking around the high ceiling, gray marble arches and columns.

"In Saudi Arabia, you would never be allowed to walk in a *masjid*. It's *haram* for non-Muslims to enter the house of worship. You see, to Saudis, their religion is the only right religion and anyone with a different faith is considered inferior."

"Really?" he said noticing the red Persian carpet where people kneeled to pray with their heads touching the ground. That was the position they felt closest to God.

"Oh yes, even Sunni Muslims who are non-Saudis are considered second-rate, but they're allowed in."

"What about the Shiites?"

"They're barely tolerated. Even they get beaten sometimes because they believe in worshiping prophets and saints and Sunnis don't. Sunnis only worship god."

"I had no idea how the Saudis felt," he admitted, noticing her smirk.

"What's funny is that if we were in Saudi Arabia, you and I would be flogged for standing next to each other in here because we aren't related."

"Where do women pray then?"

"In a separate room from men, except in the Grand Mosque in Mecca where Kabba, Islam's holiest shrine, is located. There, women are allowed to pray with men. But the government is trying to change that as well under the pretext that it's too crowded and women should have their own section." They exited the mosque, walked into a courtyard, and both put their shoes back on.

"That's a good thing, no?" he asked.

"No, men always get the better spots. Even out here, in a country where there's freedom and equality, in many mosques women have to enter from the back entrance and men the front," she told him, spotting a bench a few feet away from a fountain. "Let's go sit over on that bench where we'll have a nice view of the architecture."

"Then what happens?" he asked, sitting somewhat close to her.

"Then the women are ushered to a separate room or there is a partition that separates the men and women. In some mosques where there's no partition, men stand in front of the line, close to the *Imam* – the male prayer leader. The children are in the middle and women at the end."

"Why are women at the end?" he wondered.

"Because during prayers when men and women kneel on the floor, their shoulders cannot touch. And they can't very well put the women in front because when they kneel, their bottoms are a distraction to men."

He laughed. "Well, men do like to look at women's behinds but not usually while they're praying."

"There's more. A woman must not be heard in a *masjid*, because her voice is considered an instrument of sexual provocation," she told him, removing the scarf around her hair, folding it and throwing it in her shopping bag.

"You knew this and still decided to convert?"

"I was foolish and in love; nothing else mattered. Sahar warned me not to do it but I didn't listen."

"I hear that Muslims pray five times a day. How do they find time to get their work done?"

"I don't know. I wasn't allowed to work when I lived in Riyadh."

"But there are women who work."

"Yes, if their *mahram* allows it. Some have jobs in women's banks and women's shopping malls, but this is all new. You see, women didn't even have birth certificates until recently. They were included on their father's birth certificate, which made them the property of a man."

"I know you said *mahram* is a male relative. Would that be any male relative?"

"*Mahram* has various meanings. A *mahram* may mean a woman's guardian, such as her father or husband, whose permission is needed for a woman to do just about anything including going to see a doctor."

"A woman needs permission to go see a doctor?" he asked, looking shocked.

"Yes, even if she is bleeding to death, a doctor will not treat her unless her male guardian is with her, granting permission."

"That's horrible!"

"Welcome to the Saudi woman's world," she said sarcastically. "A *mahram* also means someone who is allowed to see a woman without her *hijab,* and in the Saudi culture that only includes those who are permanently forbidden for her to marry because of blood ties, breastfeeding or marriage ties such as her father, husband, brother, son, uncle, father-in-law and nephews."

"What about her brother-in-law or cousins?"

"They are not considered a *mahram.* And what's most unfair is that a 12-year-old brother of a 30-year-old single woman, for example, is allowed to make decisions for her and can forbid her to leave the house."

"Even though he's just a child?" He looked at her, baffled. A child making a decision for a grown woman was preposterous, he thought.

"Yes. His sex is more important than his age."

"You know, I never hear you talk about your husband. What was he like?"

"He was attractive and had no trouble finding a wife. I thought I was his one and only when I agreed to marry him."

"He didn't tell you that he had other wives?"

"No. He had two whom I never met. After a year into our marriage, he began boasting about it shamelessly. How they were much prettier than I and satisfied him more in bed," she said, tears welling up.

"That's a horrible thing to say to anyone."

"I had to have his meals ready at a precise time and, after each meal, he forced himself upon me even when I didn't feel like it."

His facial muscles tensed at the thought of him hurting her. "That's no different than raping someone."

"Yes, it is rape when a woman says no regardless of whether or not she is married, but in Saudi Arabia the courts laugh at you for bringing up such charges. A woman is obligated to satisfy her husband whenever he asks."

A black haired man with a crooked smile and a cigarette in one hand came in their direction and asked Dawn for a lighter.

"I'm sorry, but I don't smoke," she told him.

"Are you sure you don't smoke?" he asked with a thick accent, his shifty eyes fixed upon her.

"Yes I'm sure," she answered, annoyed that he didn't believe her.

"Neither of us smoke," Jason interrupted.

"That is too bad," the man said as he continued to stare at Dawn.

"Where are you from?" Jason asked, realizing that he was making Dawn feel uncomfortable.

"I'm from Dubai."

"How about that dinner?" Jason looked at Dawn, holding her hand in his to assure her that she was safe.

She looked at him confused at first but caught on quickly. "Actually dinner would be great," she said as they both stood up.

"Good luck finding that lighter," Jason said to the man and left holding Dawn's hand.

"Are you okay?" Jason asked her, noticing her worried look.

"He gave me the creeps."

"He was a strange one, but he's gone now. I think he went into the mosque."

"I guess I'm always going to be worried about someone recognizing me."

"Is that why you wear those thick glasses?" he asked her, remembering the time when he had caught her reading Chaucer without them.

"Yes."

"And your metal retainers. Are those fake as well?" he inquired, recalling the time when they had gone paragliding and she had forgotten to wear them.

She turned her gaze away from him. "Yes, I'm always afraid of being followed."

"It must be hard always looking over your shoulder and wondering who might be there. But you needn't worry anymore. You're on U.S. soil. Our judicial system will protect you."

"Will it? I'm not so sure," she said.

They walked hand in hand as though they had been lovers for a long time. The sky was starting to turn dark and the air much cooler. Pedestrians moved about with their grocery bags. The smell of fresh bread in someone's bag made Dawn's stomach rumble as she noticed a restaurant with an Arabic sign across the street.

"Let's have dinner there." Jason pointed toward the restaurant as they crossed the street.

Inside, a host led them to the only empty table in the center of the room. The small, crowded place seemed to be frequented by a Middle Eastern clientele. Jason couldn't understand anyone's conversation except for the Canadian people behind him.

"*Masaa Al Kair*" – good evening – their waiter greeted them as he used an ice tong to give them two hot towels from his silver tray to clean their hands. "Would you like something to drink?"

"Why don't you order for the both of us?" Jason asked Dawn.

The waiter looked at him with surprise. *Since when did a woman order for a man?*, he thought.

"We will have two glasses of champagne, and *jareesh* soup to start," Dawn told him.

The waiter wrote down the order and left.

"*Jareesh* means crushed wheat and is made with crushed wheat, tomatoes, dry lemon, onion and garlic."

"Sounds good to me," he said, surprised that the modest restaurant sold champagne. "You know, he forgot to give us utensils."

"We're supposed to eat with our hands as it is the custom," Dawn said, wiping her hands with the white towel the waiter had given her.

Jason followed suit and said, "And the soup?"

"It will come in a bowl. You lift it to your mouth and drink."

The waiter poured champagne in their glasses and served the soup. Jason tasted his drink and realized that it didn't contain any alcohol. It was apple juice and Sprite.

"It's a common drink in Saudi Arabia since alcohol is illegal," Dawn explained. "Thought you might want to try it."

"Are you ready to order?" their waiter asked.

"We'll have a vegetable *mutabag* and an order of *aish abulaham*."

Dawn turned to Jason. "*Mutabag* looks like a crepe filled with vegetables, but you can also order it with minced beef or cheese and sugar."

"What's *aish*?" he asked trying his hot *jareesh* soup and liking its flavor.

"*Aish abulaham* resembles a pie but the dough is made with chick peas, flour and powdered milk and the stuffing contains minced beef, sesame seed paste and black vinegar."

"And you know how to make this?"

"Yes, I know how to cook Arabic food. A good wife must know how to cook for her husband, among other things. Running a household has always been more important than having a career." She sipped her champagne.

"I remember you saying that men and women aren't allowed to work together."

"They're allowed only in hospitals. Male doctors see only male patients and women doctors see only females."

"I would imagine that the segregation must be hard on both men and women."

"Yes, but women have it worse. Take a poor mother of three, for example. The husband tosses her to the street and takes on a new wife and she has no way of supporting herself and her children."

"It must be difficult to be a single mom over there."

"Most women have been dependent most of their lives and have no work experience. The gap between the rich and the poor is huge and the poor suffer the most."

"Nowadays, it's like that everywhere, no?"

Their waiter came by with their meals.

"*Shokran*" – thank you – Dawn said.

"*Afwan*, – you're welcome – he answered.

Dawn used her hand to serve Jason the *mutabag* as she continued with her conversation. "You see over there, the problems are much bigger, especially for foreigners."

"Like yourself."

"Believe it or not, I had it better than the others. A lot of these poor Sri Lankans, Indians, Pakistanis and Filipinos who can't find work in their own country get cheated by agencies who claim that they'll find a great paying job for a large fee but once they get to Saudi Arabia, they soon find out that everything they were told was a lie."

"If they have no money, how do they pay the fee?"

"They borrow from their parents, siblings, uncles and aunts in the hopes that someday they can pay them back."

"But they never can," he said, as though reading her thoughts.

"No, and when they finally find a job, their employer takes their passports away."

"Why?" he asked, picking up a piece of *aish abulaham* and trying to eat it like pizza as a chunk of the minced meat dropped down onto his plate.

"It's the law," Dawn used her hand to scoop up the meat on her plate.

Jason followed suit. "Do they ever get it back?"

"Some do after they finished the work they promised to do, but others don't. They live in run-down buildings and get paid just enough to cover their rent. The employer bleeds all he can out of them while still hanging onto their passports. You see, an employee is forbidden to leave the country or change jobs without his employer's approval."

"How do you know all this?"

"Everyone there is well aware of this problem but doesn't talk about it much. It's cheap labor and these people are doing all the work that the Saudis refuse to do. What is disgusting is that many of these employers are filthy rich and yet they are ripping off the poor."

"There was a case out here not long ago where a Saudi visiting the U.S. on a scholarship was jailed for abusing his Filipino maid."

"She was lucky that she was on U.S. soil. Had she been in Saudi Arabia, her plight would have been ignored. These poor people go there to earn a living and end up working long days with no more than five or six hours of sleep. Some get raped by the owner of the house or by his sons."

"Aren't there laws against this?" he asked, feeling full and noticing that Dawn had stopped eating as well.

"The courts send the rape victim back to their country and the rapist is never charged. Some raped victims who become pregnant are thrown in jail as prostitutes. There are many women and children in Saudi jails as a result of rape. Remember a non-Saudi's life doesn't have much value, especially one who comes from a third world country."

Their server returned and asked if they wanted dessert. Dawn and Jason shook their heads no. He then left and came back with a bowl of water for them to clean their hands and left the bill.

"I always knew that there was oppression of women, but I had no idea that it was this bad."

"If the maids are lucky enough to escape rape, they get beaten by the wives because they're jealous of their husband's attention to them or because Arab women are angry from being pushed around by men. So they take out their frustration on their maids to whom they pay meager salaries as low as $200 a month."

"What about the human rights watch or Amnesty International? Why don't they bring this out into the light?" Jason asked, signing off on the bill.

"They have, except that no one listens. First, as soon as there's too much media coverage out in the west, the Saudis threaten to pull out their investments and western governments pressure the media to kill their stories. Second, Saudi Arabia has a ban on Amnesty International's staff and any human rights advocates from entering their country. Third, any activist from inside Saudi Arabia is either thrown into jail and tortured or prevented from traveling and communicating with the west."

"So, no one can get out and protest?" he asked as they both got up to leave.

"Public protests are forbidden and punishable to the full extent of the sharia law," Dawn told him as they headed back toward their hotel. "Sometimes women have an informal gathering in their homes to discuss problems with human rights inside their country but often there's an informant among them and as soon as the gathering gets bigger, the *mutawan* gives them a warning to close shop or pay the consequences."

As Jason listened, he realized how sheltered his own life had been. The media hardly ever covered anything on Saudi Arabia. What they did cover had been mostly positive, except for 9/11, but that story disappeared quickly as Bush decided to attack Iraq instead of going after the real terrorists.

That night Jason, tired from the flight and all the walking, fell into a deep sleep until he heard Dawn's cries. He jumped out of his bed and ran to her room. To his relief, she was only having a bad dream. Gently touching her arm, he said, "Wake up, you're having a nightmare."

"Help me, I don't want to die. Please God, don't let me die."

This time he shook her harder, "Dawn, wake up, it's me Jason. You're not going to die. You're only having a bad dream."

She opened her eyes, not knowing where she was at first. Her heart thumped against her chest; her hair and face were covered in sweat. Jason went to get her water from the mini-bar.

"Here. Drink this, you'll feel better." He handed her bottled water.

Dawn took a swig and set the bottle on her nightstand. Her body and mind were still asleep as she sat up for a while with Jason on her bed, looking distraught.

"I'm sorry to have woken you up," she said.

"I thought someone was in your room, hurting you. What were you dreaming about?"

"Nothing important."

"It must've been something or you wouldn't have been so completely horrified by it."

"I can't remember what it was," she swallowed. "I'm fine now. I just would like to get some sleep."

"You're not fine. You're shivering. What's been bothering you?" he asked with concern.

"It's late, and I'm really tired," she told him. She wished that he would stop questioning her.

"You've been acting strange ever since we arrived in Dearborn. Whatever secret you may have, can't be worse than what you have already told me." He was frustrated by her lack of trust.

"Please leave." Dawn couldn't look him in the eyes and lie, yet she couldn't bring herself to tell the truth no matter how much she wanted to share her story with him. Her secret gnawed at her guts, consumed her thoughts and separated her from the rest of society. It twirled and turned in the pit of her stomach, forcing her body to feel as if she would vomit at any moment no matter how hard she tried to control it. It was only a matter of time but the longer she kept her secret hidden, the more forceful it became until one day it would simply explode, kicking out her insides and exposing her to the world around her. Yes, a secret was a terrible thing to keep.

"You know, eventually you're going to have to trust someone," he said irritably, getting off her bed.

"That's rich, coming from a man who is petrified to make a commitment because his mother cheated on his father," she said, covering her mouth with one hand as soon as she said it. "Please forgive me. I didn't mean what I said."

"Yes, you did. And you're right. I don't let myself get attached either but at least I trust my friends enough to confide in them."

The thought of him considering her a friend moved and upset her at the same time. She was flattered that he was treating her as his equal but disappointed that he only regarded her as a friend. She wished she were more attractive to him even if she didn't want a relationship with him. *You're a confused girl*, she told herself as she watched Jason leave her room, closing the door behind him.

The next day, Jason's clients informed him that there was a problem at the Dubai International Airport due to breach of security and that all the flights had been delayed. They were to meet in the late afternoon instead of morning as it had been planned. Jason decided to take Dawn to Greenfield Village, where they rode the steam locomotive around the park for a scenic audio tour of historical homes and buildings followed by a visit to Henry Ford's home and museum. At 5:30 in the afternoon, they met with their Arab clients in their hotel suite. Room service brought them an early dinner.

The meeting and dinner went well. Dawn translated what Jason told her about the history and goals of Crawford Enterprises, the company's stability and growth in their investments over the past 20 years to convince the potential clients to use their services. After Sahar's death and the possibility of losing Husam's business, Jason had been making every possible effort to bring in new business. At the end of the evening, their UAE customers committed to purchasing a series of apartments and office buildings.

"Where did you learn how to speak Arabic so well?" one of the men asked her.

"I majored in it at school," Dawn responded.

"You must come and visit me," another one of them said to Jason, "I'll take you to the camel races. A real race with a real person riding the camel instead of those silly looking robot jockeys guiding the camels. My camel was a champion last year."

"Camel races? I've never been to a camel race," Jason said.

Dawn was disappointed that the Arab men who seemed to be progressive and modern thinkers, invested in camel races with jockeys.

What Jason didn't know was that these races, portraying the high life for the wealthy, were performed at the expense of children as young as three years old.

Funded by the UAE, oftentimes, three-and-four-year-olds were kidnapped or bought from poor families of India, Pakistan, Bangladesh, Sri Lanka and Sudan, held in bonded labor and used as jockeys because of their light weight. These children were kept in tin shacks and cramped quarters with no electricity in the desert, were given little food and abused and tortured. When there were no races, they were forced to do hard labor – typically 18 hours a day. Oftentimes, they were bitten by the dromedaries and their inner thighs were rubbed raw. Many ended up with spinal injuries and their vulnerable genitals suffered damage. After reaching the age of 10, they were considered too old to race and were given back to their families whom they no longer recognized since they had left at such a young age. Others, whose families were in jail remained homeless. Then there were those who were taken by strangers and put to hard labor or given away as rent boys – they were rented like a piece of furniture and their temporary owners were allowed to do whatever they wanted with the boys, Dawn told Jason after their guests had left.

"You can't save the world he told her. There's cruelty everywhere."

"And you don't care," she said with discontentment.

"It's not that I don't care, but why should I worry about something that I have no power to alter?" he answered, annoyed that she was lecturing him.

"If everyone thought the way you did, nothing would ever change."

"Why are you so angry with me? It's not like I'm going to rush to see a camel race tomorrow. I tell you what, I promise never to bet on one or go see one."

"Whatever," she said angrily.

He let out a big sigh and replied, "I'm going to my room and rest now. I will see you tomorrow morning."

Talk about robbing those kids of their childhood happiness, Dawn thought, slipping on her nightgown and turning on her TV.

Although child jockeys were banned about three years ago in the UAE, a huge black market still existed not only in the UAE but also in Oman, Qatar and Saudi Arabia. Supported by corporations or tribal sponsors, these illegal races, which accepted underground bets were no secret and took place in the flat desert.

"Dawn?" Jason called her name two hours later as he walked toward her room.

"Yes?" she answered throwing on a robe over her thin nightie.

"Don't forget to set your alarm for seven. I think we should pack our things, check out and have breakfast before we go to the Arab American museum."

"Okay," she nodded. She began to think that maybe she shouldn't have come to Dearborn. The city reminded her too much of Riyadh. Not that it looked anything like it but the Arab culture and her surroundings were starting to remind her of why she had decided to escape. She thought about the woman in her *burqa* and her husband. Earlier, she had been waiting for Jason in the lobby while he went into the gift shop to buy a magazine and mints. "Shut your mouth," the man was telling his wife in Arabic as he waited for the elevator. "I deal with you when we get to our room."

Dawn felt goose bumps on her skin as she wondered about what he was going to do with the woman after they had reached their room. Would he hit her? It was illegal in the U.S. but who would know? She'd be covered up when she went out. *Go to sleep*, she told herself. *Jason is right. You can't save the whole world.* She tossed and turned for an hour until she fell asleep, but her nightmare started up again.

"Somebody help. Can't breathe. I can't breathe," she wheezed as Jason rushed to her room, seeing her flat on her back and hands by her side as she wriggled, "Air, I need air."

Jason woke her up, wondering again what her dream was about. Did her husband try to drown her? Was she having a nightmare about her husband choking her? He had no idea but this time, he wasn't going to leave her. The girl was traumatized by something and he wasn't about to let her alone as he held her in his arms and rocked her. "It's alright. You're safe. I won't let anyone harm you."

They lay in bed like spoons. Dawn slowly dozed off but Jason couldn't sleep as he wrapped his arms around her, sensing the warmth of her body, taking in the sweet smell of honey in her hair and feeling the velvety smoothness of her skin. He was in love with a strange scrawny girl who wasn't even his type. At what point did this happen? He had been careful not to fall for anyone ever since his fiancée had betrayed him. When did he fall for the mystery girl? Did he want Dawn because he wanted to discover her secrets or because he truly loved her? He wasn't sure. Jason wasn't sure of anything anymore. He decided that he was going to stay with her for a bit longer and then go back to his room, but he passed out and didn't get up until morning.

The next time Dawn opened her eyes, she was lying on her belly, one leg tossed over Jason's and her head on his chest. She slowly lifted her head, moved her leg, turned to quiet the alarm that hadn't yet gone off and lay on her side to study the man in her bed. She wanted to trace his mouth with her finger and kiss the lips that had once brushed against hers in the kitchen, lips that had asked her if she'd preferred he made love to her instead of the girl waiting for him in the upstairs bedroom, lips that she wished had never kissed anyone's but hers. Her eyes shifted to the perfection of his nose and swept up to his eyes; eyes that were the most beautiful shade of green, eyes that betrayed his feelings toward her even when he acted as though he didn't care. He woke up and caught her watching him.

"Good morning," he told her groggily. "How're you feeling?"

"I feel good. Thanks for staying with me," she answered, with a look of appreciation.

"You're welcome," he told her, pushing the covers away and getting up. "I hope I didn't hog all the blankets. My girlfriends always..." and then he stopped.

"Your girlfriends always say that you hog the blankets?"

It felt strange for him to talk about his girlfriends in front of her. "I should go brush my teeth," he said.

"Stay," she blurted as he turned around and looked at her intently. "The night before last, you said that I don't trust anyone, not even my friends."

Were they friends now? He didn't want to be friends. Friends meant taking sex out of the equation, and he wasn't sure he could do that as he approached her. He wanted her then and there. He had tried hard to control himself last night, but this morning he found his willpower slipping away as he leaned over and gave her a long passionate kiss, his tongue tasting, exploring and pleading for more. Pushing her down on the covers, he slipped her nightgown above her head. He nibbled on her ears and traced the contour of her back, feeling every inch of her body down to her legs. His hands shifted to between her thighs caressing it and gliding up to her belly and the softness of her breasts. He squeezed one and then the other as he coerced her legs open.

"Please stop. I can't," she said as she saw a look of disbelief on his face. "I'm sorry, I thought I could but I can't," she told him and grabbed her robe.

"You are something you know, always luring me into your arms and then pushing me away."

"Luring? I never lured you into anything."

"Really? Weren't you the one who asked me to stay?"

"Yes, but not because I wanted to lure you into having sex with me."

"Then why, Dawn?"

"It doesn't matter, just go."

"No you don't," he said and pinned her to the wall, yanking her hair, kissing her hard and thrusting his finger inside her.

"I beg of you, stop. You don't know anything about me. I don't want to make love, not like this."

"Who said anything about love?" Not willing to loosen his grip, he relished her neck with his mouth. "This is just pure uninhibited sex. You want it or you wouldn't have lured me in here."

She slapped him hard on the face.

"You hit me," he said in shock, rubbing his cheek.

"Yes."

"Why? I'm never wrong about reading women, and you and I both know that you want me."

"So full of yourself, you are. You men are all the same – Americans and Arabs – the only difference is geography."

Her words stung more than her slap as he turned and left, but she followed him.

"I'm sorry for what I said."

"I've had enough of this, little girl. I'm not interested in playing games."

"Jason, please let me explain," she called after him as he went to his bedroom and slammed the door behind him.

She cried for the rest of the day. She cried for her mother and father. She cried for leaving her home, she cried for her misfortunes. And when she was finally tired of feeling sorry for herself, she took a shower, changed and came out of her room but there was no trace of Jason. Dawn decided to go out for fresh air and to walk through the Arab neighborhood.

At one of the stands, she bought an Arabic coffee and *kunaffa*, a dessert filled with cream and banana. She hadn't eaten one in a long time and missed it ever since she left Riyadh. She then went to sit on a bench, watching people who seemed to be going on about their day, not caring what they wore or the differences in their beliefs. She wished that Riyadh were more like Dearborn and that people were allowed to decide for themselves how they wanted to live.

That's why she loved the U.S. She may have been more conservative than others but she had choices. The choice to drive even if she couldn't afford to have a car, the choice to dress sexy, even if she preferred to dress modestly, the choice to vote even when she didn't have time to make it to the polls, the choice to live alone even if she preferred not to live alone, the choice to work, even if one day she decided to stay home, raise her children and let her husband earn money. She understood that the freedom to choose one's destiny and equality of all human beings was, is and would always be, the biggest gift a government could afford its citizens. She knew that complete equality and freedom never existed anywhere. Women still got paid less than men for the same work. Tapping of phones, reading emails, surveillance of homes, checking bank account activities and travel habits of citizens under the pretext of Homeland Security would always exist but the illusion of freedom given to citizens of western countries was far better than the oppression of people in the Middle East.

"Excuse me, will you take a picture of us?" a man with his son asked her, interrupting her thoughts.

She gave him a big smile, thinking how she was never allowed to talk to any man in Riyadh and men were never allowed to talk to her. "Of course," she said, taking his camera.

"It's easy, really. All you have to do is push this button here."

Dawn focused the apparatus and clicked the button.

"Thank you," the man said, taking his camera back. "You're from around here?"

She shook her head no. "I live in Los Angeles."

"I'm from Chicago. You enjoy your day and thanks again for the picture."

"You have a nice day too," she replied. She walked around a bit longer and then went back to her hotel but when she entered her room, she noticed that the maids had cleaned the rooms and Jason's belongings were gone. Dawn called downstairs.

"Is there a message for me by any chance? I seem to have lost my roommate."

"I apologize, it's been crazy busy here. I was just writing you a note to be delivered. Mr. Crawford checked out earlier and said you could stay as long as you wished."

"Thank you," Dawn said, feeling the sting of his actions. She began packing her belongings and called the airlines to see if she could catch an earlier flight out. She then grabbed a taxi to the airport.

On the four-hour flight from Detroit to L.A., she thought about her relationship with Jason and decided that it was time for her to get a new job and do without him. She didn't want to be attached to a man who wasn't right for her. He and his family were completely messed up and important things that should have mattered never did, such as spending time together. Instead, superficial things had tremendous value, such as excessive wealth and the way outsiders perceived them. Dawn hated the way Jason pimped himself to get more business for his father. She could still remember that night in the private room where women were all over the men and Jason offered Husam an experienced call girl. It was like being in a high-class prostitution house. No, she wanted a cleaner and simpler life, and the first thing she was going to do when she returned was to start filling out job applications.

SIXTEEN

Dawn and Jason didn't speak for a month. She tried to stay out of his way, mostly keeping to her room. A messenger would deliver documents for her to translate and if Jason needed anything, Yumiko would call her. Then one day Dawn caved and sent a note telling Jason they needed to talk, but he didn't respond.

In her free time, Dawn job-hunted on the internet, filled out several applications for a receptionist/administrative assistant position, signed up with various Web sites that offered translation services to their customers and looked for a room to rent.

"I can't find a job. I'm completely useless," she told Zoya in frustration at a hamburger joint in Old Town Pasadena.

"How long have you been searching?" Zoya asked, tapping the bottom of a ketchup bottle and pouring it over her fries.

"A month already but I haven't had a single response."

"Is that all? A month is nothing. Don't look at how quickly Jason offered you a job. He's too smitten by you to think straight."

"So, what you're saying is that I don't deserve my work," she answered angrily as pedestrians walked about outside in their shorts and sundresses on a comfortable July evening.

"No, but most people don't get to stay at someone's guesthouse for free and have a cushy job."

Dawn wiped off the hamburger sauce that had fallen on her peach dress. "I work my behind off and have earned every penny. Granted, I'm fortunate to be able to live in a nice place rent-free but...."

"Exactly, you're lucky. Why do you want to mess with a good thing? If I knew how to translate documents, I would take your job in a heartbeat." After barely graduating high school, Zoya, who didn't enjoy the academic environment, decided to work instead of continuing her education.

"I know it's very comfortable living in the guesthouse," she said, thinking of her beautiful small garden, the housekeeping service, private security and permission to access all the amenities that the Crawford mansion offered, "but sometimes, you have to get out of your comfort zone in order to grow."

"Is that your theory or some famous philosopher's? Because frankly, I think you're being an idiot," she told her in a reprimanding tone. The truth was, Zoya didn't want to lose her friendship and liked to keep things exactly the way they were.

"Think what you will, but let me ask you something: Where will you be when you're 50 or 60 years old?" she asked, finishing her burger.

Zoya shrugged. "I'm too young to worry about such things."

"You're wasting your time working as a maid when you have no family to support and every opportunity to better your life. Take some classes on the side and make a future for yourself," Dawn commented.

"I'm content with what I have."

"You can't clean homes for the rest of your life. How're you going to support yourself when you no longer have the energy?"

"Okay Mom, I'll keep that in mind." Zoya rolled her eyes and pushed her plate away so she would stop eating the fries. The waistband around her brown skirt was starting to dig into her skin.

"I know I sound preachy, but that's because I care," she replied, opening her purse to pay for her share of the meal.

Zoya threw in a $10 bill. "I know you do. It's just that I'll miss you."

"You're still planning to keep in touch with me, aren't you?" Dawn said as they both got up. "You and Fred are the only friends I have."

"Yes, but it's different than seeing you everyday," she said, almost melancholy, walking toward a side street where her car was parked.

"I know, I'm going to miss you too, but I promise to call you or at least email you everyday," she said as the two got into Zoya's old pomegranate Taurus. Minutes later they were home.

"Want to come up to my place for tea or coffee?" Dawn asked, looking for her keys as they walked toward the guesthouse.

"I would, but you seem to have a visitor."

Dawn looked up and saw Jason waiting for her in the dark, his face, anxious, his eyes, grave, and his body, rigid. It was nine p.m. "I'll see you tomorrow," Zoya said, heading toward the servant's quarters.

"What're you doing here?" Dawn asked, her face filled with surprise.

"I received a note that you wanted to talk." He had been waiting for her for the past 20 minutes, walking back and forth, debating if he should leave. But he decided to wait because he couldn't stand spending another day wondering what she had wanted to confess the morning he abandoned her in Dearborn.

"Yes, but Jason, that was a week ago and now I'm really tired," she answered, mad that she hadn't heard from him until now.

"Okay then," he said coldly. "This was the only free time I had available, and I'm not sure when I'll be able to meet with you again."

She knew he was playing a game with her but didn't care. The sooner she talked to him about her past, the better. That way, she could break free and move on forever from her old life and from Jason and his family, who constantly had ties with Saudis. "You can come in, but I don't want you to blame me for *luring* you in," she said, frowning.

"I see that word still bothers you. What is it about women and their elephant memories?"

"I'd let you know why I hate that particular word if only you'd give me a chance to explain. But Jason, I'm only inviting you in to talk."

"Don't worry, I promise to act civilized," he replied, fighting hard to conceal his attraction toward her.

"Then, come in," she offered, inviting him into her living area.

Jason sat on one of the large comfortable chairs as he eyed Dawn's slender legs and manicured toes walk toward the kitchenette. Dawn made Arabic coffee with cardamom and saffron. It was going to be a long night and they needed something strong.

She brought the ingredients to a boil and then let the coffee simmer.

"I hope you like Arabic coffee," she said and then went to her bedroom to grab a small bag and silver antique looking box decorated with faux ruby and emerald stones. She didn't know why she was about to trust him with her secret but something he had said to her in Dearborn had been bothering her ever since: "I don't let myself get attached either, but at least I trust my friends enough to confide in them." And in reality, Jason's friendship was just as important to Dawn as Zoya's and Fred's.

She poured the coffee, brought a small plate of dates to the table and took a seat on the couch opposite him.

"Thank you," he said, taking his cup.

"Here, have some dates with it," she offered. "Once you get used to it, you won't want to drink anything else."

"I doubt that," he told her, making an effort to smile. He stared at the mysterious box and the bag that she had set on the table earlier.

She noticed him looking at the objects on the table with immense curiosity. "Before I get to the items on the table, what you need to understand is the negative connotation the word 'lure' holds for me," she said, drinking her coffee. "Oppression of Saudi women is based on the belief that women's voice, looks and shape lure or entice men on purpose to get them to do things against their willpower and beliefs."

"But I always thought it was their religion telling them that they must dress that way."

"No, the religion only dictates that women should dress modestly but it is the interpretation of the religious scholars, who are all men, by the way, that forces the women to cover up."

"Now I see why you hate the word so much. I suppose that's why Saudi and other Middle Eastern women wear shapeless black material and cover their face and hair."

"The belief that women lure goes farther than just having to cover up," she told him with a serious look. "You see, if a woman gets raped, nine out of ten times she gets blamed for luring the man into raping her."

"You're joking," he commented, his eyes wide.

"I'm completely serious. Many women don't report being raped because they're afraid they'll get punished for it."

"What's the punishment?"

"Anywhere from 90 lashes and up to time spent in prison to decapitation. The beatings are carried out at 50 lashes per day And truth be told, worse things happen there and no one ever hears about them."

"Dawn, what I have a hard time understanding is why an intelligent person like you wouldn't have read up on the laws and customs of that country before marrying your husband."

A cloud of darkness fell upon her face and she sat in silence for a long time.

Jason waited patiently for her response.

"I'm not Dawn," she finally said. My name is Sahar. Sahar Al-Hijazi, not Dawn Parnell."

"The girl who died a year ago?" he asked. "I'm sorry but I find that hard to believe," He got up and paced the room. He couldn't handle her lies anymore.

She looked at him with concern and wondered if she should finish her story or walk away and pretend that she had lied to him. No, it was too late to back down now. "Please sit. Let me finish explaining before you judge me."

"This is too much. First you show up to my house as a housekeeper, then I find out that you were an educated girl who married a Saudi man and now this. When will it stop Dawn? When will the lies end?" He headed for the door.

"Husam is my husband, but our marriage was never consummated. Saad, the man you liked doing business with is my father," she reluctantly admitted.

Jason stopped in his tracks and turned around, "Why are you doing this? Why are you lying to me like this?"

"I'm not lying to you, I swear," she said, popping out a dark-blue contact lens from one eye. Her uncle had bought the lenses for her before her escape. "These match your face perfectly," he had told her. "No one will ever be able to tell that your eyes are brown."

Jason was shocked. He grabbed her by the shoulders and studied her closely. One eye was dark brown.

"You're hurting me," she told him, her face wrinkled with traces of pain.

He loosened his grip. "No, that's impossible. Sahar is dead."

She walked toward the bag sitting on the table and pulled out a box of red hair dye. "I dye my hair once a month and touch up my roots incessantly. My natural hair color is brown." She then opened the jeweled box and pulled out a photo of herself and Dawn Parnell and held it up to her face. "See this. I'm the one with the dark hair and Dawn is the red hair."

He stared at the photo. The resemblance between the two girls was uncanny.

"My name Sahar means Dawn, the time when daylight begins. My mother used to say that no matter how bad things get and no matter how many mistakes we make, tomorrow, at daylight, a new day will begin, promising new beginnings and new hopes. That's why she named me Sahar."

Jason shook his head at the impossibility of it all. He looked at the photo again. One of the girls in the picture had brown hair and eyes and a golden complexion. The other girl had red hair, dark blue eyes and a pink complexion but the shape of their eyes, lips and facial structure were similar.

"My uncle taught me how to apply my makeup so that I could look like Dawn. He gave me a pair of metal retainers and thick glasses so that I could hide behind them in case anyone had any doubts about my identity." She stopped talking for a moment to give him time to digest all the information before she continued. "Everyone thought we were related when we roomed in Barcelona. Our features were so much alike, but our personalities were completely different."

"Christ!" was all he could say. "How? How did you fool so many people? What about the story you told me about Dawn?" He collapsed back on the chair.

"Everything I told you about Dawn was true. Except that Dawn killed her husband and when her brother-in-law found out, he went after her."

"How did she kill him?"

"She, she...oh God, I told her not to marry him," Sahar said, noticing that Jason was focusing on her eyes. She must have looked bizarre with her red hair and one brown eye, she thought as she put her contact lens back in.

"Will you always be wearing those? The lenses, I mean." He was confused about his feelings toward her. He had fallen in love with a girl with red hair and blue eyes. Maybe he fell for who she was rather than what she looked like.

"I'm afraid I will have to. There will always be the fear of running into someone like Husam, who might recognize me."

"How come you don't have an accent?"

"I had an American tutor since I was five. Not only was she my English teacher but also a phonetics instructor. And I am good at picking up languages and accents. I can fake an Irish, Scottish and English accent with ease."

Jason went to the kitchenette, filled a tall glass with water and gulped it down. He stood there with his back toward her, his hands on the counter around the sink wondering what had he gotten himself into. He wanted to leave and never find out the truth, but it was too late. His curiosity got hold of him and now he needed to know everything.

Sahar felt bad for cheating him out of the truth for such a long time as she watched the tense muscles of his back and his drooped head, but she had to be sure that she could trust him. She was also fearful of disappointing him.

"Dawn tried divorcing Youssef but she wasn't allowed to go in front of a judge. She needed a *mahram* to speak for her but she had no one. Even if she had a male guardian, the court would never allow a woman to divorce her husband. The police just sent her home and told her to work it out with her husband. Then one day I went to see her. I wanted to tell her about my grandfather forcing me to marry a man I didn't love."

"Kadar is your grandfather?" he asked, still skeptical.

"Yes, Kadar's businesses weren't doing so well and he decided to merge with Husam's company."

"But why did he make you marry him?"

"I was part of the deal, you see. I was given to him as a bonus in order to create a solid relationship between our two families."

"They can do that? They can push you into marriage?"

"Yes, it's not talked about much in public, but oftentimes the family pressures the woman to make the wrong choice. It's not like here where women are free. From the day a girl is born, she's taught that her role in life is to get married and bear sons to carry out the husband's name. In return, her husband will take care of her financially and guard her from harm."

A chill went through Jason's spine and he shivered even though it was warm inside.

"I begged my family not to force me into marriage, but they wouldn't listen. When I went to see Dawn...."

"It's strange to hear you speak about yourself in third person. I mean I know that you're talking about the real Dawn...anyway, just go on."

"When I saw my friend one late morning, she seemed unusually cheerful. We talked about our past and how happy we were in Barcelona. We discussed Husam and she told me he wasn't a nice man. I told her I didn't want to marry him, and I wished we could both be free again. I cried and she said, 'Be careful of what you wish for, you might just get it.' "

Jason was starting to understand how hard it must be to live in a depressed society. "Then what happened?"

"She told me not to worry and that all would be fine. At the time I didn't understand her. I remember being angry with her. I yelled 'How could everything be fine, when I'm going to be raped by a man who I have to call my husband?' You see, I was so envious of Dawn. 'You can't even comprehend what I'm feeling,'

I told her, 'At least you married out of love.' And she said, 'Love is a curse, and I don't wish it on anyone. I promise that I'll help you and soon we'll both be liberated. But now you have to go before my husband gets back from work,' So, I left. That was the last time I saw her."

"You still haven't told me how she killed her husband."

"She killed him two hours after I left. She waited for him to fall asleep during his afternoon nap."

"Afternoon nap?"

"Yes, private businesses close from noon to 4 p.m. and resume from 4 to 10 p.m. During that time people go home, pray, eat, take a nap and then go back to work."

"Oh yes, now I remember. I've tried to call our Saudi investors at their work during those times and had difficulties," he remarked.

"Anyway, she stabbed her husband 15 times while he slept. His death was in the papers, but nothing was said of who did it."

"My God! Did she turn herself in after that?"

"No, she just sat there next to his body until his brother arrived to pick him up for work."

"Did he call the police?"

"No, a neighbor told me that the brother-in-law used the same knife to kill Dawn."

He gaped at her, his face immobile and shocked. "How…how did the neighbor know?"

"Dawn's trusted maid, who also worked for the husband's family had overheard their conversation and confided in Dawn's neighbor," she said. Her throat felt parched, her mouth sticky and her head throbbed.

"You said there was nothing about her in the papers. So what happened to the body?"

"Dawn's maid overheard the brother-in-law tell his mother that he dumped it somewhere in the desert," she said, choking back her tears. She got up and started screaming with her fists up in the air. "I'm so angry. I'm so angry at you, God. Do you hear me, damn you? You should have helped save her. There is no one to save us. No one. We women get trampled over every day, and there's no one to rescue us. If we protest, we get thrown in jail. We have no rights. We have no rights." She grabbed a tissue and wiped her tears.

Jason, who felt her pain, sat there in silence, He too wanted to cry but couldn't.

Sahar wiped her nose. "There was no escape for Dawn. If the authorities had gotten hold of her, they would've slashed off her head anyway at the Sa'ah square."

"At where?"

"It's a public place, also known as the chop chop center," she sniffled, "where limbs get cut off if a person has committed robbery or heads get chopped if someone commits murder, especially when a foreign woman whose life basically has no value kills a Saudi man whose life has a tremendous value."

"I don't understand."

"A Jew or Christian's life is worth 50 percent of a Muslim man's life, all others including Hindus are worth 1/16. An atheist's life is worth 0 percent and a woman's life is worth 50 percent of the males in each of these categories. That's how the judges base their decisions when they sentence offenders."

"So, for example, a Jewish woman's life is worth 25 percent of a Saudi man's?" Jason asked.

"Yes but there are no Jews in Saudi Arabia. They're not allowed in the country and any associations with them are forbidden." She picked up his coffee cup, "Here, let me pour you more coffee. I have a feeling we're going to be up all night."

"Er...you wouldn't happen to have American coffee in there, would you?"

"No, but I have tea."

"Tea sounds good," he told her. "Mind if I stretch my legs on the sofa?" So taken by Sahar's story, he hadn't budged and his legs felt as stiff as an iron rod.

"You needn't ask. This is your house, and I'm simply a guest," she said.

He didn't have time to tell her how much her words stung as he had a moment to think by himself. Jason had done everything possible to make her feel comfortable and to treat her as though she belonged there, but he could see now that she didn't feel that way.

While pouring the tea, Sahar regretted her big mouth. She didn't know why, but somehow she always said things to create a distance between them. Did she do it because she was afraid of getting hurt, or did she do it because she wanted to remind him about their differences? In Riyadh, her family was one of the wealthiest families in the region and Sahar had owned many properties under her name, but here she had nothing to offer him. As she reentered the room with tea and a dessert plate, she noticed his unhappy look.

Trying hard to forget her earlier comment, Jason asked, "what happened to the brother-in-law? Did he have to go to jail?"

"No, honor killings are common in Saudi Arabia and the government looks the other way. When a male relative kills a woman in order to restore family honor, it is tolerated. In Dawn's case, the brother-in-law was really taking revenge but he claimed that Dawn had been cheating on her husband and that he had gone home to confront her and she killed him to hide the truth."

"So, how did you steal the identity of the dead girl?" he asked, drinking his tea.

"You speak of her as though she meant nothing to me. She was my best friend," she raised her voice, upset at his insensitivity.

"I am sorry. Please let me rephrase my callous question – How did you assume Dawn's identity?"

"About a month before my wedding, I received a letter from Dawn's neighbor, who requested to see me. When we met at her house, she told me what happened and gave me this jeweled box with a lock that opened by using a pass code. She said Dawn's maid had given it to her."

"A pass code?"

"Dawn and I made up a pass code long ago when she opened up a bank account under my name. Three months before her death, I emptied the account and gave her the money because she asked me to. It was her savings, and I didn't ask any questions. I think she used it to plan her escape." She opened the jeweled box, took out the letter and began reading:

If you have this letter in your hand, it means that I am dead either by the hands of my husband or his family. I want you to do two things for me. Use the information in this box and the money to escape and live a happy life, and if there's any money left once you have settled in, give it to my parents along with pictures of me, the locket they bought for my 16th birthday and a farewell letter. The ashtray and the box are yours, something you can remember me by. By the way, I thought you'd be happy to know that I gave up smoking a month ago.

"You know what's ironic is that at the end, it wasn't the smoking that killed her, it was her brother-in-law," she said running her hand over the gold-plated ashtray Dawn had bought while they were shopping in Barcelona. That was the last time they had gone out together. Once Dawn got to Riyadh, her husband didn't permit her to go anywhere without him.

"Are you sure you want to continue reading your letter?" Jason asked, noticing her ashen look.

Sahar nodded, "Yes, I want you to know everything. Then we will have no more secrets between us."

You are the voice in my head. You are the sister I never had. You are my best friend, my family and the only person I have in this dark, lonely world. The only thing that kept me alive these past few years was my memories of us in Barcelona – the cafés, the shopping, waterskiing in our bikinis, horseback riding, tennis and skiing. Those were the good days that I will never get back. I know you tried to warn me not to marry my husband, but I didn't listen. I know you tried to warn me not to go and live in Riyadh and give up my freedom, but I didn't listen. And when I finally listened, it was too late, but it's not too late for you. I want you to live for both of us and be free. Do all the things I took for granted. Run on the beach, go out in the street without a mahram, *vote, drive, work and have sex with a man who respects and cares about you. I want you to live in a country where women have equal rights and men cannot decide their future. Be free my friend and live for both of us."*

Tears rolled down Sahar's face, but she did not try to wipe them. "I realize now that the last time I went to see her, she looked unusually joyful, almost like a person in denial." Sahar finally grabbed a tissue and wiped her nose. "When she told me that soon the both of us would be free, I didn't know what she meant at the time, but I do now."

"She was planning to take you with her?"

"No, she was planning to kill her husband and let me use her ticket to freedom. Goddamn fool. She was always so reckless."
She continued reading the letter:

There is a phone number here, call them, give them our pass code and they will help you. Everything has been paid up front, so don't let them tell you otherwise. I made a deal with them two months ago that if I lose my nerve, you will use their services instead. You see my dear, there's no refund. But make sure you follow through where I have failed. Don't be scared. I may be dead, but my spirit lives on and will protect you. Take my strength and use it to escape. God may have forgotten all about me but he will not forget you. Here's to hope, and al horeyat.

You friend always and forever,
Dawn Parnell

"I have read this letter at least a hundred times, but I still cry each time," she said, wiping her tears away. "I can never get used to what she sacrificed for me. She gave up her life to save me from a forced marriage. I wish now that I had never complained about Husam. Had I just accepted my obligation to my family, Dawn would still be alive, living in this country."

"You don't know that. She could have snapped and killed him anyway. I mean the guy did abuse her," said Jason, noticing the wall clock with both hands pointing to midnight.

Dawn had planned to escape and then she was going to find a way to get Sahar out of Saudi Arabia, too. But her husband had come home one day, slapping and kicking her and then forcing her to have anal sex – something she had never done before. He hurt her as she screamed but he laughed, enjoying her pain. After that he fell sleep, snoring contently. Dawn had taken a shower to cleanse herself and then taken a kitchen knife and ripped him into pieces.

"I don't know anything anymore. All I know is that I must live for both of us. I must make sure that I'm happy for both of us, otherwise her sacrifice would have been for nothing. My life would have been just like hers, had I not escaped."

Jason got up, grabbed a box of tissues from her desk and gave it to Sahar. "Do all Saudis beat up their wives?" he asked sitting back down.

"No, not all. My father loves my mom and has never laid a finger on her," she said. "And to be honest with you, I'm not sure how Husam would have treated me. I just didn't want to get married, especially not to him. I didn't love him."

"Are all women kept at home?"

"No, many fathers, brothers and husbands give women certain freedoms but life is very hard for those who want more. Things are changing but they're changing at a snail's pace."

"At least things are getting better."

"I'm not so sure. It took the Saudis 1,000 years to give women I.D. cards, which are often useless anyway. Many institutions don't honor them and ask the woman to bring two *mahram* who can vouch for her. You can't do anything without a man's permission, not even get an I.D. card or travel."

"They're not allowed to travel?"

"No, not without the proper papers signed by a man. Women can't even get a hotel room by themselves."

"Why?" he asked, thinking of the two of them rooming in Dearborn and wondering if Husam ever found out, what he would do to them.

"The ones who get rooms by themselves are considered prostitutes. A chaste woman must sign up at a hotel with another female roommate or her husband."

"How difficult life must be for them."

"They're used to it. They've been brainwashed since childhood to be subservient and to protect their virtue by covering up."

"How come you're not like that?"

"Believe it or not my parents were liberal and allowed me to study abroad and travel," she said, appreciating her parents for the first time in a long time. She missed them but knew that she could never lay eyes on them again, or contact them. It was simply too dangerous. If her father ever found out what she had done and that her mother and uncle had helped her, he would divorce Asima and kill Sahar to save his family's honor. If her government found out, they would have her deported and her head slashed; her uncle and mother would be punished as well.

"How did you fake your death?"

"With the help of my uncle and mother. I met up with a man who gave me a potion that could slow down my vital signs for 24 hours."

"I've never heard of such a thing. What kind of potion was it?"

"I don't know what was in it. He told me spies used it when caught by the enemy. It's supposed to fool the captor, thus allowing the prisoner to escape. He also said sometimes people didn't wake up."

"My God. Weren't you scared?"

"Very. My mother and uncle begged me to think twice about what I was doing, but my mind was made up."

"You were brave. What happened after you passed out?"

"I don't remember anything. I can only assume what happened. I went once to someone's funeral and know the procedure for burying someone."

"What are the steps?" he asked, curious about their customs.

"A doctor signs a death certificate, and then the body is sent to a morgue. They wrap it in a *kaffan* and…"

"A what?"

"After washing the body three, five or seven times – more if needed – they wrap it from head to toe three times if it's a man, five times if it's a woman, in a white cloth called *kaffan*, and add a non-alcoholic perfume to it."

"Do you think they washed you?"

"I doubt it. I think they probably just wrapped me. The *Imam* must have said a prayer while my family was standing – *Allahu Akbar* – God is greater than everything. At the end when the prayer was finished, everyone probably said *assalaamu alaikum* – peace be upon you."

"What happens after the prayer?"

"The mourners walk in front of the bier. It's forbidden for anyone to cry. Then they bury the body without a casket and position it so that it faces Ka'aba. A casket is only used when the soil is moist."

"What's Ka'aba?"

"It's an ancient cube-shaped granite structure located in a courtyard. The al-Masjid al-Haram, also known as the Grand Mosque in Mecca, was built around it. A set of stairs on the north side lead to the inside, which is hollow. In the southeast corner, a black stone is embedded in a silver frame. The structure is covered with *kiswah*, a black silk cloth embroidered in gold with verses of Qur'an."

"It sounds like an important structure. Does it symbolize anything?"

"It serves as a local and unifying point among the Muslims. At prayer time, *kibla* is the direction Muslims face. It is a direction that points to Ka'aba from wherever they are in the world. During Haj – a holy journey to Mecca which takes place at the last month of the Islamic year, pilgrims circle the Ka'aba as the final act of pilgrimage."

"Have you ever participated in Haj?"

"Yes. One of the five pillars of Islam dictates that all Muslims must participate in Haj at least once during their lifetime. However some never make it to Mecca because they are physically and financially unable to fulfill their obligation. In such cases they may send someone in their stead."

"Okay, so they bury you facing Ka'aba, then what happens?"

"Everyone says *Bismillah Wa A'la Milla rasulallah* – in the name of Allah, the beneficent and merciful and messenger of Allah – while they lay down the body and put bricks under the head."

"And you didn't feel any of this?"

"No, I have no memory of it. As the grave is filled, mourners throw in three handfuls of soil each.

"No headstone?"

"No, we don't mark our graves. That's why it was so hard to find mine. I was almost buried alive."

Then it dawned on him why she had screamed for help when she couldn't breathe that night in Dearborn. "That was what your nightmare was all about, wasn't it?"

"I have had many nightmares since I left Riyadh. Nightmares about my friend Dawn being beaten by her husband. Nightmares about me stuck in the grave, not being able to move or breathe, nightmares about getting caught and being sent back to face a death sentence by my father, grandfather or my husband."

"They would kill you?"

"Yes and if they found out we stayed in the same room, they would find you and get rid of you as well."

Jason rubbed his face, took in a deep breath and let it out. "You're a virgin then?"

"Yes."

"No wonder you didn't want to sleep with me. You were scared."

"Yes but Jason, we did sleep together, we just didn't have sex."

"You know what I mean."

"I didn't want to get you involved and ruin your life."

He wrinkled his forehead for a moment. "What happened when everyone left the burial site?"

"I remember waking up feeling suffocated from the scarcity of oxygen. I tried to take in a deep breath but the strong smell of dirt and the fact that I was trapped in a sheet made it impossible. Fear and panic consumed my entire body as I wiggled atrociously and screamed."

"Could anyone hear you from above?"

"I doubt it. Eventually I passed out and the next time I woke up, I heard the sound of shovels. I cried for help. I screamed, 'I don't want to die.' The men above my grave dug fast. You see, they had had trouble finding my location."

"Good grief. You could have died," he said, looking horrified. His eyes were red and his face stiff.

"They warned me that it was going to be dangerous. When they finally got to me, they pulled me up, four of them. Four men, imagine that! Four men touching my body. My husband would have been displeased. And when I think about the possibility of being caught...." She rubbed her arms to get rid of the goose bumps.

"I still can't get over the fact that you're married."

"By Saudi law, perhaps, but not in my heart. I was never married in my heart. As far as I'm concerned, I'm a single person, free to marry anyone I want."

"I suppose you couldn't get a divorce even if you wanted to. Could you?"

"No, and that's one more secret I'm going to have to live with for the rest of life."

"How did you get out of the country?"

"My uncle helped change my looks," she smiled, missing his crazy sense of humor, "and my rescuers falsified papers that gave me permission to leave Riyadh and go to Dubai under the name of Reyhana bint Abdol Majid. They coached me on how to stay calm and collected if caught."

"Did you travel by yourself?"

"No. I left with an Egyptian man who posed as my husband."

"My God, when I think about what would have happened if you got caught. It was a serious violation of international laws."

"Yes, I know. That's why you can never tell anyone."

"Don't worry, I won't. What did you do in Dubai?"

"We got a room in the western section of Dubai where there were many American tourists."

"I hear Dubai is quite progressive and modern."

"Yes, if you're in the western section where only men and foreigners are allowed."

"You mean a Saudi woman like you cannot go there?"

"No, it's *haram* – forbidden – even when a foreign woman goes to visit, hotels will not rent her a room. She either has to room with another woman or her husband."

"What did you do in Dubai?"

"I learned how to act like an American. I watched how the girls dressed, how they walked and their manners. I talked to them in clubs to see their likes and dislikes and learned their views."

"You're a fast learner. I would have never known that you were a Saudi."

"When you're desperate, you pick things up quickly. Besides, I had an American tutor at a young age and already knew how to speak English."

"What about the man with you? Did you...you know..." he asked thinking of when they shared a suite in Dearborn.

"God, no! Nothing happened between us," she answered, angry that he would even think it. "He was a professional, there to help me blend into my new life before I flew out with a group of tourists to Los Angeles."

"Why Los Angeles?"

"I met these girls one night, they talked about how great L.A. was and that there were plenty of job opportunities. They said they were looking for a roommate, and I jumped at the chance."

"You had an American passport?"

"A fake one that allowed me to travel under the name of Hope Patterson."

"Why did you change your name to Dawn Parnell?" he asked, thinking that Hope Patterson would have suited her better.

"Because when I got to L.A., I soon found out my new roommates worked for a drug dealer and were eager to recruit me so we could all afford to live in an expensive Westside apartment."

"What did you do?"

"They tried to push me to make deliveries. They said I would be making a lot of money and be able to easily support myself, but I said no. I applied for a job at a fast-food restaurant but couldn't make ends meet."

"I know living in Los Angeles can be expensive," he said sympathetically, glad that she refused their offer.

"Then the girls and their dealer started pressuring me more. They told me if I wouldn't help them out, I'd have to leave," she told him, staring at the box her friend left her. "What I forgot to tell you is that inside Dawn's box, there was a résumé she had been working on for some time with reference letters from her past employers."

"I suppose that's why you – or rather Dawn – came so highly recommended. That was one of the reasons among many that I began doubting your identity. You were so clumsy, letting the threads on the carpet get caught in the vacuum cleaner and then burning my shirt."

"Yet you never complained."

"I felt sorry for you. I didn't want to get you fired. But you kept on fouling up, like when I caught you reading with your glasses sitting on top of your head."

"To tell you the truth, you made me really nervous. You were scrutinizing me from the first day and I was afraid that you would find me out," she admitted, looking him in the eyes more freely now that he knew the truth.

"So, the only reason you assumed your friend's identity was to get a job?" he asked, hoping that she was telling him the truth this time around.

"You still don't trust me do you? You're still pondering over whether or not I'm being honest with you?"

"You haven't answered me. Was the only reason you changed your name again to get a job?"

"Not just a job but also a place where I could stay. I made a
point of it when I applied. The employment agency said they
would try but weren't promising anything. And then a space
opened up. I guess God was looking out for me."

"Are you very religious?"

"I was raised as a Muslim for 23 years. It's all I've ever known.
I'm not certain how many of my beliefs are my own and how
many are teachings of my religion."

"So I guess you can never be with someone outside of your
faith?" he asked, wishing that might not be the case.

"I don't know. My religion dictates that I cannot, but I find
myself questioning it every day."

Jason looked at her gravely. He wanted to know if there would
ever be a chance for them to be together. But how could he commit
to someone who wasn't sure? He decided to change the subject
when he noticed her studying his face. "I guess what I don't
understand is when you met with Dawn's parents in a coffee shop
in Utah. Didn't they recognize that you weren't their daughter?"

"You were there?" she looked at him flabbergasted.

"The detective I hired followed you there."

"And here I thought I was being discreet," she said, shaking her
head. "Dawn's parents knew I wasn't her. Along with my best
friend dying and my leaving my family behind, that was the worst
day of my life. I gave Dawn's mother the farewell letter Dawn had
left her, her locket and $7,000."

"I thought you said you had no money?"

"I didn't have my own money. I didn't want to use up all of
Dawn's money. I knew her parents weren't well off and wanted
them to have what was left," she said, glancing at her watch. It was
two in the morning and she was tired.

"That was very noble of you since you were broke yourself," he
told her with skepticism.

"You still don't believe a word I have told you, do you?"

"You did lie to me twice already. I need time to absorb all this
information."

She tried hard to hide her anger. The only thing that was important now was to finish her story and be done with it. "Dawn's mother started crying as her father came out of the kitchen. At first he thought I was his daughter and dropped a plate full of eggs, but with his wife yelling 'She's dead. Our daughter is dead. Kill me God, please kill me. This is all your fault,' she blamed it on her husband. At that point, he knew I wasn't Dawn and kicked me out of his diner. Dawn's mother had wanted to keep in touch with her but her husband had forbidden her to have any contact with her because she had converted to Muslim."

"How come you went to the park and not back to your hotel?"

"And you say women have a memory like an elephant. I forgot all about that until you brought it up."

"Well?"

"I went there because Dawn used to talk about that park all the time. She used to tell me about her childhood and how her mother used to take her to play in the park to cheer her up."

"To cheer her up from what?"

"If you must know," she said in a tired and bitter tone, "her father used to molest her as a child and beat up her mother."

"What a monster!"

"Yes, we all have monsters in our lives, don't we?" she said, thinking of Kadar and how he would belt her as a child if she misbehaved. "Dawn's monster was a lot worse than mine. So her mother would take her to the park, play with her and buy her ice cream as though that would make all the horrible sexual misconduct go away."

Jason rubbed his forehead and eyes. The idea of a grown man stealing his daughter's youth bothered him immensely.

"Look, I know that I will never be like your carefree friends who have had everything come easy in their lives. My life and connections are complicated and will always be so. I can understand if you would want to break loose from me," she told him, giving him the opportunity to walk out of her life forever, even though that wasn't what she really wanted.

He glanced at her with somber eyes and after a long deathly silence, said, "Perhaps that would be best. My father's company does a lot of business with your grandfather and your..." *husband* he wanted to say, "and Husam. I'm not sure where you would fit in all this. What if they recognize you? What then?"

"I understand," she told him, disparaged. Once again he had let her down by allowing business to come before their friendship.

"Don't talk to me in that condescending voice," he yelled, hoping that she would just blurt out loud how he was a failure when it came to relationships instead of staring at him with disapproval.

"What're you talking about?"

"You know what I mean. You want me to give it all up for you, but I can't."

"I think you'd better go," she ordered, realizing that he simply didn't understand her. It wasn't that she wanted him to change for her, but she wished that he had the guts to take risks and live his own life instead of living a life that his parents had mapped out for him.

"See, you do want me to give it all up," he uttered like a child who had to be right.

"Believe me when I say, I don't want you to mess up your life for me," she answered firmly. "I only want your happiness."

"I'm happy damn it. Why can't you see that?"

"If you say you're happy, then I have to believe you," she said, standing up and opening the door. "I'm glad that now you know my truth, but it's time for you to leave. I'm tired and would like to get some rest."

He gaped at her, angry that she would dismiss him just like that. He jumped up, slammed the door shut and wrapped his arm around her waist, bringing her close to him so that there was no space between them. His lips bathed hers slowly, playfully and his tongue teased and coaxed her into a prolonged erotic kiss. He loved her more than he had loved anyone, but she could destroy his family's hard work. If anyone got a whiff of her getting into this country through illegal means during a time when terrorism was at its peak, he would be considered an accessory, questions would be asked and his family name would be all over the newspapers. No, he couldn't chance it when the odds were so high.

She kissed him back with ardent desire, knowing full well that it would be their last time together. She yearned for him as he did her but their love was forbidden any way she looked at it. He was Christian and she, Muslim. He valued money and status and she, family and friends. He was naïve and she, complex. No, it would be best if they parted and didn't see each other again.

Jason picked her up and carried her to the bedroom. He undressed in front of her and she blushed at the sight of his nakedness as he lowered himself over her and slipped off her panties and her dress. His mouth caressed her breasts and shifted toward her navel and then to between her thighs but when he heard the sound of pleasure in her voice he lost all control and pushed her legs open with his as he entered her in one sharp move and felt her nails dig into his skin.

"Don't move. Relax your body," he told her.

A hot searing pain went through her and she cried for the pain he had caused her, for the family she had left behind and for her best friend's death.

"I'm sorry to have hurt you like this but it gets better the second time around." He wiped her tears away and kissed her gently.

"*Ohebbake –*"

"What does that mean," he said, thinking it sounded romantic.

"It means I love you."

Surprised at the words that she spoke, all he could say was, "What you're feeling, my dear, is lust and not love."

"No, Jason I truly do love you."

He started to move inside her slowly and gently, while kissing her and trying to get her to loosen up until he brought her to climax and then himself.

They lay in bed for a while, their legs entwined, their eyes locked as he pushed her hair away from her face, studying her.

"I wish we had met sooner," he told her, "Perhaps in Barcelona or somewhere else in Europe."

"That would have been impossible because my mother warned me long ago, 'Although I am giving you more freedom than other parents, I expect you to behave responsibly.' "

"Meaning?"

"Meaning I was to never have a relationship with strange men."

"And now?"

"And now I have violated everything I have always been taught, and yet I feel no remorse. I'm glad that it was you who made love to me instead of a husband I could never love. I wouldn't trade this night for anything."

He caressed her face tenderly with the back of his hand, feeling the smoothness of her skin, moving down slowly to her neck, shoulder and further down to her waist and to the curve of her hips. He could stay in bed with her forever, Jason thought, drawing her on top of him, guiding her to take control as he seized her lips with his, their bodies hot and sweaty and their minds trapped in ecstasy.

They made love two more times and Jason seemed not to get enough of her but he knew he had to leave. Jason got up while she was asleep, put his clothes back on and walked back toward the main house, not knowing that Mrs. Anderson had seen him go into Sahar's apartment during the night and leave in the morning. Consumed with jealously, Old Crab had been watching Jason and Sahar's every move. She was determined to find a way to eliminate her rival.

SEVENTEEN

That warm July night was the only time Sahar and Jason made love. She remembered the blood-stained sheet on her bed which she had discarded in the trash after he had taken her virginity. She was no longer untainted and for that, according to Sharia, she would burn in hell.

Now, a month later, she rarely saw Jason. He was either working or going on short trips to meet with clients. Sahar had often wondered if he still had customers of Arab or Spanish origin and, if so, why didn't he take her with him for her translation services? The paperwork and documents that were sent to her had been slowly diminishing as well. Yet her paychecks came in on time twice a month. Today, she had absolutely no work and felt completely useless and used.

She wasn't even a kept woman since he never wanted anything from her in return, she thought as she sat on a bench in a shaded area watching the fish in the koi pond. Today was the anniversary of her death and rebirth, and she missed her homeland more than ever. She didn't understand this American way of loving and leaving. Back in Riyadh, there were boundaries and rules. A man didn't touch a woman unless he wanted to marry her. Even then, he would go to her parents and ask for their daughter's hand. Did she now want what she had run away from? A man who could support her and take care of her? Had Dawn's murder been for nothing? Had all the trouble she had gone through to come to the land of the free merely a waste of time?

Jason had used her in the most contemptible manner, and she hated him for it. He had his fun with her and was now tired of her. The paychecks he sent her were nothing but a symbol of his pity and guilt. She was confused and scared. This way of western life was tough on her and would take some getting used to, she thought as she heard a familiar voice behind her.

"Dollar for your thought," Zoya blurted. It was around four in the afternoon on her day off and she was walking toward her room wearing her white short-shorts and a bright yellow shirt tied at the waist. Zoya still knew her friend as Dawn because Sahar had not confided in her.

"Don't waste your hard-earned dollar on my thoughts; they're not worth it," Sahar said, her body slouched and gaze toward the ground so that Zoya wouldn't see her tears.

"Why so grave? Where's the feisty girl who learned to stand up to Mrs. Anderson, the girl who made me laugh at Monday meetings? I know she's in there somewhere."

"I'm afraid the spirited girl has lost her oomph."

Zoya sat next to her. "C'mon tell me what's bothering you."

Sahar contemplated for a moment before she lifted her head and answered, "There is this man I care about deeply."

"Anyone I know?"

She shook her head. "No, no one you know. Anyway he and I...he and I had...." Her voice cracked.

"Had sex?" she asked, wondering why was it so difficult for Dawn to say it. To Zoya, sex was a good thing and great sex with multiple orgasms, well, bring out the cigarettes and beer, baby.

"Yes that...except that it was my...you see, I've never..."

"Never done it before?" she finished Sahar's sentence as her eyes bulged out. Zoya lost her virginity to her first boyfriend at age 18.

"Yes, you look shocked. Is that so rare?" she asked feeling inadequate in the western culture. Back home it was shameful if she lost it before marriage, and here it was weird if she hadn't already.

"Nowadays, yes. I mean some girls start fooling around when they're 13, which I think is just wrong. They should go out with their friends and have fun instead of worrying about stuff like that."

"So, he must have found me boring and left. I mean, I didn't know what to do and all that."

"Honey, men love you and leave you no matter what. It has nothing to do with you being a virgin," she told her, having had a few bad break-ups herself.

"Did you ever have problems with a man?"

Zoya burst into laughter. "My whole life. Men are difficult to figure out; one minute they're singing you a love song, the next they're in bed with some other girl."

"I don't think I can ever get used to that."

"No one does. It's all trial and error until you meet the right man. Tell me, this man wouldn't happen to be Jason, would it?" she asked, remembering the night he had been standing outside of Dawn's door, waiting for her in the dark.

"You know?"

"I had a notion it was him. Would it make you feel any better if I told you we had a thing before he dumped me?" Zoya could still remember the excuses he gave her when he broke it off – "I think you're really great," he said, "but we have nothing in common. I like sports and your idea of a workout is a 10-minute walk. I like discussing serious issues and you like to talk about which celebrity is having a meltdown. I prefer watching the news and you prefer talk shows where the guests are beating up each other. I'm looking for a woman who is more reserved. We had some fun together but I just can't see us as a couple."

Sahar stared at Zoya, speechless. She thought he really loved her and was just afraid of commitment, but this, she never expected in a million years.

"Say something," Zoya yelled when she saw her friend's flabbergasted face.

"Say something? What can I say except that I have been a fool. He must have slept with half of Los Angeles," she answered raising her voice, her face completely red with anger.

"Well, I wouldn't quite put it that way, but he's had his share of girlfriends. If it's any consolation, I do believe he earnestly cares for you."

"How can you sit here and say that, when he broke your heart just the way he did mine?"

"My fling with him was just that. I wasn't expecting anything serious," she confessed, knowing all along how quickly Jason changed girls. But Zoya hadn't seen Jason look at anyone the way he looked at Dawn. The way he protected her, one would think he was protecting a precious commodity, like the night he had been furious with Zoya for taking Dawn to the private room. In a way, she was envious of her friend and had she not been in a serious relationship herself, her envy would have turned into a strong jealousy. She was certain of it.

"Doesn't it bother you to have sex with so many men?"

"First off, let's get something straight. I haven't had sex with as many men as you think. I just get lonely sometimes and need someone to hold me." Zoya shrugged nonchalantly. "Besides, I've now been in a monogamous relationship for the past year."

"I don't know if I'm cut out for this promiscuous life," she said, glancing over at the August gladiolus, tulips and sunflowers that spread their colorful hues a few feet away from the pond.

"Look, just because a guy takes you out, doesn't mean you have to put out. If he respects you, he'll wait. You just take your time. I mean, I never kiss a man until the fifth date," she lied, because now she was comparing herself to Dawn and wishing that she had shown more restraint in her dealings with men.

"Another thing that's been bugging me is that I haven't received a single reply to my job applications nor have I found a place to live."

Sahar had used Fred and Yumiko as work references and Zoya as a personal reference. She told Fred and Yumiko not to say anything to Jason until she found a job. On her résumé, she had asked her potential employer not to contact her current employer until they were ready to hire her.

"C'mon get up," Zoya commanded, pulling her hand. "You're blocking your energy with all these negative thoughts."

"What are you talking about?"

"If you let go and relax, doors will open up. I'll guarantee it. It's no use moping around all day over things that you have no control. Let's go get pampered at a spa."

"You can afford that?" she inquired, knowing quite well how little a housekeeping job at the Crawford's paid. The richer people were, sometimes the stingier they were.

"No, but I know you can, now that you're an interpreter and, God bless my boyfriend's credit card," Zoya said, pulling a Visa out of her pocket.

"He gave you his credit card?" she exclaimed with envy, remembering all the jewelry and fabric for clothes Husam had bought her and the gifts her parents had showered her with. Back then, it had been almost too much, but now she missed not worrying about money matters and having someone else pay her bills.

"Yes, the fool is in love and wants to marry me," she replied, as they walked toward the parking garage.

"And you don't love him?"

"I do, but I don't want to get trapped. I hate to become one of those married couples that when you ask a wife to hang out, she says 'I have to talk to my husband to see what he's doing' or 'My child has a project and I need to help him out.' No thanks, I don't want to be confined."

"You mean you like to be free to do as you please," Sahar stated, getting into Zoya's car.

"Absolutely. No checking with the hubby and no kids to take care of," she said as her cell phone rang. It was her boyfriend asking her where she was, what she was doing and if she wanted to hang out with him before going out with Yumiko and her husband. "No can do. Dawn and I are going to go get pampered, but I will see you tonight. Say about eight-ish…okay…see you then…love you," she said, hanging up.

"No strings, huh?" Sahar said sarcastically, rolling her eyes.

They went to a day spa and got a massage. Afterwards they were scrubbed down, got a body wrap in seaweed and herbs and went into the Jacuzzi. Sahar had forgotten how great it felt to take care of herself. Ever since she left her parents' house, she had had no money for luxuries, but now that she was getting a better paycheck, she could afford to do this once in awhile.

"Let's go get you a nice haircut," Zoya said after they paid at the front desk.

"You're going to make me go broke," Sahar protested.

"When was the last time you did anything for yourself?" she asked as though reading her mind. "Your hair looks like a broom."

"Gee thanks, when you put it that way," she huffed as Zoya dragged her to a French salon two doors down.

The stylist layered her hair and taught her how to dry it straight to get the frizz out. He reminded her of her maid Rubilyn back in Riyadh who shampooed and fixed her hair everyday. How much she missed her and the way she clacked her tongue against the roof of her mouth when she disapproved of something Sahar had done. Too bad, she would never see her again.

"You look beautiful," Zoya said, dialing her boyfriend, Jim. "Do you have a friend we can set up with a friend of mine?"

"I don't like to set my friends up on blind dates. You know it never works out," his voice, on the other end, told her.

Sahar signaled Zoya with her hands and whispered, "No, no. I'm not going out with anyone."

"Please, do it for me. It'll be nice to have a couples' night out. Besides, wait until your friend sees Dawn. She'll knock his socks off. Ouch!" Zoya yelped because Sahar had just kicked her in the shin.

Zoya quickly brightened as she heard his reply: "Fine, fine, I'll bring him along. Anything for you, poopsie."

"Why don't you guys pick us up at the employee entrance of the mansion at eight?" Servants weren't allowed to have visitors come inside.

"I'm not going," Sahar adamantly insisted as Zoya ended the call and they got back into the car.

"You have to, you promised."

"No, I didn't. You promised. I'm not going out with a complete stranger. What if I don't like him?" She glared at Zoya.

"That's why it's called a date. Take him for a test-drive to see if you like him," she answered, pulling out of the parking space.

"You're out of your mind. I don't have a thing to wear." All she owned was casual wear and the business clothes she had purchased before going to Dearborn.

"I have plenty for both of us," Zoya said.

Once back at their quarters, she gave Sahar a sexy black dress. "You can wear this with my black heels, and I'll wear the red one. When I'm done with you, men are going to have a hard time keeping their eyes off you."

"I'm not a toy doll, you know," she said, mad that she was being forced to go on a date when all she wanted to do was to sit in her room and watch TV.

"Here I am trying to make you feel better and help you forget all about Jason and that's the thanks I get?" Zoya put her hands on her waist in a threatening manner.

"I'm sorry. Thank you, you've been great and I so enjoyed our day, but I'm not so sure about this dating thing."

"Don't worry, I promise he won't bite," she said, starting to brush plum shadow on Sahar's eyelids.

After getting ready, they walked toward the back gate where a convertible vanilla Chrysler PT Cruiser was waiting for them. Zoya's boyfriend, Jim, had slanted eyes, a flat face and a short haircut; Sahar's date, Daniel, an engineer about her age, looked like a surfer with his shoulder-length blond hair and blue eyes. They drove to a local tapas bar, where they met Yumiko and her husband Keiji, a small quiet man, already seated at a round table. Men in matador costumes and women in flamenco costumes stamped their heels to music.

The conversation was light and friendly and when dinner ended, they walked around Old Town Pasadena, a historic district filled with restored buildings where free thinkers, writers and poets such as Albert Einstein, Upton Sinclair and Andy Warhol once lived. It was a beautiful warm night and the stars twinkled.

"We should triple date more often," Yumiko said, putting her arm through her husband's as they walked past a row of red brick buildings. Zoya and Jim were walking behind them. Sahar and Daniel were in front.

"I agree," Zoya said, looking at her boyfriend and then at Yumiko.

"Me too," Daniel added, "This has been a splendid evening; don't you think, Dawn?" he asked Sahar.

Sahar's thoughts were a thousand miles away. "What?"

"We were just discussing what a nice time we've been having."

"Oh yes...me too," Sahar replied reluctantly. Although she did enjoy spending time with friends, her mind and heart were focused elsewhere. She thought of Jason and wondered what he was doing. Was he out and about with a new girlfriend and had he forgotten all about her?

"Have you always lived in Pasadena, Dawn?" Daniel asked, as they passed by an antiques and a clothing shop.

"No, I used to live in Huntsville, Utah."

"Did you?" he asked, surprised and excited. "I'm from Huntsville. Whereabout did you used to live?"

Sahar's stomach churned. Her knowledge of Huntsville was limited and all she could think of was Dawn's old address. "I lived near the Huntsville Town Park."

"I used to go ice-skating there all the time. This is incredible. Which school did you attend?"

"I...I...was home schooled," she lied. "And you? Did you go to college around there?" she asked, tremendously agitated.

"No, I left there when I was 14. My parents relocated to Los Angeles."

"And do you like it here?" she inquired before he could ask her another question.

"I do. L.A. is a great place to live," he replied, staring at her. He found himself attracted to her and wanted to get to know her better. He wanted to ask her more questions about Huntsville, but he had a feeling that she wasn't comfortable talking about it and decided not to press her.

"We should all go to Magic Mountain next weekend. Wouldn't that be fun?" Yumiko said, passing by a sculpture of a giant porcelain blacksmith.

Keiji said, "That's a bit too adventurous for me. I don't really care for roller coasters." He preferred gardening in their yard, reading and theater.

"You used to like to do things. Now all you want is to sit home and do nothing," she pouted.

"We can't join you anyway," Zoya said, "Jim and I will be out of town that weekend."

"Do you like children?" Daniel asked Sahar. "I'd like to have lots of children, at least five or six."

"That many?" Sahar asked, wondering if he would still feel that way if roles were reversed and he were the one getting pregnant.

"Yes, the more the merrier. I want to buy a large house in a nice neighborhood. I have already saved…."

He continued talking and Sahar tuned him out. She found his personality bland and his dialogue tedious. At dinner he had been infatuated with her, smiling and laughing at anything she said. She preferred Jason, who argued and gave her a hard time. This guy was too eager to please.

When the evening came to an end, they said farewell and got into their cars. Jim drove Daniel, Sahar and Zoya to the mansion. Sahar's date held her hand, which made her feel uncomfortable but she didn't protest as he walked her to the back entrance. He leaned into her and brought his lips close to hers to kiss her but as his mouth started to touch hers, she turned her face away and extended her hand. "Thank you for dinner. I had a nice time," she said, leaving him standing there without making any kind of promise to see him again.

The next day, Jason was working in his office when Yumiko gave him an envelope marked "Important." He opened it and took out a series of 8-by-11-inch photographs of Sahar and her date with a note attached to it. "I'd hurry up and make up my mind if I were you. From the looks of it, this girl isn't going to stay single for very long. – Alex." He flipped through the photos and the ones that bothered him the most were the one where the couple was holding hands and the one where his lips almost touched hers. He dialed Alex.

"I see you got the photos," Alex said with a coffee mug in one hand, a cigarette in the other and a headset over her head.

"Did he spend the night with her?" he asked, furious and tense.

"No, but it looked like he wanted to."

Jason clenched his teeth. "Did she kiss him?"

"Jason, you sound like a boy in high school. Tell the woman how you feel and be done with it already."

"Did they kiss?" he yelled, drumming his fingers on the keyboard.

"No, they didn't kiss and honestly if you weren't paying me so obscenely to baby-sit your woman, I'd quit."

"Keep an eye on them. Will you and let me know if things are getting serious?"

"Yes, boss. Anything else?"

"No, that's it for now." He couldn't stop himself from staring at her photo. Her hair had never looked so silky and smooth and her skin so vibrant. Was she falling for this boy who was closer to her age than he was? How long would it be before she slept with him? He hated himself for being so obsessed with her. He wasn't the possessive type, not even when he was engaged. But Sahar made him crazy with jealousy. He stuck the photos back in the envelope and locked them in a drawer.

Two days later, Sahar received an email from one of the companies where she had applied: *Dear Ms. Dawn Parnell, we have received your application and are interested in interviewing you for a receptionist position. Please call our office so that we can schedule an appointment. Best regards, Tom Wilkins.*

Sahar was beside herself as she jumped up and down and started dancing around. If only she could find a place to stay, her life would be complete.

Zoya knocked on her door and walked in. "What's all the ruckus about?"

"I'm going to be interviewed soon for a receptionist position," she joyfully yelled.

"Is that all? I thought you won the lottery or something."

"It is like winning the lottery for me. Now be quiet, and let me call them back."

Zoya sat there in silence while Sahar made arrangements with the interviewer.

"I hate to burst your bubble," Zoya said after Sahar hung up, "But if you do get this job, where're you going to stay?"

"One thing at a time," she answered, thinking things were starting to fall into place for her. First a job, then a place she could call her space and after that who knew? Maybe she'd go back to school and pursue her law degree since that was her goal when she had double majored in political science and English.

"By the way, Daniel, the guy you went out with the other night really likes you. He said he left you several messages, but you never returned his calls."

"Yeah, about that. He's really sweet and all...."

"But you like bad boys."

"No, that's not it. There's much I need to learn about myself before getting involved with anyone." Where everything was once certain and decided for her was now ambiguous. America, the country that now supported her independence, expected her to make decisions, find work, make money, get lodging, pay for her own medical bills, look for a mate and figure out right from wrong. No longer were there laws that dictated her path. She was a caged bird who had been fed and protected all its life and now had been set free. Will she find a home in a country where people were too busy with their own lives to worry about helping their neighbors? Will she be able to make a family of her own in a place where the roles of women and men were no longer black and white but a shade of gray? Yes, she was free, but was freedom as great as she had once thought?

EIGHTEEN

On August 25, Jason received a letter at his office from Sahar that made him livid.

Dear Mr. Crawford,

The purpose of this letter is to announce my resignation from Crawford Enterprises, effective two weeks from this date. I would like to thank you for allowing me to stay at your guesthouse. However, I have found new living arrangements and will be leaving the keys with Mrs. Anderson on the day of my departure on September 8. It has been a pleasure working for you.

My sincere best wishes,
Dawn Parnell

Shocked, he paced back and forth as he read and reread the letter. So, is that how she wants to play? Everything to him was a game. He was used to women threatening to leave but always sticking around when he refused to pursue them. The image of his mother in the arms of a stranger had marred his faith in all women and Sahar wasn't going to be any different. He didn't want to love her. He didn't want to be obsessed with her. He was Jason Crawford, a member of the board of directors of one of the most prestigious companies in the U.S. and no Crawford ever begged, especially not to a woman who was threatening to leave.

He was certain that Sahar wasn't going to abandon him. She was in love with him and had said so the night they made love. And that's what had scared him the most – those awful words – *I love you*. Sex with a woman didn't involve intimacy but saying that he loved her too was out of the question, he thought as he finally sat down. He picked up a paper clip, unwound it and started playing with it. He called his friend George with whom he had a special bond – they could not see each other for a whole year and still be able to pick up where they left off.

"Hi, it's Jason."

"Hey, how the hell are you?" George answered while driving in his car. He had kept in touch with Jason through email and had told him that their mutual college friend, Ladan, got a teaching job in Los Angeles and was planning on moving, and that he too was thinking about relocating to L.A.

"Are you in the L.A area or South Beach?"

"I'm driving in South Beach."

"Feel like bar-hopping to meet some girls? I was thinking about flying out to Miami tomorrow."

"Who are you running away from this time?" George asked, as he made a left turn in his dark cherry convertible Jaguar toward an exclusive jewelry store that catered to celebrities and affluent clientele.

"What do you mean?" he frowned. He hated how well George knew him.

"You always want to go pick up a girl when you're escaping from a relationship that's becoming too serious."

"Did I ask for your opinion? A yes or no would suffice."

"Sounds serious. Anyone I know?" George laughed.

"I'm hanging up now," Jason answered angrily.

"Wait, don't hang up. I'm sorry for intruding on your private life, but the truth is I think I'm insanely in love and have lost all my marbles."

"In love? With whom? Wait don't tell me. It's Ladan, isn't it?" Jason asked, remembering her picture on George's dresser when he had visited him four months ago.

"I guess you always knew we would end up together, didn't you?"

No, I didn't, especially not after she dumped you in college and married a Cuban instead of you, Jason wanted to say. "I take it you have been dating her for a while. When were you planning to tell me?" he asked, raising his voice, upset that he was just finding out.

"I was going to call you later on today but you beat me to it. You see I asked her last night to marry me and we're flying out to Vegas this weekend."

"Marry you?" *Have you lost your mind?* he was tempted to say. "Isn't this a bit sudden?" he asked, forgetting the reason he had called George.

"I never stopped loving her even after she got married. I guess that's why I didn't get into a serious relationship with anyone."

"And are you sure that she loves you?" He inquired, concerned about his friend getting hurt again.

"Two weeks ago when she came over to my apartment for dinner, she told me she was in love with me. We ended up spending the night together and the following night and the following...."

"I get the picture. But why Vegas?" he asked, aiming the paper clip toward the trash and tossing it.

"We decided not to spend our money on a wedding and save it to buy a nice house."

"What will you do with your condo in South Beach?"

"I'm planning to sell it. We're moving to L.A. I switched to a different department at work so my job no longer requires traveling."

"That's a lot of changes," Jason said bitterly, because he was losing his only single friend.

"It all happened so quickly," he replied, pulling into a parking lot. "My fiancé's sister is going to be a witness. She's quite a looker. Want to come to Vegas and meet her?"

"No. I have no intention of getting involved with my best friend's soon-to-be sister-in-law. I have enough problems on my hands as is."

"That's right, I forgot. You like to pick a flower wherever you go," he said, parking his car.

"You used to be like that. I suppose this means that we can never go out together to meet girls."

"No, but we can still go out and have a drink."

"Well, this has been the most disappointing day," he said, picking up another paper clip.

"Hey. I thought you'd be happy for me."

"Oh I am. Truly," he answered, swiveling in his chair.

"Are you sure you don't want to join us?" George asked, getting out of his car, flipping on his alarm and walking out of the parking lot.

"Yes, I am. Weddings have always spooked me."

"Well, if you change your mind, we'll be staying at the Four Seasons in Vegas this weekend. Got to run now. I'm meeting Ladan at a jewelry store to pick out our rings."

"Talk to you later," Jason said. *Damn! Why did he have to go get married and ruin everything?*, he thought. His intercom buzzed. "Yes?"

"Your clients from China just arrived. I put them in the conference room," Yumiko informed him.

"Thanks. Be there in a minute," he said, throwing on his jacket. As he left his office, he decided he wasn't going to contact Sahar. In fact, he was going to make every possible effort to put her out of his mind.

Sahar, who was offered a job a week after her interview, was able to rent a bedroom inside an elderly woman's home. Her friend Zoya was right, Sahar thought as she finished packing her belongings. When she stopped thinking negatively, doors opened up for her. She had been trying for a long time to find an affordable one-bedroom apartment, but the rents were too high for her budget. And now, she believed herself fortunate to have found a place at all. She fastened the lock on her worn-out suitcase, zipped her stuffed duffle bag and went downstairs.

As she walked toward the back entrance of the mansion, her taxi was waiting – except that wasn't all. Jason was there looking grave and, when her eyes fell upon him, her heart skipped a beat. She then became angry with herself for loving a man who had treated her so shabbily.

He approached her and put his hands around her shoulders. "I know I've been a complete ass, and I'm sorry. Please don't go."

She squeezed the handle of her suitcase tightly. "There's no reason for me to stay."

"Am I not enough of a reason?" he cried out.

Her knees started to wobble and her heart turned into putty. She dropped her bags and they hit the gravel. *Don't let him manipulate you*, she reminded herself.

The cab driver put her luggage in the trunk.

"You have some nerve to twist my heart so shamelessly," she told him, indignantly. "For a long time I've been wondering what I did wrong, thinking that you didn't want to have anything to do with me because of my past or because I wasn't exciting enough for you. And here you are on my last day asking me not to leave. I have no idea what to say."

"Say yes, you'll stay," he told her, his eyes were glued to her, afraid that if he stopped concentrating on her, she would suddenly disappear.

The driver couldn't help himself silently root for Jason. *Say yes, you stupid fool. Consider all the money he has. You'd be set for the rest of your life*, he thought biting his tongue.

"And if I said yes, what then? Will I eventually end up like Tiffany or Madison?"

"Why does everything have to be black and white with you? Life doesn't offer guarantees and happily-ever-afters. Life is unpredictable."

"Oh, I see. So what you're saying is 'Stay and let's see what happens.'"

"Exactly. That's the best offer I can give you."

Sahar took a long look at Jason and then at the overwhelming mansion. Although she also came from a rich family, she had learned to appreciate a simpler life. The Crawford lifestyle was too much for her, the hypocrisy of it all, the superficial parties, the rich wives with plastered smiles who flaunted their expensive jewels as the world struggled with a hunger crisis. Men pursued young girls and valued their careers and pricy luxuries more than their families. Worse, Sahar might end up like Madison, hanging on to an on-and-off-again relationship until Jason grew weary of her. At best, she would become a Cynthia, unhappily married and bored out of her mind. No, she deserved better than that.

"I love you Jason, but sometimes love isn't enough." Reaching in her purse and pulling out a business card and pen, she scribbled a note. "My address and phone number are on the back of this card. We can always be friends."

"What if I don't want to be your friend?"

"That would be too bad since I don't know many people out here and could use your friendship." She knew she had to leave right then and there or she would lose her courage all together and end up living in a place where there was so much waste just the way it was in her own country. The poor starved to death and lived dreadful lives while the obscenely wealthy squandered all the resources that they were blessed with.

"At least tell me why. What is it about me that is forcing you to flee?"

"It's not you, it's…"

"Don't…don't patronize me with an overused line. You owe me at least an explanation."

"I'm leaving for many reasons. One is that I'm too comfortable in your house."

"And that's a bad thing?"

"No, but when I'm there and the gates are shut, I forget all about the outside, become lazy and lose my desire to want to make a difference in a world that could use my help."

"Your help? That's an arrogant assumption, isn't it?"

"Tell me this, when was the last time you ever took a risk for yourself or for anyone for that matter?"

"What do you mean?"

"You've stayed in this house your entire life, instead of venturing outside to see how the rest of the society lives." She hated to tell him this because her intention wasn't to separate him from his family, but she thought he could be so much happier if he pursued his own dreams.

"I like it here. Everything functions just as it should, giving me ample time to focus on my work."

"Work that you don't even like. You went from college straight to working for your father without ever asking yourself what makes you happy."

"Most people would kill to have my job."

"Yes, Jason, most people would, but what good is doing a job you don't even enjoy?"

He raised his voice. "If you mean following a foolish childhood dream of making computer games, that ship has sailed."

"It's never too late to turn it around," she said, cupping his face with her hands. She kissed him gently on the lips. "Goodbye, Jason. I will always love you. Remember that no matter what happens." She left him standing by the entrance that led the way to the house he no longer had an interest to live in, as she got in the taxi and drove away.

NINETEEN

For the past month, Sahar had been working for an entertainment law firm in Pasadena. Her job was to answer phones and sort the mail. The owners, all Jewish, were polite and treated her with utmost respect. She found herself wondering why her country had been so adamant about not allowing Jews in and forbade its citizens from having any kind of contact with them.

She worked five days a week, starting at 7 a.m. and finishing at 4 p.m., when she took a bus to nearby Lacy Park, where she enjoyed strolling through the rose arbor, sitting on a bench and watching people. From there, she took a 20-minute walk to San Marino, an upscale town, where she rented a bedroom in a townhouse owned by a woman named Elham. At 79 years old, Elham, had her good and bad days. A caretaker named Millie from Alabama, stout, with dark-brown skin and black hair, came in every morning to help her bathe, clean the three-bedroom house, do grocery shopping and drive her to doctor appointments or on errands. In the afternoons she would leave, and Elham would fall into a depression from loneliness.

Elham's small townhouse, located in a serene neighborhood, had a dining and living area that looked onto a purpled-flowered jacaranda-lined street. A petite back patio offered a view of an ivy-covered wall that was shared with the building's other occupant. Sahar still remembered when she had seen the inside of Elham's home for the first time – white leather sofas and chairs covered in transparent plastic, a glass-topped dining table and an oval coffee table sitting on top of two matching tangerine-and-tan Persian carpets, and a square-shaped dimly lit kitchen.

When Sahar got home, she found Elham, taking a nap in the downstairs bedroom that was once a guestroom. She had moved downstairs when her arthritis worsened, and it was difficult for her to navigate stairs.

Upstairs, Sahar's room had two small windows that faced the street. There was a rectangular closet with a gliding mirrored door and a double bed with a pine frame. Her space wasn't as nice as the guesthouse where she used to live, nor was it as dingy as the maid's quarters where she once stayed.

Every day after work, Sahar would stick her head in the doorway and ask Elham how she was feeling.

The answer was always the same. "*Salam dokhtaram* – hello my daughter – I, the same. My arthritis, you know." Elham was from Rasht, Capital of Gilan, a province situated along the Caspian Sea in northwestern Iran. Her long hair, once blond, was now short and cotton-white, and her sparkling azure eyes had faded to powder blue.

"Can I do anything for you?" Sahar would ask. "*Na Azizam*, no my dear," Elham would answer. "Just don't get old." Her back had a hump from osteoporosis, so she wore easy-to-slip-on loose dresses, belted around her thick waist, and dark-tan support hose.

After a month of the same routine, Sahar became weary and depressed herself. Answering phones all day and coming home to an empty room became boring. She thought of her grandfather and the injustice of how she had been treated, of her father and how angry she was at him for not standing up for his family, her mother and her two sisters whom she loved and missed and her uncle who had often made her laugh.

She was so deep in thought that the loud ring of the phone sitting on top of her desk startled her. "Hello?" Sahar said, but no one responded. "Hello?" she repeated, but again, nothing. She hung up and went to grab the box Dawn had given her when she realized that she had forgotten to code it since the night she confided in Jason. Sahar opened it and noticed that some of her items were out of order and wondered if they had been jumbled during her move from the mansion to Elham's house. She pulled out a picture of her family by the pool. Her uncle had taken it on her 17th birthday in Riyadh.

The phone rang again but this time she let her machine get it. The caller didn't leave a message. She picked up another photo. It was when she was with Dawn at her new home in Riyadh. A servant had taken the photo of the two sitting in the kitchen, eating *sahruba* – vanilla cookies. They were both giddy in the picture. Dawn had her arm around Sahar's shoulder, and Sahar had leaned her head against Dawn's. Sahar was not engaged and Dawn had just moved in their new house still unexposed to the soon-to-be-inflicted cruelties by her husband.

Sahar yearned for her own home in Riyadh where she could never return. She felt ashamed that her country, which was supposed to be a model for Islamic states, was the biggest human rights violator in the world. If they couldn't get it right, how could their followers? She remembered the inhumane way her friend had been treated. Had it not been for Dawn, Sahar would have been trapped in an abyss. But what had she done for Dawn? Nothing. Nothing at all, she thought and started checking her emails to see if someone needed a document interpreted. Ever since she had signed up with an online translation company, she had received a few responses and was able to make extra cash. But today there was nothing in her box. She signed off and began surfing the net to kill time when her phone rang again.

She picked up the receiver and yelled, "Listen to me whoever you are, either speak up or stop calling me."

"It's me Zoya. Why so grumpy?"

"Sorry, Zoya. Someone has been calling me for the past few days and hanging up. How are you?"

"Oh, not so great. Thought I should check up on you and see how things are outside of the Crawford prison."

"I take it that you're not happy there."

"Mrs. Anderson is driving me nuts. We're having another one of those dinner parties and she's walking around making everyone's life miserable. Listen, I'm going to have to call you back. She's glaring at me for using my cell phone. Bye."

Sahar went back to playing on her laptop – the one that Jason told her she could keep when he had it messengered over to her place. She wondered what he was doing at that very moment. He had always been on her mind, no matter how hard she tried to forget him. By now he probably had a new girlfriend. She hadn't heard from him since she left his house. He must have moved on, but why couldn't she? *I must stop thinking about him,* she thought, and began searching various charities to distract herself. Maybe if she filled up her extra time with helping others, she wouldn't have the time to dwell on him.

Her phone rang again. It was Zoya.

"Won't you get into trouble for calling me again?"

"No, the Old Crab couldn't fire me even if she wanted to. We're short of help. Besides, now she's too busy yelling at the new girl," Zoya replied, smoking a cigarette behind the gymnasium, out of Mrs. Anderson's view.

"I can never understand why the Crawfords don't replace her with someone nice. If they get rid of her, then maybe the help would actually stay instead of quitting every month," Sahar said, checking out a charity that delivered meals to the elderly.

"You're probably right but now with Jason gone, I doubt that there's anyone left in this house with enough sense to fire her."

"Jason's gone?" Sahar asked, moving away from her desk and sitting on her bed to give Zoya her full attention.

"Oh yeah, I forgot to tell you," she said, tapping her cigarette ashes to the ground, "He doesn't work for his father anymore. He took Fred with him and left."

"Fred's gone too?" She should have made an effort to keep in touch with him. "Did he say where he was going?" she asked, wanting to see him.

"Oh yes, he said he preferred working for Jason more than anyone else. So, wherever Jason is living at the moment, I suppose that's where Fred is."

"What was Jason's reason for leaving?"

"I heard him get into a heated argument with his father over a client and decided he wanted to go his own way," she answered, blowing smoke into the air.

"Do you remember the name of the client?"

"Who....something. He had an odd name."

"Husam?"

"Yes, that's it. You know him?" she asked with curiosity.

"Remember that man who was going to force me to go to his hotel that night when you rescued me?"

"That's him?"

"I'm afraid so. Did you hear any part of their argument?"

"Apparently, Jason found out that this Husam was into illegal dealings. I really couldn't understand all of the conversation. Something about him funding camel races and trafficking children into Saudi Arabia. Although I don't know what one has to do with the other."

"That dirty son of a..." she bit her lip. "Did you happen to find out what Jason was going to do after leaving his father?"

"That I don't know. I haven't heard or talked to him for a month now."

What Sahar didn't know was that Jason was now living in a home in pristine Madison Heights, in Pasadena, a 15-minute drive from where she lived.

"Well, I am happy for him. He had every right to quit."

"You still love him, don't you?"

Sahar didn't answer.

"I can tell, you know," she said, walking back toward the house, "It's in your voice whenever you speak of him."

"What I feel for him isn't important. He and I can never be," she replied, getting up to turn up the air conditioner. Pasadena was always scorching hot in summer.

"I suppose you're right. He does have fancy friends and you and me, we're just...."

"We're just what? Inferior because we don't have money?"

"You know how it is with rich folks," she said.

"Listen to me, Material things come and go. It's education and knowledge that will always stay. I told you once before, you should get out of that house and make a life for yourself."

"I'm trying. After you left, I signed up for a beginning class at court reporting school. I was told once I graduate, I can make good money and work decent hours."

"That's wonderful. I can't tell you how proud of you I am," she said, both happy and envious of her friend. She still was looking for that right job.

Zoya glanced at her watch. "Well, I'd better go. My break is over."

"Thanks for calling."

"Let's get together soon. I'll call you."

Inspired to do something that would make her happy, Sahar began surfing the internet again until she found the name of an abused women and children's shelter and decided to call it. It was Solution Women and Children's Center. She may not be able to save the world or have the power to change her country but she could at least reach out to the community around her.

A few days later, Sahar showed up at the shelter's volunteer orientation meeting and then was interviewed by one of the administrators.

"I am interested in volunteer work in the evenings and on weekends," she told the interviewer, a middle-age African American woman who sat on the opposite of her dented work desk, looking over Sahar's résumé.

"Do you have a psychology or counseling background?"

"No."

"Have you ever worked at a suicide hotline?"

"No, but I'm very good with working with people."

"Would you be interested in working the phones? You will be making cold calls to a list of prospects in order to raise funds."

Sahar thought about it for a moment and said, "I'd rather be working with the women and children in person."

"I'm sorry, but you don't have necessary credentials. You would need counseling experience or formal education."

"I'm educated. I have a degree."

"Yes, but your degree was in pre-law," the woman said, removing her glasses and rubbing her eyes. The administrator fell into silence as she sat back in her chair and tapped her pen on her desk.

"Please? You see, my friend who died recently had an abusive husband and...and...." A lumped formed in her throat and she couldn't talk.

The interviewer, who felt her pain, glanced over her résumé again and said, "I see that you are fluent in Spanish."

"I am. I once worked as a translator."

The interviewer scratched her head. "Maybe I can place you in the legal advocacy department. Many Hispanic women suffer from abuse. The problem is they often don't speak English and we have a hard time communicating with them."

"What would be my duties?" Sahar asked.

"You would go through a training program to learn how to deal with issues related to law enforcement and the judiciary including orders of protection, court support and advocacy. I hope you're a quick learner."

"Oh I am. I am. Thank you. Thanks a million."

"You don't have the job yet. We have to do a background check and get back to you."

"Background check?" she asked nervously.

"Yes. Is there a problem?" she looked at her inquisitively.

"No. No problem. I just thought that since this is volunteer work..."

"We are very careful about whom we hire. You will hear from us within two weeks."

Three weeks later, Sahar began her training and soon after began volunteering twice a week at the shelter after work. Her job was to provide information to participants to obtain an injunction for protection, supplying attorney referrals, giving emotional support to participants, and administrative duties such as helping women fill out legal forms, mailing newsletters and filing.

TWENTY

Jason changed into a cream Polo shirt and brown pants in the upstairs bedroom while Fred prepared his breakfast downstairs. It had been two months since he left his parents' mansion and moved to the swanky Madison Heights neighborhood of Pasadena. His home made of glass and concrete exterior, had a vaulted ceiling with open beams, black marble floors and a pewter staircase that swirled up to a semicircular bookshelf and Jason's bedroom with a wraparound balcony overlooking the peach, plum and pomegranate trees adorning his yard and the magnolia-lined street. Downstairs was Fred's room, the living and dining area and a breakfast bar with stainless steel appliances.

The buzzer on his intercom went off. "Breakfast is ready sir," Fred announced.

"Thanks Fred. Be right down," he replied, slipping on his mocha canvas shoes.

Not caring much for the rest of the Crawfords, Fred had volunteered to live with Jason. He kept house for him, cooked, watered the plants and the quaint garden, took clothes to the cleaners, marketed and ran errands on a daily basis. Fred actually had the house all to himself for most of the day because Jason was always working. When he came home, he ate, watched a little TV and went to sleep. It was the perfect arrangement for the both of them.

Jason went downstairs, greeted Fred and sat at the breakfast bar, eating his goat-cheese omelet and croissant and reading the morning paper. His home, decorated with minimalist furniture, had a Sputnik scone-shaped chandelier, plain rectangular walnut dining and coffee tables and a Philippe Starck-designed yellow sofa.

Fred started to walk outside to cut some rosemary from the garden for dinner when Jason stopped him.

"Fred?"

"Yes sir?"

"Could you buy some doughnuts for tomorrow's breakfast? I'm suddenly in the mood for some jelly doughnuts."

Fred looked at him perplexed. Since when did his boss eat doughnuts? "Certainly sir. Is there anything else you would like?"

"Yes. I would like for you to start calling me Jason," he replied, drinking his freshly squeezed orange juice."

"Sir?" he looked at him with wide eyes.

"We're no longer at my parents' home and I see no need for formalities here. We're simply two bachelors living in the same home."

"Forgive me sir, but I don't feel comfortable calling you by your first name."

Jason chuckled. Fred was old school and he knew he couldn't change him overnight. "Very well, then. If you're ever in the mood to call me by my Christian name, please feel free to do so. I will not be offended."

"Thank you, sir. I will take that into consideration."

When finished with his meal, Jason left for work. His new firm, C&M games, a computer games and virtual reality company was in a 10-story green-tiled building in Studio city, about a 10-minute drive from Universal Studios and 30 from where he lived. He sold his Zermatt chalet to fund the company for the next two years. After the fallout with his father, he contacted George and asked him if he was still interested in forming a partnership. George was now married to Ladan, and was living in their condo in downtown Los Angeles.

"I don't know, buddy. Ladan and I are still looking into buying a house and starting a family," he answered nervously, rubbing his top lip. "I'm too afraid to take the risk."

"Then don't quit your job. I run the place during the day and you can come in and help out after work and weekends until it takes off. Then you can quit."

Jason's startup company made video games as simple as ones for DVD and as complicated as virtual reality games using headsets, handheld wands, joysticks and data gloves that allowed users to navigate through a virtual three-dimensional computer-generated environment. He soon planned to expand and add real world environments for educational purposes.

"But you haven't written a single program for the past 14 years. How're you going to manage?"

"Don't worry about me. I have hired a husband-and-wife team who graduated at the top of their class from the engineering and computer science department of UC San Diego. I'm paying them a good salary and a share of the profit in exchange for their expertise. If they're as good as they say they are, we can make them our partners and expand the firm."

"I have to talk to Ladan about this. She handles all of our finances."

"Do that and get back to me," Jason told him.

A few days later, Ladan agreed to the arrangement. She got the job she wanted, teaching chemistry and physics at the USC, and wanted her husband to have his own company, recognizing that it had always been his dream. She knew Jason and followed his progress as his reputation and business savvy made headlines. It was only a matter of time that C&M would thrive.

"Okay buddy, I'm in. I will keep my current job and will drop by after work and on weekends to help out," George said.

Jason was in charge of managing the day-to-day activity of the firm, George was the head of production, overseeing the programs and testing for glitches and two senior software student volunteers helped the husband-and-wife team. Everything had happened so fast, Jason thought as he reached his office and his petite Hispanic assistant in a black and gray dress greeted him.

"And how are you this fine morning?" Jason smiled, looking happy. Unlike a few months ago when he dreaded managing the Crawford enterprises, he actually looked forward to going to work everyday.

Jason had leased a furnished four-room executive suite on the building's first floor. The entrance had a reception area with comfortable leather chairs, contemporary art and a glass coffee table that rested on a light gray carpet. There was a conference room that seated eight people, two rooms with oak bookshelves and desks and one large virtual lab equipped with devices such as computers, a big screen, head mounts, cyber gloves, shutter glasses that looked like dark goggles, motion tracking device, video and sound projector.

"I'm doing well, thank you for asking," she said, handing him a message from Alex, about a progress report on Dawn. Jason hadn't told Alex about Sahar's real name and her nationality.

He went into his office, closed the door behind him and dialed Alex.

"Good morning Alex, this is Jason returning your call," he said, relaxing in his chair, pulling out some paperwork from his briefcase and turning on his PC.

"You'd never guess who dropped in at the shelter where I volunteer," Alex announced, sitting behind her desk, emailing a client.

"Dawn? Dawn's working there now?" Ever since she left, his life felt completely empty. He dated to keep up appearances at parties and society functions, but he never took a girl home with him. After Sahar, he felt nothing toward any of them and no matter how beautiful or successful his dates were, he only had eyes for one girl.

"No, she still has her receptionist job but she's volunteering at a shelter twice a week. Dawn's quite nice, you know."

"You're not supposed to talk to her. Suppose she finds out who you are?"

"Relax. I didn't speak to her personally. I overheard people talking about how helpful she was. She brings toys for the children and gives hope to women who walk in."

"Is she seeing anyone?" He wanted to see Sahar for some time but decided against it. Commitment petrified him and yet he had a hard time letting her go. Sahar wanted a guarantee that he would be by her side forever and he wasn't sure if he could do that. So, he remained in limbo, keeping busy and trying not to think about her until each time Alex updated him with a progress report.

"No, she's not with anyone."

"Keep an eye on her and make sure she stays safe." He still had Sahar followed for two reasons. First, he wanted to make sure she had told him everything about herself and wasn't holding out on him. Second, he was afraid for her, especially since she lied to the U.S. government. He was scared of what they would do to her if they ever found out.

"No, problem," Alex said.

TWENTY-ONE

Sahar's work at the shelter was rewarding. She helped file complaints against abusive husbands and referred women to lawyers who did pro bono work. She also took training workshops about domestic violence and sexual assault offered by the shelter to broaden her knowledge. At nights, she would pull out her friend's picture and speak to her about her progress. "I wish there were a way for you to see it all. I wish you would know that the sacrifice you made was not a waste and, most of all, I wish you were right here by my side."

Then one day, on a cool, October afternoon after work when she wasn't volunteering, she got home early and found Elham crying.

"Are you okay?" Sahar asked, sticking her head in the doorway of her bedroom.

"*Salam dokhtaram* — I'm not so good today," she told her, embarrassed.

"Where is Millie? Why didn't she take you to the doctor?" Sahar asked with a concerned look.

"I am not sick. I am sad."

"You want to talk about it?" That was all she needed to ask, because Elham then poured her heart out.

"I have no family to love me. Nobody loves me."

Elham had been living in the U.S. for 11 years and lost her husband three years ago to a heart attack. Back in Iran, they had a successful tile-and-window installation business. Long before retiring and coming to America, her husband had invested his savings in bonds, precious metals and petroleum. So Elham had plenty of money and the only reason she rented out the room in her house was that she was afraid to be alone at night.

"I like you," Sahar said, thinking how pretty she must have looked when she was younger. She had large beautiful eyes, long lashes and high cheekbones.

"I like you too, but you always busy and I no want to bother you."

Elham had friends, nieces, nephews and two sisters-in-law, who all were superficial. They used to visit her when she threw big parties in restaurants and was in good health but when she became ill, no one bothered coming by and her circle of friends slowly diminished. Now they were all waiting for her to die to see how much they would each inherit.

"It's no bother." Sahar smiled.

"Do you know how to play *Passoor*?"

Sahar shook her head no.

"It's Iranian game. Very easy. I show you," she said, pulling out a deck of cards.

Sahar sat on Elham's bed as she handed her four cards, took four for herself and dropped four to the floor.

"You drop one card and if your card and the ones already on the floor add to eleven, you pick them up. All the faces pick a matching face."

"What if my card doesn't add up to eleven?"

"Then you leave it on floor and my turn to play."

"Okay, let's do it," she said enthusiastically. She brought out a five and picked up a six.

In Saudi Arabia gambling was forbidden and considered satanic, even when one wasn't playing for money but Sahar didn't care. She was tired of all the dos and don'ts. She just wanted to break the rules and experience life.

"Very good," Elham said and used her king to pick up another king.

"You know, I remember everything. Like picture in here," she said tapping her finger on her temple.

"I wish I had a photographic memory," Sahar said, dropping a card to the ground.

"Sometimes. Not good."

"Why? It's a gift."

"Sometimes better to forget," she nodded, recalling how her husband died in her arms at the hospital, the scent of his skin, his gray unshaven face, the smell of alcohol the nurse used to wipe his skin before inserting the I.V. in his arm and the unbearable odor of disinfectant used to clean the floors. "Yes, sometimes better to forget."

"I know what you mean," Sahar replied with empathy. She too had a vivid memory of her past, which, at times, she wished she could forget.

Elham dropped a jack on the floor and picked up all the cards except the faces.

Soon Sahar realized that the rules of the game were more complicated than what she anticipated as Elham beat her at two hands.

"Elham?" Sahar said, writing down the score on a sheet of paper.

"*Baleh, azizam* – yes dear?"

"Have you ever considered doing volunteer work?"

"My arthritis, you know."

"I have a perfect job for you at the shelter, if you're interested. You never really have to stand on your feet and your housekeeper can drop you off there and pick you up later."

"What I do?" she asked, both excited and afraid to try something new.

"All you have to do is stuff envelopes and address newsletters. You can also sit behind the register at their thrift shop. That way you get to meet people."

"No, not good," she suddenly blurted, too nervous to meet new people.

"You can always quit if you don't like it. I'm not sure if they need anymore volunteers, but I can put in a good word for you."

"I think. Okay?"

"No, no thinking. The best thing is sometimes to just jump in and get your feet wet."

Elham chewed the inside of her mouth for a moment, nodded her head from side to side and said, "I try one time."

"I'll call them right now," Sahar offered and called immediately to see if there was anything available.

Thanks to Sahar's help, Elham became a volunteer, worked three days a week and forgot all about her arthritis and loneliness while at the shelter. Millie, too, was grateful to Sahar, because Elham's mood lifted and now she didn't have to listen to her complain all day and could accomplish more around the house.

"I feel good today. I want to make you tea," Elham told Sahar one afternoon.

"Are you sure? I don't mind...."

"Sit, sit," Elham said, pointing at her bed.

Sahar did as she requested as she shuffled through the gossip magazines lying on her bed. She looked at the cover of the first one, then a second and third to see which looked more interesting but when she got to the *Pasadena Society Pages*, her face froze. There he was, handsome as ever, in a tux, with his hand around the waist of a beautiful model. The headline read: "Jason Crawford III and Isabella da Pontedera." The caption read: "Da Pontedera, a sought-after model in Europe and America was a man's dream and a woman's nightmare." Sahar dropped the paper on the bed and ran upstairs.

"Where you going?" Elham asked, "I thought we play *Passoor*."

"I'm sorry, but I don't feel very well," was all she could manage to say as she went to her room and shut the door.

Baffled, Elham stood at the bottom of the stairs with her jaw open and a teapot in her hand. She had never seen Sahar so distraught. What could have possibly upset her so, she thought as she went back to the kitchen, grabbing Sahar's cup, which Jason had given her in Zermatt, and poured tea in it. Elham decided to go to her bedroom to see what triggered the girl's bizarre reaction when she spotted the *Pasadena Society Pages*. There was a photo of a handsome man with a tall young blond on the cover and underneath was a page number. She turned to the page, put on her glasses and read the article. It talked about how Jason Crawford had recently opened up his new company, C&M Games, with his friend George Maloney. Elham recalled Sahar's apartment application and the name Crawford Enterprises, the company where she once worked. She flipped back from the article to the cover and looked at Jason's picture once again and was able to put two and two together. "Oh dear," she sighed, heading upstairs slowly and with difficulty. She knocked on Sahar's closed door.

"*Ebtaed anny*," she blurted by accident the way she used to order Rubilyn to go away.

"I don't understand."

"Please, go away."

But Elham was Iranian and in her culture, people never went away. They were a nosy lot who didn't understand the words, "I need my space." Such words simply didn't exist. Everyone was in each other's business for better or worse. Elham opened the door and went in only to find her tenant on her bed, turned on her belly and crying her heart out.

"*Dokhtarm*," she said, moving toward her to caress her hair, "The man in the photo, who is he?"

"I don't want to talk about it."

"You and he were lovers? No?" It had to be, thought Elham. Why else would Dawn suddenly be in such a foul mood?

Sahar lifted her head and said, "You know, it's terrible of you to butt into my personal life."

She then buried her face in the covers.

"He not worth your tears."

"What do you know?" She let out a loud cry.

"I was young too. I had heartbreaks," she said, remembering her boyfriend who married her sister, and her second boyfriend who spent her money like there was no tomorrow. "Man I love marry my sister. Then, I love another man who only want my money."

"That's terrible," she said, turning to her side, sniffling.

"If I marry, I lose everything. He spent money, money, money."

"So, what did you do?"

"I married a good man. No children. I try but no. It was only us. He died three years. God bless him," she said, folding a sweater that was on Sahar's bed.

"I'm sorry. How come you don't have any pictures of him around?" she asked, forgetting about her own problems.

"Too, too much pain. No want to see. I lonely sometimes. I miss him...Hey Baba," she sighed and looked out at the dark blue sky, the stars glinting down at her.

"I miss Jason all the time."

"You call him. Talk to him," she suggested. "One time, I very angry. I fight my husband. No speak six weeks. Now, I sorry. Too much time I be angry with him. Now he gone and me sorry. You call him."

"No, I don't belong in his world," Sahar said, recalling all his beautiful, sophisticated dates.

"You're like the girl in picture. Better." Elham encouraged her.

"You think so? She's flawless," she replied wishing that she were as pretty as the girl on the cover.

"Perfect is boring. You look, you look, nothing wrong...eh...flaws are good. Never cry for man who doesn't love you."

"What about unconditional love?" she asked, hanging on her every word.

"Na, no such thing. Always condition attached. You should get someone, too."

"I don't want to go to bed with different men every night."

"Not what I said. You date. You have dinner, have fun, he bring you home, say goodnight."

Sahar burst into laughter.

"Why you laugh at me?" she asked, offended that she was making fun of her.

"Which planet are you from? Date a man a few times and he expects more."

"I don't understand this new generation. Always hurry about everything." She frowned.

"There's something you should know about me," Sahar said, wanting to confide in her about her past. Her gut feeling told her that she could trust this woman. She reminded Sahar so much of

Rubilyn – her kind heart, the way she wanted to make everything better and how she always wanted to feed her.

"You make baby with this man?" she asked, thinking maybe she was pregnant and that's why she was so sad.

"Nothing like that. But I want you to know the truth about me."

Elham nodded and Sahar began telling her story about Dawn, her abusive husband and her friend's horrifying death. She talked about her family, her forced marriage to Husam, her dangerous escape from Riyadh and her relationship with Jason.

"*Hey khodayehman…hey khodayehman,*" – my God…my God, Elham said after Sahar finished explaining. "Very hard. Very hard." She put one hand to her face as she bit her lip and shook her head from side to side.

"I miss my family but can never go back. You're my family now. You, Zoya and Fred, except I haven't seen Fred since I left the Crawfords."

"You don't look Arab," she said studying Sahar's features.

"I do when my hair isn't dyed and I remove my contacts," she said and fell into silence for a long moment before she blurted, "Do you hate me?"

"Hate you?" Elham asked with surprise "Why?"

"You know, I'm a Sunni and you a Shiite."

"Governments, politicians and religious men make everybody fight. They want war and money, money, money. Me, you, people working, we don't care. Sunni, Shiite, all same."

"That's too bad, isn't it? I mean all my life, I've been taught that we're the superior race and here I am finding out that on the outside no one cares."

"My country, before revolution, everybody friends. Many jobs, many people – Christians, Jews, Muslims. French schools. American schools. People celebrate Eid Noruz, Christmas, Rosh Hashanah."

"In my country, no one has ever been allowed to practice anything but the Muslim religion. Christians sometimes practice Christianity in their homes, but if caught, they'll get punished by the *mutawan*. They're not even allowed to wear a cross."

"I know. Your country very conservative. I was afraid to travel to your country. An Iranian husband and wife walk on the streets in Riyadh, hold hands, arrested."

"I'm not surprised. Women and men are not allowed to touch in public. Even when they're married," Sahar said, getting off her bed. "I feel better now. You mind if we go downstairs?"

"Okay," Elham replied as the two headed down.

"You know, I've been meaning to ask you, the white van parked outside of your house. Do you know who it belongs to?" Sahar inquired.

"Many week, I ask my neighbors. They say no have van. I said to police many times about van. When they come, van gone." A week later, she complained to the police and filled out a report but nothing came of it.

"Did you happen to get the license plate number?"

"No. No plate."

"No license plate?" Sahar asked in surprise.

"Nothing."

"It's been there at all hours of the day for the past week."

"I call police right now," Elham offered but as soon as she called them, the van was gone. "Let's have *faloudeh* instead of tea," Elham recommended.

"What's that?"

"It's an Iranian sorbet," she explained, spooning it into two cups.

They went to Elham's room to eat but as soon as they sat down, two police officers showed up at the door and rang the bell.

"That's probably the police. I'm really not comfortable having a run-in with them," Sahar whispered.

"Go upstairs. I talk to them," Elham said, going to open the door.

"Oh good, you're here," she told the police.

"You reported a white van parked outside of your house for weeks but we couldn't find it," one of the two officers told her as they stood in the doorway.

"There was but they left."

"Did you happen to get the license number?" a tall broad-shouldered officer asked.

"No."

"Year, model?" his female partner asked.

"I don't know cars. It looked…you know…a white van," Elham replied.

"Did it have any labels on it like the cleaners, food delivery or something like that?"

"No, no labels."

"There's really not much we can do unless you can give us more information," she said.

"Sorry, I don't know more."

"Here's my card," the female officer said. "Call me if they come back. You have a nice day ma'am."

When they left, she locked the door and Sahar came back down as the two sat on Elham's bed.

"What did they say?"

"They can do nothing. Van left."

"Don't you think it strange that as soon as you call the police, the car disappears?"

"Yes but don't worry. I live here 10 years and no problem. *Khodah bozorgeh* – God is great," she declared, raising both hands up toward the sky.

"Yes, God is great but I don't understand how that's going to help us," Sahar said, impatiently.

"I mean God protects us."

"Really, Elham. You sound just like the people from my country."

"God protects the innocent."

"Truly? You believe that?"

"Yes, truly."

"Then tell me this," Sahar said, frowning, "where is God when women get flogged and decapitated for having sex with unrelated men? Where is God when prisoners are tortured until they confess to crimes they never committed? Where is God when the *mutawan* let 15 girls burn in fire because they were not clothed properly?"

"They did that?" Elham asked with a shocked expression on her face.

"On March 11, 2002," Sahar said, still remembering that date clearly in her head, "a fire broke out due to an electrical shortage at a school in Mecca. Firemen confronted the *mutawan* in order to rescue 15 girls but they wouldn't let the girls come out because they didn't have their *abayas* and veils. When the girls tried to push their way through, the *mutawan* beat them and pushed them back. All 15 were burned to death because they were not dressed properly. One of the girls was a friend of my sister's. Where was God then? Hmmm?" Sahar asked.

"I feel very bad for them."

"I feel bad, too. I feel bad that this hair, face and body I was born with are considered a menace to the willpower of the opposite sex. I feel bad to have lived in a world where women's rights are nonexistent. I feel bad for so many things that I can do nothing about," she said, going to the bathroom to splash water on her face.

Minutes later, she came out and said, "Elham, let's play *Passoor*. As Jason once said to me – 'Live in the present.' All I have is right here, right now. You, me, our friendship and a deck of cards."

"Okay. We play. Maybe I let you win," she smiled and started dealing.

TWENTY-TWO

One evening, a few days after the police had dropped by, Elham was in her room watching television and Sahar, upstairs in her terrycloth pajamas, was writing a letter in her journal.

My dear Dawn,
Life in Los Angeles has been most interesting. I volunteer at a women's shelter and have also started this Web site about oppression of women in Saudi Arabia. I'm trying to start a petition, asking California's senators to initiate a bill that would put sanctions against a country that mistreats women so abominably. Five people have signed the petition so far. I know, what you're thinking – that I'm a fool to think things will ever change – but it's a start. Next month, I'm setting up a table in front of a grocery store in Pasadena so that I can collect more signatures and make people aware of women's plight in that ...

"FBI, open up," Sahar heard banging from downstairs and hid her journal in-between her mattress. She hurried down with light footsteps to look through the peephole. "Oh my God," she whispered and ran to Elham's room.

Elham, hard of hearing, said, "What's the matter?"

"There are two men outside claiming they're the FBI."

"Maybe they ask about the white van." The van had vanished after the police had shown up at Elham's door four days ago.

"No, they look Middle Eastern. They may be after me," she said, shaking from fear.

Elham picked up the phone to call the police but her line was dead.

"I have ladder," Elham said, going through her closet, "You go up and jump over wall."

"No. I cannot leave here without you."

"You are young, you can jump. I can't."

"I am not leaving here without you. You don't know these people. If I escape, they will torture you to get answers. Stay in your bedroom and lock your door."

"You stay here too."

"No. I have to go. I have to do the right thing and face my fate. Please, lock your door and don't come out until they have taken me."

Outside, two men with fake badges, looked at each other, nodded their heads in a cool manner and pulled on ski masks. One shot the lock with a silencer and burst into the house.

Elham peered out of her bedroom, worried about Sahar.

Sahar stood in front of Elham, frightened. "Please don't hurt her. I will go with you. Just don't hurt her."

One of the men grabbed Sahar and put a handkerchief laced with chloroform over her mouth. The other man went after Elham, who started screaming, but he shut her up quickly by slapping her. She hit her head against her dining room table and fell to the floor. He anesthetized her so that she wouldn't get up for a long time and checked the rest of the house to see if anyone else was home. He took Sahar's laptop and purse. Luckily, he didn't find her diary or the box where she kept her letters and photos, several passports, IDs, credit cards and cash. Sahar usually kept those in her hamper with dirty laundry tossed over it. The other man surveyed the outside, making certain there was no one on the street.

Parked in Elham's driveway, a chauffeur of a black Mercedes popped open the trunk as his accomplices dragged Sahar's body out and dumped it inside. Then they got into the car and drove away.

Hours later, Elham woke up groggy, not knowing where she was. She lay in a white room on a bed covered with white sheets. One of her fingers was inserted in an apparatus and connected with wires to a machine that tracked her pulse. She opened and closed her eyes several times, her vision still blurry, and then it all came back to her – the men bursting in and grabbing her and Sahar.

A man with dark skin and crew-cut sable hair, seated on a chair, stood up and approached her. He had been waiting impatiently for the past hour for her to wake up.

Elham yelled, "No. No, please don't hurt me." She had a bruise on her cheek and a bump on her head.

"Please. I'm not going to hurt you. You're at Huntington Memorial hospital. I'm Detective Johnson with the Pasadena police, he said, showing his badge. Your neighbor called us. She said she heard someone screaming at your residence."

Fifteen minutes after the kidnappers were gone, the police had shown up and found Elham passed out on the floor. They called the paramedics who transported her to a nearby hospital for observation.

"I screamed. They took her. They took her."

"Who did they take?" he asked, pulling out a note pad and pen from his pocket.

"Sah...Dawn. They kidnapped my tenant, Dawn."

"Last name?" he asked and jotted down her name.

"Parnell."

"What is your name?"

"Elham Moulook."

"Will you spell that out for me please?"

Elham did as he requested.

"Do you remember what the men looked like?"

"Big. Muscular."

"What did he look like?"

"Who?"

"The man who attacked you."

"I don't know. He had mask."

"What kind of mask? Pantyhose over his head? A face mask?"

Elham shook her head no. "A black mask."

"A ski mask?"

"Yes. A ski mask."

A nurse came in to check up on Elham. She asked her how she was feeling and if she wanted anything. Elham asked for water.

"Anything else?"

"No. Nothing," she shook her head, disappointed that she couldn't remember anything.

"Did they speak? Have a deep voice? An accent perhaps?"

She put her finger to her mouth and tapped it on her lip.

"What is it?" the detective asked.

"Nothing...well, before come in, Dawn looked in hole...you know small hole in door."

"A peephole?"

"Yes. That. Peephole. Dawn said men looked from Middle East. They break lock. Come in. They don't speak. They put towel like this on Dawn," she said, putting her hand over her mouth, "then I scream. They hit me. Then...I remember nothing."

"Can you describe Dawn?"

"Nice girl. Quiet. Tall, Red hair, dark blue eyes."

"You have a picture of her at home?" the detective asked her.

"No. No, picture."

"Does she have any family? Friends?"

"I don't know. We no talk much," Elham lied. She was scared to give out any more details and give away Sahar's identity.

"Okay. You rest up. I will run a check on your tenant to see why someone is after her."

"I am scared."

"Don't be. If they wanted to harm you, they would have done it last night. It is not you they want."

"No. I am scared for Dawn."

"We will do everything we can to find her."

"I want to go home now. I want to go home," she said, hating her surroundings. The last time she had been to a hospital was three years ago when her husband died.

"You should rest here until tomorrow."

She started feeling anxious. "My door. They broke the lock."

"There is an officer set up outside of your house. He'll stay there until you return tomorrow. Do you have any relatives you want me to call?"

She thought of her nieces, nephews and two in-laws but didn't want to get in touch with them. They were like leeches, waiting for her to die. "No. I have no family."

When the detective and nurse left, Elham reached for the phone and called Millie, her caretaker. She explained all that had happened in the past several hours and asked her to pick her up from the hospital in the morning. She then pressed a button and her bed started shifting forward until she was sitting upright. She turned on the TV. Jay Leno was on, making fun of the economy and gas prices. Her mind drifted as she thought about how she could help find Sahar. She remembered Jason Crawford. Sahar had told Elham that she and Jason were the only two people she had confided in. She had to call him and seek his help, but where would she find his phone number? Elham recalled the name of his company – C&M Games – and dialed the operator.

"Excuse me sir, there was a very strange message on our machine when I got in this morning," Jason's young secretary told him the day following Sahar's disappearance.

"What was it?" he asked, curiously.

"A woman with a thick accent going on about someone named Dawn being kidnapped. She left her name and two phone numbers." She handed him a pink Post-it.

Jason took the note calmly, looked at it and said, "It's probably a crazy person with nothing better to do." He crumpled the paper and tossed it into the trash.

"I thought so as well." His secretary returned to her desk.

Jason dug into his trash, picked up the note and called Elham, but he was told that she had already checked out of the hospital. He tried her home but the line kept on ringing and no one picked up. He called Alex at her office.

Alex had been checking up on Sahar twice a week, making sure that she was alright. Last night, she had been working on another client's case and hadn't slept a wink. She was about to go home when her phone rang.

"What the hell am I paying you for?" Jason hollered.

"What're you talking about?" She yawned, rubbing her gray eyes that could barely stay open.

"Dawn has been kidnapped. You were supposed to keep an eye on her."

"What! I've been following her around for a long time now and haven't seen anything out of the ordinary. She goes to work, stops at the shelter and spends time with her landlord."

"Where were you last night at 10?"

"Working on a case. I checked on Dawn yesterday. Everything seemed to be fine. The white van was nowhere in sight and...."

"What white van?"

"There was a car always parked on the street but they stopped parking there and never came back," she said, pouring herself a cup of last night's coffee to keep awake.

"Did you happen to run a check on the car?"

"I couldn't. There was no license plate, but I did follow them once to a house in North Pasadena. I found out that it belonged to a doctor who rented it out to a businessman."

"And?" he asked, pacing his office.

"There was nothing out of the ordinary. I took pictures of three men getting out of the van and had the police run a check on them but nothing negative came up."

"If anything happens to her, I'll make sure you never get another job, you hear me?" Jason had been living in limbo, not wanting to make a commitment and not quite ready to let Sahar go, but the thought of losing her forever was the wakeup call he needed.

"Hold your horses and your threats. I'll find her, but you need to stop lying to me and tell me the truth about her."

Jason cleared his throat. "I'm not sure what you mean." Sahar had made him promise not to tell her story to anyone.

"Come off it, will you? I've been at this job for too long to know when something stinks." When she heard nothing, she added, "Look, if you want my help, you'd better start singing."

Jason then told Alex everything he knew about Sahar.

"What have you gotten me into? No wonder you have been paying me without questioning the bills."

"Please, I need your help," he begged, putting one hand through his hair and squinting outside at the muddy-looking air.

Alex heard the desperation in Jason's voice and felt sorry for him. But it wasn't just that. She was also worried about what would happen to Sahar if she didn't help her out. "Okay, I'll stay on it but before I go, is there anything else I should know?"

"I received a call from Elham about Sahar being kidnapped. I tried calling her, but there was no answer."

"What's her number?" Alex asked, grabbing a pen and paper.

"I have two numbers here, but the first number isn't any good. I was told that she already checked out of the hospital. Poor woman. They must have hurt her," he said, giving Alex the second number. "Don't forget to call me as soon as you know anything."

"Ya, ya," she said, hanging up and dialing a college friend of hers who now worked for the FBI. Alex emailed her the photos of the three men she had on file but again, nothing turned up.

She called Elham but no one was picking up. Alex called the phone company to have the line checked and they told her that the line was out of order. She decided to drive out to Elham's house, hoping that she would find her there.

Twenty minutes later when she arrived, she found a locksmith working on the door.

"You have a visitor," he said to Millie, who came to the door.

"Who are you?'" Millie put her hands on her waist and glared at Alex. Ever since she found out what had happened to Elham, she was very protective of her.

"My name is Alex Rosenberg. I'm a detective and would like to talk to Elham."

"Have an I.D. on you?" she asked looking her up and down, checking out her red stiletto heels, black leather pants and white cotton sweater.

Alex reached in her pocket, pulled out her detective's license from her wallet and showed it to her.

"A P.I.? Shoo…she's not up to answering anymore questions," she replied with her Alabama accent. "She already talked to a detective last night and this morning she was questioned by two police officers."

"But…."

"I say, you'd best get going."

"Just tell her that I work for Jason Crawford."

"Who is at the door, Millie?" Elham asked as she got off the sofa shuffling toward the door in her sheepskin slippers and floral housedress.

"Some lady named Alex claiming to be a detective working for some guy named Jason Connelly."

"Crawford. Jason Crawford," Alex repeated.

"Let her in," Elham said when she heard his name.

"C'mon in," Millie said to Alex. "Sorry about my manners but you can't be sure of anyone these days."

"No problem," Alex smiled, getting a kick out of Millie's feisty personality.

"Please sit." Elham pointed at a chair.

Alex noticed her bruised cheek and felt bad for her. "Did you know your phone isn't working?" she said, sitting down on the cushy seat as her pants stuck to the transparent plastic covering.

"Telephone company come today to fix. They say wait all day."

"Yep, that's the phone company for you. Can you describe to me what happened last night?"

Elham explained everything in detail. When she was finished, Alex got up and looked around the downstairs area. "Was anything missing?"

"No." Elham shook her head.

"Where is Dawn's room?" Alex asked, uncertain if Millie knew who Dawn really was.

"Upstairs to the right," Millie said.

"May I?" Alex asked, pointing toward the stairs.

"Go ahead, but you ain't gonna find anything," Millie replied. "The girl's room is clean as a whistle.

Alex checked Sahar's room. She found a pen on her bed and wondered what Sahar was doing before the kidnappers had arrived. There was a printer on her desk but no computer. How odd, she thought, looking under her bed, in her closet and the bathroom. The girl didn't own much.

"Did she have a purse?" Alex asked Elham when she went downstairs.

"Large navy one. Everyday, she put over shoulder when come home."

"What about a PC?"

"No understand."

"You know, a computer."

"Yes, small, like this," Elham showed her with her hands.

"A laptop?"

"Yes. That."

"They're both missing," Alex said, reaching in her wallet and pulling out a business card and minuscule pen. She wrote on the back of the card and gave it to Elham. "My cell and office phones are on the front, and I jotted down my home number on the back. If you can remember anything else or need to get in touch with me, you can call me 24/7. Keep your doors locked, and don't let anyone come in."

"She be okay?"

"I am not sure."

Elham looked at her, worried.

"I will try hard to find her. I promise."

TWENTY-THREE

Alex grabbed her keys from her purse and opened the trunk of her car, pulling out her wireless laptop. Setting it inside, she lit up a cigarette and called Ryan at his office. No one really knew what exactly Ryan did because he worked on covert operations. In fact, Alex wasn't even certain if his real name was Ryan. All he had told her was that his job was to analyze information provided by the covert CIA officers who were in charge of intelligence collection.

Alex needed to find out who the kidnappers were and the dangers involved. "If I send you three photos, would you run a check to see if anything comes up?"

"Oh, it's you," Ryan said, unenthusiastically. Six feet tall, he had short wheat-color hair, a clean-shaven face and a pale complexion. "You know, you could at least say hello before asking for something." Alex never called without wanting something from him in exchange for sexual favors. Had she not been so satisfying in bed, he wouldn't be taking her calls, he had often told his friends. But deep down, he did care for her even if she irritated him.

"Hello Ryan," she said and repeated her request. "If I send you three photos, would you run a check to see if anything comes up?"

"Forget it. You got me in a whole lot of trouble the last time," he answered, getting up to shut a glass door so that no one could hear his conversation. The last time he helped Alex, he interfered with an FBI operation. When Ryan's boss found out, he suspended him without pay for two months.

"Please, a girl has been kidnapped," Alex said.

"Let the police handle it," he gruffly insisted, dropping two Alka-Seltzers into a glass of water and downing it. Alex not only gave him heartache but also heartburn.

"I can't get them involved," she hissed through clenched teeth. Even when she asked her contact in the police department and her FBI friend for help, she asked them to keep it under wraps.

"Then I can't help you," he said, hanging up.

She called him back. "Why the hell did you hang up on me like that?" She emailed him the photos from her laptop.

"Look Alex, you're bad news. You did me a favor once and I've been paying for it ever since."

"Just open the attachments. This is a matter of life and death."

"Everything with you is always a matter of life and death," he groaned.

"If you do this, I'll do anything you want," she said devilishly. "I'll even go on a date with you."

"You mean like the last three dates when you didn't bother showing up?" he huffed.

"I'm running out of time here, just look at the damn email," she answered, completely losing her cool.

"I must be crazy for doing this," he grumbled as he fed the photos into his database for a match. "I mean you don't even appreciate me. If you get me fired, I'm going to hunt you down and kill you myself."

"Ya, ya. So, what did you come up with?"

"Just a second," he told her, reading their files. "You're in way over your head. Give me the address, and we'll take care of it."

"I can't do that."

"Who's the girl they've snatched and what do they want with her?"

"You're asking me things I cannot answer. Who are these men anyway?" she asked, ready to take notes.

"One of them is a cleaner."

"You mean the person who cleans up a mess after someone gets killed and gets rid of the body?" she asked, shocked.

"Yep."

"Holy shit!" she said, putting out her cigarette.

"Come on now, be a lady, will you?" He crinkled his nose, wishing that Alex had a regular job like a teacher or an accountant. This whole P.I. business wasn't becoming to her.

"Who are the other two?"

"Give it up, Alex. She's probably dead by now."

"It's not in my nature to give up, and you have no right to tell me what to do. I don't work for you," she said, angrily. "I asked a simple question. Who are the other two?"

"Your questions are never simple. But if you must know, one of them is a Saudi pilot."

"Why would a pilot get involved in all this?"

"I don't know. Suppose you tell me."

What Alex and Ryan didn't know was that Husam, who had ordered the kidnapping, had no intention of killing Sahar because he wanted to find out who had helped her escape. Besides, why should he kill her when the Saudi courts would gladly do it for him? All he had to do was to surrender her to the Riyadh police and explain how she had violated their marriage contract. The courts would then throw her in prison, torture her until she disclosed the names of the people who helped her escape and then give her the death sentence.

"Who's the third kidnapper?"

"He is a hit man on the CIA's most wanted list, and that's all I'm allowed to tell you," Ryan said, changing screens.

Husam had hired the hit man and the cleaner in case things went wrong. He had told the kidnappers if anyone got in their way, shoot to kill.

"Is he an Arab, too?" she asked, making notes.

"No."

"Where's he from?"

"Uh-uh, you give me something, and I give you something back," he replied with an obnoxious tone that irked her.

Alex hung up.

"Alex? Alex?" he screamed. *Damn fool*, he told himself. *She's going to get herself killed. Maybe that would be a blessing. No, I like the idiot too much.*

Alex had a hunch that Sahar was abducted by the three men in the white van and since she knew where they lived, she decided that that was the first place where she would look. From her car, Alex called Ethan, a P.I. friend of hers and asked for his help. He was a big guy who looked like a bodyguard. All he had to do was sit in the car, ask no questions and wait for her when she went in to rescue Sahar. They waited for nightfall as Alex drove toward a house which was situated at a corner of a wide street. There was a black Mercedes and a white van parked in the driveway.

She parked on a street where she had a diagonal view of the house as she peeked with her night vision monocular that could spot people 450 feet away. Inside, the cleaner was watching television, and the other two were playing backgammon. She drove past the house and killed her engine. Ethan helped push her car into an alley that gave access to a glass-paned pine door and a plain pine door at the back of the property.

"Remember to stay in the car, no matter what happens. If I don't come out in 10 minutes, leave and call Ryan. Do not try to rescue me," she said, handing him Ryan's phone number.

"Who's Ryan?"

"A friend of mine who is resourceful and that's all you need to know."

Ethan looked at his watch. It was nine o'clock. "Let me help you," he insisted.

"No," she said adamantly, "I have no intention of getting both of us killed."

Ethan nodded with a worried look and went to sit in the driver's seat.

Alex seized the opportunity to pick the lock on one of the back doors. She glanced through the glass-paned door and saw a laundry room that led to the kitchen. The other door seemed to be the back entrance of a room with a two-by-eight-foot-wide rectangular window with lace curtains. Looking around her, Alex noticed a medium-size plastic patio table and several chairs. She grabbed the table, put it underneath the window and climbed on top. Luckily, the curtains weren't fully closed, so a small slit allowed her to look inside. She saw Sahar lying on the bed, lifeless. No one else was in the room with her.

She climbed down from the table and began picking on the room's lock. Nervous, she dropped her pin to the ground but after several tries, she was able to unlock it. But before entering, she heard one of the men open the entrance door to the room and yell to the other two, "Yeah, she's still out." The door closed.

A drop of sweat glided down her face and her body shook with fear. *Alex, what the hell you are doing here?* she asked herself as her heart thumped hard against her chest. *You can get killed and no one would care. No, I have to do this. I can't let this girl die or worse, get tortured.*

To ascertain that the man had left the room, Alex mounted the table once again and saw only Sahar. She climbed down and mustered all the courage within her and opened the door. Alex saw Sahar lying on her back on a bed. She went to her and shook her. Sahar moved her head weakly, opened her eyes halfway and closed them. "Goddamn it, wake up," she whispered, shaking her hard.

Sahar opened her eyes but everything was blurry and her head felt fuzzy. The men had drugged her every four hours. The last dose had been administered three hours ago. She had no idea what was going on when Alex glided her arm underneath her shoulder and helped bring her to a seated position.

"Jason sent me to rescue you," she whispered, "We have to hurry."

Sahar gave her a blank look. She could hear Alex but her words weren't registering.

Alex turned Sahar so that her legs were hanging over the edge of the bed and slipped on her slippers. She then put Sahar's arm around her shoulder and her own arm around Sahar's waist as she lifted her to a standing position. "Please, you have got to help me out here," Alex panted. Sahar tried hard to put one foot in front of the other as the two quietly snuck out the back door. Ethan was thrilled to see them alive as he rushed out and helped put Sahar in the back seat. Then he and Alex pushed the car out of the alley and onto the street.

Sahar slept and Alex drove. She called Ryan from her car and gave him the location of the house. In exchange for the favor, she asked him not to tell anyone about the kidnapping.

"Oh and if you happen to find a laptop and navy purse, could you hang on to them until I collect them from you?"

"I ought to report you to the authorities and have your license pulled is what I should do," he reprimanded her.

"Ya, ya. Pick me up for dinner next Friday at seven and I'll show you just how much I appreciate you," she said.

"You better be there when I pick you up or say farewell to the laptop and purse," he said and hung up.

Alex put her cell phone back in her jacket pocket.

Ethan turned his head from the passenger seat and looked at the sleeping Sahar. "Who is she anyway?"

"Trust me, the less you know, the better. I just need you to help me get her up to my apartment, and then you can be on your merry way."

Alex parked her car on the second level of her apartment's subterranean parking lot in the Silver Lake area, east of Hollywood. Ethan scooped up Sahar from the back seat.

"No, put her down. She has to be able to stand up on her own," Alex said, concerned that someone would see him carrying her. "C'mon wake up. We're home," she shook Sahar who could barely open her eyes.

"I'm tired," she mumbled.

"You can sleep later. I need you to do your best to walk. We'll help you," Alex said as she and Ethan both supported Sahar and the three walked toward the elevator. The door opened and they got in but not before they greeted Alex's elderly neighbor.

"Good evening, Mrs. Langley," Alex said.

Mrs. Langley, a stiff nosy widow, gave the three of them a strange look and replied, "Good evening."

"Slumber party," Alex chuckled. "My young cousin had a bit too much to drink and asked me to pick her up."

Her neighbor raised her eyebrows and tightly smiled.

Alex hummed uncomfortably until they finally reached her floor. "Goodnight," she said to Mrs. Langley and continued helping Ethan guide Sahar to her apartment.

Once inside, Ethan cringed at the messiness of Alex's place. Her one-bedroom apartment looked like it hadn't been cleaned for months. Clothes and shoes were strewn everywhere along with books, files, empty cheese-puff packages, chocolate wrappers and empty beer cans.

"Sorry, haven't had time to clean up. Just put her on this purple chair for now," Alex said, removing her laundry basket that had been sitting there for the last two days.

Alex reached in her pants pocket, removed her wallet and dropped it along with her keys on a tray in the kitchen where she usually kept them. She cleared the clothes, books and files off the sofa and dumped them in the already cramped hallway closet. She then opened the sofa into a bed, went to her room and came back with fresh linens, a blanket and pillow and made the bed. "Okay Ethan, now lay her down here."

Ethan removed Sahar's slippers and pulled the blanket over her.

"Thank you. You have been an immense help," Alex told him. "I'll mail you a nice fat check tomorrow."

"You sure you don't want me to spend the night? I can sleep on the chair."

"Thanks, but we'll be just fine," she assured him.

When he left, she bolted her door and called Jason.

"I have your package safe and sound," she told him, going on to explain how difficult the rescue had been.

"That was truly stupid of you, Alex. You should have called me immediately when you found out about the identity of the three men and asked for help," he said, seated on his sofa.

"I suppose you think you can do a better job than I," she said sarcastically.

"No, but I could have used my connections to help you out."

"It's a done deal. The least you can do is to thank me."

Jason rubbed his temples. His head throbbed and every inch of his body ached when Alex was explaining what had happened. "Thank you Alex. I'm sorry for criticizing you."

"Forget about it."

"I want to talk to Dawn," he said, still not used to calling her by her real name.

"She's resting. They drugged her pretty heavily. You can talk to her tomorrow."

"Then, I'm coming over. I want to be there when she wakes up."

"Don't worry Jason. I will take good care of her. I'll bring her by tomorrow, say around 10."

"Are you certain they didn't follow you to your apartment?"

"I'm positive. One of the kidnappers is on the CIA's most wanted list. I gave his location to a friend of mine who works for the CIA. The abductors are probably in custody as we speak," she said looking at her watch. They won't be getting in your way anymore. We'll talk tomorrow."

"Goodnight," he said reluctantly and hung up.

Her phone rang again. It was Ryan calling from his office. "We got two of the men but couldn't find the pilot. Thought you should know."

"Goddamn it!" Alex said.

"I can send two of my men to keep an eye on your place."

"No," she said, wanting to protect Sahar's identity. At least the hit man and the cleaner were out of the way.

"Damn you Alex, who are you protecting? The President?" he asked, hurling his pen at the wall. "This is not a game, I tell you."

"I know this not a game, you moron. We had a deal. I give you the men on your wanted list and you ask me no questions."

"Fine," he responded angrily." If you get killed, I'm not attending your funeral."

"You worry too much. The pilot doesn't know who snatched their victim."

"For your sake, I hope you're right. Call me if you run into trouble. I'm going home now."

"Thanks baby. Can't wait to see you," she said, throwing him a kiss.

Even though she was exhausted, Alex decided to stay awake in case Sahar woke up and had questions. She changed into her red pajamas, made herself a cup of Cuban coffee, picked up Somerset Maugham's *The Razor's Edge* and settled in a chair to read.

At four in the morning Sahar woke up, disoriented. She stared at the gray ceiling, at the silver blinds covering the windows and the small kitchen facing the sofa bed. She sat up, feeling dehydrated. Then her gaze fell upon a woman slouched in a chair wearing reading glasses with her eyes shut and a book resting on her chest. Bits and pieces of her memory started to return. The Middle Eastern-looking men pretending to be the FBI, Elham, chloroform and then it all went dark. She recalled lying on a bed in a room and a tan-skinned man giving her an injection as she fought him before passing out. Someone yelling 'Wake up. You must wake up.' She looked at Alex. She had helped her escape. But why? Why would she risk her life for her?

Sahar got off the sofa to get some water when her foot hit an empty beer can that rolled into the kitchen.

The noise woke up Alex who jumped up, yelling, "Who is there? Who is there?"

Sahar stared at her, petrified.

"You're up," she said with surprise.

"Who are you?"

Alex walked toward her and extended her hand. "I'm Alex Rosenberg, hired by Jason Crawford to look after you," she said. But when she noticed the frozen look on Sahar's face, she dropped her hand. "I can see that you're shocked. Please sit and let me explain."

Sahar did as she asked and sat on the sofa bed while Alex recounted the last 24 hours.

When she finished, Alex said, "You don't look so well." Sahar's chalky complexion looked as though all the blood had been drained from it, and she was shivering. "Why don't I give you some fresh towels and clothes, and you can go take a nice hot shower? Then I'll make you a cup of chamomile tea and a sandwich. You must be starving."

"Thank you, but I'm not hungry. I'm parched. All I care for is a glass of water."

Alex grabbed a small bottle from the kitchen and gave it to her.

Sahar gulped down every drop. "Did Elham seem okay when you saw her? Did they hurt her?"

"She had few bruises on her face but…."

"Oh God," Sahar said, covering her face and shaking her head. "I should never have escaped from Riyadh. I have put too many people in danger – the people who helped me, my mom, my uncle, Jason, Elham and now you."

Alex felt sorry for her and didn't know what to say. She got up, grabbed some towels and a pair of sweats from her bedroom drawers and set them in the bathroom.

"Thank you for risking your life for me," Sahar called out to her, "I don't know how to ever repay you."

"Forget about it. You're safe, and that's all that matters," Alex replied, handing her a new toothbrush. "Go on now, go shower. It will help relax you."

"I had no idea that Jason was having me followed."

"He loves you. He just doesn't want to admit it."

"Yet, he never as much as called me when I left the mansion."

"Contrary to what we women think, men are complex creatures. Maybe someday the two of you can sort things out."

"I think I will take that shower now."

"Mind if I go to bed?" Alex asked. "I have been up for two days."

"Please, go rest. I will try not to make a lot of noise."

"Don't worry about that. I have a feeling that this time around, not even an earthquake would wake me up."

Sahar went into the bathroom and let the steaming water run over her body as she thought about all that happened since her kidnapping. She knew Alex was naïve to think that she was safe. In fact, not only was she in trouble but so were Jason and Alex for helping her. She had to leave L.A. and go somewhere where no one knew her. Even if her pursuers found and killed her, at least the people she cared for would be protected.

After her shower, she changed into the clothes Alex left her, brushed her teeth and dried her hair. Sahar checked on Alex, who was sound asleep in her bedroom, and then went into the kitchen for more water. She looked in one of the cabinets, found a huge beer mug and filled it with tap water. As she drank, she looked around for a note pad and found a large one next to the Yellow Pages and the tray where Alex kept her keys and wallet. Sahar took $60 from the wallet, looked at her driver's license and jotted down her address. She then wrote Alex a note and called a taxi service. Throwing on Alex's jacket hanging by the door, she slipped her feet into a pair of tennis shoes, which were a size too big, and left.

TWENTY FOUR

The taxi took Sahar to Lacy Park. The air was fresh and cool; the sun had risen just before six a.m. and several joggers were making their way around the grassy perimeter. She recalled the man who had helped her escape from Riyadh – his black mustache and thick lips, his small eyes and the missing pinkie on his right hand.

"We work with other underground organizations all over the world," he told her. "If you ever get into trouble in the U.S., page this number and someone will call you back, but remember to use a public phone and only call in case of dire emergency."

Sahar walked over to a phone booth near a water fountain and dialed the number she had memorized by heart. She punched in the telephone number of the park phone followed by a code and hung up. Five minutes later, the phone rang and she picked up.

"What is your great-grandmother's name?" a man asked in Arabic.

"Mind your own business," she said.

"How do I like to drink my tea?"

"With a cup of vinegar and a tablespoon of pepper."

"If you could fly, what would you be?"

"A pteranodon."

"Good morning, Sahar. Give me your location, and I send someone to pick you up."

"I'm at Lacy Park in San Marino. I can meet up at the west entrance where the rose arbor is located."

"In 30 minutes, look for a dark, metallic-green Ford Escape, license plate 913XKJ," he said. The phone went dead.

Dawn started walking toward the arbor while repeating the license plate number and car model to herself so that she wouldn't forget. After a waiting for what felt like an eternity, the SUV pulled in front of her and she got in.

"Tell me what happened?" A chubby middle-aged man with thinning hair and a friendly smile asked her as he drove off.

"You're an American?" she asked with surprise, noticing that he had no accent and that his fair skin was sunburnt.

"No, I'm not," was all that he offered.

"What is your name?"

"Don't have one but you can call me Clark. Now, tell me how you got caught?"

"Long story. The short version is that I think my husband recognized me at a gathering and has been having me followed ever since. I was kidnapped. Someone helped me escape but I'm afraid that Husam will not rest until he takes his revenge."

"Are you certain that your husband is behind it?"

"No, but I can't think of anyone else who would want me dead so badly."

"What is it that you want us to do for you?" Clark asked, making a right turn into a narrow street.

"I need to leave Los Angeles and go where no one can find me."

The driver scratched behind his ear and said, "How much money do you have?"

"I don't have anything on me right now. My money is sitting in a box underneath a pile of clothes in a laundry basket."

"Now, that is a problem."

"Please. I need to get out of here. Staying here is jeopardizing many lives."

"I'm going to need a $5,000 down payment."

"If I give you that, I will have nothing to live on. I can give you $3,000 and the rest in installments after I get a job."

"Sorry but that's not how we work," he said, seeing her desperate look as he drove toward East L.A.

"Please," she begged. "You're my last hope."

He stared at her in silence and then at the road in front of him. "Well, once in a while we help people with no money."

"Does this mean you accept my offer?"

"Yes," Clark said irritably, "Just tell me how can I get my $3,000," he asked, parking in front of a white office building with a For Lease sign in a rundown neighborhood of South Central Los Angeles.

Sahar was scared. For all she knew, this man could take all her savings and not even help her. But what choice did she have? She didn't want to ask for anyone else's help. She gave him Elham's name and address. "How are you going to convince her to let you in?" she asked, watching him get out of the car. Sahar followed.

"Let's talk later," was all he said as the two went up a set of stairs. He used his keys to unlock the rusted-steel front door and the two walked toward an elevator that creaked as it went up. They stopped on the third floor, walked down a hallway and entered a room with only a desk and two chairs. He turned the light on. The room had a beige carpet, dark blue curtains that were drawn and a musty smell. There was a clipboard holding blank sheets of paper, a bunch of pens sitting on top of a metal desk, a 1960s black dial phone with no redial button, a yellowed newspaper, a package of Twinkies, a 24-pack of root beer and a sleeping bag.

"Why are we here?" she asked, afraid that he was going to harm her.

"I need you to stay here while I go get your box," he said, sitting on one of the chairs. "Who is Elham?" he asked, popping open a soda.

"She is my landlord. The kidnappers drugged both of us when they broke in to snatch me."

"Does she know who you are?" he inquired, unwrapping a Twinkie.

"Yes, I confided in her."

"You should know better than to go shooting off your mouth to everyone," he said, with a disapproving look.

"She's not everyone," Sahar replied, raising her voice. "We have become good friends."

He grabbed the clipboard and began writing.

"How are you going to get my box? You're not going to harm Elham, are you?"

"Sahar, you're either going to have to trust me or leave right this minute," he said, losing his patience.

Sahar nodded. "I am sorry, but Elham is dear to me. She has been hurt once because of me. I don't want anything else to happen to her."

"Nothing will happen to her," he assured her and continued writing until he finished. "Here," he said, handing her the clipboard. "Copy this letter word for word and then sign it."

She looked worried but began writing. "Why can't I just call instead of writing her?"

"Because her telephone may be tapped."

When Sahar finished, Clark looked over the letter and said, "I thought I said to copy it word for word. What is this journal you talk about in here?"

"It's just a notebook where I write down my thoughts. I miss my family and my friend, Dawn. To relieve my stress I write about it."

"Are you mad?" he said angrily. "Didn't the men who helped you escape teach you anything? You are never to keep a journal of any kind."

"Stop yelling at me. You have no idea what it's like to leave one's family and never be able to see them again," she said, bursting into tears.

"Alright." He took the letter from her. "I have to go. Don't peek through the curtains because someone might see you, and don't open the door to anyone. I have a key to get in."

"What should I do then?" she said, wiping her tears with her sleeve.

"Take a nap or something," Clark told her, looking at her exhausted face.

When he left, Sahar wrung her hands, paced the room, sat on a chair, got up and moved about again. She felt imprisoned and helpless. So many thoughts ran through her mind. What would happen if someone found out that Jason and Alex had helped her? What city was she going to end up in and how would she start a new life again? She was tired of trying and was losing all hope for a normal life.

At eight in the morning, watching from the tinted glass of a black Lexus parked next to a curb a few houses before Elham's house, the pilot, Husam and Emad saw a courier get off her bike and drop a yellow envelope through the mail slot of Elham's door. From the kitchen, making porridge, Millie heard the envelope hit the floor. She went to pick it up and put it on a tray along with the porridge and a cup of tea for Elham, who was watching a rerun of *The Andy Griffith Show* in bed.

"I'm going to go to the grocery store now," Millie said.

"Okay, buy potato chip for me," Elham said.

"You know potato chips are bad for you. I'll make you air-popped popcorn when I come back," she said.

Elham grimaced. Air-popped popcorn tasted like chalk to her. She picked up the envelope Millie had brought her, opened it and pulled out a letter. She put on her glasses and began reading.

My dearest Elham,
So much has happened to me since I was taken away, but let me assure you that I am safe. In order to protect you, I'm not going to give you details of my whereabouts and all that has occurred. But there is one last favor I am going to ask of you. There is a journal under my mattress. I need you to destroy it. There is also a box underneath a pile of clothes in my hamper. I want you to take it out and put it in a laundry bag along with my clothes. Today, at 10 a.m., a dark red van with the inscriptions – Hector's Dry Cleaning – will come by. Give the driver my belongings and tell no one. This is the last you will hear from me. After you read this letter, make sure you shred it. You will always be in my thoughts, and I will miss you very much.
Love,
Sahar

Elham pushed her breakfast away, got out of bed and slowly walked upstairs. She pulled out Sahar's pink journal from under her mattress, opened it and compared her handwriting to the one in the letter. She wanted to be sure that it was Sahar who had written it. After Elham ascertained that the writing was Sahar's, she followed the instructions, pulling out her clothes from her drawers and the ones hanging in her closet and putting them in a taupe canvas laundry bag. She took out Sahar's box from underneath a pile of dirty clothes in her hamper and enclosed it with the rest of her belongings and dragged them, along with the journal, downstairs.

Elham put the canvas bag in the hallway closet and turned on her gas fireplace. She burned Sahar's letter and the pages in the journal and threw the pink plastic cover in the trash.

When Millie got back, she unloaded the groceries and noticed a burning smell in the house. She looked around and saw that there was a fire going. "Did you know that your fireplace is turned on?" she asked Elham who was looking through a *People* magazine on the living room sofa.

"I was cold," she said.

"Since when?" Millie said, knowing well that Elham always complained about being warm but rarely about being cold.

Elham shrugged and repeated, "I was cold. You buy potato chip?"

"Yes, yes but you can't eat it all at once." Millie had a soft heart and couldn't refuse Elham anything.

When she finished putting the groceries away, Millie said, "Okay, time to take your bath."

"Maybe later," Elham said, waiting for the van.

"Are you feeling alright?" Millie asked.

"Yes. I am fine."

"You sure are acting strange, first with that fire going and now you don't want to take your bath."

"You water plants. I read," Elham demanded.

"Umm...Umm...Umm...you're acting mighty strange," Millie said, going into the kitchen and filling up a watering can from the sink and turning on the faucet.

Outside, Husam, Emad and the pilot listened through a device that picked up conversation from a mile away. Two weeks ago when no one was home, they had put hidden microphones under the upstairs and downstairs furniture in Elham's home.

When Millie finished, she opened up a silver trashcan with her foot and noticed a pink plastic sheet inside that looked like a cover of something. She pulled it out and said, "What's this?"

"Trash. No good," Elham said.

"Didn't this belong to Dawn?" she asked, remembering seeing it once on her bed when she was vacuuming her room.

"No good. Trash," Elham repeated as the doorbell rang.

Elham looked outside through her peach curtains and saw Hector's Dry Cleaning van.

"Who is out there?" Millie asked.

"Dry cleaner."

"Dry cleaner? Since when do you have your clothes picked up?" Millie always took the clothes to the dry cleaner herself.

Elham went to the hallway closet and pulled out the taupe bag. She dragged it to the front door and opened it.

A man with a dark mustard jumpsuit with an emblem said, "Thank you. We'll have it back by this afternoon." He then left.

"What was in the bag you gave him?" Millie asked.

"Millie you ask many, many question. I take my bath now."

The pilot, Husam and Emad became suspicious after listening to Millie and Elham's conversation, so they followed the van until the driver stopped in front of a white building. They watched Clark get out carrying a large box as the van drove away.

"Should I follow the car?" the pilot asked Husam in Arabic.

"No, we'll stay here," Husam said, trusting his instincts.

After Clark went in, they got out of their car and walked up to the steel door but it was locked. Husam kicked the door out of anger.

"Stop that. Let's wait in the car until he comes out," Emad suggested.

"I'll go check to see if there is a back entrance," the pilot said, but after he looked, he shook his head no. So they waited.

Alex woke up from the sound of her phone ringing and looked at the clock. It was almost 11 a.m. "Shoot. I must have fallen sleep," she said, answering the phone.

"Alex why aren't you here?" Jason asked. He had been waiting for her since 10.

"Sorry, I overslept. I hadn't slept for two days."

"Will you check on Sahar to see if I can talk to her?"

"Hang on," she said, going into the living room. She checked the sofa bed and there was no sign of her. "Oh my god!"

"What's the matter?" he shouted.

"Uh...uh..." she said, rushing to the bathroom to see if Sahar was there. *Not here either. Where the hell is she?*

"Alex, talk to me. What is going on?" Jason demanded, his voice full of fear.

Panic consumed every inch of her body. "Uh...Uh...I am sorry but..."

"But what. goddamn it?"

"She isn't here," she replied reluctantly, feeling as though the room was spinning around her.

"What do you mean she isn't there?" He sensed a sharp pain radiating through his chest, making him feel as though he couldn't breathe.

Alex looked around the living room once again. There was no sign of forced entry but something was amiss. "My jacket is gone," she slapped her head, remembering that she had hung it by the door the prior evening.

"I knew I should have come by last night," he hollered.

Alex ignored him and hurried into the kitchen to see if her wallet and keys were still there when she noticed Sahar's note. "Oh shit..."

"Oh shit, what...oh shit what, Alex?" He screamed feeling completely helpless on the other side of the receiver.

"There's a note," Alex said, picking it up with shaky hands and reading it.

To Alex,
I want to thank Jason and you for saving my life, but I have put too
many lives in danger and it is time for me to leave Los Angeles.
Please do not look for me and tell Jason I said goodbye. He is
better off without me. I borrowed your leather jacket and $60 from
your wallet. Once I settle somewhere I will mail them to you and
the clothes you so kindly let me borrow. I am truly grateful for
your hospitality. Give my love to Jason.
Dawn

"Not smart of her to run away like that…no money but $60…how far is that going to take her," he said, putting his hand through his hair and pacing his home like a madman. "You have to find her," Jason demanded, angrily.

"Let me think," Alex said, falling into silence.

"Alex?" he shouted, "Are you there…Alex?"

"I'm here…I'm here…calm down…I can't think straight with you yelling at me. She must've gone to Elham's to get her things. But why would she risk that? She knows that would be too dangerous," she said, rubbing her chin.

"She said in her letter that she has already put too many lives in danger," he said, his face tense and his head throbbing with pain.

"What's your point?" Alex asked with exasperation.

"I don't think she's going to ask for anyone's help."

"If that's the case, she isn't going to get far on $60," she said, biting her nail, upset at herself for falling sleep and at Sahar for leaving.

"That's true," Jason said, sitting back on the sofa and tapping his foot on the floor, nervously.

Alex looked at the tray again and furrowed her brows. "My cell phone is missing."

"You think she took it?" he asked her, going to the bar, pouring himself a shot of whiskey and downing it. Sahar's disappearance was driving him crazy. He never drank so early in the day.

"I don't know. I mean had she taken my phone, she would have told me so in her note, wouldn't she?...My jacket is missing." She blurted, excited.

"For crying out loud, I'll buy you a new jacket Stay focused, will you?"

"You don't understand. My cell phone was in my jacket. I usually put it in the tray when I get home but last night I forgot."

"What are you planning to do? Call her? She isn't going to pick up."

"No, that's not what I was thinking. My cell phone has a GPS system. All I have to do is call a friend of mine and he can track her down. Gotta go. Will call you later." She immediately called Ryan at his CIA office.

"Ryan, this is Alex and I need your help."

"I'll be right there."

"No silly, I'm not in any danger. I need you to track down my cell phone."

"What?" he asked, sitting behind his desk, drinking his espresso and sifting through his mail.

"Please, just do it."

"Just a minute," he said while he began running a trace on his computer. "Your cell phone is in Southeast of downtown L.A."

"Then that's where I'm going. Give me the address."

"I'm looking at the address and it's not in a safe neighborhood. Let me go with you."

"Hurry up then," Alex said impatiently.

"I'll be there in 15 minutes," he told her.

Alex called Jason and updated him.

"I'm coming with you," he told her.

"No way, I'm not in no mood to bail you out of trouble too. I'll handle it myself."

"I'm keeping my cell phone on," Jason said. "Call me at any hour, day or night."

"Ya, ya," Alex said. When Ryan arrived, she hopped in his specially equipped silver BMW.

"Your phone is now moving west on the 10 freeway," Ryan said, reading the trace he put on her cell.

"Let's get on the freeway, then," Alex said.

A taxi drove Sahar to Los Angeles International Airport and stopped at the American Airlines terminal. Clark had given her new luggage, taken out his share of the money from Sahar's box, leaving her $2,500. Sahar had a pair of everything – passports, ID cards and credit cards that the Egyptian man who had helped her escape had given her under the names of Dawn Parnell and Hope Patterson. Clark bought Sahar a one-way airline ticket to Fort Collins, Colorado, under her old alias, Hope Patterson.

Sahar walked in the terminal and stood in line to check her luggage but when she saw Husam and Emad running toward her followed by Alex and Ryan behind them, she left the line, leaving her luggage behind and moving quickly toward the security check point.

Inside, Emad yelled, "Stop that woman, she's an imposter. I said stop her, she is a fugitive."

Several security guards heard him and began walking toward Sahar. Husam and Emad grabbed Sahar's arms and pulled her out of the security line. Some of the passengers began staring at them to see what was going on. Alex, who had been watching the whole thing from afar, turned pale as the security guards began questioning them.

"Ryan, can't you do something?" she asked him.

"This is out of my jurisdiction and is now the responsibility of U.S. immigration and Homeland Security. If I get involved, I could lose my job."

Alex frowned.

"I don't know anything about this girl," he explained. "My boss has no idea that I'm running around, helping you save someone who may be a threat to our country."

"She's not a threat," Alex said, watching the officers escort Sahar, Husam and Emad through double doors that led to an immigration security office.

The pilot, who had been waiting outside witnessing his boss, the interpreter, and Sahar get apprehended, casually walked away hoping he would not be identified

"I am truly sorry that I can't help you," Ryan said, feeling guilty. "I can get fired if I do."

"I understand," said Alex. "You have already done a lot for me and need to get back to work. Thanks for everything."

"Are you sure you don't want me to stick around with you?" he asked her, looking concerned.

"Yes. Go on," she said, walking toward a row of public telephones. She used her credit card and called Jason.

"Sahar's in trouble and needs your help," she said, quickly explaining to him what had happened. "If you or anyone you know has a contact in national security, now would be the time to use it."

"Stay with her. I'll see what I can do."

"Didn't you hear me? They took her to another department. I can't get in there without a pass."

"Stick around and I'll find a way to get you a pass," he said.

"If you send someone, I'm wearing a light-blue jean jacket, standing by the phones at the American Airlines terminal," she told him before hanging up.

Jason called his father, and a woman with a nasal voice answered.

"I'm sorry Mr. Crawford is in a meeting."

"Then get him the hell out of the meeting. This is his son, it's an emergency."

"Just a minute, please," she said, buzzing her boss. "Excuse me sir, I have your son on line three. He says it's an emergency."

"Put him through," Drew replied, wondering what the emergency could possibly be. Jason had never interrupted any of his meetings before.

"Need you to call your friend Arnold Reef at Homeland Security and help me out," Jason asked as soon as his father picked up the call.

"What's all this about?"

"Someone I know is in a whole lot of trouble at the airport. They might deport her...."

"Hold on," he told Jason. He then put the phone down, turned to his associates gathering in the conference room and said, "I'm sorry but I'm going to have to cut this meeting short." He went into his office and shut the door.

Drew picked up Jason's call and said, "You were saying?

"Look there isn't much time, so I need you to stay focused and take some notes," he said.

Drew pulled out a pad of paper and a pen from his drawer.

Jason gave a short version of Sahar's story – the death of her friend Dawn, Sahar's forced marriage to Husam, her fake burial and her entry into U.S. under a false name. He also told his father that he had done a thorough background check on her, her record was clean and Alex had been following her when Sahar got caught. He told Drew where Alex was waiting and described her so that someone could help her gain entry to see Sahar. "Please, you have to help her."

"I can't get involved in this. Our company could stand to lose a handsome sum of money if Husam ever found out that I helped this girl."

"Andrew, I have never asked anything of you my whole life," he replied, remembering how his parents never showed up on parents' night, his tennis matches or any significant occasions. "I grew up on my own, studied without your help and worked at a job I hated when you needed me. Can't you, for once in your life, do right by your son?"

Andrew rubbed his chin in contemplation. If he did this, he risked losing Husam's business. If he didn't do it, he would lose his son. "I'll make the call to Arnold since he's the deputy director of U.S. citizenship and immigration services, but I can't promise anything. I'm not going to lie to you, but she's in deep and only a miracle can help her at this point."

"Call me on my cell phone. I'll await your call," he said, filled with anxiety and stress. The asking was the easy part but the waiting, unbearable.

"Promise me not to go to the airport," Drew warned. "I don't want Husam finding out that we're involved in rescuing her."

"But I want to see her."

"I mean it son. If you want my help, please don't complicate things any further until you hear from me."

"Fine," Jason replied, reluctantly.

Andrew called Arnold. "How are you doing Arnie?"

"I'm doing great. I haven't seen you since your anniversary party. What can I do you for?" he asked, knowing very well that a call from Andrew was hardly ever a simple social call.

"Listen, there is a girl in the custody of LAX security. I want you to tell them to release her and make it all go away," he ordered without blinking an eye.

"And why would I do that?" Arnold huffed, even though he knew he owed Drew a huge favor but would never admit it unless he absolutely had to.

"Because you owe me a favor," he said, as though reading his mind.

"Do I?" he answered coyly.

"Remember how I used my contact to save your behind from an SEC investigation when you purchased $18 million worth of the bogus bird flu antivirus?" Andrew knew that Arnold's scheme to make the rich become richer by creating a panic to buy the antivirus would make its stock rise profusely.

Arnold picked up a green rubbery tension ball on his desk and started squeezing it. "That was long time ago and frankly I didn't do anything wrong."

"Come now, you knew that within weeks the government was going to appropriate another $1 billion exclusively for that drug and that the drug company owning the antivirus was planning to sell the patent to a global company,"

"What's your point?" he inquired with a raised voice.

"My point? My point is that you made a 720 percent return on your investment when the stock climbed on something you knew was bogus. I can inform the government anytime and your career would be over."

"Okay so you helped me out but there's no record of it," he responded ungratefully.

"Well, I can make the investigation come back. All I have to do is leak the information," he bluffed, although the paper trails and phone records were destroyed long ago.

"I thought you said your source shredded all the evidence," he said, squishing the ball in his hand much harder this time.

"I never said that. I said I can make the investigation into your finances go away and I did. Now, you need to do something for me."

"Let's hear it," he said, annoyed.

Drew told him about Sahar's plight and the men who were after her.

"What's her name?"

"Sahar Al-Hijazi," Drew said, looking at his notes, "also known as Hope Patterson also known as Dawn Parnell."

"What airline was she going to fly on?"

"American."

"I'm going to put you on hold for a second," Arnold said, and punched in an extension that buzzed the associate director of national security. "There is a Dawn Parnell also known as Hope Patterson in the custody of the LAX immigration department. Supposedly she was getting on an American Airline flight. Get ahold of them and tell them to keep her there and the two men involved until they hear from me."

"I'll do it right away," the associate director said.

Arnold picked up Drew's line, "Okay I'm back. I put in a call so that immigration will detain the girl until they hear from me. He started doing a background check on his computer, "Sahar Al-Hijazi died about a year ago...Dawn Parnell...I have lots of Dawn Parnells here. Birthday?"

"I don't know. She's about 21, maybe a little older, red hair, blue eyes. Somewhere about 5-feet-10-inches tall."

Arnold began looking at all the Dawn Parnells born after 1980. "There's a Melissa Dawn Parnell, Andie Dawn Parnell..." he said and put in more data, "here it is – red hair, blue eyes, 5-feet-9-

inches tall, left the U.S. for Barcelona and then for Saudi Arabia but after that there is no record of her. Oh yes…here it is…she now works for a law firm in Pasadena. Why don't I have a record of her entry into this country?" He frowned.

Because that's not really Dawn. That's Sahar, who entered the country under the name of Hope Patterson and later changed her name to Dawn Parnell."

"Where is the real Dawn Parnell?"

"She was killed in Riyadh by her husband."

"That's unfortunate," he said, continuing to search his database, "I do show a Hope Patterson entering the country about a year ago…Well, she is a clever girl. I see nothing negative in the files here but then again, many sleeper cells have perfectly clean files."

"My son had her fully checked out and says she is clean. I love this country as much as you do. I wouldn't be asking if I thought she was a threat to our security. You know what would happen to this poor girl if she gets deported."

"Why such an interest in someone so inconsequential if she is indeed inconsequential?" he asked with tremendous curiosity.

"Because my son is in love with her," Andrew confessed, finally beginning to understand his son. He had heard Mrs. Anderson complaining about Jason meddling in the cleaning schedule because of Dawn and his wife telling him time after time about their son being smitten by Dawn, but at the time he believed Jason just had a big appetite for women, any woman. Now he knew better. It wasn't just any woman his son wanted. He wanted the dead wife of one of the most influential businessmen in Saudi Arabia. Why couldn't he just fall for a good old American girl? He didn't have that answer, but he was going to help him all the same.

"I see," Arnold uttered. *How ridiculous to be going through all this trouble for love when love was nothing but a momentary madness,* he thought. But he still had to give in to Drew's demand if only to save his own behind. "I'll try to help but it's going to be hard."

"I don't want to hear the words 'I'll try.' Did I say that when you needed my assistance?"

He sighed loudly. "I'll send someone down there to see what's going on."

"So, I have your word that you'll help her?"

"Yes, you have my word. Just remind me not to ask you for a favor again," he responded, angry that he had to go out on a limb for a girl he didn't even know.

"Oh, and I need you to send someone to American Airlines to pick up Alex Rosenberg so that she can she can gain entry to see Sahar."

"Who is she?"

"She is a private detective my son hired. She has been following Sahar everywhere. She can help out and answer any questions your men may have." He gave him a description of her.

Arnold ran a check on his computer for a list of P.I.'s. "Self employed…no children…works for a woman's shelter… proficient in Krav Maga… no prior convictions. Blond hair, gray eyes, 5 feet 8 inches, 130 pounds….I'll have one of my men pick her up on his way to see Sahar."

"She is wearing a light-blue jean jacket, waiting by the phones at the terminal."

Jason hadn't left his home all day as he waited impatiently by his phone. He couldn't even think about work until Sahar was home safe and he couldn't go to the airport because his father had asked him to stay put. Fred, who had been hearing bits and pieces of his conversation since yesterday, prodded him about Dawn so Jason finally gave in and told him everything. It actually felt good to confide in Fred, Jason thought as he tapped the arm of his chair with one hand and flipped the channels on his TV remote with the other to distract himself.

At one in the afternoon the phone rang. Fred, who was mopping the floors, stopped and stared nervously as Jason took the call.

"Hi son. Arnie is sending one of his men to bail out your girl. You can count on it. He'll also find Alex."

"Thanks. I'm going to go the airport and wait for her."

"No, you cannot."

"Why not?"

"Because I need a favor from you."

"Anything. All you have to do is ask," he said, grateful that his father had helped him.

"I need you to…." Drew hesitated as he loosened his tie. It felt as though it were choking him. "When this is over, I need you to not to pursue Sahar."

"What are you talking about?" He furrowed his brows.

"I have given the matter some thought, and I just don't think your involvement with this girl is wise. Look at all the trouble she has caused you."

"I'm sorry, but I can't stop seeing her. I will do anything you want except let her go."

His father put his hand over his face and shook his head. *What a mess.*

"Are you there?" Jason asked. "You're mad at me, aren't you?"

"No. I am not mad. I just wish that you had fallen for a different girl."

"You mean for someone like Cynthia?"

"Touché," Drew said, knowing very well that his marriage to her had been a mistake, but he too had once been in love with his wife.

"If you are worried about your image, I promise not to bring Sahar over to the house."

"I am not worried about my image, but you need to understand that Husam is heavily invested in our enterprise and if he finds out that I or you had helped Sahar, I'm not sure what he would do. At the very least I need you to put some time and distance between the two of you."

"So, what do you suggest?"

Drew thought about it for a long time. "Will you not get in touch with her for a month until this whole thing blows over? I don't want Husam finding out that we were involved in rescuing her."

"A whole month?" he asked, frustrated. "I don't know if I can do that."

"Please," his father begged. "Do this for our family's safety and our business."

"What if she tries to get in touch with me?"

"Instruct Fred and your secretary to tell her that you're out of town or make up some other excuse."

"Fine," Jason said, reluctantly. He knew he had to do right by his father even if he didn't like it.

"Thanks son. I understand how hard this must be for you."

After hanging up with his father, Jason said, "Fred, Break open that 12-year-old bottle of bourbon I brought back from Bardstown, Kentucky, and pour it into two glasses, no ice. We can both use it."

TWENTY FIVE

Sahar sat in a holding room all by herself, waiting for the worst. Husam and Emad were kept in a separate holding room as a young female immigration officer, from the U.S. Department of Homeland Security, studied them all from behind a two-way mirror. She then went in to question the men. Each room had ivory brick walls, long plywood tables and few gold metal chairs with plastic mustard seat cushions.

"Tell me who the girl is you're accusing of falsifying her identity?"

By three in the afternoon, Sahar's luggage had been turned inside out and an interrogator found two passports in her possession – one identifying her as Dawn Parnell and the other as Hope Patterson.

"Her name is Sahar Al-Hijazi, the wife of my employer, Husam. He doesn't speak English very well."

"Then who's Dawn Parnell?" the investigator asked as she made notes on an official form.

"She was an American who killed her Saudi husband. Dawn and Sahar were friends."

"And where is this American? Is she in a Saudi jail? Was she deported to the U.S?" she inquired, surprised that the incident never made it to the news. But then again not much about Saudi Arabia was ever revealed to the American public.

"Who knows?" the translator shrugged as though she were just a pebble on the beach. "She disappeared."

"Just like that? Poof into thin air?" she asked, upset at his callous behavior. She studied him closely to see if he was lying.

"We don't know, and we don't care," he admitted at last. After all, who gave a damn about a stupid foreigner, especially a female one. "Our concern is the girl you're holding."

"Ask your employer what he's planning to do with her once she's in Saudi Arabia." she asked, concerned for her well-being.

She knew that no matter what this girl's predicament would be, if she were a Saudi citizen, she would have to be surrendered to the Saudi authorities.

"Em…," he said, nervously.

"Ask him," she demanded firmly.

Emad relayed the message and replied, "He says he refuses to answer to a woman."

"Excuse me?" she uttered, eyes wide, not believing her own ears.

The translator nudged his boss and told him in Arabic to answer the question.

"Tell her I will not answer to some low-level American whore. I want to talk to a man in charge."

"I'm sorry ma'am, but do you have a male supervisor or someone who is above you in rank?" Emad asked.

The officer understood Arabic and answered in his language, "Oh, I see your problem. Because I'm a woman or, as your boss puts it, an American whore, I'm inferior."

Emad shifted in his chair.

"Fine. I'll be back with someone else," she said, exiting the room.

Amused by Husam's behavior and wanting to get to the bottom of what was going on, she asked a subordinate with years of experience to help out. "Here, put this jacket on," she told him as she removed it from another employee, "It'll make you look like you're above me in rank."

"This is why I love working for you, never a dull moment," he said, playing with the toothpick in his mouth as he put the jacket on.

"And take that toothpick out of your mouth for God's sake. You look ridiculous."

"This is how you speak to your superior officer?" he teased, looking distinguished with his salt-and-pepper hair.

"Go on, get in there and see what you can find out." She then asked an assistant to run a check on Husam Abdol Samad and Emad Zamad. Sahar Al-Hijazi, Dawn Parnell and Hope Patterson.

It was a messy case, and she wasn't looking forward to dealing with it.

The new investigator opened the door and saw Husam whisper to Emad. He looked over his boss's notes and asked, "Can you tell me, who's Hope Patterson?"

"His wife, Sahar Al-Hijazi," Emad answered, "After faking her death, she escaped Riyadh under the name of Reyhana bint Abdol Majid and from there came to the U.S. under the alias Hope Patterson. Once she was in U.S., she took on her best friend's name, Dawn Parnell."

From the other side of a two-way mirror, the woman who had first questioned Husam asked an assistant to find out the identity of Reyhana bint Abdol Majid.

"Would you explain how she faked her own death?" he asked, thinking this case just kept on getting more complicated by the minute.

Husam took his fist, smashed it on the table in front of him and said in Arabic, "I don't have time for this shit. I want my wife back, you hear me? I want her back."

Emad told his boss that if he didn't calm down, he could end up in prison. He then turned to the interrogator and said, "I'm sorry. My client has had a long day and is tired. He apologizes for his behavior."

The interrogator observed Husam's violent temper and wondered what he would do to the girl after he had her in his possession. "Tell your boss, another outburst like that and he'll be thrown in a cold, coffin-like cell for the night without food, water or his clothes."

The translator relayed the message in the hope of scaring Husam and making him shut the hell up. He had no intention of joining him in a coffin.

Husam decided to calm down and responded in Arabic.

"My employer apologizes and says he will cooperate. He says if you don't believe him, you can ask the girl to remove her contact lenses. Her true eye color is dark brown and so is her hair. She has a brown mole on the right side of her lower back."

"People color their hair and use colored contact lenses all the time. It doesn't make them fugitives. And as for the mole, you may have seen it on her while she was in a bikini walking around on a public beach."

"We can give you her blood sample and you can match it with the Saudi authorities' data files," Emad offered.

When Husam had Dawn investigated several days after the Crawford party, he sent an inside person, pretending to be an electrician, there to repair wiring on the house. The snitch asked one of the new maids about Dawn and since the maid didn't know her, she directed him to Mrs. Anderson. Old Crab was only too happy oblige as she told him all that she knew. The snitch then told Mrs. Anderson that Dawn may have falsified her identity. He bribed her to keep an eye on Dawn and report to him any bits of information she could find.

The night Mrs. Anderson saw Jason go into the guesthouse and leave the following day, enraged her. She waited for Dawn to leave her place before sneaking in to find evidence to prove that Dawn wasn't who she said she was. She found the sheet sullied with blood in a garbage bag, contacted Husam's snitch and gave it to him to run a DNA test.

"And you have found her blood, how?"

"Sahar was a virgin when one of your American citizens violated her," he answered, with disgust. "We have the blood-stained sheet to prove it. You can run a DNA test and see for yourself," he added, remembering that Mrs. Anderson told his snitch that she had found the sheet the morning after Jason spent the night at Sahar's. Husam had immediately jumped to the conclusion that the stained sheet was the result of intercourse and ran a DNA test to confirm that Dawn Parnell was indeed Sahar.

As soon as he said this, the woman who had first questioned Husam, and been listening to the interrogation from another room, was about to talk to Sahar herself when she was interrupted by one of her assistants who said, "Sahar Al-Hijazi is his wife. She was supposed to have died from an aneurysm the night of their wedding."

"Well, according to him, she faked her death. If that's the case, I can't say that I blame her. I would too if I had to live with that chauvinistic pig. I want you to have someone look into Dawn Parnell's disappearance," she said and left to talk to Sahar, who showed no signs of nervousness.

Sahar recalled what the Egyptian man who had helped her escape tell her: If caught, you must relax your entire body and show no fear. People can smell fear from miles away and once they know they have you, it's all over.

The interrogator leaned forward, rested one elbow on the table and her cheek on her fist as she stared into Dawn's eyes and tapped her pen rhythmically on the table. She then dropped her pen, sat back and let out a sigh. "I want you to think carefully about what I'm about to ask. What color are your eyes?"

"Blue," Dawn cleared her throat, "I mean dark blue."

The interrogator made a note on her form. "And you hair? Is that your real hair color?"

"No, my real hair is brown and I color it red, but that's not exactly a crime is it?"

"No, it's not, but having two different passports with your photo on each is," she said holding out the passports. At that moment, a man in a black suit and tie walked in and held out his badge. "Homeland Security. I'll take it from here."

"Excuse us," the interrogator told Dawn and glared at the intruder as she walked toward him, grabbed him by the sleeve and took him outside. "I also work for Homeland Security. This is my investigation. You have no right to interfere."

"As a matter of fact I do," he said, taking an envelope out of his pocket and removing a letter from it. "I have a letter from the CIA director. The girl has been working for them undercover, and they don't want us questioning her."

"What? This is preposterous," she said, reading the letter. "What do you suppose I should do with the man who claims to be her husband?"

"Get your investigator out of there, and I'll wrap this up as quickly as possible."

She waved her hand and said, "Your call." She knew something wasn't right and it seemed that someone with a lot of clout was bailing this girl out. In a way, she was glad that the girl wasn't going to be deported. She knew what Saudis did to unfaithful wives.

The first thing the man claiming to be working for Homeland Security did was to check that Sahar wasn't harmed. "You have some powerful people looking out for your interest young lady," he told her.

"I'm not sure I understand what you're talking about," she answered.

"Your friend Jason called his father, who called the higher ups, who called me to bail you out. Welcome to America," he said.

"Does that mean...does that mean..." she burst into tears. It had taken her tremendous effort to hold back her fear. "Am I free to go?"

"There are a few things we should go over. You can no longer identify yourself under any other name except for Dawn Parnell."

Sahar nodded her head in agreement.

"We have never met. The Department of Homeland Security was never involved in helping you. You may never contact anyone in Saudi Arabia nor should you ever travel anywhere in the Middle East. You'll have to pretend to be a good old American girl going about your life. We'll issue the real Dawn Parnell a death certificate."

"Wouldn't that complicate my life?"

"No. Dawn Parnell is a common name and your fingerprints, dental records and genes are different than hers," he said, taking her picture with a small digital camera. He then fingerprinted her. "You will get a new birth certificate and Department of Motor Vehicles ID in the mail. If you have any other IDs in your possession, you need to hand them over."

"Everything I had was in my purse and my suitcase."

"In that case, Alex is waiting to drive you home where your friend Elham waits."

"How do you know Alex and Elham?"

"We're the government. We know everything."

"Thank you," she said with appreciation.

"Go on now. She's outside," He got up and opened the door for her.

Back in a holding room, Husam waited impatiently as a man with a laptop entered. He opened it and began typing.

"Who are you? What happened to the other man?" Emad asked.

"The other man was hungry and went to lunch. I, on the other hand, am your biggest nightmare…go ahead and translate that to your boss."

Emad swallowed and did as he asked.

"I have opened up a file here for both you and Husam. If either of you ever come within 500 feet of Ms. Parnell, you will be denied access to our country. Am I making myself clear?" What he was actually typing on his laptop was a text message to his boss and one to Andrew Crawford, letting them know that Dawn, or rather Sahar, was safe. As far as banning Husam from the country, he had no power to do that.

Emad translated what he was told.

Husam's face turned beet red as he got up and said to his interpreter, "Come on let's get out of here. I will hire someone to get her."

"Oh and did I forget to mention that I worked inside Saudi Arabia for seven years and speak Arabic fluently?" he told Husam in Arabic.

"You speak Arabic? Not possible," Husam blurted.

"Yes, very possible. I'm asking you nicely to disappear and am warning you for the last time: If as much as a hair is missing on that girl's head, I will personally destroy your lives. For your own interest I suggest that you move on and forget about her." He then called to one of the security officers: "Please escort these gentlemen out of the building. We're all finished here."

Husam and Emad grabbed a taxi. On his way back to his hotel, Husam sat in silence, thinking and planning for a long time. He decided that someday, somewhere, he would get his revenge but now was not the time. He needed to have a different plan and no longer had the intention of complaining to the Saudi government or to Sahar's family. In fact, he wasn't going to tell anyone that Sahar was still alive. His goal was to kill Sahar one day and save his honor. He didn't want the U.S. government working out a deal with the Saudi government as was done in 1999 with the Bahrain government when a Bahraini princess ran away with a U.S. soldier. Sahar not only committed adultery but also made a fool of him by faking her death. He would wait. He would wait for months and perhaps years until he had a foolproof plan before he made one last attempt at ending her life.

While waiting for Sahar, Alex used a phone in one of the offices to call Jason to let him know that Sahar would be released shortly.

"Jason, it's Alex."

"How is she? Is she alright?" he asked from his bathroom phone, his voice panicky.

"Ya, ya, she's fine. A suit with dark glasses from Homeland Security picked me up, didn't really tell me much about himself but asked a lot of questions about Dawn, Sahar and Husam," Alex said, looking around the room for an ashtray. She could really use a smoke, she thought, noticing a sign that said: Thank you for not smoking. "Oh man," she said out loud.

"What's the matter?"

"Nothing," Alex said, reaching in her pocket for nicotine gum. "Anyway, the Homeland Security guy drove me to a gray stucco building. He flashed his badge and we got in. We went through several security checkpoints and he asked me to wait for him in a hallway while he went to get Sahar. I asked one of the security personnel if there was a phone I could use and she directed me to one of the offices."

"So, you haven't seen Sahar," he said, washing his hands and looking in the mirror at his messy hair, the bags underneath his eyes and his tired dull face.

"No, not yet but I should go and wait for her in the hallway. I'll call you again when she's released and you can talk to her."

"Ummm...well...Now that I know she is going to be fine, there's something I must take care of. I will call her myself," he lied because he knew his father didn't want him to contact Sahar.

"Okay then, we'll talk soon."

After her conversation with Jason, Alex called Elham to inform her that she found Sahar and would soon be bringing her by. She then met with Sahar in a hallway.

"How are you?" Alex asked, looking at her jaded face and sallow complexion.

"I'm happy to be freed."

"What happened to you? Where did you go after you left my place?"

"Let's talk later," she said as two security officers escorted them through a series of corridors toward a white exit door. Outside, a metallic blue Chrysler Aspen gave them a ride back to the airport. Alex rented a car instead of taking a taxi. She needed to talk to Sahar in private without a third person listening in on their conversation.

"Tell me what happened to you after you left my apartment. Who helped you get money to buy an airline ticket?" Alex asked.

"I cannot tell you every detail because I have been sworn to secrecy, but I will tell you as much as I am allowed to tell." She began explaining.

When Sahar finished, Alex said, "I thought my life was complicated. Yours is much worse."

"I am glad that now I don't have to worry about being deported," she said, staring at Alex for a moment before she spoke. "I will never be able to repay you nor Jason for what you two have done for me."

"Hey, don't sweat it. I was just doing my job."

"No, Alex. You went beyond the duties of your job, and I don't know if there are many people in the world like you."

"Okay, okay, enough of this sentimental crap. You're going to get me teary. By the way, you have my cell phone."

"Your cell phone? But I only took...."

"My jacket has a pocket inside with my phone."

"Sorry." She wrinkled her nose. "Your jacket is in my suitcase and my suitcase is...."

"In the trunk," she said finishing off her sentence. "I have an idea, what if I first take you to Jason's home before dropping you off at Elham's?"

"No, that's not necessary."

"Are you sure?" she looked puzzled.

"Yes I'm certain. I can tell from the look on your face you think I'm being ungrateful. But you see, as much as I love Jason, I truly don't think I'm the right woman for him."

"Then who is right for him?" she asked, turning on her right hand signal to change lanes.

"Someone he can show off on the covers of magazines and gloat about to his friends and family about her successes." She still hadn't forgiven him for flaunting his Italian model girlfriend on the front page of a magazine.

"You really think he's that shallow?" Alex inquired, having a hard time believing Sahar.

"No, I don't think that at all. He's really kind and caring when he wants to be, but he's always worried about what outsiders think," she said, remembering how he had treated her in Zermatt when Tiffany and her friends showed up.

"I'm sorry, but the man I work for and the person you're describing are two different people. The man I work for has been worried about you for months. He had me follow you since...."

"Since Utah?"

"You know?" She asked, surprised. Alex had been so careful to stay out of Sahar's sight.

"He told me he had an investigator on my back."

Alex rolled down her window and lit up a cigarette.

Sahar didn't particularly care for people smoking in her presence but this time welcomed the fumes. The way Alex was inhaling and puffing smoke in small ringlets, reminded her of Dawn. "Didn't it ever occur to you why he had me followed for so long? He didn't trust me. He wanted to make sure I wasn't lying to him about my identity. He wanted to know for certain that I wouldn't be the cause of his family's disgrace," she tearfully explained, recalling the way Cynthia looked at her when she found them playing tennis at the mansion.

"But you did lie to him at first and pretended to be Dawn Parnell."

"I didn't have a choice. I still have no choice. My escape was illegal and if my government ever finds out, they'll push to have me extradited and dealt with accordingly. What's worse is the shame I would bring my family for faking my own death and for refusing to accept my duties."

"You mean your duties as a good wife?" she smiled satirically. If there was one thing Alex hated, it would be living a boring, conventional life.

"My duty to be a good wife was branded on my forehead from the day my mother gave birth to me. But you see, my fate is no different than the fate of many girls who are often as young as 11 years old."

"That's child molestation."

"Many are from Afghanistan, Pakistan, India, Iran, you name it. Oftentimes they're kidnapped or bought from families who can't make ends meet. The younger the girl, the better. Men as old as 60 look for wives in their early teens or younger."

"That's terrible." Alex pondered the injustice of it all. "What's interesting is, I have never seen our president point to Saudi Arabia for violation of human rights and yet he has no problem pointing fingers at China, Russia, Cuba and Iran."

"It's not in his best interest since his wealth and the wealth of his family depends upon our oil and on us purchasing his planes, artilleries and goods. Besides, foreign airplanes sit inside our borders, monitoring the Middle East like hawks, protecting their assets and resources that don't even belong to them at the cost of losing human lives. And it's not just your president. Many presidents, prime ministers and kings before him have looked the other way when it's not profitable for them to do otherwise."

"I suppose this is part of the reason you don't want to be with Jason," Alex replied, beginning to understand.

"His family's strong ties with unscrupulous businessmen bother me. I truly believe the Crawfords would do anything just to get more business and Jason is their son, after all. When push comes to shove, he would be there to help them out."

"I think you need to give him more credit than that. Look at how far he went to protect you from Husam."

"I've thought of that. His actions, often contradictory, have always confused me." She recalled the night when she had revealed everything to him and he stated that perhaps it would be best for him to stay away because of business.

For the rest of the ride, both sat in silence, reflecting on all that had happened in the past week. Sahar stared out the window at cars swooshing by, wondering if she should give the man she loved another chance. Alex lit up another cigarette, thinking how badly she needed a vacation.

"Well, here we are," Alex said when they reached Elham's home.

"Would you like to come in? My landlord is a wonderful hostess."

Elham had been waiting anxiously on the living room sofa, looking outside through her curtains ever since she found out that Alex was bringing Sahar home. When she saw the car pull up, she shuffled to the door.

"No, I should get going. I haven't slept much for the past few days and need my z's."

Sahar extended her hand to shake Alex's. "You've been wonderful and if I hear of anyone looking for an investigator, I will definitely have them call you." She fetched her bag out of the trunk, returned Alex's money, jacket and phone to her and waved goodbye. She was about to ring Elham's doorbell when the door opened.

"Oh, I am happy to see you," Elham greeted her.

"And I am thrilled to see you. "

"Your friends Fred and Zoya are here," Elham said, observing the look of surprise on her face.

"We were worried sick about you," Fred said as he and Zoya jumped off the sticky plastic-covered sofa to hug her.

"Fred overheard Jason's conversation on the phone and couldn't rest until he knew the entire story. Then Fred called me and swore me to secrecy," Zoya confessed.

"So much for secrecy, Now, everybody knows," she said with a tired voice, dropping her luggage near the staircase.

"No, just us three and Jason."

"And my mom, uncle, Husam, his translator, the thugs who kidnapped me, Alex the investigator and the Homeland Security man and God knows who else. You guys might as well start calling me Sahar."

"Sahar? That's a pretty name," Fred said. "Does it mean something?"

"Ironically and coincidentally, it means Dawn. I was being cynical when I said you can call me Sahar. You must always address me as Dawn. I am now officially Dawn Parnell, an American citizen."

"Well Dawn, come sit with us and tell us about your escape."

As tired as she was, she couldn't refuse. They were her friends and surrogate family who now knew everything about her hidden past. She suddenly felt overwhelming relief as she revealed her story.

After Jason heard from his father, and later, Alex, that Sahar was home safe, he felt at ease. Ever since her kidnapping, he hadn't been able to shut his eyes for more than five minutes as he collapsed on his bed. Now that he had broken his business ties with his father and had a place of his own, it was time to bring her into his life. However, he had to wait one long month before he could do that. She had helped him see his life for what it was – full of people who really didn't care about him as much as they did status and clout. When he walked into a restaurant, he always got the best table. Packed hotels always found him a room. Friends invited him to extravagant parties only to ask for favors later. And his parents had hurt him more than anyone else. He had always thought that he would end up just like them and accepted the idea. But now, he realized that he needed someone who would always stay by his side. Sahar was that someone.

TWENTY SIX

The month following her run-in with the law, Sahar's life went back to the way it was before the kidnapping. She worked, stopped at the park, played *Passoor* with Elham and volunteered at the shelter. She often picked up the telephone to call Jason, only to hang up before the call went through. He helped save her life and if she wasn't in love with him and only thought of him as a friend, she would have called him. But in her gut she sensed danger – the feeling that Husam would never give up until he got rid of her – and she was afraid. Sahar had already put Jason through hell. If she were going to be killed she wasn't about to put him in harm's way. Yet, there was no one she would rather be with.

"How is Jason?" she asked Fred. They were seated at a local café on a Friday afternoon, drinking chai lattes and gabbing about the past.

"Oh, he is fine. He's in China on business." Fred lied. Jason told him about the promise he made to his father. Tomorrow a month would have passed and Fred wondered what his boss was planning to do.

"Is he seeing anyone?" she prodded, using her hand to brush crumbs from the blueberry muffin they were sharing to the floor.

"I don't know. He doesn't bring home his dates," Fred said, clearing his throat. Jason had warned him not to reveal anything until he had a chance to talk to her himself. Yet Jason had been driving Fred crazy by asking him several times a day whether or not Sahar tried to get in touch with him. The answer was always no.

"Well, I hope he is happy," she replied sadly.

Fred felt horrible lying to her. He knew how Jason felt about Sahar, and frankly, he didn't mind if the two of them got back together. His boss had changed immensely ever since he left the mansion. He no longer hung around any of his old friends except for George, who was happily married. All the women he once dated had disappeared from his life and Jason seemed more down to earth and friendlier. Fred still remembered the day when Jason found out that Sahar was safe. Jason invited Fred to join him on the sofa and toast her safety. Jason would have never done that in a million years had they stayed at the Crawford mansion. "So, what's your schedule like tomorrow?" Fred asked, changing the subject.

"Tomorrow I'm setting up a table outside Pavilions grocery store to get signatures on a petition, protecting human rights in Saudi Arabia."

"What a great idea. What time? Which Pavilions?" he asked with curiosity.

"From 10 in the morning until 4. It's going to be at the one on Fair Oaks, in South Pasadena. Why? Did you want to stop by?" she asked enthusiastically.

"Maybe I will and surprise you."

"That would be nice. To tell you the truth, I am kind of nervous. I could use the support."

"Somehow, I have a feeling that you'll be alright by yourself. Your strength and resilience always amazes me."

"Thanks for the vote of confidence."

"You're quite welcome."

The following day, Sahar set up shop outside Pavilions to collect signatures asking California senators to speak up against the violation of human rights in Saudi Arabia and to support a bill to put sanctions against that country. It was a beautiful November day, the California sycamore behind her had shed its yellow and golden leaves on the ground, a mockingbird chirped above and, as the year was gradually coming to an end, the air was filled with promise. She had printed up pamphlets regarding the treatment of Saudi women and foreigners in her country as she stopped each shopper and said, "Excuse me, do you have a minute to sign this form?" Some shoppers hurriedly picked up pamphlets, others slowed down to listen to what she had to say and signed the form. Then there were those who said they had to think about it. One of the women wearing a shirt that said "My Body, My Choice" stopped by to talk to her.

Jason, who had been watching Sahar from afar, shook his head and chuckled. If the "My Body, My Choice" lady ever teamed up with Sahar, there would be no stopping them, he thought as he saw the woman sign the form and exchange business cards with Sahar.

He had been upset with Sahar for the longest time because she never bothered calling him. He had almost given up on her had it not been for Fred, who told him last night about how hurt Sahar looked when he told her that he wasn't sure if Jason was seeing anyone. Jason began moving toward the table as Sahar looked up.

"What are you doing here?" she asked, thinking how handsome he looked in his pale green round-neck shirt hugging his body, and his light blue jeans.

"Is this how you thank the man who rescued you from ill fate?" he bantered, excited at the sight of her. With the exception of her not wearing her glasses and retainers, nothing about her had changed – same red hair pulled back with butterfly hairpins, same simplicity in her sundress that stopped above her knees, same angelic eyes – and he liked that.

"I've been meaning to call you but…."

"But?"

She didn't know what to say.

"That's okay, if Mohammad can't go to the mountain, then the mountain…well you know the rest."

"Thank you," she said, with a voice filled with love and gratitude. "Thank you for all that you have done for me."

"And what makes you think I did it for you?" he replied, with his hands in his pockets.

"Then who did you do it for?"

"Me. What would I do without you setting me straight all the time?"

"I don't know," she smiled at him for the first time in a long time. "You're hopeless."

"Maybe not as hopeless as you think. I'm running my own computer game company now."

"Yes I know. I saw a picture of you with Isabella da Pontedera," she said, bitterly.

"Nothing happened between us," he told her with apologetic eyes, wishing that he hadn't dated anyone after her.

"That's okay. You'll eventually find someone else you like, you always do."

"I've already have found her," he answered, staring into her eyes.

"Good for you. Now, please go away. I have work to do." The nerve of him, showing up here after a whole month and wanting to chitchat about another girl, she thought.

"You're that someone, you idiot," he said, grabbing her by the waist and making her melt in his arms like putty.

"Let go of me. I'm not your girl."

"Yes, you are. You were always my girl. I won't let anyone else have you. Not even that blond you double-dated with Zoya."

"How dare you? How dare you violate my privacy when you go off with woman after woman," she said, trying to wiggle out of his arms but his grip was too strong.

"Sahar…."

"Don't call me that, someone might hear you," she said, missing the sound of her old name. The truth was she yearned for many things in her past but was glad that at last she had her *al horeyat*. Her freedom had come at the high cost of living in exile forever and never seeing her father, mother, sisters and uncle again but she hoped that someday things would change in her country. She hoped that someday when she was walking down a street, she would run into her family. Hope. There was always hope. If a person didn't have hope, he or she had no reason to live.

"Dawn, I never slept with anyone after you. You're the one I want. You're the one I have always loved from the first day you entered my house with those awkward glasses and your shy stance."

A store security guard came up and said, "Is this man bothering you?"

Sahar shook her head no. She then turned to Jason and tearfully said, "Did you mean what you just said? You won't keep searching for someone better?"

"What for, when I have always had her under my nose but was too stupid to notice."

She scrutinized his face to see if he meant it and wasn't just saying words that he would later regret.

"Will you marry me?" Jason blurted, jolting both of them. He had come there to talk, to tell her how he felt and how much he had missed her. The marriage proposal was never on his agenda but the sentence came out of his mouth with incredible ease.

"Marry you?" She pinched herself to make sure she was awake.

"Yes. Will you marry me?" This time he was better prepared for the words that formed on his lips. He knew she was the one for him and felt a delightful tingling throughout his body.

"Aren't you supposed to kneel and pull out a ring when you ask?" she bantered.

"Don't go anywhere." He ran into the store.

Sahar waited impatiently as he came back with a box of large, colored paperclips. He uncoiled a white one and shaped it into a ring.

Several shoppers stopped to see what was going on.

"I don't have a ring because I had no idea what I was going to say to you to make you see how much I love you. And I hurt my knees playing tennis, so I can't kneel. But my beautiful Dawn of Saudi, will you accept this as a temporary ring?" he asked, holding it out. "Until I buy you something nice. You see, I'm afraid if I wait, I'll say something to make you mad and then you'll change your mind."

"Jason," she said, extending her hand for him to slip the makeshift ring on her finger, "nothing you'll ever say will anger me enough for me to leave you. And yes I will marry you." She glided her hands around his neck and kissed him with ardent passion as the few onlookers around them began clapping. But neither Jason nor Sahar heard anything but the beating of their own hearts.

"*Ohebbake,*" he told her as he kissed her again.

"*Ohebbake kasiran,*" I love you more, she answered staring into his glinting eyes and brushing her nose against his playfully. "You know," she added with a smile, "now that you've kept me from my volunteer work, will you at least help pass these pamphlets around?"

"We're not even married yet and you're already putting me to work," he said jokingly, not wanting to let her go. He then stopped a man pushing a shopping cart. "Excuse me, would you like to sign this petition to protect human rights in Saudi Arabia?"

Dawn watched her fiancé persuade the man to sign up, thinking how content she finally was with her new life. She thought it unusual that soon she would be married to two men since she never did get a proper divorce from Husam. But who cared? If Saudi men were allowed to have more than one wife, then Saudi women should be allowed to have more than one husband.

Author's Note and Readers Guide

Author's Note

Iran, also known as Persia, has never had an Islamic government in its 2500-years of history until 1979 when the French, British and U.S government decided to do a regime change and replace the Shah of Iran with Ayatollah Khomeini. When that happened, the Iranian civil laws were replaced by sharia – the Islamic code of law. Today's Iranian government has been modeled after the Saudi government from their rule of law to their sentencing to their court system to oppression of women. Therefore, when foreign governments criticize the Iranian justice system, in essence they are criticizing the Saudi justice system.

However, the abuse of human rights in Iran is a walk in the park compared to the abuse of human rights in Saudi Arabia and the reason is simple – Iranians are not Arabs. Although one cannot deny the Islamic influence of Arabs on the Persian population, one must also recognize that Iranians are independent thinkers and not followers. They have their own belief system, their own language and their own way of doing things, no matter how hard the religious hardliners of Saudi Arabia try to change that by issuing a Fatwa, labeling them as "Infidels" because Iranians refuse to adhere to the Saudi way of life.

Saudi Arabia, a country that is 76 years old, has always been ruled by religion, fear and secrecy. Today, there are many modernists in the Kingdom who are desperately seeking change if only the Western governments would help support their hard journey to freedom. Currently, The Saudi government unlawfully detains activists who are advocates of reform. The kingdom has no penal code and judges are religious scholars with inadequate legal training. According to Human Rights Watch, officials make arbitrary arrests and abuse human rights from oppression of women to inhumane treatment of unskilled workers from third world countries to slavery to unjust criminal justice system to lack of legal council for defendants to statements extracted by torture of prisoners to sentencing of preteen children to death to human trafficking.

Women have no rights and are considered the property of a man. Housekeepers are often raped and put to work seven days a week, 16 hours per day, locked up in a home or in a bathroom with their wages withheld for a period of a few months to 10 years. If they escape and file a complaint, they face imprisonment or lashing for false countercharges of theft, adultery or witchcraft. As a result, many are afraid to file a complaint against their employers.

According to Amnesty International, people living in the kingdom are arrested, locked up and are not told why. They are not allowed to contact anyone outside the prison, are refused legal council and are tortured until they sign a confession to a crime they did not commit. Foreigners are not provided with translators. Unaware of the date of their sentencing, they await their punishment in fear everyday as they watch other prisoners being tortured in front of them. The punishment they face may be flogging, amputation of limbs or death.

According to Human rights watch, in 2007, Saudi Arabia executed three people for crimes committed while younger than 18, including a 15-year-old boy who was only 13 at the time of his alleged crime. Saudi officials arrest and detain children trafficked for begging and often deport them to conflict zones such as Somalia or Chad without tracing their families or ensuring that their return is safe. And yet, leaders such as the U.S. President George W. Bush, France's President Nicolas Sarkozy, Germany's Chancellor Angela Merkel and England's Prime Minister Gordon Brown shake hands with the Saudi king and keep quiet about the human rights abuse.

The influence of the Saudi Arabian government and religious hardliners is not limited to their own country. The Kingdom has an appalling control when world governments criticize or interfere with their actions. On April 9, 1980 when *Death of a Princess*, a film directed by Anthony Thomas about the granddaughter of Prince Muhammad bin Abdul Aziz who was killed by her family because she married a man her family did not approve of, aired on ATV in the United Kingdom, it provoked an angry response from the Saudi government. Export orders began to be cancelled. The movie was immediately banned in the UK. The U.S. as well received enormous political pressure from Saudi Arabia, to censor its broadcast. After much delay, the film was broadcast by the PBS program. No other major television station picked up the movie and a DVD has not been available to date.

Fast forward to September 11, 2001 – with the help and connections of Prince Bandar bin Sultan bin Abdul Aziz, the Saudi Arabian ambassador to the United States, Saudi royals and members of the Bin Laden family immediately fled the U.S in a secret airlift authorized by the Bush administration. Fifteen of the nineteen hijackers who had attacked the U.S. were not Iraqis nor were they Iranians. They were Saudi militant Islamic fundamentalists. A year later, after attacking Iraq and blaming Iran for the unrest in Iraq, President Bush failed to mention that 50 percent of the people who killed by suicide terrorism in Iraq were Saudi fundamentalists who believed that martyrdom guaranteed one's entrance into paradise.

In England, the Saudi government has a fearful power. If you walk around London, you may think you have stepped back to the Middle East of the 6th century. Women in their abayas and veil move about with their shopping bags from some of the most exclusive stores that not even the average British can afford. Ironically, one of the principles behind the Salafi Sunni religion is to live a modest life and help the poor and although this principle has never been enforced, their leaders have no problem enforcing the oppression of women under the pretext of religion. The majority of mosques in England and around the world are owned and operated by the Saudi government. And there has been a push for some time by the Kingdom for the sharia to be incorporated into the British court system to resolve disputes among Muslims.

On July 4, 2008, UK's mail online news reported that Britain's top judge, Lord Philips, said the sharia should be used in Britain. He said that Islamic legal principles could be employed to deal with family and marital arguments and to regulate finance in Britain. What Lord Philips failed to comprehend was that many Muslim women left their countries to escape sharia. According to CBN news, the head of Church of England was in support of sharia as well. As a result of Britain bowing to Saudi Arabia and sharia, polygamy, domestic violence, forced marriages and honor killings in the English communities has increased.

Banaz Mahmod, a Muslim living in London fell in love with a boy her parents did not approve. Her family beat her and she ended up in a hospital. She recorded a video from her hospital bed the first time her family tried to kill her. She went to the British Police four times asking for help before she disappeared. In a letter to the police, she even named the people who were planning to kill her. The British police ignored her because they thought they should respect ethnic diversity and not get involved. Benaz was finally murdered by her father and uncle, stuffed in a suitcase and buried in a backyard in Birmingham, south of London. Her father and uncle had ordered her killing because she had fallen in love with a wrong man and shamed her family.

On September 15, 2008, according to Times of London, Britain adopted the Islamic law. Rulings issued by a network of five sharia courts are now enforceable by the full power of their judicial system. However, the Saudi influence does not end there. In Australia, Indonesia, France and America, the Saudi government and private Saudi donors donate an obscene sum of money to universities, mosques, libraries and prisons to promote the Salafi version of Islam that denies equal rights to women, is intolerant of all other Muslims and is unwilling to accommodate other religions.

The Saudi influence even reaches to the genocide occurring in Darfur, a Western region of Sudan rich in oil, natural gas, uranium, gold and oil. In order to understand this, it is important to travel back in time to when the Janjaweed, known as Arab tribesmen with a gun on a horse, migrated 12 centuries ago from the deserts of Arabian Peninsula to Africa. They Islamized the Africans, taking hundreds of thousands of them as slaves. Today, those who class themselves as "Arabs," and have dark tan skin consider themselves racially and culturally superior to the Africans who have black skin.

The Janjaweed militias have been terrorizing millions of Africans in Darfur by raping their women and killing their men and children while world governments sit back and watch. In the beginning, they killed the Africans for farmlands and water. Today, they are killing them because of oil and ethnic cleansing. The militias burn villages, gang rape women and kill children and men in order to instill fear and push them out of their homes. Once the Africans leave, the families of the Janjaweed Arabs move in. The Islamic government of Darfur is supported by Saudi Arabia and thus, world leaders have done little to stop the genocides.

According to the Daily Star of Lebanon on April 10, 2006, The Arab league supported the Sudanese government and rejected international military involvement in Darfur. Saudi Arabia is a member of the Arab league. Already there exists a Saudi Arabia – Darfur relation in the field of real estate which includes agriculture, animal, petroleum, power and transport field as well as banking services but Darfur Africans will never benefit from any of it.

It is important to note that the intention of this book is not to criticize anyone's religion and nationality because those by themselves are not the problem. It is the manipulation of religion and nationality by soulless leaders, self-serving religious hardliners, a handful of obscenely wealthy families who control world governments and believe in population control, ruthless conglomerates whose main concerns are accumulation of wealth and a selected group of unconscionable foreign bankers that are the problem. The average citizen who practices his or her religion goes on about their day, working, raising their family and helping others.

Unfortunately, the fault of those who do not have a conscience bears a heavy burden on the rest of the society. To these people, nothing matters and they are willing to sell their souls to the highest bidder. They would do anything for money such as keeping quiet about oppression of women and human rights abuse, recruiting innocent teens and sending them to fight wars that do not exist, robbing their country of resources and committing acts of genocide.

Although fighting corruption and injustice may be an overwhelming task, we can no longer afford to walk around with blinders. By joining organizations such as Amnesty International, Human Rights Watch, SaveDarfur.org, Action Against Hunger and thousands of other associations which are in terrible need of funding and volunteers, we can help. We all need to come together as a society and do more.

–Homa

The Dawn of Saudi
Readers guide

For more information regarding The Dawn of Saudi, please visit www.thedawnofsaudi.com. To learn more about the author, visit her at www.homapourasgari.com.

Discussion Questions

1. In many countries where there is no separation of church and state, the human rights abuse is overwhelming. Why do you think the author decides to set the scene in Saudi Arabia as opposed to say Egypt or Afghanistan?

2. Discuss the word "Lure" and its ramifications on the Saudi court decisions in terms of rape and molestation.

3. Name at least three things that Dawn and Sahar have in common.

4. Discuss Dawn before and after marriage. Do you consider her ignorant or naive and why?

5. Sahar could have lived an incredibly comfortable life. Why do you suppose that she decides to give all that up?

6. What about Saad? Is he a man of conviction or someone who goes with the flow? How does Kadar influence Saad?

7. Could Asima have done things differently and protected her daughter from an unwanted marriage? Does she or any woman living in Saudi Arabia have the power to change their destinies? Discuss.

8. Why must Saudi women cover up? Why are they not allowed to drive or ride a simple thing called a bicycle?

9. Do you feel that the Saudi government will change in terms of human rights abuse and oppression of women in ten, twenty or thirty years from now? Discuss.

10. In your opinion do money, natural resources, sophisticated architectures, mansions, numerous advanced hospitals, freeways, paved roads, fancy airports, large shopping malls and charitable organizations within a country make it a modern country or is there something else built into the system of a government that needs to be addressed first? And if so, what is that something?

11. Discuss Jason's transformation of character before and after he falls in love.

12. How did Jason's upbringing affect his decision making in terms of his relationships and work?

13. What does the word *mahram* mean? List those who are considered *mahram*.

14. What does the word *haram* mean? Name at least three things considered *haram* for Muslims that the protagonist ignores.

15. Discuss sentencing of prisoners in Saudi Arabia. How is the sentencing for the same crime different for a Saudi man, a woman, a foreigner from a western country and a foreigner from a third world country? Are they all treated equally? Discuss the value of a person's life based on percentage points.

16. Discuss tolerance for other cultures and religions within the Kingdom. Why do you think is their government fearful of the influence of foreigners on the Saudis?

17. Why does United States have a military base inside Saudi Arabia? How do the Saudis feel about this?

18. Discuss Camel racing and their impact on children. What do you feel is the responsibility of Western countries that trade with countries that disregard human rights?

19. Can you name another country that is much more invested in Saudi Arabia than the U.S? What would happen to its economy if the Saudis decided to divest?

20. What do you think world governments should do about the human rights abuse within the kingdom? Can they dictate to Saudi Arabia how to run their country? Should they use diplomacy? Should they simply look the other way for the sake of profit? Should they decrease their dependence on oil, invest in new energy technologies and divest in that country? What options can you think of? Discuss.